A BOLD, SWEEPING NOVEL OF ONE MAN AGAINST THE WORLD

He was Adonis. He had everything a mortal human could desire, but his taste of the suffering on earth would make him a rebel to his own kind. For he would attempt to leave the unimagined splendor of the space colony to help mankind on the earth below. . . .

COLONY

The first novel of colonies in space

"An idea whose time has come."
—*The New York Times*

"A BEAUTIFUL STORY AND FULL OF PROPHETIC VISIONS."
—Frank Herbert,
author of *Dune*

COLONY

BEN BOVA

PUBLISHED BY POCKET BOOKS NEW YORK

Another *Original* publication of POCKET BOOKS

**POCKET BOOKS, a Simon & Schuster division of
GULF & WESTERN CORPORATION
1230 Avenue of the Americas, New York, N.Y. 10020**

Copyright © 1978 by Ben Bova

ISBN: 0-671-42882-9

First Pocket Books printing July, 1978

10 9 8 7 6 5 4

POCKET and colophon are trademarks of Simon & Schuster.

Printed in the U.S.A.

To Barbara

Not at a crisis of nervousness do we stand now, not at a time for the vacillations of flabby souls; but at a great turning point in the history of scientific thought, at a crisis such as occurs but once in a thousand years. . . . Standing at this point, with the vista of future achievement before us, we should be happy that it is our lot to live at this time and to participate in the creation of tomorrow.

—V. I. Vernadskii,
1932

I do not wish to seem overdramatic, but I can only conclude from the information that is available to me as Secretary General, that the Members of the United Nations have perhaps ten years left in which to subordinate their ancient quarrels and launch a global partnership to curb the arms race, to improve the human environment, to defuse the population explosion, and to supply the required momentum to development efforts. If such a global partnership is not forged within the next decade, then I very much fear that the problems I have mentioned will have reached such staggering proportions that they will be beyond our capacity to control.

—U Thant,
Secretary General of
the United Nations,
1969

EARTH-MOON LIBRATION POINTS

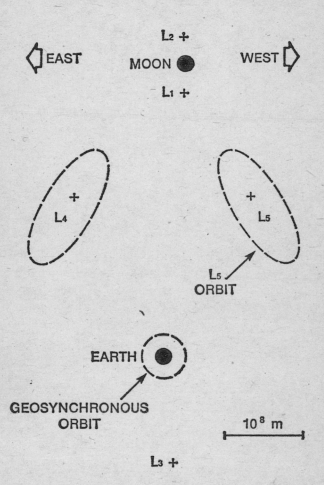

BOOK ONE

May, 2008 A.D.

WORLD POPULATION:
7.25 BILLION

The concept, the design, and even the term "Island One" stem from research led by Professor Gerard O'Neill at the old Princeton University back in the Seventies. He originally envisioned Island One as a space colony up at the Moon's orbit, constructed in empty space out of materials scooped from the Moon's surface. His colony would house ten thousand permanent residents. It was huge by the standards of the 1970s, and people gaped at the idea. But actually his Island One was no more massive than the ocean-going supertankers that used to haul oil around the world, back when there was oil to be hauled.

That was O'Neill's dream, and lots of people scoffed at it—but not the corporations. And right around the turn of the century, when they finally decided to build a colony in space, the corporations made O'Neill's thinking look *small*.

—Cyrus S. Cobb,
Tapes for an unauthorized
autobiography

· CHAPTER 1 ·

"Slow down!" she called. "I'm only a city girl."

David Adams stopped and turned back toward her. They were climbing a grassy slope that wasn't very steep. Young slim-boled maples and birches stood every few feet, so that you could grab them and pull yourself along.

But Evelyn was out of breath and starting to feel angry. *He's showing off*, she thought. *The muscular young male in his Garden of Eden.*

Laughing, David extended a hand toward her. "You said you wanted to see the whole colony."

"Yes," Evelyn said, puffing, "but I don't want to get a heart attack doing it."

Grasping her wrist firmly, he helped pull her up along the climbing path. "It gets easier up ahead. The gravity slackens off. And the view is worth the effort."

She nodded, but said to herself, *He knows he's handsome. Good muscular body; firm backside. That's why they picked him to guide me, no doubt. He gets all the female hormones popping.*

David reminded her of the Hawaiian beachboys who had invaded England's holiday resorts lately: the same strong, sleek body; the same wide-boned handsome face with the big bright smile. He was dressed for the outdoors, something Evelyn had never expected: rough shorts, loose-fitting sleeveless shirt open to show his smooth muscular chest, soft-skinned hiking boots. Her own short-skirted business suit looked perfectly proper in an office or a restaurant or anywhere civilized, but out here it was terribly out of place. She had already taken off the vest and stuffed it into her shoulderbag, but still she was overheated and sweating like an animal.

4

That smile of his is dazzling, though. There was something else about him, too, something . . . different. *Could he be the one?* she asked herself. *Could I have stumbled onto him already? What a coincidence that he'd be assigned to be my guide.* But another voice in her head warned, *There's no such thing as a coincidence. Be careful!*

Those blue eyes and that golden hair. What a combination. And the slightly olive cast to his skin: a Mediterranean gene. Can they engineer your complexion, too? Still, there's something. . . . *He's got that filmstar look to him,* Evelyn realized. *Too perfect. Not a thing out of place. No blemishes, no scars. Even his teeth are white and straight.*

"Careful here," David said. He slid an arm around her waist to help her jump over a tiny gurgling brook that cut across their path.

"Thanks," Evelyn murmured, disengaging his arm. *He knows he's a hunk,* she told herself. *Don't let that angel face take you in, old girl.*

Silently they climbed through thinning stands of oak and spruce, all neatly arranged, evenly spaced. *Like his bloody teeth. They should have sent a blooming Girl Scout on this job, not a reporter.*

David watched her as they climbed the steadily ascending path. *Why did Cobb pick me to show her around?* he asked himself. *Does he think so little of the work I'm trying to do that he wants me to put it aside and play Boy Scout with a newcomer?*

With an effort, he kept the resentment out of his face as he watched her struggle in her open-toed shoes to keep up with him. On impulse, he tongued the communicator switch built into his rearmost molar and whispered to himself, deep down in his throat where no one could hear it except the miniaturized transmitter implanted there: "Evelyn Hall, new arrival last week. File, please."

It took four paces along the grassy path before the microscopic receiver implanted behind his ear whispered back: "Evelyn L. Hall. Age twenty-six. Born London Complex. Attended state schools in London area. Graduate of Polytechnic University, Plymouth. Degree in journalism. Employed as researcher, later reporter, International News Syndicate. No other employment history. Physical data . . ."

David shut off the computer's voice with a click of his

tongue. He didn't need her vital statistics. He could see that she was almost as tall as his own five-eleven and had the full, ripe kind of figure that meant she faced a constant battle against overweight. Her thick honey-colored hair curled over her shoulders; it was badly tangled right now. Sea-green eyes that were alive, intelligent, inquisitive. A pretty face. She looked almost like an innocent child except for those probing, restless eyes. Still, it was a sweet face, vulnerable, almost fragile.

"I wish they'd told me we'd be mountain-climbing," Evelyn grumbled.

David laughed. "Come on. This isn't a mountain. We didn't build any mountains into this side of the colony. Now, if you really want to climb . . ."

"Never mind!" She pushed a matted mass of hair away from her eyes.

Her suit was ruined, she knew. Grass-stained, soaked with perspiration. That bastard Cobb. The "mayor" of Island One. This was all his idea.

"Get to see the colony," the skinny old fart had boomed, as if he were haranguing the multitudes. "I mean *really* see it. Walk through it. Experience it. I'll get somebody to show you around. . . ."

If this is how he treats every new arrival, it's a miracle anyone stays up here to live. But Evelyn wondered, *Or is he giving me special treatment because he suspects what I'm here for?* For the first time in her life she realized that investigative reporting could be not only dangerous, but damned fatiguing.

She tagged along behind the muscular young woodsman through forest and stream, over hill and glade, her clothes in a mess, her shoes utterly ruined, blisters searing her feet, shoulderbag thumping against her hip, and her disposition unraveling more with each painful step.

"Not much farther," David said. His cheerfulness aggravated her. "Feel any lighter? The gravity falls off pretty quickly up here."

"No," she snapped, not trusting herself to say more. If she told him what she really thought of all this woodsy lore, they'd have her packing back to Earth on the next shuttle.

David was walking alongside her now. The path seemed to have flattened out considerably. At least the walking was

6

easier. Evelyn saw that there were head-tall bushes along both sides of their path, gorgeous with huge, pumpkin-sized blossoms of fantastic vibrant reds and oranges and yellows.

"What are these?" she asked, her breathing almost back to normal.

David's pleasant face wrinkled for a moment. "Umm . . ." He made a clicking sound with his tongue as he stared at the flowers.

Some P.R. man, Evelyn thought. *He takes me on the royal tour and he doesn't even know . . .*

"They're a mutated form of the common hydrangea," David said, his head oddly cocked to one side, as if he were listening to something as he spoke. *"H. macrophylla murphiensis.* One of the colony's earliest geneticists was a gardener by hobby and he tried to establish a new line of show flowers that would not only produce spectacular new colors, but would also be self-pollinating. He succeeded too well, and for more than three years his modified hydrangea bushes threatened to overrun much of the colony's farming lands. With the help of a special team of biochemists and molecular biologists, the mutated shrub was confined to the upland regions at the far end of the colony's main cylinder."

He recites like a bloody robot, Evelyn thought.

David smiled at her and said in a more normal tone, "The amateur gardener's name wasn't Murphy, by the way. He refused to have his own name identified with the new variation, so Dr. Cobb named the plant after Murphy's Law."

"Murphy's Law?"

"Hasn't anybody explained Murphy's Law to you? 'If anything can go wrong, it will.' That's Murphy's Law." More seriously he added, "It's the first and most important rule of living up here. If you're going to make your home here, remember Murphy's Law. It could save your life."

"If I'm going to make my home here?" Evelyn echoed. "Is there any doubt about that? I mean, I've been accepted for permanent residency, haven't I?"

"Sure," David said, looking innocently surprised. "It was just a figure of speech."

But Evelyn wondered, *How much does he know?*

They resumed walking, with the spectacularly flowered

bushes screening both sides of their path. There wasn't much scent from the flowers, but something else was bothering Evelyn . . . something was missing.

"No insects!"

"What?" David asked.

"There are no insects buzzing around."

"Not very many," David said, "up here. We have bees and such down in the farmlands, of course. But we've worked pretty hard to keep pests out of the colony. Flies, mosquitoes . . . disease carriers. The ground we're walking on has earthworms and beetles and everything else the soil needs to stay alive, of course. That was one of the colony's biggest problems, at first. It takes a lot of living creatures in the soil to make it fertile. You can't just scoop dirt from the Moon and spread it around the colony. It's barren, sterile."

Evelyn asked, "How long have you lived here?"

"All my life," David said.

"Really? You were born here?"

"I've lived here all my life," he repeated.

A tremor shuddered along Evelyn's spine. *He is the one!* She asked, "And they've got you working on the P.R. staff?"

"P.R. What's that?"

She blinked at him. "Public relations. Don't you even know . . ."

"Oh, that!" He grinned at her. "I'm not on the public relations staff. We don't even have one, outside of Dr. Cobb himself."

"Then you just guide newcomers all the time?"

"No. I'm a Forecaster . . . or I'm trying to be."

"A Forecaster? Now what in heaven's name . . ."

But her question was blown away as they stepped around the final turn of the trail and she saw the view.

They were standing near the rim of a high hill. A breeze should have been blowing up this high, but if there was one, Evelyn didn't feel it. The bushes that had screened their path were behind them now, and she could see the whole colony laid out before her.

Island One.

From up on the crest of the hill Evelyn could see the fertile green land stretching out before her, long swaths of wooded hills, gently curving streams, grassy glades, little clumps of forests, a scattering of buildings, blue lakes glittering in the sunlight. She almost felt as if she were falling, pulled off her feet by the broad open vista of greenery that reached on and on, until its farthest distance was lost in haze.

She could see the clustered spires of a village and the white sails of boats skimming across one of the larger lakes. Here a bridge delicately spanned a river, there a set of gossamer wings glided easily in the clear, clean air. Far off in the blue-hazed distance were neat rows of cultivated farmlands.

She knew that Island One was a huge cylinder hanging in space. She knew that she was standing inside a long, broad, man-made tube. Numbers from her background briefings played through her head. The colony was twenty kilometers long, four klicks wide. It rotated every few minutes to keep an artificial form of gravity inside the cylinder and make everything feel Earthlike. But the numbers were meaningless. It was all too big, too open, too vast. This was a *world*, a rich, verdant land of beauty and peace that defied every attempt to measure and define it.

A whole world! Green, open, clean—shining with hope and room to walk in, to breathe in, to play and laugh in, the way Cornwall and Devon had been before the gray tentacles of the megalopolis had swallowed all the green hillsides.

Evelyn could feel herself trembling. *There's no horizon!* The land curved up. It reached upward, dizzyingly, sweeping higher and higher. She lifted her head and saw through the bluish, cloud-flecked sky that there was more land above her, straight overhead. An inside-out world. She swayed.

Slashing across the open green land were long gleaming swaths of brilliant light. The solar windows. They ran the length of the colony's cylinder, steel-braced glass that brought in the sunlight reflected by the huge mirrors outside the colony's mammoth tubular body.

It was all too vast to comprehend. Hills, trees, farms, villages curving up over her head, lost in the hazy blue of the sky, up, up, swirling around over her head in a full circle, green land, shining window, more green land. . . .

She felt David's arm around her shoulders.

"You were getting dizzy. I thought you might fall."

Weakly, gratefully, Evelyn said, "It's . . . it rather staggers one, doesn't it?"

He nodded and smiled at her, and suddenly she was angry again. *Not you! It doesn't stagger you! You've seen this every day of your life. You've never had to fight your way through a city queue or put on a breathing mask just to get through the streets alive. . . .*

"It's a breathtaking sight, all right," David was saying, as calmly as a newscaster reading a weather report. "All the pictures in the world can't prepare you for this."

She heard herself giggle. "Columbus! This would have driven Columbus mad! It was difficult enough for him to get people to believe that the world is round. But if he had seen this—this world—it's inside-out!"

Knowingly, David said, "I've got a telescope at my place if you want to actually see people standing upside down with their heads hanging toward you."

"No," Evelyn said quickly. "I don't think I'm ready for that yet."

They stood at the edge of the hill's steep dropoff. It was eerily quiet. No birds chirping. No trucks rumbling along a nearby highway. Evelyn forced herself to look upward again and see the land curving over her head, forced herself to accept the fact that she was standing inside a man-made cylinder more than twelve miles long, a giant tube hanging in space a quarter-million miles from Earth, landscaped, filled with air, an engineered paradise that housed an elite few of very rich people—while billions lived in misery on the tired, crowded old Earth.

"Anything else you'd like to know in the way of statistics about the colony?" David asked. "It's just about the same length as Manhattan Island, but since we can use almost all the inner surface of the cylinder, we actually have more than four times Manhattan's area . . ."

"And a hundredth of its population!"

If David were stung by her retort, he barely showed it. "One of the benefits of living here is the colony's low population density," he said evenly. "We don't want to get into the same strangling situation that the cities of Earth have gotten themselves into."

"What do you know about the cities of Earth?" she demanded.

With a shrug, he said, "Not much, I guess."

They lapsed into silence again. Evelyn turned back to see the view. *All that open space. They could take in a million people. More.*

Finally David held out his hand to her. "Come on," he said. "It's been a hard day for you. Let's go get a drink and relax."

She looked at him. *Maybe he's human, after all.* Despite herself, she smiled at him.

"Up this way." He pointed along another trail that wound off into the trees.

"More climbing?"

He laughed. "No. Just a short walk from here. Downhill, mostly. You can take your shoes off if you like."

Gratefully, Evelyn slipped them off her burning feet and hung them by their heels on the strap of her shoulderbag. The grass felt soft and cool. David led her along a winding path, past more of the strange, flaming hydrangea bushes, and along the bank of a stream that tumbled downslope toward the forest they had climbed through.

She's got a big chip on her shoulder, he thought as they walked. Of course, she hadn't been prepared for the trek up here. *Cobb surprised us both with that move. He's full of surprises.*

Then he recalled the look on her face when she had first seen the view of the whole colony. *That was worth all her complaints.* Surprise, wonder, awe. It was worth spending the whole day away from his work. *But why would Cobb pull me away for this tour-guide task? I'm so close to putting it all together, to understanding where it's all leading . . . and he makes me spend a day in the woods.*

Evelyn watched David as they walked. He seemed so relaxed, so sure of himself. She wanted to trip him or drop a worm down the back of his shirt just to see how he'd react.

He doesn't think it's worthwhile, David was thinking. *He's never thought much of Forecasting. But he never interfered with my studies before. Why now, when I'm so close to putting together all the basic interrelationships? Is he afraid that I'll find something he doesn't want me to know?*

The trees were farther apart now, mostly pine with a few white-boled birch scattered among them. Pine scent filled the air. Rocks, gray and pitted, showed through the thick grass now and again. Some of them were shoulder high, although most were much smaller.

"What peculiar-looking rocks," Evelyn said.

"What?" David broke out of his musing.

"These rocks . . . they look odd."

"They're from the Moon."

"But the entire colony is built from lunar materials, isn't it?"

"It is. Just about every gram of material here—from the outer shell to the oxygen we're breathing. All scooped from the lunar surface and refined here in our smelting plants. But we brought these rocks in without processing them at all. Our landscaping people thought they'd help make the ground look more interesting."

"You must have had a Japanese landscaping team," Evelyn said.

"How did you know?"

She laughed and shook her head. *Score one point for our side!*

"Well, here we are," said David a moment later.

"Where?"

"Home." He spread his arms and turned slightly. "This is where I live."

"Out in the open?"

They were standing beside a wide pond, where the stream they had been following pooled its waters temporarily before resuming its flow down to the forest. Birches and pines stood off a short way from them. The ground was soft with grass and ferns, although outcroppings of rock showed through here and there. Toward David's right was a huge boulder, much taller than he was.

David gestured toward the boulder. "This is my house. It's plastic . . . made to look like a rock. It's not very big inside, but I don't need much."

This tricky bastard has brought me up to his place!

David misinterpreted the look on her face. "Sure, I spend a lot of my time outdoors. Why not? It never rains unless we get a two-day warning. The temperature never goes below fifteen degrees—that's nearly sixty on the Fahrenheit scale."

"We use the Celsius scale," Evelyn snapped. She looked around dubiously. "You sleep out here?"

"Sometimes. But mostly I sleep inside. We're not Neanderthals."

Yes, and I'll wager your bed is big enough for two, isn't it?

"Look," he said to her, "wouldn't you like a nice, relaxing bath? I can throw your clothes in the cleaner and fix you a drink."

Evelyn weighed the probabilities swiftly in her mind. The idea of soaking in a hot tub was too good to miss. Her burning feet would never forgive her for passing it by.

"The bath sounds fine," she said. *Maybe afterward, after I get my clothes on again, we can think about a drink.* A pang in her stomach reminded her of how long it had been since brunch.

David guided her around the fake rock. A plastic door was set into its face so cunningly that she had to look closely to see the hairline crack outlining it.

Inside it was a one-room bachelor's pad. Thick carpeting of reddish gold, cream-colored curving walls. No windows, but a pair of blank viewscreens hung over the desk that was set to one side of the door.

The middle of the room was dominated by an open fireplace and funnel-shaped flue over it: red on the outside, soot-black inside. On the other side of the fireplace was a king-sized, low-slung bed.

Ah-hah! thought Evelyn. *A waterbed, at that.*

There was a spare, utilitarian kitchen alcove, a small, round table with just two straight-backed chairs, and several oversized Oriental pillows strewn on the floor. No other furniture.

It was neat, clean, but austere. Not a thing out of place. *Like his damned teeth.* No books. Not a scrap of paper anywhere in sight.

David went to the bed and touched the wall there. A door popped open to reveal a closet. Rummaging in it briefly, he pulled out a shapeless gray robe and tossed it to Evelyn. She plucked it deftly out of the air.

"Nice catch," he said.

Don't you wish, she answered silently.

"Bathroom's through there." He pointed to another nearly invisible door. "Throw your clothes back out here and I'll put them in the cleaner."

With a nod, Evelyn walked into the bathroom. David

headed for the kitchen alcove, wondering, *What's she so edgy about?* He opened the cabinet above the sink.

The bathroom door banged open and she was out, glaring at him. "There's no tub in there! No shower! Nothing!"

David stared at her. "You don't bathe in the john, for God's sake. That's what the pond is for."

"What?"

Feeling exasperated, he explained, "You clean yourself with the vibrator—that shiny metal thing on the flexible hose hanging on the wall in there. It flakes off your body dirt by using sonic vibrations and vacuums the stuff up as it comes loose. Same way this thing cleans your clothes." He tapped the ultrasonic cleaning machine set into the cabinet below the sink. "Water's too important to use for washing."

"We have tubs and showers in my quarters," she said.

"You've been in the quarantine quarters. This morning they moved you to a permanent apartment and there's no tub or shower in it. You'll see."

Evelyn looked confused. "But you said I could take a bath. . . ."

"In the pond—after you're clean."

"I don't have a swimsuit."

"Neither do I. There's nobody around here to spy on us. The nearest neighbor is more than five kilometers away."

Her expression hardened. "And what about you?"

"I've seen naked women before. And you've seen naked men, haven't you?"

"You haven't seen *my* naked body before! And I don't care what your tribal customs are up here in this New Eden of yours; I don't prance around exhibiting myself!"

Oh, hell! David thought. *An English prude.* "All right, all right," he said, making conciliatory gestures with his hands. "I'll tell you how we'll work it out. You hand me your clothes through the door of the bathroom . . ."

She looked as suspicious as Dr. Cobb did whenever a delegation from Earthside wanted to come up to "inspect" the colony.

". . . and I'll put them in the cleaner. Then I'll go out and jump in the pond."

"In the buff?"

"In the who?"

"Naked."

He shrugged. "If it makes you feel any better, I'll keep my shorts on. All right with you if I take off my boots, though? The environmental protection people get really nasty when you go swimming in dirty boots."

She nodded without changing expression.

Cold fish! "All right. I'll clean myself with the vibrator outside and then get into the pond. Now, when you're ready to come in, you yell. I'll turn my head, shut my eyes, put my hands over my eyes, and dive underwater. All right? Then, once you're safely in, if I haven't drowned we can have a nice relaxing swim. The water's always warm, you know. And I'll stay two hundred meters away from you at all times. All right?"

Evelyn could feel a grin tugging at the corners of her mouth. "That pond isn't two hundred meters wide."

"Well, I'll do my best," he said.

He looks so damned sincere, she thought. "I don't mean to be prudish," she said, 'but back home we simply don't bathe naked with strangers."

"You've got a right to your own folkways," David said. "Everybody skinnydips here. I didn't stop to think that it might shock you."

Feeling a bit foolish, but still apprehensive beneath it all, Evelyn went back into the bathroom, shut the door tightly, and started stripping off her sweaty clothes.

Whose scruples am I worried about? she asked herself. *His, or my own?*

Then she reminded herself that it didn't matter; she was here to get a story, and once she got it she would leave Island One.

Then she smiled. *It would make a much better story if I could see what he's like without those silly shorts on him.*

Our conclusions are:

1. If present growth trends in world population, industrialization, pollution, food production, and resource depletion continue unchanged, the limits to growth on this planet will be reached sometime within the next hundred years. The most probable result will be a . . . sudden and uncontrollable decline in both population and industrial capacity.

—Meadows, Meadows, Randers, and Behrens,
The Limits to Growth,
Universe Books, 1972

· CHAPTER 2 ·

Dennis McCormick planted his fists on his hips and glared at the dusty parking area. Every last truck and car was gone.

"Damn!" he said to himself. "I thought those sneaky bastards were getting to like me."

The blood-red sun of Baghdad was touching the horizon, turning the cloudless sky into a bowl of molten copper. *Hot enough to melt copper, pretty near*, Denny thought, mopping his sweaty face. Ordinarily he didn't mind the heat, but now he was angry that his work crew had left him nothing—not even an electrobike—to get back to the hotel with. He'd have to walk through the heat of a dying Baghdad afternoon.

At least the *shamal* had stopped blowing its blast-furnace breath across the construction site. The air was still and desert-dry in the hot sunset.

"God damn it!" he muttered. "I'm going to break Abdul's ass for him. He knows better than to leave me stuck like this."

What really disappointed him was that he had convinced himself that the Arab workmen had finally accepted him. They had become friendly over the past few weeks. *Maybe they just forgot*, he told himself. *Keeping track of the motor pool isn't their bag, after all.*

He glanced back at the construction site. The palace was finally beginning to take visible shape. Even the women who came down to the riverside for their daily chores and gossip could see that something magnificent was being created. They would stand for hours and watch the work progress. The riverfront wall was finished at last, high and smoothly curving. The towers at either end would be capped before the end of the week.

With a sigh that was half satisfaction, half irritation at the thought of walking back to the hotel, Denny mopped his face again and started off toward the bridge that spanned the Tigris. Sweat trickled down along his red beard and throat, down his ribs. But soon the sun would be down and the blessed relief of night would be here.

As he walked through the dusty, bare construction site, he started tapping out numbers on the keyboard of his wrist communicator. He squinted at the tiny display screen. It all checked out. The project was still slightly over the budget, but considering the way things had started, all was going very well, indeed.

The Iraqi construction crew had grumbled and sulked at working under a foreigner. (Not just a foreigner, *Imshalla*, but an infidel, a Christian—an *Irishman!*) Slowly, grudgingly, they had come to respect him. Gradually the jokes and whispers behind his back had dwindled. They never seemed able to understand that a man of Irish descent could be a Canadian. To them, he was the *Ah-reesh*. But then they had started calling him the Caliph's architect, a Suleiman among builders.

"And if they love you so much," Denny said to the sun-reddened rooftops and spires across the river, "how come they didn't leave you a car to get home in?"

But they had seen their own work begin to produce solid, beautiful reality, and they had responded to it with Arab pride and enthusiasm.

("Reconstruct Haroun al-Rashid's palace?" he had blurted out to his boss. "But nobody knows what it looks like."

("Don't let that bother you, my boy. The archaeology eggheads will guide you, and there'll be plenty of local 'experts' who'll be glad to give you advice."

("Come on, Russ, this is crazy . . ."

("No, it's politics. The World Government wants to Do Something for the Hashimite side of the Arab world, just like we're helping the Saudis. Otherwise, we've got troubles in the desert. Baghdad needs a facelift, new capital inflow, new industry."

("Then let me build an industrial complex for them, the way we did in Dacca."

("Not this time. You're going to reconstruct the palace of Haroun al-Rashid, the *Arabian Nights* Caliph. That's the key to revitalizing their economy, according to the computer forecasts."

("You mean you're going to turn Baghdad into another damned glorified amusement park, like Elsinore."

("Don't knock it, Denny, me boy. It brings in tourism and more commerce than industrial developments that the locals don't have the training to handle. Do a good job with this one and you'll get the next plum dropped right in your lap."

("And what might that be?"

("Babylon. The Hanging Gardens and all. We're going to reconstruct the entire ancient city, just the way the Greeks have recreated their Acropolis."

(And Dennis' mouth had watered, just as his boss had known it would. Denny had been bitterly disappointed that the Greek Government would not allow non-Greeks to work on the Acropolis project, despite the World Government's financing of the project.

("Babylon," his boss repeated. "The Iraqis have become very proud of their cultural history lately. They want to rebuild their past glories. Do a good job on the Caliph's palace and they'll beg to have you head up the Babylon project.")

The numbers flickering on Denny's wrist communicator were automatically transmitted back to World Government headquarters in Messina by satellite relay. *We'll be finished here by the end of the year,* Denny thought. *Then it's Babylon. And after that, the biggest plum of them all: Troy.*

He looked back at the palace he was building. The setting sun threw blood-red light over the new walls. Denny raised one arm over his head and watched the long shadow of his reaching fingers almost touch the base of the wall.

He turned back toward the bridge and the slow-moving Tigris. The old city of Baghdad lay on its other bank. Wafting through the still, stifling air came the high, keening wail of the muezzin's call to evening prayer—amplified by reedy-sounding loudspeakers: "Come to prayer, come to prayer. . . . Come to the house of praise. Allah is Almighty, Allah is Almighty. There is no God but Allah. . . ."

The International Hotel's terraced towers rose above

the low, colorful tile rooftops and domes of the old city. A shower, fresh clothes, and—best of all—a couple of icy beers were waiting for Denny at the hotel.

The shortest way to the hotel lay through the *suq,* the noisy, odoriferous, crowded, sweaty, wonderful bazaar that had been the center of Baghdad's life since long before Haroun al-Rashid himself. It was a dangerous place for strangers, easy to get lost in, easier still to lose your wallet. But Denny had gone through it many times, and everyone knew that he rarely carried more than a few *fils* in his pocket.

Still, men had been killed for a few *fils*—or less.

It was cooler under the high vaulted arches of the *suq.* Even where stonework or colored glass did not roof over the streets, tattered old tarpaulins kept out the day's sun and heat. But the dirt streets stank of urine and animal dung.

The crowds seemed thinner than usual. And quieter.

Prayer time, Denny told himself. *And most people are going home for the evening meal.*

All the shops were open, as usual. They always were. The shopkeepers ate where they sat or went upstairs briefly to be fed by their unseen wives. Denny stalked down the narrow, twisting street of the metalsmiths, unconsciously pacing his steps to the eternal din of the hammers banging out their deafening rhythm. Each shop displayed its wares on the street. Huge copper coffeepots—the three-gallon *ghoum-ghoums*—dominated the displays.

The beggars were all in their usual places, on every corner, against every wall, young men and old squatting in the dirt, their faint, nasal entreaties for alms in the name of Allah sounding like a poorly made tape recording.

Hardly any corpses in the street, Denny noticed. A better day than most. And the usual gangs of children were nowhere in sight. Ordinarily they swarmed around any foreigner on the theory that all foreigners were rich. They begged for cigarettes or coins, offered to be your guide, your bodyguard, your pimp, your whore. Now they were missing.

It made Denny feel uneasy, as if a many-trussed bridge were lacking one supporting beam. A discrepancy that you might not notice consciously at first glance, but you'd know something was wrong.

A gypsy girl was dancing on the corner of the street of the fruit vendors. There was the inevitable tea shop on the same corner, one of Denny's favorites. So he pulled up a rickety chair and sat at one of the outdoor tables.

The girl was young, no more than fifteen, and if she had a woman's figure it was well hidden beneath the swirling folds of her *dishdasha*. But her face was unveiled and beautiful in that eager, fleeting moment between childhood and maturity.

She swayed and spun, dancing barefoot on the dirt street to the reedy sound of a lone wooden flute played by an even younger boy squatting crosslegged against the tea shop wall. A half-dozen men stood across the street watching. No one was sitting at the outdoor tables except Denny.

"The Caliph's Builder!" said the rough-bearded old man who ran the tea shop. "What can I bring for you this day?" Months ago he had decided to speak International English for Denny, whose Arabic was a pain to the ears of any man of refinement.

"Beer," said Denny, knowing it was hopeless.

"Alas," said the shopkeeper, playing his side of their game flawlessly, "Allah in His wisdom has forbidden civilized men from imbibing."

Denny smiled without taking his eyes off the gyrating girl. "Ah, but I'm not a civilized man. I am a barbarian from a dark and northern land, where the cold forces men to drink alcoholic spirits."

"It is a sad life for you, then?"

"I have few complaints. But tell me, isn't it true that the Koran forbids the followers of Islam to drink of the fruit of the vine?"

"Truly." The old man was watching the dancing girl, too, but his wrinkled face showed no sign of emotion.

"But beer, my friend, is not made from grapes. Might not then a barbarian—or even a civilized man—partake of it freely?"

The old man looked down at Denny and grinned. His teeth were tea-stained and rotting from sugar. "I will see what can be done." He hustled back inside his shop.

Knowing that "what can be done" would be a glass of sweetened tea, Denny followed the proprietor with his eyes. He saw that several men were peering out of the shop's heavily curtained window. He got the feeling that they were watching him, rather than the girl.

The reed flute wailed on, and the girl continued her dance. Her face was beaded with sweat. But no one threw a coin. None of the watching men even smiled.

The proprietor came out with a copper tray bearing a solitary bottle of beer, already opened, and the long type of glass that he usually served tea in.

"Allah has seen fit to provide you with beer," he said, putting the glass and bottle down on Denny's table.

Denny was too surprised to ask where it came from. They never had beer in the *suq*. At least, never before.

"Praise to Allah," he said. "And to you."

The old man bowed slightly, then retreated back into his shop. Denny poured the beer and tasted it. An Eastern European brew, unchilled.

But it's beer, he thought gratefully, swallowing.

The girl finished her dance with a final swirling flourish and sank to her knees in the typical beggar's supplicating posture. The Arab men across the street simply moved away, ignoring her. She looked at the flute player—*Probably her younger brother,* thought Denny—with a sad-eyed glance. Slowly she got to her feet and pushed a sweat-matted curl of hair from her forehead.

"Come here," Denny called to her.

She turned hesitantly. Denny crooked a finger at her.

"Come on, sit down." He patted the seat of the chair next to him in case she didn't understand English.

She came to the table and stood on the side opposite Denny, looking wary, almost frightened.

"Do you speak English?" he asked, trying to smile so that she wouldn't be afraid of him.

"Yes."

A child's voice, high and uncertain. Her face would have been beautiful if she had been clean. Huge dark eyes, long lashes, rich sensuous lips. But all caked with street grime.

"Sit down. You've worked very hard. Would you like a glass of tea?"

She sat in the chair next to Denny, close enough so that he could smell her rancid body odor. Her younger brother remained squatting on the dirt a few paces away.

The old man came out again, and Denny asked for tea for the girl. "And do you have any more beer?"

"I will see."

"And something for our dancer here to eat—a sweet cake, at least."

The girl neither smiled nor acknowledged the offer of tea and sweets in any way. But her eyes continually flicked from Denny's face to her brother's and back again.

"What's your name?"

"Medina."

"Is he your brother? He looks a little like you."

"My brother. Yes."

"I'd like to give you something for your dancing." He reached into his pants pocket.

"No." Her eyes widened. "Please."

"It's just for your dancing," Denny said. "I don't expect you to do anything more for it."

He pulled a crumpled *fils* note from his pocket and put it on the table.

"No," she said, looking genuinely frightened. "I cannot. It is bad luck."

"But why were you dancing? Didn't you want them to give you money?"

"Yes."

"Then take this."

"It is bad luck!" she whispered fiercely, more to convince herself, Denny thought, than anyone else. He saw that her slim hand, the nails cracked and blackened, was creeping toward the wrinkled bill lying on the table, almost as if the hand had a will of its own.

"Why bad luck?" Denny asked.

"Death is on it . . . on you."

He could feel his eyebrows climbing toward his scalp. "Death? What do you mean?"

She took her eyes away from the money and looked straight into his. *She'll break a lot of hearts with those black, black beauties,* Denny thought.

"One hears things in the *suq*."

"Such as?"

"There will be a tall Christian, with a red beard, a foreigner who builds the Caliph's palace . . ."

Denny nodded. "That's me."

She glanced desperately around her, across the now-

24

empty street, back toward her patient, unmoving brother, into the eye-filled dim window of the tea shop.

"He will not leave the *suq* alive."

"What? What do you mean?"

"These are the whispers I have heard today. The tall Christian with the red beard will not leave the *suq* alive."

He tried to laugh, but he found that his throat was unaccountably dry. "That's nonsense," Denny said, reaching for the beer bottle. It was empty.

"It is the truth," she whispered.

"But who would want to kill me? And why?"

She had no answer.

Suddenly impatient, Denny banged his empty bottle on the table. "Shopkeeper!" he bellowed. "Where're the drinks?"

The old man came out of the shop empty-handed. He was no longer smiling. He yelled at the girl in Arabic. Denny could recognize the first two words, "Begone gypsy!" and a reference to the *Ah-reesh*. The girl scampered away, her brother following her down the narrow twisting street.

"Sir, you should not let them take advantage of you. They will beguile you with fanciful tales and steal all your money."

Denny got to his feet. He pulled the remaining few *fils* from his pocket and tossed them on the table. "That's all the money I have. She couldn't have taken much."

The old man stared for a long moment at the bills, then at Denny. His eyes were red-rimmed and sad beneath their shaggy white brows. "Perhaps you should go back the way you came and not try to walk through the *suq* this evening. It is an evil time, filled with bad forebodings."

He knows about it, too! "Maybe you're right," Denny said. He moved away from the table.

"Your money," the proprietor called out.

"You keep it," Denny said, "for the beer . . . and your advice."

He walked briskly away from the tea shop, back along the street of the metalsmiths, leaving the old man standing there. He glanced over his shoulder in time to see three burly looking men in black *dishdashas* and checkered turbans shoulder their way past the proprietor, following him.

Even the normal banging of the metalsmiths was quiet now. The sun had set, and there were few lamps lit along the *suq*'s narrow street. It all looked dark and ominous.

Is this really happening, or am I letting the legends of this place get to me? Denny asked himself. *A skinny gypsy kid gives me a line of chatter and now my hands are shaking.*

But when he looked back, the three men were still following him.

Why me? What the hell is going on here?

As he walked, he tapped out his office number on his communicator. The office computer answered with winking red letters on the tiny display screen: PLEASE LEAVE YOUR NAME, THE TIME, AND THE NUMBER WHERE YOU CAN BE REACHED. WE WILL CALL YOU BACK IN THE MORNING.

Denny growled a curse as the message began to repeat itself in Arabic script.

Calling the local police would be a joke. They never came inside the *suq* unless there was a body already bleeding in the mud.

He quickened his walk and punched out the number of his crew foreman. No answer. The Office of Antiquities, which supervised the work on the palace. Another automated answering tape.

The men behind him had also quickened their pace. They were getting closer. And Denny realized that by heading back toward the construction site he was only giving them a better chance to get at him. No one would be there. They could kill him on the bridge or at the site itself. They could bury him under one of his own walls and no one would ever find him.

He broke into a sweaty jog and tapped out the number of the local World Government office. The red letters on the communicator's display screen answered: YES?

He held the electronic wristband to his mouth and gasped into his miniature microphone, "Security office. Emergency!"

Instantly a deep male voice answered, "Security."

A human being, at least!

"This is Dennis McCormick, from the . . ."

He skidded to a stop and nearly slipped in a puddle in the dirt street. Three more men were standing up ahead of him, blocking the street.

"Yes, Mr. McCormick?" He heard the tiny voice from his wrist. "What can we do for you?"

26

Nothing, Denny realized.

He glanced around and saw a flight of ancient stone steps climbing the face of the building to his left. Instantly he was racing up them. The men below shouted and ran after him.

Denny got to the roof of the building and started running. He couldn't go far because the roof ended about thirty meters ahead in a blank wall that buttressed one of the arches spanning the street below.

He dashed to the wall, turned, and saw all six men rushing toward him. *That means there aren't any on the street below.* He jumped without a second thought. It was a two-story fall, but the dirt was soft and Denny rolled expertly to absorb the impact.

Then he ran, not back toward the construction site, but deeper into the *suq.*

The old man, he thought furiously as he ran for his life. *Did he set me up for this?*

In the darkness of the twisting streets Denny was soon lost. But at least he saw no one following him.

If I could find the street of the metalsmiths . . . or even the carpet shops . . .

But the streets were dark and the shops were shuttered. Not a soul in sight. Denny had never seen the *suq* closed up tight before. It looked as if the whole area had been abandoned. But he knew they were all inside, behind the bolted doors, waiting for the final outcome, waiting for his life to be snuffed out. And none of them would raise a finger to help him, the foreigner, the man marked for death.

He wanted to shout his rage at them all, but instead he walked swiftly and silently along the empty streets.

And then he saw a pair of men lounging against the wall up ahead. Instinctively, Denny ducked into a cross street and flattened himself into the first black doorway he could find. He waited, heart pounding.

Sure enough, they came stalking past, long slim wicked knives in their hands.

Denny slipped out of the doorway and headed back along the street he had turned out of. He glanced up at one of the rooftops and saw a checkered turban disappear not quite fast enough to evade his eyes.

Sweet Christ! They're all over!

As he approached the next street he hesitated. A glance behind him: no one. He pressed against the rough wall and took a cautious peek up the cross street. The same two he had evaded moments ago were coming toward him. One of them was peering into doorways, the other striding straight down the street toward the corner where Denny waited. The Arab had a hand-sized radio held up to his ear.

Denny took a deep breath, clenched his fists, and waited. *This won't be like a construction gang brawl,* he warned himself. *These men are out to kill you.*

As the Arab reached the corner, Denny leaped out and kicked him in the groin. He howled and doubled over. Denny smashed his fist into the back of his neck before he hit the ground. Then he picked up the knife.

The one up the street started yelling and running toward him. Denny held his ground and even took a step toward his enemy. The man suddenly halted several paces away, knife drawn.

Sure, you can afford to wait while your buddies come to help carve up the goose, can't you?

With a bellow of fury that he didn't realize he had in him, Denny charged the confused would-be assassin. The Arab tried to back away, but Denny launched himself into a football block, knocked the man's legs out from under him, rolled free, and sank his knife into the man's shoulder. He screamed and dropped his knife.

For an instant Denny's knife hovered at the Arab's throat. He could see the man's eyes, wide with pain and terror.

Denny spit in his face, took his knife, and raced away down the street. *Wish I had learned enough Gaelic to curse them all properly!*

He turned a corner blindly and ran until his chest felt as if it would crack open. Then he stopped, bent over, hands on knees—knife in each hand—and panted painfully, trying to catch his wind.

He looked up and through the arches along the wall to his right he could see the nearly full Moon riding serenely in the dark sky. *Stop grinning at me,* he said to the Man in the Moon. High overhead, the steady bright star that was Island One climbed toward zenith.

Maybe I can get a call through now. . . .

But as he looked around he saw that it was too late. A man was standing on a rooftop nearby, speaking into a hand-held radio. Denny saw that he was boxed into a sort of courtyard, an open area bounded by high walls and the shuttered fronts of shops. Three streets opened up before him. He could see that along each one of them a crew of assassins was walking slowly, steadily toward him.

Three . . . five . . . eight in all. And the bastard on the roof makes nine. Nine to one. Not good. I must be damned important to them for all this. But why? Why me?

Somewhere in the back of his head he was marveling that he felt no fear, no despair, not even anger that someone had gone to such lengths to kill him. He was trembling, but with an anticipation that was almost joyous.

Jesus, God, he thought, *we really are pagan warriors underneath all that politeness and chat.*

And then he yelled an incomprehensible battle cry and charged toward the middle street, where there were only two men waiting for him.

They stood their ground. As Denny came to within a few paces of them he threw the knife in his right hand, forcing one of the Arabs to duck, then leaped at the man and ripped at him with the dagger in his left. He heard a scream of pain and realized it was his own. Hot searing agony flashed through his body. His legs went out from under him and he was down on the ground with a sea of grinning teeth and those long evil knives above him.

A light flashed in his eyes, blindingly bright, and suddenly the knives and faces disappeared.

Moaning, clutching the hot, blood-wet slash in his side, Denny flopped over onto his belly and tried to see through pain-swimming eyes what had happened.

The lights were from the headlamps of a car. *A car? In the* suq? Someone in a black uniform . . . *a chauffeur?* He bent over Denny, peering at him intently. He turned and called something in rapid Arabic over his shoulder. A voice from the car answered.

The chauffeur grabbed Denny under the armpits and hauled him to his feet. Denny yelled with the pain of his wound and clamped both hands over it.

"Walk!" the chauffeur urged into his ear. "Quickly!"

Something inside Denny's guts was pulling him apart with red-hot pincers every time he took a step. He leaned heavily on the chauffeur, who, despite his much smaller size, held Denny upright and half-dragged him toward the car. Even in the dizzying pain Denny could see that it was a huge black limousine. *Who the hell uses these ancient zeppelins?* he wondered through his agony.

Somehow the chauffeur got the back door opened without letting Denny collapse and eased him into the car. It was hellfire to move, but at least doubling over to get inside the doorway seemed to mollify the pain a little.

Someone else was in the back, reaching out to help bring him into the car and get him stretched out on the rear seat. He lay there, his strength suddenly gone, and felt the chauffeur tuck his legs inside the car. Then he heard the door slam. It was dark inside, too dark to see. A woman's voice said something in Arabic, something about a physician. The car lurched into motion and Denny passed out from the pain.

When his eyes opened again he was lying full-length along the rear seat of the limousine and the woman was kneeling alongside him, her face still hidden in shadows. The windows must have been down, because a dark night breeze was playing with her long hair and touching Denny's own face with its cool stroke.

Or is she stroking my face?

"I must be delirious," he muttered.

"Shh! Be still. We will have a physician for you very soon." Her voice was low, almost throaty.

He felt the movement of the limousine as they sped through the night. Looking out through the windows, all he could see were the facades of tall modern buildings whipping by. *Rashid Street?* he wondered. They were far out of the *suq*, at least.

"I must be . . . bleeding all over . . . your upholstery," he said weakly.

"It is nothing."

They drove past an open square where the moonlight fell on her face. She was the most exquisitely beautiful woman Denny had ever seen. Dark, almond-shaped eyes. High cheekbones and the strong-yet-delicate jaw and nose of Arab nobility.

30

An Arabian angel, straight out of the Koran's promises of Paradise.

Maybe I'm dead, Denny thought, *and they've shipped me to the Moslem heaven by mistake.*

He had no intention of complaining about the error.

They called themselves *the* World Government, but they didn't do all that much governing, and there were certainly places on Earth where they didn't govern at all. Boardrooms of the major multinational corporations, for example.

De Paolo was an admirable man, in his way. He saw to it that the World Government got all the credit for halting the arms race and destroying all the nuclear weapons. But if you ask me, it was the big corporations—like the ones that built Island One—that finally realized that nuclear war was bad for profits. Once they went bearish on military R&D, the World Government could "persuade" the nations to give up their nukes.

But we got in a situation where the big nations (read: corporations) were using their economic power against the little nations, while the World Government stood helplessly in the middle. It was a World War, all right, an economic and *ecological* war, with weather manipulations and other environmental weapons being used in secret. And sometimes, not so secretly.

We in Island One belonged to the corporations, of course. Whether we liked it or not. . . .

—Cyrus S. Cobb,
Tapes for an unauthorized autobiography

· CHAPTER 3 ·

Wrapped in a sky-blue terry-cloth robe, David stood at his kitchen alcove, rummaging through the cabinets. But his eyes were actually on Evelyn.

Their swim had been fine, and now she seemed much more relaxed as she sat by the crackling, pine-scented fire, an oversized coral-red bath towel pulled around her, staring into the flames.

"Liquor's one of the items we don't produce for ourselves," he was telling her. "We have to import it all. Mostly, we bring in Old Moon Juice from Selene. I hear it's a combination of homemade vodka and rocket fuel. But I've got some Earthside wines here someplace . . . and a bottle of Tennessee sour mash."

Evelyn leaned back on the big pillows she had arranged for herself on the floor. "Do you mean to say that no one up here has his own little still bubbling away?"

David shook his head. "Not that I know of."

"I don't suppose you have any thieves, either."

Grinning, "And no tax collectors."

"Small wonder they call it Paradise."

He turned his attention fully to the cabinets and found the bottles. "Here we are. California chablis or . . ."

"Chablis will be fine," Evelyn said.

"It's not very cold. I could chill it for you."

"No, it will be fine as it is."

David busied himself for a moment with glasses. "What about dinner? You have your choice of rabbit, chicken, or goat."

"Goat?" Her face screwed up in distaste.

"Don't knock it if you haven't tried it. Tastes better than mutton . . ."

34

"I doubt that."

". . . and goats are very useful animals up here: scavengers, milk providers, fiber providers, meat providers."

"I'll take chicken, all the same."

David poured her wine into a frosted glass that he pulled from the freezer. Then he mixed himself a whiskey and water. He walked over to the fireplace and bent down to hand Evelyn her drink. He felt the heat of the crackling fire singeing the hairs on his bare arm.

She reached for the wineglass with one hand, keeping the other one clutching the towel together. Inwardly, David grinned at her ideas of modesty. The coral-colored towel covered like a sarong, leaving plenty of soft white skin exposed: shoulders, arms, thighs. *Her throat is beautiful*, he thought, wondering what it would be like to kiss it.

Instead, he went back to the kitchen and pulled a pair of chicken dinners from the freezer. He slid them into the microwave oven, then set the timer.

Sitting on the floor beside Evelyn, he said, "All right, dinner will be ready in a half-hour."

"That long?"

"Could be done in three minutes, but I thought you'd like to enjoy your drink and the fire first."

A strange look crossed Evelyn's face. Finally she blurted, "David, I'm *starving!* I've had nothing to eat since eleven this morning."

"Oh, for . . . I'm sorry." He scrambled to his feet. "I didn't think . . ."

"Aren't you hungry?"

"Yes, a little. But I can go for a long time without eating."

"Well, I can't."

He sliced some cheese and found a packet of wafer-thin crackers and brought them to her. They sat by the fire, watching the dancing flames. David grinned to himself as Evelyn's munching drowned out the crackle of the burning logs. The warmth of the fire and the inner glow of the whiskey started to relax him, make him feel happy. He was close enough to stroke Evelyn's bare shoulder by merely reaching out his hand slightly. Close enough to smell the faint clinging scent of her perfume. But he refrained from touching her. *No telling how she'd react.*

Before long he was lying on his back, talking about his Forecasting work.

"Then it's not at all like predicting the weather," Evelyn was prompting.

"Nothing like it," he told her. "Forecasting—the kind of Forecasting I want to do—is to pull together all the economic, social, technological trends and actually predict what the future will be—in detail . . . enough detail to make the predictions useful."

"Useful to whom?" she asked.

Shrugging, "To whoever wants them. The Board, I guess."

"The Board?"

"The group that owns Island One," David said. "Five of the biggest multinational corporations on Earth combined into a special company to construct Island One."

"Ah, yes . . . and the World Government has been trying to make them give up ownership of the colony and turn it over to the people of the world."

"Not much of a chance of the Board giving in to the World Government—not when the Board controls all the energy beamed back to Earth from the Solar Power Satellites that we've built."

"Hmm." Evelyn propped her head up on her fist, her bare white arm a vivid contrast against the bold Oriental pattern of the pillow she was reclining on.

"Are you a good Forecaster? Do your predictions come true?"

"I haven't started making predictions yet," David said, "not for public consumption. What I'm trying to do is to *understand* all the forces at work. Then the predictions will fall like rain . . . naturally."

She cocked an eyebrow at him. "But surely you must have made some predictions . . . now and then."

"Well . . . some."

"Such as?"

He thought a moment. "I came to within a half of a percent of last year's Gross Regional Products for Western Europe, Eurasia, the Mideast, and North America. I was a little off on China and Southeast Asia. And I didn't make Forecasts for South America or Africa; too much political turbulence there."

"Rather dry stuff, actually," Evelyn said.

"Important stuff, though."

"I suppose so."

"People need to know GRP's if they're going to make effective regional plans."

She toyed with the tufting of his robe. "Make a Forecast for me, something that's a bit more interesting."

David sipped the last of his drink, then said, "Well, at the rate Island One is constructing new Solar Power Satellites, we'll be able to supply the entire Northern Hemisphere with . . ."

"No, no," Evelyn said. "Don't give me numbers and statistics. How about a political Forecast?"

"Politics is crazy," David said. "Too many variables."

"But it's so important. You really can't make accurate Forecasts, can you, if you don't include the political factors."

"No, that's true."

"And you have thought about political Forecasts, haven't you?"

"Yes."

"What do you do, put all the data on a computer?"

"Computers are part of it," he said.

"And what does your computer tell you about the political situation?"

He looked at her. She was smiling at him, her bare shoulders and thick blonde hair catching the glow of the firelight.

"Well," he said at last, "there's a worldwide reaction against the World Government going on right now. It's rather small and disorganized, but it's going to erupt into violence soon. Latin America will be the first place to feel it. Then Africa, I think. Whole nations will try to secede from the World Government. . . ."

"But they can't!"

"They will if they're strong enough, and if the right factors come together," David said.

"What factors?"

He shook his head. "I wish I knew. That's what I'm trying to find out. There's an interrelationship between per-capita income and political stability, of course. But it's much more complicated than that. Weather patterns seem to be affecting political stability, especially in the poorer nations, where a bad storm can ruin their year's crop. . . ."

"But surely the World Government won't let individual nations break away. We'd be right back where we were under the old United Nations."

"There's nothing the World Government can do to stop them, short of declaring war against them."

"But will the corporations allow nations to declare independence? After all, they've invested so much money in nations such as Argentina and Brazil . . . and in Africa, too."

David blinked. "The corporations? They're not involved in politics."

"Hah!"

"Peripherally, maybe," David said. "But the World Government would never allow the corporations to have enough real political power to be a force. . . ."

The dinner chime sounded.

"Guess we'd better get up and eat," David said.

With obvious reluctance, Evelyn broke off the discussion. "I suppose I should put my clothes back on."

"It's not a formal dinner," David joked.

"Are they in there?" She pointed to the cleaning machine.

David took the clothes from the machine and handed them to her. Evelyn disappeared into the bathroom. He put dishes on the table and opened a bottle of Chilean claret.

As he took the steaming dinners from the oven, Evelyn came out, fully clothed. He held her chair for her, then poured the wine. They clinked glasses and she dove into the meal.

David watched her eat. *Like a bird,* he told himself. *A vulture.*

Several times she tried to restart the conversation about his Forecasts, but David slid off the subject each time. He was thinking about the political power of the corporations. *The Board controls all the energy beamed down from the Solar Power Satellites,* he realized. *That's political power! How stupid of me not to see it that way sooner. No wonder Dr. Cobb is trying to move me into another area.*

"The food's delicious," Evelyn said, looking just a bit annoyed at his silence.

"I really didn't do anything except set the oven's temperature gauge," he confessed. "The dinners are prepackaged. You can get them in the stores down in the villages."

And where would rebels such as the revolutionaries in Latin America get their arms and munitions? If the corporations wanted to weaken the World Government . . .

Evelyn was admiring a drumstick. "Better than anything I've had in Merrie Olde England in some time, I can tell you."

"It's all fresh food," he said, forcing himself to pay attention to her. "No preservatives or other gunk. You can do things that way when you've got only a small population to take care of."

Dabbing at her lips with her napkin, Evelyn asked, "Doesn't it bother you that you're living so well while so many billions of people on Earth are hungry and miserable?"

"I don't know. I haven't thought about it much."

"But you should."

"What about you?" he countered. "Won't it bother you to live here and leave all those miserable billions behind you?"

Her ocean-deep eyes stared at him in surprise for a moment. Then she looked down at her plate, almost guiltily. "Yes, I suppose it should bother me," she said in a whisper.

He reached across and took her hand. "Hey, I was only teasing you."

"It's not really very funny, is it?"

"But look," David said, "we're doing great things up here, things that will help those people back on Earth. We're building the Solar Power Satellites . . ."

"To provide energy for the rich people who can afford to buy it."

David put his fork down on his plate with a clink. "Well, somebody's got to pay for the construction and operations costs. The satellites don't build themselves, you know."

"So the rich get richer while the poor go on starving."

How can you argue with this woman? "What about

the molecular biology work we're doing up here? They're developing specialized bacteria that'll fix nitrogen for cereal grains, like wheat and barley. You won't need any fertilizers! That'll make food much cheaper and easier to grow—and environmental pollution will be lessened . . ."

"And the rich corporate farms will get it first and use it to squeeze out the poor individual family farmers. The starvation in the poor nations will be worse than ever."

"You've got a one-track mind!"

"And you've never been to Earth. You've never seen the poverty, the hunger, the despair."

He had no reply for that.

"You ought to go down there," Evelyn insisted. "Go to Latin America or Africa or India. See them starving in the streets."

"I can't," David said. "They won't let me."

"They won't . . . who won't let you?"

He shrugged. "Dr. Cobb. He makes all the decisions around here."

"Dr. Cobb? Why won't he let you visit Earth? He can't hold you . . ."

"Oh, yes, he can," David said. *I shouldn't have mentioned anything about it.* He felt suddenly miserable. *Now she's going to want to know everything.*

"But how can Cobb prevent you from leaving Island One? You're a free citizen, you have your rights!"

David raised a hand. "It's a long story, and I really can't go into all the details."

She looked furious for a moment. Then her expression softened into mere curiosity. "Do you mean that it's private information? Or is it some sort of company secret that Cobb holds over you?"

"I can't go into it," David said.

"Really?"

"It's all right," David tried to explain. "I have no complaints. I have a very good life up here; you're entirely right about that. Maybe too good. But I watch the TV news, and of course my Forecasting studies keep me in touch with everything that's happening on Earth."

"It's not the same," Evelyn said. "Economic data and technical reports aren't the same as *being* there."

"I know," he said. "Maybe someday . . ."

She let the subject dissipate like smoke wafting away

into thin air. David felt grateful. They finished the meal in silence.

As David was putting their plates into the cleaner's clip-on rack, Evelyn said, "I've got to get back to my quarters. It's been a long, hard day, and tomorrow they begin my orientation tours."

You could stay here, David thought. But he said, "All right. I'll take you home."

He went into the bathroom to change into a fresh pair of shorts and a pullover shirt. As he came out, Evelyn suddenly asked, "We're not going to have to walk all the way back, are we?"

He saw the almost-frightened look on her face. With a laugh, he answered, "No . . . no. I've got a bike. Don't worry."

She let out a huge sigh of relief, then picked up her bag and slung it over her shoulder as David opened the front door and held it for her.

It was night outside. The colony's solar mirrors were angled away from the windows. Once David let the front door click shut they were plunged into utter darkness.

"No stars," he heard Evelyn mutter. "I can't see a thing!"

He took her arm. "It's all right. Your eyes will adjust in a minute."

They stood in silence. Finally David said, "See? Over there to your left and up a bit . . . lights from one of the villages. And overhead, that's a shopping arcade. Down there is your apartment complex."

"It's . . . yes. I can see them." Her voice was a disembodied shadow, shaky and nervous.

David tried to reassure her. "Some people have drawn constellations from the lights overhead . . . you know, they connect up the patterns the lights make, like drawing a connect-the-dots picture. One nut even started basing horoscopes on them."

She didn't laugh.

"Now you stand right there and don't move. I'm going to get the bike. I'll only be a few paces away."

"All right." But she didn't sound very confident about it.

David walked partway around his "rock" and reached for the switch that opened the garage door. *Could it be*

*that they never have real darkness back on Earth? I
thought the cities were always covered by so much smog
that they could never see the stars.* The garage door slid
up and the light from its fluorescent walls glowed gently.
But Evelyn ran over toward him to stand in the pale light
as he wheeled the bike out of the narrow, closet-sized
garage.

"It's not a two-seater," he said. "You'll have to ride
behind me and hold on."

"It's better than walking," she said.

David swung a leg over the saddle and sat down, then
helped Evelyn onto the bike. She had to hike up her knee-
length skirt to get astride the seat.

"Ready?"

She put both arms tightly around him. There was nothing else to hold on to. "Ready," she said. Her breath
tickled the back of his neck.

David touched the starter and the bike's electric motor
purred to life. Taking hold of the handlebars, he kicked
the bike into gear and they started rolling down the trail
that they had hiked along that afternoon.

"Aren't you going to close the garage door?"

"No need to," he said, raising his voice slightly to get
it above the breeze that blew in his face. "No thieves
here, remember?"

"Why should there be?" Evelyn retorted.

The bike couldn't go fast, but it was good to be moving, to feel some wind, to feel her arms around him, her
cheek against his back. He drove in silence, the bike's
motor humming, the single headlamp throwing a pool of
brightness against the otherwise black countryside.

On a sudden impulse, David turned off the main trail
and started bumping down a crossroad. "Something you
ought to see," he called over his shoulder. "You sounded
disappointed that you couldn't see any stars from inside
the colony."

"I've got to get home," she said.

"This will only take a minute or two." They were on
a climbing path now, going along the switchbacks that
crisscrossed up the steep slope. David knew he could cut
straight up the slope on this bike if he kicked in the
motor's reserve battery power. But not at night. And never
with a passenger who could get bounced out of the saddle.

Finally they reached the level and David saw the lone lightpost of the parking area. He stopped the bike beneath the post, remembering Evelyn's shudders in the dark, flicked out the kickstand, and helped her off the bike.

"Down this way," he said, leading her to the heavy metal hatch of the observation blister.

There were no lights inside the blister, of course. That would have made reflections on the big curving bubble of plastiglass and ruined the view. They stepped through the hatch, and as David closed it, the wan light of the parking area was closed off from them.

For the second time that day, David heard Evelyn gasp.

It was like stepping out into space. The plastiglass blister bulged out from the curving wall of the colony's massive cylindrical shell. They were surrounded by the totally clear plastic of the observation blister. In the sudden darkness it seemed as if there was nothing at all between them and the stars.

Evelyn reached out, tottering. David held her close.

"I thought I was falling." Her voice was a breathless whisper in the darkness.

"The gravity's pretty light up here," he said without letting go of her.

"Good Lord! It's so . . . dazzling! Beautiful! The stars . . . there must be millions of them!"

David could have given her an exact count with just a flick of his communicator, but he stayed silent. He gazed out at the universe, at the stars that glittered like diamond dust against the infinite black of eternity, and tried to see it all through her eyes. He couldn't. But he could feel the pulse racing in her wrist, and his own heart started to beat faster.

"They're moving! Turning!"

"We're turning," David explained softly. "The whole colony is revolving slowly, to keep a feel of gravity inside. That makes it look as if the stars are rotating around us."

"It seems so strange. . . ."

He smiled at her in the darkness. "Just a minute or two and the Moon will come up."

It rose slowly, majestically, a nearly full Moon that bathed the dome with its cold brightness. David could see

Evelyn's face clearly now; her lips were parted in a joyful smile. She seemed genuinely excited.

"But it doesn't look the same," she said. "It's the same size, but it looks different."

David said, "We're the same distance from the Moon that the Earth is; that's why it looks the same size."

"But I can't see the Man in the Moon."

"That's because we're sixty degrees off the Earth's angle of view. We're seeing parts of the Moon that you can never see from Earth. Look—see that big bull's-eye down near the bottom? That's *Mare Orientale*. Up to its right, just near the equator, that's the crater Kepler. And Copernicus, next to it. You can see both of them from Earth."

"I see lights!" Evelyn said.

"The strip mines on the Ocean of Storms . . . where all the material for this colony comes from."

"Where's Selene?"

"Too far East; we can't see it. Besides, it's almost entirely underground. There's really not much to see of it."

"Oh." She sounded disappointed.

"Dr. Cobb picked the L4 location for the colony so that he could see *Mare Orientale*. He thinks it's the most beautiful formation on the Moon."

"It's . . . impressive, certainly."

"Years and years ago, when people first started thinking about space colonies, they always assumed the first ones would be built at the L5 location, on the other side of the Moon. But Dr. Cobb talked the Board into putting it at L4—strictly for aesthetics' sake."

Evelyn grinned at him. "And the Board—those grubby old moneychangers—they accepted his aesthetic reasoning?"

"No." David laughed. "But Dr. Cobb told them that if they placed their colony at the L5 position, they'd have to stare at the backside of the Moon, which is not only kind of dull to look at, but is filled with Russian placenames, like Tsiolkovsky crater and *Mare Moscoviense*. The Board is still anti-Communist enough to be swayed by silly arguments like that."

"I can imagine," Evelyn murmured.

They stood together as the Moon floated sedately past them. David called out landmarks that meant almost nothing to her: the "physicists' corner" where the craters Einstein, Roentgen, Lorentz, and others were bunched; the bright rays of Tycho; the rugged highland mountains that gleamed so brilliantly; the flat, dark expanse of the Ocean of Storms that lapped against the highlands.

Finally the Moon rode out of sight and the dome was plunged into darkness again, with only the stars to watch them.

David held Evelyn in his arms and kissed her. She melted into his embrace for a breathless, wordless moment. Then she gently pulled away.

"I do have to get back. Really." She sounded almost apologetic.

For a heartbeat's span of time David thought of pressing her. But then he heard himself say, "All right. Let's get back to the bike."

"It was beautiful, David. Thank you."

He pulled the hatch open. "Thank you," he countered.

"For what?" she said, surprised.

"For enjoying it," he said.

She shivered as they walked back toward the bike.

"Are you chilled?"

Evelyn nodded and clasped her arms around herself. "I thought you said it never gets cold here."

"This isn't cold. But here." He unzipped the saddlebag on the bike and pulled out a goat-hair poncho. "Put this on. Don't want you catching cold your first night here."

"Especially after spending a week in quarantine," Evelyn said, "before they'd let me come out here."

She pulled the poncho over her head. "What about you?"

"I never catch cold," David said. "I'm immune."

"Immune?"

He nodded as he started the bike. "They built immunities to every known disease into me."

The bike started rolling and Evelyn clutched at his strong, muscular body. Burying her face against his broad back, she told herself, *He's the one, all right. All I have to do is get him to open up, to talk freely.* She nuzzled her cheek against his back. *It should be a lot of fun.*

When they reached the village where the administration offices and apartments were, they stopped under a softly glowing streetlamp for Evelyn to rummage through her handbag and find the paper with her new, permanent address written on it.

"They just whooshed me in there this morning, from the quarantine quarters," she muttered as she went through the bag's mysterious assortment of contents, "and I didn't even have time to catch my breath before Cobb rang me up. . . . Ah, here it is!"

David checked the address and apartment number, then drove down two more quiet streets to a graceful, flat-roofed, five-story structure studded with balconies that seemed to float unsupported in midair. Lights were burning in the windows of the village buildings, but hardly anyone was walking in the streets, even though the hour was hardly late by Earth-city standards.

Evelyn didn't say a word as David walked her through the front lobby of the apartment building and into its only elevator. He touched the button for the third floor as she smiled at him.

They walked to her door and she opened it with a touch of her fingertips against the identification plate.

"Would you like some tea or something? I don't know what they've stocked in my kitchen."

"There's probably real coffee," David said. "We grow our own, you know."

"I'm not surprised." She pulled off the poncho and dropped it on the living room couch. Gesturing to the travel bags sitting just inside the open door to the bedroom, "I haven't even had a chance to unpack."

David saw that the bed was made, though. Ready for immediate occupancy.

"Excuse me a moment," Evelyn said, and she headed into the bedroom. A moment later she came back, grinning. "You're right. The toilet has one of those sonic buzzers, but neither tub nor shower."

"They must have told you about it in the orientation lectures," David said.

"I suppose I didn't pay proper attention."

David sat on the couch and folded the poncho as Evelyn puttered around the coffeemaker. It was a small apartment, typical for a newcomer: one bedroom, a living room, kitchenette, bath. No frills. At least she had a balcony and windows that looked out onto greenery. But, then, everybody did.

Before he realized it, she was sitting next to him and they were sipping coffee and talking.

"Don't you get lonely up here?" Evelyn was asking. "I mean, everybody else can go back to Earth and visit friends or family. You must be terribly lonely, stuck here all the time."

"It's not that bad," he answered. "I've got some friends."

"Is your family here, too?'"

He shook his head. "I don't have any family."

"Oh, they're back on Earth, then."

"No," he said. "I . . . there just isn't any family."

"You're all alone?"

"Well, I never thought of it like that before. But, yes, I guess I am all alone."

For a moment Evelyn said nothing. *She looks like a scared little kid,* David thought.

"I'm all alone up here, too," she said, very softly. "It . . . it frightens me to be away from all my friends and family."

He tilted her chin up toward his face and kissed her. She clung to him for a moment, and then her mouth opened and she was suddenly fiercely passionate. He felt her body pressing into him and he held her tightly. They leaned back, stretching side by side on the couch, and he began to pull the dress down from her shoulders.

"It doesn't come off that way," she whispered, with the hint of a giggle in her voice. She sat up briefly as he stroked her smooth, lithe legs and pulled the dress off over her head. Another quick movement of her hips and she was naked. He started to pull at his own shirt.

"Shh." She kissed him, then whispered, "Let me do it. Lie back and close your eyes."

She took a much longer time undressing him than herself, but David didn't care. He felt her hands, her body, her tongue over him. The sweep of her thickly curled hair against his thighs—he reached for her, pulled her up to him. She straddled his body as she had straddled the bike's seat and he exploded inside her.

Somehow he found himself in the bedroom with her under a softly caressing sheet. She lay beside him, head propped on her hand, the other hand lightly brushing his torso.

"I must've dozed off," he mumbled.

"Um-hmm," she replied, then leaned over and kissed him. He responded, and they made love again.

Then they lay together in the bed, and he stared up at the shadowy ceiling.

"You're not afraid of the dark now?" David asked.

"No, this is good darkness. I can feel you next to me. I'm not alone."

"I'll bet you always slept with a Teddy bear when you were a kid."

"Of course," she answered. "Didn't you?"

"I had a computer terminal next to my bed. And the viewscreen was set into the wall on the other side of the bed. I read about Teddy bears, though. Christopher Robin and all that."

"Have you always been alone?" Evelyn asked.

"Well, not alone, really. I've always had lots of people around me . . . friends, Dr. Cobb . . ."

"But no family."

"No."

"Not even a mother?"

He turned on the pillow to look at her. There was no way to see her expression in the darkness, only the Moon-like sheen of her hair and the curve of her bare shoulder.

"Evelyn," he said slowly, "I'm not supposed to talk about it. They don't want to make a big sensational news story out of me. The media would come swarming up here like a pack of wolves."

"You're the test-tube baby."

His breath sighed out of him. "So you know."

"I suspected. I was in the news media back on Earth. We'd heard rumors for years."

"I'm a genetic experiment," he said, "of sorts. I wasn't born the usual way. I was gestated in the bio lab here. I'm the world's first—and only—test-tube baby."

For a long moment she was silent. David waited for her to say something, ask more questions. But nothing. Finally he asked, "Does that bother you? I mean . . ."

She stroked the side of his face. "No, silly boy. It doesn't bother me. I was just wondering . . . why did they do it to you?"

Bit by bit he told her. David's mother had been one of the construction crew technicians who had built Island One. She had been killed in an accident, her chest crushed by a weightless but inexorably massive steel slab that had broken loose from its rigging while she had been guiding it into place in the colony's outer hull.

Before she died, she gasped out to the medics that she was more than two months pregnant. "Save my baby," she begged. "Save my baby." She never had the breath to tell them who the father was.

The biology team was already at work in one of the first of the colony's specialized pods, engaged in recombinant DNA research that had been bogged down Earthside by smothering government restrictions and frightened mindless mobs that wrecked laboratories in the name of Frankenstein. The colony was far from being finished, but the biologists jury-rigged a plastic womb for the fetus and sent back to Earth for the equipment they would need to keep it going.

Dr. Cyrus Cobb, the flinty anthropologist who had just been named Director of the colony—to the surprise of everyone except the Board and himself—combed every corporate laboratory within the Board's command for the right equipment and specialists to keep the fetus alive. The unknown, unclaimed, unborn baby became the pet project of the biomedical experts.

The biochemists nurtured it; the molecular geneticists tested its genes and improved them beyond anything an ordinary human being could have dreamed for. By the time the baby was "born," it was as healthy and genetically perfect as modern science could make it.

All strictly illegal on Earth, or extra-legal, at least. But at the still-unfinished Island One there was no law except that of the Board, and it was administered with even-handed finality by Cyrus Cobb, who ruled with an iron hand and a steel mind. Cobb saw to it that the baby was physically perfect and then undertook its education from infancy.

"So you never knew a mother or father," Evelyn said, her voice low, her breath tickling David's ear.

He shrugged under the sheet. "I've never known my mother, of course. Dr. Cobb has been all the father anyone could ask for."

"I wager . . ."

"No, he has. He's a fine old man. And then some. Sometimes . . . well, sometimes I wonder if he isn't my real father, you know, biologically."

"That would be wild!"

"To you. To me it's all perfectly normal."

"But you've never had a family, no brothers or sisters or . . ."

"No family quarrels, no sibling rivalries. And I've had the whole scientific staff of the colony to mother-hen me. They still think of me as something between their mascot and their prize pupil."

"Prize possession, you mean."

"They don't own me."

"But they won't let you leave the colony, won't let you go to Earth."

David thought a moment, remembering all the reasons Cobb had given him. *He wasn't being cruel to me. He wasn't!*

"See," he said to her, "I'm still a pretty important piece of scientific knowledge, on the hoof. They're still studying me, finding out how all their work has turned out. They need to study me into full maturity to see . . ."

"You're fully mature," Evelyn said, patting his thigh. "I can tell them all about that much of it."

He laughed. "Yes, but there are other complications, too. I don't have any legal status down on Earth. I'm not a citizen of any nation, I don't have any records there, I haven't paid any taxes . . ."

"You could become a citizen of the World Government," Evelyn said firmly. "Just sign a simple form."

"Really?"

"Of course."

He tried to picture himself on Earth, at the World Capital in Messina.

"Yes," he said. "But once the news media found out who I am, they'd treat me like a freak."

For a long moment Evelyn didn't respond. Finally she said, in a nearly inaudible whisper, "That's true enough."

Dad came back from Minneapolis this afternoon with the signed papers. The farm belongs to the power company now. Instead of growing wheat, the land's going to sprout antennas to receive energy from space.

Mom cried, even though she tried hard not to. But the way the weather's been acting all spring, crazy, there wasn't much Dad could do. He explained it all to us so many times; I think he was trying to explain it so that Mom would forgive him. Not that she's mad at him, but . . . well, the farm's been in the family six generations and now it's going to strangers, to some company that won't even use the earth the way it's supposed to be used, for growing things.

It's still raining. Eight days straight. Even if we had planted the seed'd be washed away by now. No wonder the banks wouldn't give out a dime. Of course, knowing that the power company wanted our land— and our neighbors'—didn't make the banks want to help us any.

The rain is awful. Just pours and pours. Never seen anything like it. And Mom and Dad—the rains have washed them away, too. Taken all the color out of them. All the life. Just washed out and away.

—The journal of William Palmquist

· CHAPTER 4 ·

The old city of Messina lay bleached-white and dozing under the harsh Sicilian sun. Olive groves still fringed the city with intense green, and the Mediterranean glittered an impossible blue. Across the Strait hunched the bare brown hills of Calabria, worn and poor as the threadbare shoulders of the region's peasants.

New Messina was also cleanly white, standing on the hills above the old city. But the new towers were of plastic and glass and shining metal. They rose straight and high, proud monuments to the new World Government. They stood aloof from the ancient, exhausted, impoverished city. No beggars dotted its streets. No filthy children, bellies bloated with hunger, wandered along its broad avenues.

Glass-enclosed walkways connected the towers of the World Government buildings. The men and women who worked in those towers never had to expose their skins to Sicily's blazing sun. They never felt the breeze from the Mediterranean, never sought the blessed shade of a sidewalk awning, never walked the dusty, winding streets and breathed the contamination of poverty and disease.

Emanuel De Paolo stood at the window of his office on the top floor of the tallest tower in the World Government complex and stared out at the tiled roofs of the low, humble buildings of old Messina. At first glance, De Paolo looked little different from the silent, bitter-eyed old men who sat endlessly in the doorways and *cantinas* of the old city. His skin was swarthy, his thinning hair dead-white, his eyes as dark and suspicious as any peasant's.

But instead of the fleshy, heavy features of the native Sicilian, De Paolo's face was fine-boned, almost delicate.

He was a slight, frail-looking man. But those black embers of his eyes were alive and alert. Bitterness was in those eyes, a weariness born of more than four decades of watching his fellowmen play their games of power and treachery and greed.

Once he had been Secretary General of the United Nations. When the World Government had been built out of the UN's ashes, he became its chief administrator. His title was Director. Around the world he was called Dictator. But he knew better; he neither directed nor dictated. He ruled. He struggled. He survived.

His aide, a young Ethiopian law student, quietly let himself into the Director's office and stood at the door, waiting for De Paolo to notice him.

The aide frowned worriedly. The Director was standing at the window again, just staring out at—what? The dirty old city, with its flies and beggars and brothels? The sea? The mountains? He did this too often nowadays. His mind was drifting. After all, the man had passed his eighty-third birthday. He had borne the burdens of world leadership for many, many years. He should rest and pass the responsibilities on to younger men.

"Sir?" he called gently.

De Paolo turned slightly, as if slowly rousing from a dream.

"Sir, the meeting is ready to begin."

The Director nodded. "Yes. Yes."

"The conference room is ready. The gentlemen have arrived."

"Good."

The aide walked swiftly across the large, deeply carpeted office and went to the closet set into the paneling of the far wall.

"Which jacket would you prefer, sir?"

With a shrug of his frail shoulders, De Paolo answered, "It makes no difference. They will not be impressed by my wardrobe." His voice was soft and melodious, a mellow old guitar speaking human words.

The aide pursed his lips and studied his superior for a moment. De Paolo was wearing his typical open-necked shirt and comfortable slacks. The shirt was pale gold, the slacks dark blue: his favorite color combination. His only decoration was a silver Aztec medallion hanging on an almost invisible chain around his neck: the gift of the Mexican people, many years ago. The aide picked a soft blue cardigan jacket and went to help the old man into it.

"I was watching the rainclouds," De Paolo said as he shrugged into the jacket. "Over the mountains, you can see the clouds build up, then turn dark, and then begin to shower down rain. Have you ever watched them?"

"No, sir, I have never done that."

"Never have the time, eh? I keep you too busy."

"No! I didn't mean to . . ."

De Paolo smiled gently at the young man. "Never mind. It's just that . . . I always wonder as I watch the clouds: Are they natural formations, or were they made by one of the weather-modification teams?"

"It's impossible to tell, sir."

"Impossible, yes. But important to know. Extremely important."

"Yes, sir."

"Don't humor me, *paco*," De Paolo said with some iron in his usually gentle voice. "They are fighting a war out there—undeclared, unacknowledged, but a war, nonetheless. Men and women are being killed. Children are dying."

"I understand, sir."

But the Director shook his head and muttered on, "We prevented the nuclear war. World War Three never happened, thanks to the satellites and the lunar rebels in Selene. We destroyed the old United Nations, but we saved the world from nuclear holocaust. You would think that the nations would be glad of it, grateful. You would think they would fall on their knees and thank God for saving them from annihilation!"

"They have disarmed . . ."

"They made a great show of destroying their nuclear weapons, yes. Because we threatened to ruin the weather for them if they did not. Because their missiles were useless against the laser weapons in the satellites. Because *we* guard the planet now, and make it impossible to use missiles and nuclear bombs. But now they have learned to manipulate the weather for themselves. And they use that as a new weapon against each other. The fools."

"It has never been proved, sir."

"Phah! Do you think the droughts in your country are natural?"

"It *is* a severe drought, sir."

"And the winter that North America went through? And this spring? The floods in China? All natural disasters?"

"It is possible."

"But not likely. We are in a war, I tell you. World War Four. The weapons are secret, silent, environmental weapons. An ecological war. They damage each other's weather, attack crops and water tables and rainfall levels. Starving a man to death kills him just as surely as shooting him."

"We require more evidence that they are doing this, sir, before we can act."

"I know. I know. What worries me, what keeps me from sleeping at night, is their next step. They play with the weather now. Do you realize what the next step in an ecological war will be?"

The aide went silent.

"Disease," said De Paolo. "Biological warfare. Viruses. Bacteria. New diseases created in laboratories, new diseases with no cures. It is coming. I know it is. I know the way they think, the way they act. We must stop them. We must prevent it."

"But how?"

The Director shook his head. "If I knew that, do you believe I would spend my afternoons staring out at the clouds?"

The aide almost allowed himself to smile. But that would not have been polite. An aide does not smile at his superior unless he is invited to, even though the aide may be delighted to see that his superior is not really becoming senile, after all.

The Ethiopian went to the door to the conference room and opened it. De Paolo stepped through. Six middle-aged men rose to their feet. De Paolo smiled perfunctorily and gestured them to be seated. He himself took the padded leather chair at the head of the polished ebony table as his aide sat quietly behind him in a sculptured plastic chair by the wall. Only one seat along the oblong conference table was empty.

"Colonel Ruiz was called away just a minute ago to

take an urgent phone message from Buenos Aires," said Jamil al-Hashimi, the representative from the Middle East.

"El Libertador's revolutionaries are stirring up trouble again, I bet," said Williams, the North American representative. He was the most handsome man at the table, and the youngest. His skin was the color of milk chocolate.

"I hope he will not be too long," said the Director.

"We must not be too optimistic about that," said Kiril Malekoff, the Russian representative, in flawless International English. "The good colonel rarely concludes a conversation very quickly."

The others around the table chuckled politely.

As they exchanged the meaningless pleasantries while waiting for Ruiz, De Paolo thought to himself, *How similar they all look, yet how different. The New Internationalism in all its paradoxical colors.*

Each man had come from a different part of the world: tobacco-skinned Arab, brown Chinese, black African, redhaired Russian, blond Dane, and the darkish American. Yet they all wore the same type of conservatively cut grayish suit. The colors of their clothing varied less than the colors of their skin. And they were all men. *We still do not allow women to rise to the level of the Executive Council. That would be too cruel.*

After several minutes, De Paolo said, "I fear we shall have to begin without Colonel Ruiz."

The chatter around the table faded and they all turned expectantly toward the Director.

"I have called this extraordinary meeting of the Executive Council to discuss personally with you the results of your investigations into unauthorized and illegal weather modifications. What have your intelligence services uncovered?"

They looked at one another, reminding De Paolo of six little boys suddenly faced with a tough question by an uncompromising old schoolteacher.

Chiu Chan Liu spoke first, his round, flat face revealing nothing of his inner emotions. "We find it impossible to investigate illicit weather modifications while my nation is being torn by civil war. I can report that *my* government is not involved in such weather alterations, although we have suffered severely from them. Our rice harvest was forty percent below the predicted yield—forty percent."

"Do you believe the Taiwanese may be altering your weather?" asked Victor Andersen, the Danish representative. The glasses he wore were not for vision, but to disguise his hearing aids.

Chiu waved a hand. "No, no, they haven't the technology. Our scientific strength remains loyal to the Central Government. The Taiwanese could never produce the trained manpower and machinery for large-scale weather modifications."

"True enough," murmured Jamil al-Hashimi. Of the entire group, he was the true aristocrat: a proud-faced sheikh who traced his line back to the son of Mohammed.

"But they could buy what they need," Malekoff said. "The multinational corporations are not above selling military technology to the highest bidders. Perhaps they are selling weather modifications, as well."

Al-Hashimi said, "They are not."

"Can you speak with assurance for all the multinationals?" Malekoff asked, a quizzical smile playing about his thin lips.

"I can speak with assurance about my own corporate holdings, and I have investigated the operations of the other major corporations. The directors of these enterprises understand fully that weather alterations are not only illegal, but impractical as weapons. They are bad for business; they interfere with making profits."

Malekoff gave a grunt that might have been a laugh. "So the capitalists desist from weather modifications on moral grounds. Interfering with profits is a mortal sin to them!"

Al-Hashimi replied evenly, "But not to Communists. Creating havoc with the world's weather would fit well with the Marxist-Leninist theories, would it not?"

"It would not!" Malekoff roared, suddenly red-faced.

"No bickering," De Paolo said. His voice was soft, yet it stopped the incipient argument before it could go any further.

"Am I to understand, then," the Director went on, "that none of you has uncovered any evidence of illegal weather alterations?"

Kowie Boweto, the African representative, hunched his massive shoulders as he leaned forward on the table and said, "It's the corporations—those big multinationals.

They're not selling weather technology to the individual nations. They're using it themselves. *They're* fighting this war—against us! Against the World Government!"

Andersen blinked behind his glasses and said softly, "That's a completely unproven assumption."

"And a very dangerous one," said al-Hashimi, "if you are implying that I have lied. . . ."

"No, not at all," Boweto countered. "But your fellow Board members know you are a member of the World Government's Executive Council. Do you think they are telling you the complete truth?"

"I have investigated thoroughly," al-Hashimi insisted, his voice ominously low.

"But they have means to stifle any investigation. A weather-modification team could be hidden away in some remote corner. It takes only a few men, very little equipment, and some computer time."

De Paolo said, "But why would the corporations do such a thing? It seems unlikely . . ."

"Because they are out to destroy the World Government!" Boweto said. "Or at least reduce us to a position of impotency. *They* want to rule the world, and they have the power and the money to do it, if we allow them to."

"I can't believe that."

Boweto clenched his heavy black fists on the tabletop. "Why won't the corporations allow our representatives up to Island One? They have a complete stranglehold on the energy beamed to us from the Solar Power Satellites. *They* built the satellites, *they* place them in operation, and *they* decide who will receive the energy here on Earth, and at what price. We have no control over them at all, utterly none. Are we a World Government, or are we a helpless bunch of blathering old men?"

Al-Hashimi's eyes were blazing, his lips a thin, bloodless line.

But Williams grinned at the African. "Now, wait a minute, brother. I'm worried about the corporations, too. But they built Island One. We didn't. They build the Solar Power Satellites. We don't. It's private property, legally and legitimately."

"And they sell the United States energy at a price you can afford," Chiu murmured.

"Island One is rather out of this world," Andersen said,

coming as close to making a joke as anyone at the table had ever heard him do. "We can hardly claim jurisdiction over it by *fiat*."

"They have a stranglehold on our energy," Boweto repeated. "And who knows what else they're doing up there, where we can't watch them? They have very sophisticated biology laboratories up there. How do we know they're not preparing mutated viruses for germ warfare?"

De Paolo asked, "Do you actually believe that Island One may be a base for developing biological weapons? Ecological weapons?"

"How do we know?" Boweto countered. "They could be doing anything they like up there, completely safe from our eyes."

Williams nodded. "There's that old story about the test-tube baby they made. . . ."

"We cannot base our actions on rumors and fears," Andersen insisted.

"Is there any evidence of this?" De Paolo asked, looking around the table. "Any evidence at all?"

"Only their refusal to allow us to inspect Island One," Boweto replied.

Malekoff leaned back in his chair. "It *is* suspicious."

De Paolo focused his gaze on al-Hashimi. "Could you use your influence to allow us to visit Island One?"

The sheikh said slowly, "It has been the policy of the governing Board to keep Island One out of politics altogether. That is why official visits from all governmental agencies have been denied."

"But surely," De Paolo coaxed, "seeing the suspicions that such a policy has aroused . . ."

"I will see what can be done," al-Hashimi said.

"Very well," De Paolo said, thinking, *And while he is delaying us, we must find some other ways of penetrating Island One. Our intelligence services will have to find an able espionage agent somewhere, one who is reliable. . . .*

Williams said, "I'd like to bring up another topic, one that Colonel Ruiz wanted to discuss, I know."

"El Libertador?" Malekoff asked.

The American's eyebrows rose. "He's causing trouble in Russia?"

With a shrug, Malekoff said, "Even in the workers' paradise there are misguided youths who think it is roman-

tic to cause mischief. We have had a few incidents . . .
nothing serious, minor sabotage."

De Paolo listened to them. Even though he had not seen
his own native Brazil in nearly a generation, news of *El
Libertador* was constantly bombarding him. A charismatic
leader, a brigand, an underground revolutionary, a rebel
against the gray authoritarianism and sameness of the
World Government.

"It seems that we are beset with movements against us
from both outer space and underground," De Paolo said
softly. No one laughed.

"El Libertador's no joking matter. He's not just some
underground Robin Hood hiding in the hills," Williams
said, thoroughly mixing his metaphors. "Even the urban
guerrillas—the Peoples' Revolutionary Underground—are
looking up to him as a sort of spiritual leader."

"He is becoming the symbol of freedom and defiance of
authority in much of Africa," Boweto said. "The PRU
groups there admire him greatly."

"It is more serious than that," Chiu said. "The Peoples'
Revolutionary Underground is a hodgepodge mixture of
youngsters who are dissatisfied with the societies in which
they live. Their actions have been violent, but uncoordi-
nated. A feeble swarm of gnats, more bothersome than
dangerous. Young rebels, who give themselves romantic
names, such as Scheherazade. But if they attach themselves
to *El Libertador* and become a disciplined world force, the
PRU could become a plague of poisonous wasps."

"Nonsense," Malekoff snapped. *"El Libertador* is little
more than a romantic legend. He represents a nostalgic
sentiment for a return to nationalism."

"He's a lot more dangerous than that," Williams said.

The door to the conference room slid open, revealing
Colonel Ruiz standing there, his face ashen, his eyes red
and tear-brimmed.

"My friends . . . the government of my nation has fallen.
There has been a coup. My fellow leaders have all been
shot or imprisoned. My own family is being held hostage
against my return to Buenos Aires."

Everyone but De Paolo bolted from their chairs to surround the stricken colonel. They helped him to a seat. The
Director's aide brought a glass of water to the man.

"Get him some whisky!" Williams demanded.

"Who overthrew your government?" De Paolo asked, raising his voice to cut through the confusion. "We had no reports of any political unrest in Argentina, except for . . ." His voice trailed off.

Colonel Ruiz looked up. "Except for *El Libertador.*" His face was twisted in shocked agony. "True. Yes. It is him. He has taken my country in one stroke. All of Argentina in his. How long can it be before Uruguay and Chile go over to him? How long before Brazil?"

Jamil al-Hashimi sat in impassive silence in his air-conditioned limousine and watched his security men fan out in all directions across the helicopter pad. They all wore the distinctive Hashimite robes and checkered turbans. They all carried short-barreled, deadly laser handguns.

The World Government owns the airfield, al-Hashimi thought, *and is responsible for its security. But the World Government has many enemies.* He smiled to himself. *Truly, if a man places his life in the hands of others, he values his life very little.*

The white-and-red helicopter fluttered out of the blindingly bright sky and landed near the limousine in a whirlwind of blowing dust and grit. Al-Hashimi accepted a turban from the bodyguard in the limousine's front seat and, pulling the cloth over his face as he would in a sandstorm, walked quickly to the helicopter.

As the aircraft took off, heading for the yacht anchored in the harbor, al-Hashimi turned to the pilot sitting beside him and said in Arabic, "Did you check this craft thoroughly?"

The pilot, his face obscured by the helmet and visor he wore, grinned toothily. "Yes, Excellency, very thoroughly. It is pure."

Nodding, al-Hashimi took his palm-sized tape recorder from his jacket pocket and began speaking into it in English, a language the pilot did not understand.

"To Garrison in Houston. Hand-deliver by the most reliable route.

"De Paolo is now concerned that Island One may be a headquarters for biological weaponry research. Boweto is absolutely paranoid about our refusal to allow inspection

61

of the space colony. Expect increased surveillance and strong espionage attempts.

"De Paolo's main concern continues to be the weather modifications. I suggest we terminate this phase of the operation as quickly as possible, before they can find a leak.

"We should make stronger ties with *El Libertador*, through the same channels that have been providing him with the matériel he has used so far. Under no circumstances should *El Libertador* be allowed to make conciliatory gestures toward the World Government, or vice versa."

Despite intense efforts by national and World Government police, the Peoples' Revolutionary Underground commandos who seized a World Government armory in Athens last week are still at large.

Led by a woman who calls herself Scheherazade, the PRU forces—mostly teen-agers or men and women barely in their twenties—looted the armory of several hundred modern automatic rifles, sub-machine guns, and assault rifles. No trace of the PRU commandos or of the weapons has yet been found.

Scheherazade herself, however, proclaimed over an underground radio broadcast yesterday that the weapons would be used "to continue the battle against the World Government oppressors."

—News broadcast,
28 May 2008

· CHAPTER 5 ·

Evelyn gripped the edge of the padded couch and tried to look relaxed and calm. She was in misery. The commutersphere—a round little spacecraft that chugged from the colony's main cylinder to the work pods that were ringed around it—floated along at less than one-fifth normal gravity. It was just enough weight to keep the passengers in their seats, and Evelyn's stomach on the queasy edge of rebellion.

The twelve trainees and their lone guide half-filled the commutersphere's rows of padded couches. Everyone else was strapped in and lying back in apparent comfort. *They're probably just as sick as I feel,* Evelyn told herself. *But they hide it better.*

She tried to put her heaving stomach out of her mind and concentrated on her goal for the day: getting into the second cylinder.

Island One was actually two mammoth cylinders, tethered together by cables that served as a sort of deep-space trolley for shuttling people back and forth from one cylinder to the other.

But while the main cylinder, where she and David and everyone else lived, seemed completely open to view from one end to the other, no one whom Evelyn had yet encountered would admit to ever being inside Cylinder B. It was apparently off-limits. *To everyone?* Evelyn asked herself. *Impossible.*

There was something in Cylinder B that They—Cobb and his cronies—didn't want people to see. So Evelyn was determined to see it.

If she survived the bloody orientation tour.

No matter how her brain insisted she was floating comfortably in the zero-gee environment, Evelyn's stomach *knew* that it was falling endlessly. Her breakfast threatened to make a reappearance.

The low-gravity rides in the commutersphere didn't help much. Neither did the view through the circular ports set into the sphere's shell: stars drifting past, and every few seconds the blue beckoning sphere of Earth swam by. *It never looked so good when I was on the ground,* Evelyn thought.

They docked with the next work pod, a bump that made her shudder.

"This pod spins at one gee," their guide called out as they unstrapped from the couches, "so be prepared for normal weight."

A couple of the trainees actually grumbled. The dolts *enjoyed* low gravity.

The twelve of them filed slowly through the hatch, all of them dressed in featureless gray jumpsuits and wearing I.D. badges pinned to their chests.

Their guide, a lanky, solemn-faced man whose hair was just starting to gray at the temples, stood by the hatch in his blue jumpsuit, already lecturing to them: "This is a farming pod, one of several agricultural centers among the work pods. While most of the colony's staple crops are grown in the cultivated areas inside the main cylinder, we use several of these outer pods for experiments in developing new crops, or for specialized types of agriculture, such as tropical fruits."

Some farm, Evelyn thought as she went through the hatch and looked around the pod's spacious interior. *It looks more like an overgrown weed patch inside an airplane hangar.*

The pod was a bare metal enclosure, spherical in shape. The farming area was a strip of plant-choked soil that went completely around the central region of the sphere. Evelyn looked up overhead and saw plants and dirt looking down at her. Blazingly bright sunlight was pouring in from circular windows set into the metal walls on either side of the cultivated strip. It was hot and muggy inside the pod, and the dazzlingly bright sunlight instantly started a headache behind Evelyn's eyes.

"Here in the pods," their guide was saying, "we can control the air mixture, temperature and humidity, the gravity, and even the length of daylight." He gestured to the windows and Evelyn saw that they could be closed with metal shutters that flanked each of them.

Since the colony's position at the L4 location kept it in sunlight eternally, it was a simple matter to control the length of day. In the pods, opening and closing the shutters determined "day" and "night." In the main cylinder, the big solar mirrors were programmed to provide a twenty-four-hour cycle.

"Thus, we can set up virtually any kind of growing conditions that we wish, without disturbing the Earthlike day-night cycle and other living conditions inside the main cylinder."

I still say they look like weeds, Evelyn insisted silently.

"In this pod," the guide went on, his face intensely serious, "we are studying the growth of parasitical plants that might attack out food crops or cause allergic reactions among susceptible colonists. Weeds, in other words."

Evelyn barely suppressed a laugh.

She turned to look at her fellow trainees, six women and five men—none of them over thirty. *They all look so deadly serious, as if their lives depend on every syllable that this bore utters.*

Then she realized that in a very literal sense their lives did indeed depend on the knowledge they were gathering. They were planning to live in the colony; they had no desire to return to Earth.

But why do they have to look like missionaries? Can't they smile once in a while?

Over the past few days, Evelyn had done precious little smiling herself. After her first day of hiking through the main cylinder, and her night with David, she had settled down to the typical trainee's routine of study and exploration. David had called several times, and she had finally agreed to have dinner with him on Friday evening. *Don't get too close,* she warned herself. *Fun's fun, but you're not going to stay here that long. Don't let yourself get burned, old girl.*

At last their guide had finished his lecture and started herding them back into the commutersphere.

"Sir?" one of the trainees asked. "I don't see any people here. Is this farming pod completely automated?"

"As much as possible," the guide said, stone-faced. "The

pods don't have as much shielding against harmful cosmic and solar radiation as the main cylinder does; therefore, we try to keep human exposures in the pods down to a minimum."

Thanks so much! Evelyn thought.

If any of the other trainees worried about the radiation dose they were receiving, they failed to show any outward concern. They dutifully filed back toward the hatch of the commutersphere, with so little conversation or chatter that Evelyn thought she might as well be back at Our Lady of Sorrows catechism school, studying under the scowling nuns for First Holy Communion.

Then she realized she had another low gravity ride ahead of her. *Just when my stomach's starting to calm down.* At least it would be the last one of the day, she hoped.

She felt a tap on her shoulder.

Turning, she saw that it was the guide, looking at her intently. He had a lean, serious face. *If only he'd smile, he might be handsome.*

"You seemed to be in some distress during the low-gee portions of the tour," he said.

For half an instant Evelyn wondered if she should deny it. But she decided that trying to brazen it out would be worse than admitting to the weakness. Obviously he had been watching her turn green.

"I'm afraid that my stomach doesn't approve of low gravity." She tried to make it sound light, bantering.

The other trainees had moved past them, like a little row of automatons, and gone through the docking hatch into the commutersphere.

"We're not supposed to give out medication to trainees," the guide said, fumbling in his jumpsuit pockets, "but I don't think there'd be any harm in this."

He took out a small plastic pillbox and removed a white capsule from it. Handing it to Evelyn, he said, "This'll keep your stomach under control. The flight back to the main cylinder takes about fifteen minutes and we'll be under less than one-fifth gee most of that time."

Evelyn stared at the capsule in her hand, then looked up at him. "That's . . . very kind of you."

He smiled at last, and his face turned into a craggy set of furrows. "My name's Harry—Harry Bronkowski."

"Thank you, Harry."

He peered at the badge on her jumpsuit. "Evelyn Hall."
"That's me."

He walked with her to the commutersphere's hatch, got her a plastic squeeze-bulb of water, and sat on the padded couch next to her for the entire flight back to the cylinder, talking all the way about his life, his work as a teacher and guide, his hobbies, how lonely life can be for a bachelor.

Evelyn noticed several of the women throwing her angry glances. *You can have him,* she told them silently. *Spacesickness would be better.*

Once they arrived back at the main cylinder, the trainees had a two-hour lunch break. They could eat at the cafeteria in the five-story-high training center or stroll down to the village to have lunch at one of the tiny restaurants there. Evelyn told everyone that she was going back to her apartment for a nap rather than risk any more food on her uneasy stomach.

She left the training center and headed in the direction of the apartment complex. But she went only a few dozen meters down the footpath. Then she stopped and looked back toward the terraced, pastel-colored training building. Her fellow trainees were out of sight; they had gone their separate ways toward lunch.

Evelyn walked carefully around the building to its far side. She passed the open windows of a kindergarten class singing nursery rhymes. *No room for them in the regular schools?* she wondered. *Or is this a special class?* Finally she found what she was looking for: an entrance with stairs leading down to the underground subway tube.

The train platform was empty. Evelyn peered down along the tubeway. No train in sight. She paced the platform nervously, waiting. *The sensors in the turnstile automatically signal the computer that there's a passenger waiting to be picked up,* she recited to herself. Looking down the tube again, *So where's the bloody train?*

Then she saw a flash of light down the tunnel, and almost before she realized it the train was gliding silently up toward her. It was only one car, of gleaming anodized aluminum. Quickly, she peeled the green trainee's sticker from her I.D. badge and carefully put it inside her jumpsuit pocket.

The train doors hissed open and she stepped aboard.

She thought the car rocked slightly on its magnetic lifters as she stepped in, but it was so slight that it might have been her imagination.

With a whoosh of smooth acceleration the train started up again. There was only one other passenger in it, a dark-haired, square-faced man sitting up at the front of the car, placidly munching on a sandwich.

Lunch is where you find it, Evelyn thought, sitting on the bench nearest the door she had entered.

The train made no other stops, but rushed in almost total silence down the length of the colony's cylinder. Smiling, Evelyn thought of her first day and how painful the trip had been on foot.

As the train slowed to a stop, she got up and waited for the doors to open. The other passenger came up alongside her and dropped the plastic wrapping from his sandwich into the disposal bin set into the car's wall. He was slightly shorter than Evelyn, but very solidly built. A fleck of mustard was on his chin.

"Are you lost?" he asked. His voice had a hint of a Continental accent to it.

"No," she answered, glancing at the job code symbol on his badge. A stylized pair of wings: he was an astronaut. "What makes you think I'm lost?"

"I never saw you down here before. You are not an astronaut or a flight controller; I would have remembered someone as beautiful as you."

Evelyn smiled at him, the kind of smile that she used to make men think she liked them.

"And you certainly do not look like the type of woman who works on the construction crew." He bulged his arms and puffed out his chest to give the impression of a heavyweight.

Evelyn laughed. "I'm new," she said as they stepped off the train and started walking toward the escalator that led upward. "I'm working for the communications media—you know, the television and the news sheets."

"Ah, yes?" He smiled. "You are going to do a story about us adventurous rocket-jockeys?"

"I'm just getting my bearings now. But as soon as my orientation period is over . . ." She let him finish the promise in his head.

"Marvelous! My name is Daniel Duvic." He tapped his

I.D. badge with a forefinger. Nodding, Evelyn told him her name.

The escalator seemed endless, an eternity of moving metal stairs that climbed off into some unseeable limbo.

"How well do you react to zero gravity?" Duvic asked. "We shall be almost weightless by the time these stairs reach the top."

"Oh," Evelyn said weakly. "I'll manage, I suppose."

She could feel her stomach dropping away again. Instinctively, she grabbed at the moving railing.

"Ah, yes," Duvic said, smiling at her. "You will manage perfectly."

Of course, he decided to be her big, strong protector and took her by the arm. She let him. The pill that her guide had given her must have helped, because her innards didn't seem quite so fluttery. Still she moved on rubbery legs as they stepped off the escalator at last and entered the metal-walled airlock area. *There's no solid floor under me,* Evelyn felt, even though she could see the tiled flooring and its colored strips of Velcro to catch your boot soles and make walking easier. She still felt as if she were dropping through emptiness. Like falling out a window.

Heavy steel hatches were set into the metal-walled corridor every few feet.

"This entire area is a series of airlocks," Duvic explained. "Spacecraft dock just a few meters beyond these walls, unload passengers and cargo, take on cargo. All these hatches seal themselves automatically if the air pressure should drop. Otherwise, this whole section could lose its air . . . *pffft!*—that quickly."

"But where is everybody?" Evelyn asked. "I thought this was one of the busiest places in the entire colony."

"It is," Duvic said, "but that does not mean that we require crowds of people. Computers and machines do much of the work."

Still firmly holding her by the arm, Duvic led Evelyn into the spaceflight control center, a dim, hot, crowded cubbyhole jammed with half a dozen technicians wearing headsets and sitting at consoles, watching the communications screens while murmuring into their pin-mikes and tapping out commands on the intricate keyboards in front of them. The only light in the room came from the eerie green and orange displays on the viewscreens.

One major screen dominated a whole wall. It showed a full-color picture of one of the factory pods, hanging in empty space a few dozen kilometers from the colony. The pod had split in half, neatly dividing along a straight seam and opening like a clam. It was disgorging a fully assembled Solar Power Satellite, an ungainly conglomeration of metal arms, shining black solar cells that resembled square wings, and microwave antennas that looked to Evelyn like the bulging eyes of some grotesque bug.

"Mon enfant," Duvic said over the humming cacophony of the flight controllers. "I am going to tow that ugly thing back to Earth and place it into a twenty-four-hour Clarke orbit."

Despite herself, knowing that the time for slipping into the colony's Cylinder B was ticking away from her, Evelyn watched the Solar Power Satellite edging slowly out of the gaping factory pod. It was like watching some huge ungainly metal spider emerge from its egg.

Finally, Duvic broke the spell. "I must get into my flight suit. We run on a very strict schedule."

So should I, Evelyn answered silently. "I must be getting back," she told him.

"Will you be all right by yourself?"

"Yes, thank you."

"Do you have an apartment, or have they given you a house of your own?"

"You can reach me through the training center," Evelyn said cautiously.

"Ah." He smiled, accepting her caution. "I would like to see you again. Under normal gravity."

"Lovely. Call me at the training center."

As gracefully as she could, with the Velcro matting clinging slightly to the soles of her boots and her stomach still insisting it was dropping down a chute, Evelyn made her way out of the control room.

But not back to the escalator that led to the tube train and the colony's main living areas. Evelyn wanted to find the cab that rode the cables connecting the two cylinders of the colony.

She checked each hatch along the metal-walled corridor. There was a small printed card on each hatch, bearing an identification code, except for the last hatch, at the end of the row. Its card said only: AUTHORIZED PERSONNEL ONLY.

The multicolored buttons of an electronic lock were set just below the card. Evelyn tried to open the door just by turning its hand latch. No go. The hatch was definitely locked.

She looked over her shoulder along the empty corridor as she reached into a pocket of her jumpsuit. So far everything she had done could be explained away as simple ignorance. She could bat her eyes at a man like Duvic and get away with being in places she shouldn't be.

But not if they see this. Evelyn took a palm-sized scrambler and placed it against the electronic lock. The microcomputer inside the scrambler took four seconds to decode the lock's combination and display it in tiny red glowing numbers for Evelyn. She touched the buttons in the proper sequence. The hatch popped open a crack, with a gust of stale, metallic-smelling air sighing out of it.

Every nerve tingling, Evelyn stepped into the coffin-sized elevator cage and pulled the hatch shut. The controls were also locked, but the scrambler quickly decoded it. The plastic cover over the control keyboard swung open and she saw that there were only two buttons, marked A and B. She pushed B.

And waited for something to happen.

If the elevator cab were moving, she couldn't detect it. She stood in the claustrophogenic cab, bare metal walls closing in on her, and tried to ignore the feeling of falling, falling that would not leave her.

Suddenly she realized that she was floating off the floor, almost bumping her head against the ceiling. Forcing down the hot surge of panic that boiled up into her throat, she reached out and pushed her hands against the walls as hard as she could. Solidity. Taking a deep breath, she wormed her way down and touched her boots to the floor matting again.

I will not scream, she commanded herself.

Then she felt the slightest of jars, and the elevator hatch popped open. Somehow she had gotten turned around and the hatch was now behind her.

Stepping out, she saw she was in another metal-walled corridor, identical to the one in Cylinder A. *Or am I still in A? Maybe the elevator didn't move at all!*

Slowly, cautiously, she shuffled down the featureless corridor, keeping her soles in touch with the Velcro underfoot, one arm stretched out to brush fingertips against the cold metal wall. It was like an old, old nightmare, walking alone, in total silence, down a corridor that was familiar, yet different, knowing that something dreadful waited ahead—or maybe was walking just behind you.

She whirled about. Nothing there. *Stop it! You're being silly.*

She passed a control center, the exact duplicate of the center Duvic had shown her. But through its heavily tinted window she could see that this one was empty, silent, crypt-cold.

The escalator that led down to the tube train was silent and still. A long climb down. But when she put her foot on the first step, the escalator hummed to life and started moving. Evelyn nearly lost her balance, but she hung on to the rail with both hands and let the moving stairs carry her down to the train platform. A single car was waiting there, also dark and dead-looking. But as she pushed through the turnstile, the car lit up and its electric motor began to purr. The doors slid open. *Come into my parlor, said the spider to the fly,* Evelyn thought. Still she stepped into the train.

The train started up automatically. Evelyn stood by the door, and the train—sensing a passenger on its "next stop" treadle—glided to a stop at the next station. Getting off, Evelyn found the stairs that led up to the surface. She climbed slowly, pausing every few seconds to listen for sounds of life. Nothing. Not even the echo of her own steps.

That frightened her more than the thought of being caught.

At last she reached the surface. It looked like a garden, with huge bushes of garish tropical flowers blocking her view in every direction. A winding footpath led off among the shrubbery, and Evelyn followed it. Palms and vine-decked tropical trees towered above her. It was like walking along a jungle trail—but in total silence. Not a bird calling. Not an insect buzzing. Not even a breeze to sway the huge trees that loomed overhead. And no sounds of people at all.

The path wound along a ridge, uncannily similar to the hillside where David had first shown her the panoramic view of the main cylinder. She stopped, heart racing, and looked out.

A tropical world. Jungles, hills covered with huge exotic trees, mountains off in the distance, flowers everywhere. Rivers, waterfalls, deep pools, a big lake in the center with sandy beaches fringing it.

Up overhead, more of the same. The man-made Samoan paradise curved all the way around the cylinder's inner surface. A vast Hollywood set for a tropical island spectacular. All it lacked was a smoking volcano—and life.

There were no buildings. No roads. No sign of human habitation.

Evelyn pulled a slim pair of electro-optically boosted binoculars from her pocket. Nothing. No villages, no bridges, no buildings. Not even a bird flying.

Island One's second cylinder, big enough to house a million people or more, was a tropical paradise. And totally empty.

The revolutionary spirit of this new century has manifested itself in many ways. All across the world, the downtrodden masses have decided that they must take their fate into their own hands and wrest power from their oppressors. In the poor nations of the Southern Hemisphere, massive civil unrest will lead to the overthrow of oppressive governments and the creations of new regimes sympathetic to the plight of the underdog. In the rich industrial nations to the North, disaffected young people are taking up the torch of revolution, for themselves and their less fortunate brethren.

They call themselves the Peoples' Revolutionary Underground. The vested interests whom they oppose call them terrorists. Their children and grandchildren, who will live in peace and freedom because of their struggle, will call them liberators. There is no higher accolade possible.

—Attributed to Colonel Cesar Villanova,
known as *El Libertador*, when his
Revolutionary Army marched into
Buenos Aires,
30 May 2008

· CHAPTER 6 ·

When he awoke, Dennis McCormick was convinced that he was in the Moslem version of Paradise—or, at the very least, on a movie set for an Arabian Nights scene.

The bed he lay on was wide and low, draped with silks that wafted gently in a warm breeze. The room was splendid with long, luxurious sofas and brightly colored pillows. Heavy, rich carpets with the intricately colored patterns of Isfahan and Tabriz covered the floor. Through the long, open windows he could see slim, fluted columns, and beyond them, the rooftops of Baghdad, spires reaching heavenward like supplicating fingers, the blue-tiled dome of a mosque.

The sun was setting, turning the sky to flame and throwing scarlet rays across the rooftops.

Denny tried to sit up, but a searing pain in his side forced him back down on his elbows with a surprised grunt. Looking down on himself, he saw that he had been clothed in silver-threaded silk pajamas. He dropped flat on his back and felt his side. Someone had bandaged his wound.

A woman appeared in the doorway: slim, dark-skinned, but with startling light blue eyes. She was swathed in a colorful dress that covered her from chin to toes.

She's not the one from the car, Denny thought. *Not beautiful enough.*

The woman disappeared without saying a word, closing the door silently behind her.

Denny stared at the tiled ceiling: the colored mosaic twined and meshed hypnotically, geometric fancies that obeyed the Moslem edict against portraying living creatures while still producing a beauty that was spellbinding.

Maybe I imagined her, he said to himself. *Maybe I was delirious.*

Himself answered with, *And how did you get here, then? Is this a hospital room, do you think?*

He laughed, and he felt a twinge in his side for it. "Not very likely," he answered aloud. "There aren't hospitals like this anywhere on Earth."

The woman appeared again, this time with a tray of covered dishes. Without a word, without even looking up to meet Denny's eyes, she rested the tray on the floor beside his bed, knelt on the carpeting, and took the cover off a bowl. The aroma of hot, spiced soup wafted up and Denny suddenly realized he was ravenous.

He tried to sit up but the pain stopped him again. "Damn!" he gasped, angry at his weakness.

She touched a hand to his shoulder, a wordless gesture that told him to lie back. Denny saw that she was only a kid, a teen-ager. She began spooning the soup into his mouth, holding his head up slightly with her free hand behind his neck.

It would have been incredibly sensual if he hadn't been so hungry. Denny lay there, feeling helpless but not caring about it, as she fed him, bit by bit, a meal of soup, kebab, and fruit. Nothing to drink but water, though.

If this really was heaven, they'd have ale, Denny thought. *A pint of lager, at least.*

The girl was putting her last empty dish back on the tray when the door opened and a gray-haired man walked into the room. He stopped at the foot of the bed and stared intently at Denny. The girl took her tray and scurried out of the room.

As the door closed once more, the man bent his head slightly in the barest of bows and said, "I am Sheikh Jamil al-Hashimi. This is my house. You are welcome in it."

"Thank you," Denny said. "I'm Dennis McCor——"

"I know who you are," said al-Hashimi.

He was not a tall man, but he radiated authority and self-possession. He had the aristocratic, high-boned face of a true sheikh. His skin was the color of fine light tobacco. His clothes were Western: a white business suit and a pale salmon open-necked shirt.

"We've never met before," Denny said.

"My people took the liberty of examining your clothes

and your wallet when you were brought here. I have heard of you, of course, and have spent many evening hours contemplating the palace you are building across the river."

"I hope you like what you see."

The faintest flicker of a smile crossed al-Hashimi's face. "I have examined your drawings, and the artist's renditions of the completed palace. It will be very beautiful—if it is ever completed."

"If . . . ?"

"This attempt on your life. I fear it is a reaction against the palace."

"Against the palace?" It was damned awkward, trying to carry on a conversation while on your back.

Al-Hashimi nodded slightly. "You have heard of the Peoples' Revolutionary Underground? Apparently they are not pleased with the idea of such a castle."

"But the Iraqi Government . . ."

Raising a hand, al-Hashimi said, "I am part of the Iraqi Government—and of the World Government, as well. I understand what our official program is. But you must understand, Mr. McCormick, that the PRU is opposed to the World Government . . . and to any national government that has joined the World organization."

"But what's that got to do with the castle?"

"Perhaps they see it as a travesty of their history . . . or as a commercial venture that degrades our people. More likely, since it is a World Government project, they are determined to stop it. Their reasoning never runs very deep."

"And they think they can stop the project by killing me?"

Al-Hashimi spread his hands in a Semitic shrug. "A few cutthroats are cheaper than explosives."

"Who are they? Can't we talk to them? Explain?"

"I am trying very hard to discover just who they are. And when I do, there will be no talking, no explanations."

A sudden memory made Denny's insides feel hollow. "I think maybe some of my work crew is in with them."

"Probably not," al-Hashimi said, "although the PRU can intimidate most people into at least a tacit cooperation."

Some people, Denny thought. *Like the whole* suq.

"Since they have apparently marked you for death, you will remain a guest in my house, where you will be safe."

"What about construction of the palace?"

Al-Hashimi's nostrils flared. "That can wait. It is considered polite, even in barbarous nations such as Canada, to thank a host for the offer of hospitality."

Denny was too surprised to be angry. "I do thank you. I didn't mean to be impolite. It's just that I'm concerned about the palace construction."

The sheikh relaxed visibly. "I quite understand. I will not detain you here longer than is necessary. In the meantime, my home is yours. Whatever you wish, you have merely to ask for."

"I am deeply grateful," said Denny. *Better keep a tub of blarney around, to keep this one buttered up.*

With another slight bow, al-Hashimi said, "If there is nothing else you require at the moment . . ."

"One thing," Denny interrupted.

The sheikh's eyebrows rose a millimeter. "Yes?"

"How did I get here? I . . . I remember being cornered by those . . . cutthroats, as you called them. I remember fighting with them, and one of them must have struck me. But then . . ." He let the sentence dangle, realizing he didn't quite believe his own memory of the exquisite woman in the limousine.

A slight expression of distaste showed on al-Hashimi's haughty face. "You were found by a young lady . . . an overly emotional, very romantic young lady who should have taken you to our excellent city hospital, but instead brought you to her home."

"Her home?"

"The young lady is my daughter. She was in the *suq* after nightfall, a foolish thing for her to do. When she saw you fighting she ordered her driver to break up the melee. The would-be assassins fled as the car approached, thinking it was the police, no doubt. She found you bleeding in the street and brought you here."

She really exists! "How . . . how long ago was that? How long have I been unconscious?"

"The fight occurred last evening. You have slept this entire day. The physician said it was good for you to sleep."

"Your daughter saved my life."

79

"Yes."

"I would like to thank her."

The sheikh's whole body stiffened. "That will be impossible. She is about to go away, to continue her education. She is going to Island One."

It was two days later when Denny learned that the sheikh had lied to him.

The only people he saw in his luxurious room were the serving girl and the doctor. There was a huge wall-sized viewscreen, so he could watch worldwide television and even talk face-to-face with his boss back in Messina and his crew foreman across the river at the construction site. The boss looked upset that the construction schedule might slip; the foreman looked guilty and promised to drive the men just as hard as Denny would himself.

The wound in his side was healing quickly, but they still wouldn't let him out of the room. Denny was able to get up and walk across the room by the second day, although he felt woozy by the time he clutched the handle of the door.

Opening it, he found a husky young man with a pock-marked face sitting in the hall outside, a cigarette dangling from his lip, a lurid pornographic magazine on his lap, and a huge black pistol buckled to his hip.

The guard stared at Denny for a moment, then jabbed a forefinger at him. The gesture was unmistakable: *Get back inside where you belong.*

"So I'm a guest whether I like it or not," Denny mumbled in English. But he closed the door and stayed in his room. He didn't feel strong enough to argue.

Denny found himself spending the cooler hours of the morning out on the terrace beyond his windows, sitting among the fluted columns that held up the roof and watching the mists rise from the river and dark green groves out beyond the edge of the city.

That's when he saw her. Down in the courtyard of the big five-story house, his third morning there, he watched a sporty electrobike screech through the gate and skid to a stop. The young woman driving it hopped off and pulled the crash helmet from her head. Long black hair cascaded to her shoulders. She tossed her head and glanced upward. Denny saw her face. It was her.

Her father came charging out of the house just at that moment, speaking to her in low, rapid French. *So the servants won't know he's yelling at her.* Denny couldn't catch the words five floors up, but he knew the tone: Papa was chastising daughter for driving through town recklessly—and staying out all night.

She laughed and shrugged in a very French way and pecked at his cheek. He stood there helplessly as she strode into the house.

Later that day, when the serving girl brought Denny his lunch tray, he asked her, "Can you speak English?"

He had tried to speak with her before, but she always responded with nothing more than a startled, wide-eyed stare and a mumbled phrase of Arabic that was the local version of "I don't understand."

She shook her head.

"Very well, my girl," Denny said cheerfully. "In that case we'll just put some modern miracles of electronics to work on the problem."

He tapped out a set of numbers on his wrist communicator and linked it to the wall-wide viewscreen across the room.

INTERNATIONAL TRANSLATION SERVICE glowed in bright yellow letters across the screen as a female voice said, "I-T-S. May we help you?"

Denny knew it was a computer speaking. He ordered, "English to Arabic, and reverse, please. Conversational. Baghdad dialect, if there is one."

"Certainly, sir." The computer already had Denny's billing code; that had been part of the information he had to punch into the communicator to make the call.

"What is your name?" Denny asked, looking at the girl.

The viewscreen showed the question in flowing Arabic script, as a masculine voice—not too different from Denny's—asked the question in that language.

The girl stared at the screen, then looked at Denny.

"Don't be afraid." Denny smiled at her. "I just want to know your name."

The screen repeated his words in Arabic.

"Irene," she said in a tiny voice. She pronounced the last vowel.

"But that's a Greek name."

"You won't tell Sheikh al-Hashimi that I spoke with

you? He ordered me not to speak with you at all, even though I have no English."

"I won't tell him. There's nothing to be afraid of."

"I am Greek," Irene said. "I work for al-Hashimi as a household servant, for wages. My father is a tax accountant for the sheikh."

Denny sat himself down on the bed and leaned back. "Well, I'll be damned! Would you rather talk in Greek? The computer can do that, you know."

"It is my own language," she said. "I also speak French, and some Italian."

"Greek," Denny said. "It'll be easier for you."

Within a few minutes, she was sitting on a chair next to the bed and they were not only friends, but conspirators.

"Al-Hashimi picked me to serve you because I have no English. For some reason he does not want any of the household staff to speak with you. If the guard outside the door knew . . ."

"Why is that?" Denny asked, automatically lowering his voice. "Am I a prisoner here?"

"I do not know. The sheikh is concerned about protecting you. I think he is also concerned about his daughter, the one who brought you here."

"Concerned about her? What do you mean?"

"He is a father who wishes to protect his daughter from men. Very old-fashioned, when it comes to his daughter."

"Oh. That's why . . ."

"He is not so old-fashioned about himself," Irene added.

"How many wives does he have?"

With a troubled shake of her head, Irene answered, "He had only one wife, and she died years ago. But he has many lovers, boys as well as girls. He has shown some interest in me, but his daughter has protected me from him."

"What does your father think about that?"

Her face went grim. "My father will do whatever he is told to do. His eyes can be closed by money."

"But the daughter lives here," Denny said.

"For now. She will be going into space very soon. The sheikh wants to send her to Island One, to live and study there."

"She's a scientist?"

"No," Irene answered, laughing. "And she has no desire

to leave Baghdad. They have been arguing about this for weeks. It is quite a scandal. Arab daughters are not supposed to argue with their fathers."

"She's strong-willed, is she?"

"She was educated in Paris and Italy. They put Western ideas into her head."

Denny chuckled back at her. "I'm glad for that. What's her name?"

"Bahjat. And she has been forbidden by her father from seeing you."

"Now, did I say . . ."

"You are in love with her," Irene said, her eyes sparkling with delight. "The entire household knows that she saved your life and brought you here. It was her blood that saved you."

"Her blood? You mean a transfusion?"

"Yes. Otherwise you would have died. The sheikh was furious when he heard of it. The blood of an al-Hashimi, given to an infidel! He was furious."

Her blood is flowing in me. "But that doesn't mean I'm in love with her," he said to Irene.

"Then why are you asking me all these questions about her?"

Denny thought a moment, then countered, "Why are you risking your job to answer my questions?"

"Because . . ." She hesitated. ". . . Because it is all very romantic. Bahjat has tried to see you, you know."

"Really?" His voice nearly cracked, like a teen-ager's. "I . . . well, of course, I'd like to see her very much . . . to thank her properly, of course."

"I will tell her so."

"Good!" Then he realized. "You're not going to tell her that I'm in love with her, are you?"

"Certainly. What else?"

"But it's not really true! How do I know . . . I mean, I've never said a coherent word to her."

Irene smiled knowingly, picked up her tray, and flounced out of the room.

Women, Denny snorted to himself. *That's all they think about—romance. Soft in the head. Now she's going to have the whole household buzzing about me. The old sheikh'll probably throw me out into the alley and let those thugs finish their job on me.*

But he found that he was grinning. And his heart was pounding as hard as if he'd run a mile. Then he realized that he hadn't touched a morsel of the lunch that Irene had brought him. But he didn't care. He wasn't the slightest bit hungry.

"Holy damn!" he murmured to himself. "I *am* in love with her!"

Denny spent the afternoon pacing his plush prison room. He went out to the balcony a hundred times, even in the blazing sunlight of the afternoon. But the courtyard below was empty. The whole city seemed to be drowsing in the heat.

He thought about phoning his crew foreman, but he realized that he wouldn't be able to concentrate on work. He just didn't care about it—not now.

Finally, with the heat of the afternoon soaking through him like an inescapable doom, he threw himself on the bed, still in his pajamas, and dozed off. His last conscious thought was of childhood admonitions, back in Newfoundland, against even involuntary masturbation.

It was dark when he awoke. The opening of the door snapped him out of a dark, sweaty dream. It dwindled away into subconsciousness, like the winking out of a television picture.

He sat up on the bed.

A woman was bringing him his dinner on a silver-inlaid tray. But this was not Irene: she was taller, and she wore a silken shawl over her head. Her face was in deep shadow.

Don't be silly; it can't be her.

But his pulse was racing.

She put the tray down on the low table halfway across the room, then came up to the bed. Slipping the shawl down over her shoulders, she smiled at him.

In the faint light from the windows he saw that it was Bahjat, as dazzlingly beautiful as he had remembered her. She was a picture out of the Arabian Nights, a raven-haired, flashing-eyed, slim-waisted Scheherazade. Beauty and intelligence and love shone in her face.

Denny tried to speak, but his voice choked.

She put a finger over his lips and whispered, "I can

84

only stay a moment. The physician tells me that you are healing rapidly. I am glad."

"I wanted to thank you . . ."

She shook her head slightly. "Such a beautiful red-haired *Ah-reesh*. How could I let you die?"

She leaned over swiftly and kissed him. But as Denny moved to embrace her, she backed away and retreated toward the door.

"I will return to you," she whispered. And then she was gone.

There are striking similarities between the aging and death of cities and the aging and death of stars, such as our Sun.

As a star ages, it loses its nuclear energy sources. It begins to swell and becomes a Red Giant. But even as it is expanding, its core is becoming dense, hot, and degenerate. Ultimately, when the star runs out of energy, it collapses. Our Sun will one day become a White Dwarf star. For stars more massive than the Sun, the collapse triggers a supernova explosion that destroys everything except the tiny, hot core. And if the original star was *really* big, even this seething core vanishes entirely into what astronomers call a Black Hole.

As a city ages and loses its energy sources (taxpayers), the city begins to swell. We call this urban sprawl. But, just like a star, the city's core is becoming denser, hotter, degenerate. Ultimately the city will die. The bigger the city, the more likely that its death throes will include an explosion. Very large cities, such as New York, will probably explode so violently that there will be little left. Not even a Black Hole.

—Janice Markowitz,
The Evolution of Cities,
Columbia University Press, 1984

• CHAPTER 7 •

They had him set up just right.

It was way past midnight and the streets should have been empty. Nobody in his right mind walks the streets of Manhattan after dark, especially alone. Nobody but rats, and maybe a stray cat that thinks it can handle itself.

Daytime, Manhattan was still livable—in places. But at night you barricaded yourself into your room and slept with your guns within easy reach.

Lacey had the job of trailing the sucker.

The dude was black, and he wore the right kind of clothes: blood-red shiny plastic jacket with the sleeves torn off, tight-ass bullfighter pants, heavy boots that're good for stomping or running. But the clothes were *too* right, like somebody'd handed him a uniform. And they were new. Instead of fitting into the First Avenue scene, he stood out like a hooker's pointed bra.

The giveaway, though, was the fact that he cruised the avenue only a couple of blocks from the old UN building, never any farther. He wanted to be where the other white-asses could watch him on their cameras and listen to what was said with their long-range pickups.

White-ass, Lacey grumbled to himself. *I could pick him off just like that.*

The sucker was a cop. Not just a regular cop: they knew what the rules were and left the Neighborhood Associations alone, so they could run their turfs like they should. This dude was a World Government cop. And he wanted to meet Leo himself. *Talk* with him, for Chrissakes.

And Leo had laughed and said, yeah, let's do it, let's talk with the turkey. *What the fuck for?* Lacey wondered.

But when Leo says do, you do. No matter which association you're with, no matter who's got a war going on with who. Leo didn't give many orders, but when he did, you jumped.

Lacey squinted down First Avenue. A wind was coming off the river, carrying the stench of garbage with it. The ruined old stump of the UN building looked like a blackened, cracked ghost in the sad moonlight that managed to filter through the clouds. Lacey shivered. People lived in these old buildings around here and took their chances with the rats that honeycombed them.

JoJo and Fade were up ahead of the dude, scouting out the territory, making sure the mother was by himself. Didn't want to set up Leo. *Fuckin' World Guv'mint's tried t' nail him more'n once.* But Leo was always too smart for them.

The tiny radio stuck in his left ear crackled, and Lacey heard Fade whisper, "Okay up here."

Lacey grunted, then asked into the toothpick mike he had clamped between his teeth, "JoJo? Whatcha got?"

"Biggest damned cockroach you ever saw. But nothin' else."

"Okay. Stay covered." Lacey took the toothpick from his mouth and stuck it behind his right ear, then stepped from the doorway he had been huddling in and walked out in the open, along the bluishly lit sidewalk, toward the stranger.

The turkey strolled along, hearing nothing behind him. *Shit, man, I could snuff you right now an' you'd never know what hitcha.*

But instead he dutifully jogged up behind the dude and said out loud, "C'mon."

The guy jumped a foot off the pavement and whirled around. There was a mean-looking pistol in his hand.

Lacey made a sour face. "You wanna see Leo or you wanna get zapped?" JoJo and Fade had him in their sights, of course.

"You're from Leo?" The gun didn't waver, and the dude's voice was firm. *Pretty gun.* Lacey made a mental note for future reference.

Instead of answering, Lacey said, "Le's go, man. This way." He jerked a thumb toward the darkness of Forty-fourth Street.

The man tucked his gun into a holster under his armpit. "Okay," he said. "You lead."

Lacey started walking, thinking about how he might be able to get that gun for himself before the night was over.

Leo had set up the meeting in the apartment building run by the local Association. It was falling down and most of the windows were gone, but up on the top floor things were still pretty good. They even had electricity.

He was a big man, Leo. *Bigger'n anybody*, thought Lacey. With a grin to himself, he added, *Bigger'n any two bodies.*

Leo was sitting in a tattered old armchair, his immense bulk lapping over the sides of it, threatening to split the chair apart like a bomb blows out a building. His hands were the size of Lacey's head, his arms thicker than most kids' chests. He looked fat, but it was the kind of fat that wrestlers have. He was strong enough to lift a car right off its rear wheels, and he could break bones the way other guys snapped the tops off beer cans.

And he was *black*. Not Lacey's own caramel color, or even the darker chocolate of JoJo. Leo was African black, as dark as they come. The wop kids called him *melanzana*, eggplant, because of the deep purplish-black of his skin.

The cop from the World Government looked white alongside Leo. He stood there fidgeting on the roach-chewed rug, looking around at the bare walls with the plaster going, the cracked and sagging ceiling, the windows that were painted black so snipers couldn't see a target through them.

Finally he looked at Leo, who was sitting easy, a can of beer almost lost in his big fist.

"Hello, Elliot," the man said.

"Elliot?" Leo roared a giant laugh. "Who the fuck you callin' Elliot, man? What kinda name's that?"

The cop didn't answer.

"The name's Leo, white-ass," said Leo in a nice purr of a voice, just like the big cat he named himself after. "Leo. An' don't you forget it."

"All right . . . Leo."

"Tha's better."

Strangely, the World Government cop grinned. "Can we talk?"

90

"Sure, man. Tha's why we here, ain't it?"

The cop nodded toward Lacey and his street-brothers. "What about them?"

"No problem. Ain't nothin' you gotta say they can't hear."

The cop pursed his lips. He looked at Lacey, Fade, and JoJo, then back at Leo. The big man sat back in his chair, smiling genially. *He ain't even gonna let the dude siddown,* Lacey thought. He glanced over at Fade, who took one look at Lacey's grin and nudged JoJo in the ribs.

"Okay," the cop said at last. "We're bringing you back in. Orders are that it's time for you to come in from the cold."

"Fuck orders," Leo said, easy and pleasant, still smiling.

"This isn't a joke, Elliot. They mean it. They're afraid you're going sour, turning native."

"They's right, man."

The cop made enough of a move with his right hand for Lacey to pull his own heat from his scruffy jacket and take a step toward him.

But Leo lifted one massive finger and the cop froze where he was. Lacey stopped in his tracks.

"Listen to me," the cop said. "If you don't come back now, voluntarily, they'll drag you back."

"Take some draggin'," said Leo.

"They can do it. You know that."

Leo slowly got to his feet. It was like a dark storm cloud rising. "No, they only *think* they can do it, Frank," he said in a kind of voice that Lacey had never heard out of him before. He sounded almost like the cop! "I've learned quite a bit about how things go out here in the streets, quite a bit about power—how to get it and how to use it. Power does not reside in government bureaus and agencies. There's no power in those long corridors between offices or among those faceless, interchangeable automatons that you report to. Power is *here,* in the streets, in the cities, among the people who are hungry enough, scared enough, mean enough, desperate enough to fight."

The cop staggered a step backward. "You're talking nonsense. Madness!"

"Am I?"

"You can't survive out here without us, Elliot. The

91

melanin treatments, the steroids, the hormones—they'll cut off your supply."

Leo shrugged massively. "I've got other sources, Frank. I don't need you people anymore."

"But you can't fight the World Government!"

"Can't we?" Leo advanced on him, step by step, and the cop retreated. "*You* are the World Government, here in this room. If I asked these boys behind you to wipe you out, how long do you think you'd stay alive?"

He backed into Lacey's gun. Lacey's hand trembled with the anticipation of squeezing the trigger.

"No," Leo commanded. "Let 'im go. Send this white-ass back where he come from."

"You're crazy, Elliot. The drugs must be affecting your brain. They'll come and get you . . ."

"Shee-it, man." Leo's voice went back to normal, and Lacey felt better for it. "*We* gonna come an' get *you*. We got more soldiers than you got, more guns, too. An' we know how t' use 'em. All over the world, man—the under-dogs are gonna knock off the white-asses, wherever they are."

"That's crazy. Impossible." But the cop sounded scared and weak.

"Take 'im back where you found 'im," Leo said to Lacey. "An' see he gets back okay. No funny stuff. I know he got a fancy gun on 'im. See he gets home with it still on 'im, catch?"

Feeling disappointed, Lacey tucked his own gun inside his belt and nodded. "I catch, Leo."

Lots of people have called me a dictator—and worse. I suppose there may be some truth it in. Island One is a democracy, legally. We have an elected council and every important issue is put to an electronic vote by the entire population of the colony. It's easy enough to do that when the population is small and everybody's wired into the communications net.

But a democracy works only as well as its citizens want it to. Most citizens are too busy doing other things to care much about how their community is being managed.

See to it that they have jobs, that their garbage is collected regularly, and that the communications media are under your control. Then you can become a pretty effective dictator yourself, even in a democracy. . . .

—Cyrus S. Cobb,
Tapes for an unauthorized
autobiography

• CHAPTER 8 •

"Empty?" David asked. "What do you mean, it's empty?"

He and Evelyn were seated in one of the last rows of the crowded theater. Down on the circular stage, an exquisite ballerina and her muscular partner were holding the capacity audience spellbound with a magnificent *pas de deux* from "Sleeping Beauty."

"It's empty," Evelyn whispered to him, paying no attention to the dancers. "The whole bloody cylinder is empty."

Keeping his eyes on the stage, David whispered back, "It's a hollow shell?"

"No. It's landscaped. It's filled with a tropical jungle. But nobody's living in it! Nobody at all!"

The dancers were with the Bolshoi Ballet Company. They were performing in Moscow. Their images were being transmitted electronically to Island One, where three-dimensional holograms made them appear as solid and real as if they were actually physically present on the colony's stage.

A two-way computer feedback loop allowed the Island One audience's reaction—mostly applause and shouts of *"Bravo!"*—to meld with the reaction of the live audience in Moscow, so that there was emotional feedback between the colony's audience and the performers, as well.

David turned and looked at Evelyn. She was watching his face, paying no attention to the ballet.

"Well?" she asked. "What do you think?"

"Let's get out of here."

They had to push past a whole row of irate balleto-manes, who growled and snarled as David and Evelyn stumbled over their toes. Finally they were out in the aisle. Evelyn strode toward the exit. David cast a final glance over his shoulder at the lovely dancers.

Wish I could control my body that well, he thought. He had briefly tried dancing and found that he was much too self-conscious for it. Even in the zero-gravity sections of the colony, where overweight grandmothers could execute maneuvers that no Earthbound ballerina could even hope for, David had decided that ballet was not for him, emotionally.

Outside the theater, he walked with Evelyn along a leisurely, winding footpath that led through one of the colony's scattered villages and back toward her apartment complex.

"How do you know all this about Cylinder B?" David asked. "It's a restricted area."

With a slightly impish grin, Evelyn confessed, "I was there. I snuck in."

"You what? When?"

"This afternoon."

Most of the village shops were still open; it was early evening. David saw an outdoor café and gestured Evelyn to one of its drum-sized round tables.

"How did you get in?" he asked as they sat down. "Access isn't permitted unless . . ."

"I broke in," she said simply. "I had to find out what was going on in there, so I cracked a couple of electronic locks and went in to take a look."

David's thoughts whirled. He sagged in the chair, not knowing what to say next. *Broke in? Cracked the locks?*

The speaker grille set into the tabletop buzzed. "May we serve you?"

Evelyn flinched in surprise, but she immediately recovered herself. "Whisky and soda, please," she answered.

"With ice?" the speaker queried.

"One cube."

"Any particular brand of whisky?"

"No, just a good unblended one."

"Thank you. Our sensors detect two persons seated at this table. May we serve you?"

"Sensors?" Evelyn looked slightly puzzled.

"A glass of rosé wine, please," David said softly.

"Would you care to make a selection from our wine

list?" A small square section of the tabletop lit up, revealing itself as a viewing screen.

"No, thanks. Just a glass of the local rosé. Any year except the most recent one will do."

"Yes, sir."

The screen light went off. Evelyn tapped a fingernail against the speaker's tiny grille. "Is it off? Can he listen to us?"

David shook his head. "It's a computer. The whole café is run electronically. Even the waiters are robots."

He pointed to one of the "waiters." It looked to Evelyn like one of the tables, a hips-high plastic drum that had somehow gotten loose and was rolling through the café on its own. A tray of drinks was resting on its flat top. It stopped at a nearby table and the quartet of people sitting there helped themselves to the glasses and pitchers.

"That's a robot? I've never seen one before."

Evelyn watched as the robot trundled its way back toward the bar, inside the building, neatly threading its way through the scattered outdoor tables and the crowd milling around the building's entrance.

"I know the cafeteria at the training center is almost completely automated," she said. "Are all the restaurants in the villages, also?"

"Most of them. People don't come to Island One to take menial jobs. Our engineers had to develop these special-purpose robots. They're not very bright, but they can do limited kinds of jobs. We're starting to sell them back on Earth. Makes a little extra profit for the colony."

"Take more jobs away from people who need the work," Evelyn muttered.

"It makes more jobs for the people who will build and service the robots," David countered.

"The rich get richer. You can't expect a busboy who's had no education to become a computer technician."

"You can if you give him the education he lacks."

"Fat chance! By the time he's twelve he's unteachable. Bad nutrition from before birth, bad family upbringing, bad schools—if any . . ."

She stopped as the robot rolled up to their table, bearing a tray with their two drinks on it. David did the honors after tapping out his credit number on the robot's flush-set keyboard. It hummed briefly, winked a green light that confirmed the transaction, then said, *"A votre santé!"*

Evelyn smiled at it. The robot backed away from the table, then turned on its trunnions and rolled off.

"How pleasant," Evelyn said, watching it.

"Why did you go snooping into Cylinder B?" David asked. "You could have gotten into serious trouble. Dr. Cobb has expelled people from Island One for less."

For a moment Evelyn looked undecided. She took a sip of her Scotch, then put the glass down firmly on the tabletop.

"David," she said, "I never intended to remain in Island One indefinitely. My application for permanent residence here is a fraud. I'm a news reporter, and I came here to find a story and then return to Earth to tell it."

He felt his insides congealing into ice. "About me. You wanted to do my story—the test-tube baby is now a fully grown man."

She nodded slowly, lips pressed together into a bloodless white line.

David stared at her, trying to grasp what he felt inside himself. Fear? Anger? Neither. He felt pain, he felt hurt. Bitter disappointment. Shame. *You stupid fool! And you thought she really cared for you.*

"Well, you got your story the first night. I hope you enjoyed it. Everything you always wanted to know about the manufactured man, including his sex life. Was I any good? Do you want me to pose for photos?"

"David, please . . ."

"Why did you stay on?" He could feel the ice inside him melting under the flames of growing anger. But he was more angry at himself than her, and he knew it. "Why didn't you leave the following day? You had everything you came for. God, even Dr. Cobb made it easy for you. He threw you in with me."

"That was a coincidence."

"Sure."

"Cobb doesn't dream that I'm a snoop. The reason I had to pose as an applicant for permanent residence is that he won't let news reporters into the colony."

"Well, you don't have to stay any longer," David said, his voice going husky in his throat. "You can leave on tomorrow's shuttle."

"Not yet," she said firmly.

Just get up and leave, he told himself. *Go away and stay away from her. Hide out up in the hills or go home and lick your wounds in private. Don't make a public ass of yourself.*

But instead he asked her, "Why not yet?"

"I didn't leave after . . . after our first night together because I started to realize that you're a real person, a living human being, with feelings and . . ." She reached for the whisky again, touched the glass, but didn't pick it up. "Well, I had a tussle with my conscience about you, and my conscience won. It doesn't happen often, you know."

"What does that mean?" David asked warily.

She picked up the drink and took a hard swallow of it. "It means that I decided that perhaps I could find another story while I was here. A story that didn't involve you."

"And if you didn't find another story, you already had mine to take back to Earth with you."

"But I *did* find another story, David."

"Did you?"

"Cylinder B!" She hunched forward eagerly. "It's a blooming tropical paradise, but there isn't anyone there! Not even a bird or an insect!"

David shook his head. "They'd have to have birds and insects to maintain a jungle environment. You simply didn't notice any."

"But where are the people? Why is it empty? What's Cobb doing with all that empty space? You could house a million people in there, easily. Two million! More, possibly."

"And turn the paradise into a slum."

"Why is it empty?" Evelyn demanded.

"I don't know."

"But you can help me to find out."

He leaned back in his chair and fixed his gaze on his untouched wine. "Now I understand. If I help you to unravel this mystery, then you'll have a story about Island One that's bigger than the test-tube baby story. Right?"

"I'm sure of it!" She nodded excitedly.

"And if I don't help you, you've still got *my* story. You can go back to Earth and sell my story to your bosses."

An unhappy frown creased her brow. "I don't want to do that, David."

"But you will if you have to."

"If I have to . . . I don't know what I'll do."

But I know, David said to himself.

The Board never met in a single place. Its five members never came together under one roof. But they saw each other regularly, and they had their meetings at least once a month even though they stayed continents apart.

Electronics linked them. Three-dimensional holographic picturephones allowed them to meet face to face, as if they were all in the same room. The five wealthiest men in the world sent their holographic images by laser beams to relay satellites that they privately owned and kept for use only by themselves. It was an expensive way to communicate, but it assured complete privacy, total security. And even at that, it was still a thousand times cheaper than any form of personal travel. And infinitely faster.

T. Hunter Garrison sat in his powerchair in a corner of his penthouse suite atop the Garrison Tower in Houston. Once, six decades earlier, he had played the role of Ebenezer Scrooge in a community college theatrical production. Now he looked the part: wispy white hair fringing a bald dome, narrow-eyed hawkish face with skin like badly wrinkled parchment, liver-spotted hands that would have been gnarled with arthritis if they didn't possess so much money and power.

The top floor of his Tower was Garrison's office, his playground, his home. He seldom left it. He seldom had to. The world came to him.

Now he sat back in his powerchair and faced a corner of mirrors that stared back at him with a crooked, knowing smile. He touched a keyboard built into the chair's armrest and the walls seemed to fade away, to dissolve into images of other rooms, other places.

Hideki Tanaka was obviously at his summer estate, far from the teeming crowds of Tokyo. He was a bluff, open-handed man, much given to smiling and laughter. But his eyes were as cold as a professional killer's. Tanaka was sitting outdoors on a delicately carved wooden bench. Garrison could see graceful, slim green trees and a painstakingly raked sand garden beyond the industrialist. Far in the distance hung the breathless symmetry of snow-covered Fujiyama, trembling in the blue mist.

Tanaka nodded his head in a polite bow and made a few poetic remarks about the beauty of the approaching summer. Garrison let him ramble on as the other mirrors three-dimensionalized into hologram scenes. Three more of the screens did so, but the final one stayed stubbornly flat and reflective.

"All right," Garrison said, cutting into Tanaka's meaningless chatter, "what about this coup in Argentina? How come we didn't know about it beforehand?"

"El Libertador has become a force to be reckoned with sooner than we expected," Tanaka said. "He has used our assistance to good advantage."

"But he's such a righteous pain in the arse," said Wilbur St. George, the Australian member of the Board. He was at his desk in Sydney, as usual, a no-nonsense scowl on his beefy face, an unlit pipe clamped in his teeth. The window behind him looked out on Sydney Harbor, with its breathtaking opera house and high-arched steel bridge.

"He's a useful pain in the ass," Garrison countered.

Kurt Morgenstern, in Cologne, shook his head. He was a wary-eyed little man, pasty-faced and flabby-looking. But he controlled most of the industrial power of central Europe.

"He will not accept our suggestions," Morgenstern said. "My people have tried to . . . er . . . guide him. But he refuses to listen."

"May the gods protect us from men who know they are in the right," Tanaka said, grinning.

"Same tale I've been told," said St. George. "He's a bloody fire-eating revolutionary. Won't listen to reason. Can't be trusted."

The final mirror dissolved to show Jamil al-Hashimi, who was reclining on pillows in the private compartment of a splendidly luxurious travel van. Despite his languid pose, his face was pale with tension.

"Sorry to be late for our meeting," he said. "I had urgent personal business to attend to."

"We were talking about this *El Libertador* fella," Garrison said, letting his rasping voice slide into the Texas accent of his youth. "D'you think we can use him more directly for our own purposes?"

Al-Hashimi shrugged. "It may be possible, but I doubt it. Certainly he has a wide following among these youthful revolutionary groups. . . ."

"The Peoples' Revolutionary Underground," Morgenstern said with obvious distaste.

"They are vigorous and shortsighted," al-Hashimi said, "but they have fastened onto the idea that the World Government must be brought down."

"That makes 'em ideal for us," Garrison said.

"But they are dangerous fanatics," Tanaka warned. "The PRU hates us—the corporations—as much as they hate the World Government."

"So does *El Libertador*," St. George pointed out.

"I still think they can all be useful to us," Garrison insisted. "Okay, so *El Libertador*'s a stubborn idealist who thinks he's gonna change the world. Hates our guts. He still takes money from us, and equipment—whether he knows it or not, whether he admits it or not. Long as he's tearin' down the World Government, he's on our side, and we ought to help him all we can."

The others nodded.

Al-Hashimi said, "The PRU is much the same. I have had some success in turning their local group here in Iraq to our own goals. One of their leaders accepts money from me. And advice."

"And one day he'll slit your bloody throat," St. George grumbled.

Al-Hashimi smiled coldly. "He will not live that long, I promise you."

"Well, then," Garrison said, "I suggest we continue supportin' *El Libertador*. Funnel money to him. Get our weather boys to set up conditions in the nations around 'im that'll shake up the local governments and make their people unhappy with the World Government."

Morgenstern shook his head unhappily. "The misery that we cause. Every time we do this kind of thing, I wonder . . . people are dying because of us! Is it so necessary? Must we cause floods and droughts? Look at the typhoid epidemic that is now sweeping India and Pakistan."

"Can't be helped," St. George said.

"But we caused it!"

"Only indirectly. If those bloody wogs had decent medical services . . ."

101

"And some control of their population growth," al-Hashimi added.

Morgenstern still looked sorrowful. "We tamper with the weather. We kill people who never have a chance to help themselves. Why? Are we so desperate that . . ."

"Yes!" Garrison snapped. "We *are* desperate. That's why we fight. If we just sit back and let the World Government have its way, we'll all end up in the poorhouse. The whole human race will be degraded into a bunch of whinin', starvin' dogs. The whole world will get to be like India—poorer'n dirt."

"I know what the computer projections have shown . . ."

"Damned right," Garrison said. "The World Government's policies will bankrupt us all. That's why we've got to use every means at our disposal to get rid of the World Government. Use the PRU, use *El Libertador*. Use anything and anybody."

Despite his perpetual smile, Tanaka asked, "But would it be wise to help *El Libertador* to take over more nations? After all, when he does so, we lose those nations' productive capacities and their labor pools."

"And their markets," St. George added.

"Who the hell cares?" Garrison countered. "You could take all of South America away from our production pools and markets and what do we lose? Ten percent?"

"Brazil by itself is ten percent," Morgenstern pointed out.

"So it's a price we've got to pay," said Garrison, "a damned cheap price, at that."

"It would be a significant share of my market," Morgenstern insisted.

"Mine, too, but we'll make it up to you. You'll be compensated. Besides, a revolutionary regime never lasts long. After *El Libertador*'s helped put the World Government to rest, his own house of cards'll collapse. Then we'll have *all* the world markets—on our own terms!"

Morgenstern brightened, but not by much.

Garrison scratched his chin briefly, surveying each of his four comrades. "Gentlemen," he said, "the time has come for us to take all these half-baked revolutionary movements and weld them into a single movement that'll put the World Government out of business."

"That would cause untold bloodshed," Tanaka said, "and chaos."

"Yeah, but the alternative is to let the World Government put *us* out of business," Garrison retorted. "And none of us is gonna allow that to happen without a fight."

They all nodded, most of them reluctantly, glumly. But they agreed.

"Okay," Garrison went on. "We've had Operation Proxy sittin' in the computer files for years. Now's the time to activate it, get Island One into the act, and move to get all these revolutionary hotshots into a coordinated worldwide attack."

"A global civil war," Morgenstern whispered. His face looked even whiter than usual.

"About Island One," St. George said. "That man Cobb up there won't like what we're doing."

"He does what he's told," Garrison said. "He has no choice in the matter."

"He is a very independent man," Tanaka said. "Are you certain he can be trusted?"

"I don't trust anybody. I *control* him."

"I've got a snoop up in Island One, you know," St. George said. "She doesn't know it, of course. Thinks she's digging up a scandal for International News."

Garrison laughed. "Cobb'll send her packin' inside of a month."

St. George sniffed. "We'll see."

"In the meantime," Garrison said, "I want each of you to contact these PRU groups in your own local areas. My organization's got a couple of sleepers already planted among the nuts here in the States. One of 'em's in New York, I know. It's time to turn 'em loose. Time to fight fire with fire."

The sports complex in Island One was for participants only. Dr. Cobb would not permit professional teams of athletes into the colony, although anyone was free to watch pro athletics on television from Earth. There were no auditorium seats in the gymnasiums of the colony's sports complex, only facilities for participants.

"No vicarious violence," Cobb told all newcomers. "No organized teams, no organized competitions, and no organized betting. I won't have it."

Competition and betting went on, anyway, as Cobb knew it would. But it was on an amateur, pick-up basis.

The gymnasiums, pools, and other sports facilities were built into the far endcap of the main cylinder, completely across the colony from the spacecraft docking area and not far from David's house. The sports complex climbed the hills of the endcap, so that participants could choose the gravity they wanted to exercise under—from normal, at the foot of the hills, to zero, at the center of the end-cap.

Zero-gee sports were three-dimensional. Where "up" and "down" had no physical meaning, floors, walls, and ceilings became merely playing surfaces to bounce off. Handball became a particularly tricky game, and until Cobb insisted that the courts be enlarged beyond their Earthly regulation size, more Island One residents were hospitalized from handball-incurred injuries than from work-related accidents.

Cobb himself enjoyed the zero-gravity game.

"Gives an old duffer like me a chance against these muscular youngsters," he would say. Then the old duffer would go out and trounce the over-eager young men.

"Don't let it get you down," he would say afterward, grinning viciously through the sweat streaming down his face. "I won't tell anybody."

David knew all of Dr. Cobb's moves, and most of his tricks. He had played with Cobb in zero gravity since childhood, and he had long ago learned that if he remained cool and concentrated on the ball, his younger reflexes and greater endurance would beat the old man. Usually.

But thoughts of Evelyn and the blank wall the computer had thrown around access to data about Cylinder B were filling his mind now.

The hard rubber ball whizzed past his ear before he even realized that Cobb had returned his last shot. Whirling in midair, David saw the ball carom off a corner of the ceiling and hurtle away from him. Flailing like a floundering swimmer, David barely managed to get to the ball and whip it toward the far wall.

Out of the corner of his eye he saw Cobb hanging upside down a few meters away. The old man loved to disconcert his opponents with crazy maneuvers. A long, lean scarecrow of a man, Cobb had often been compared with the classic New England Yankee in his physical appearance. Whipcord-thin. And stringy-tough. To David he always looked like the schoolbook pictures of Uncle Sam—without the goatee and flowing white hair. Cobb's hair was white, but shaved so close to his scalp that he almost looked completely bald.

His face was an unsmiling weathered mass of crevices as his eyes followed the ball's path. *Like New England granite,* David often thought when he studied Cobb's face. Strong, unyielding, enduring.

The old man kicked his legs like a swimmer as the ball came toward him. A blurringly fast flick of one hand, and it was David's turn to chase the ball and try to return it. He missed and sailed into the wall, banging his shoulder against the thick padding.

"That's game!" Cobb yelled triumphantly.

Gliding over toward David, the old man asked in his gravelly, gruff voice, "Hurt yourself?"

"No," David said, rubbing his shoulder. "I'm all right."

The ball was still bouncing off the walls, losing momentum with each impact and slowing down.

"You haven't played this lousy in months. What's eating you?"

David had learned long ago that there weren't many secrets he could keep from Dr. Cobb. "Why is access to Cylinder B restricted?" he asked.

"Oh, that." Cobb let out a weary sigh. "She's pumping you for info on B, is she." It wasn't a question.

"She?"

"Evelyn Hall—this news hen from the International Syndicate. She snuck into Cylinder B yesterday. Thinks she's a master spy, I suppose."

"You know about it?"

"I watched her doing it," Cobb said. "There isn't anything going on inside this colony that I don't see; you know that."

"Then you know about her and me," David said, feeling suddenly sheepish.

Cobb reached out and tousled David's sweaty hair. "Hey, I don't poke into people's private affairs. I keep my eye on everything public—like snoops who set off intruder alarms when they break into restricted areas."

"Why did you make me be her guide on her first day here?" David asked.

Cobb shrugged in his sweat-darkened gym suit. "I thought it was about time you started meeting people from outside the colony, learn how to deal with them."

"But she was here to find out about me!"

"I figured as much. Thought I'd save her the trouble of tracking you down, and give you an opportunity for dealing with somebody who wanted to manipulate you. I thought you'd see right through her."

"I didn't."

"She manipulated you pretty well, huh?"

Despite the flush he could feel burning his cheeks, David grinned. "Yes, she certainly did."

"How do you feel about it now?"

"Confused," David admitted. "Puzzled. She wants to know what's going on in Cylinder B. She wants to do a story about it, back Earthside."

Cobb turned and pushed off the wall with one foot. Heading for the ball, which was now drifting slowly across the court, he called back, "Nothing's going on in B. It's unoccupied."

"Why?" David floated out after him.

"Because the Board wants it kept that way. They own the colony; their money built it. They've got a right to use it the way they want to."

"But why would they want to keep it empty? To waste all that room?"

Cobb plucked the ball from midair and twisted his body around to face David again. "It's not being wasted, son. We just got the orders to start building houses there."

"Oh." Somehow David felt relieved. "What kind of housing? How many?"

Cobb grinned at him. "Mansions. Five of them."

"Fi—— . . . only five? In the whole cylinder?" David's voice was a stunned, high-pitched squeak.

"That's what the Board ordered. Five great big mansions. The cylinder'll still look empty even after they're finished."

"But why . . . what do they . . ."

Arching an eyebrow, the old man asked, "Do you see any statistical correlation between the fact that the Board has ordered five mansions and the fact that there are five

—count them, five—members of the aforesaid Board of Directors of the Island One Corporation, Limited?"

David blinked at him.

"C'mon, son." Cobb slid an arm around his shoulders. "Time for a shower."

"No, wait." David shrugged loose. "What are you driving at? What do you mean?"

Cobb's face was utterly serious. "You want to be a Forecaster. If you look at the data for the world's economic and sociopolitical trends, what do you see?"

With a shake of his head, David answered, "There isn't any single clear trend."

"There sure as taxes is!" Cobb snapped "Chaos. Apocalypse. The World Government is trying to maintain some sort of global stability, but there are revolutionary movements everywhere. From *El Libertador* in South America to the PRU in the Middle East, the World Government is in trouble, deep trouble."

"But what's that got to do with Island One?"

"We're the escape hatch, son. The men on the Board can see a worldwide collapse staring them in the face. The World Government could go under. Chaos and revolution could break out anywhere—everywhere. Those men want a safe retreat for themselves and their families. They've reserved Cylinder B for themselves."

"And they'll let the world collapse around them?"

"There's nothing they can do to prevent it, even if they wanted to."

"I don't believe that!"

"Well . . . there is one thing," Cobb said. "After the Board comes here to live, we can shoot anybody else out of the sky when they try to come up here and invade us!"

BOOK TWO

June, 2008 A.D.

WORLD POPULATION:
7.26 BILLION

The curse of the twentieth century was National-ism, the antiquated and dangerous idea that individual nations are entirely sovereign and may do whatever they wish. In international commerce, Nationalism led to enormous inequities among the nations; the rich died of overeating while the poor starved. In international politics, Nationalism twice devastated the planet with World Wars and was responsible for the long, bitter struggle known as the Cold War, which was terminated only with the enforced founding of the World Government.

Today, in the burgeoning years of the twenty-first century, the curse of Nationalism is still humankind's greatest threat to peace, reason, and stability. Many benighted people would return to Nationalism and turn their backs on their World Government. More importantly, many of the world's wealthiest individ-uals and corporations see the World Government as a threat to their positions of wealth and power.

They are entirely correct!

—Emanuel De Paolo,
    Address to the opening session
    of the World Legislature,
    2008

· CHAPTER 9 ·

Cyrus Cobb's office was like the inside of an insect's complex eye. It was a theater in reverse, with only one man where the stage should be, sitting at a podium-like desk on a high, swiveling, plush-backed stool. Instead of tiers of seats for an audience, there were tiers of viewing screens, dozens upon dozens of them, row after row, each showing a different part of the mammoth colony. From where he sat, like some stern old Yankee schoolmaster, with his stubble of white hair catching the screens' light like a miniature halo, Cobb could see virtually every public area of Island One.

A pair of technicians were replacing a cracked pane in the huge windows that ran the length of the colony. A meteorite no bigger than a grain of sand had grazed the pane. Automatic sensors had alerted the repair crew, which worked full-time keeping the windows airtight and clear.

Electrically powered harvesting machines were clanking down a long row of corn, their multijointed arms plucking the ripe ears from the stalks, other attachments cutting down the emptied stalks and mulching them.

A teen-aged girl was soaring in a bright red-and-yellow hang glider, spiraling upward toward the center line of the vast cylinder, where the spin-induced gravity was effectively zero and she could float easily until she got hungry enough to come back to the ground.

One of the automated processing plants, out among the work pods, was silently and efficiently vaporizing a ton of lunar rocks and converting the gaseous chemicals into antibiotics and immunological agents for sale back on Earth. A lone supervisor sat at a bank of controls and

112

looked at—yawning—the inhumanly complex spiderwork of metal and glass. The plant's computer kept a micro-second-by-microsecond watch over every gram of material and erg of energy used by the plant.

Down in the lower left area of his theater-office, five of Cobb's screens showed views of the lush tropical scenery of Cylinder B. Nothing moved there. Not yet.

Cobb himself hardly glanced at the screens. They were so much a part of him that he could sense when all was well and when something out of the ordinary was happening, something that needed his attention.

He was dictating into his desktop communicator: ". . . no matter what the World Government thinks they have a right to do, or how much pressure they put on us. We will permit no—repeat, no—inspection tours of this colony by any—repeat, *any*—representative of the World Government whatsoever. The real problem is not so much their official requests; it's their unofficial attempts at espionage. . . ."

He looked up at a viewscreen perched near the ceiling. David was on his electrobike, racing pell-mell down the dirt road that led to the Administrative Center building.

Cobb almost smiled, then glanced at the digital clock set into the desktop. He resumed dictating his memo.

Exactly fourteen minutes later, the red light flashed on the communicator's tiny box. Cobb touched it, then asked gruffly, "What is it?"

"It's me." David's flustered, worried face filled the viewscreen that was dead center of Cobb's desk. "I'm here in your outer office. I've got to talk with you."

"I know," Cobb said, looking at the boy from beneath his shaggy white brows. "Make yourself comfortable. I'll be out in a minute or so."

The outer office was for show, for receiving visitors and chatting quietly without the viewscreens staring at you like a thousand curious eyes. Cobb had no secretary, no assistants, no staff of flunkies cluttering up his Directorate. Why waste valuable human minds in tasks that computers could handle so well? Typing, filing, sending messages, finding people by phone, searching the data files for information—computers did that better than people could, without coffee breaks, calling in sick, asking for raises, or boredom.

Visitors were often surprised that they had to announce themselves to the Director of Island One. No leggy secretary to smile at them. No officious assistant to make them wait while he decided if The Boss was ready to receive them. You just came into the outer office and picked up the phone for yourself.

It was a plush-enough office: suede-covered couches and chairs gleaming with aluminum and chrome; handsome three-dimensional pictures of Island One's construction days on the walls; thick carpet manufactured in the colony; a room of warm browns and reds, with a few highlights of yellow.

Cobb let the door click shut loudly enough to make David whirl about and face him.

"What's your problem, son?"

For a moment, David didn't know what to say, where to begin.

"I've checked the standard Forecasts . . . the overall picture . . ."

Nodding, Cobb said, "And you found that I was telling you the truth. The world's heading for superdisaster as fast as it can get there."

"It's starting already!"

"That's right."

"And I never saw it," David said, dropping onto one of the couches. "I'm one helluva Forecaster, aren't I?"

Cobb went over and sat beside him. "I've kept your nose pretty close to the grindstone, son. It's my fault as much as yours. You can't see the Big Picture when you're hunting down the Gross National Product of Bolivia and cross-indexing it with . . ."

"I saw all the data," David said. "I had it all at my fingertips. But I never put it together before."

"Maybe you didn't want to," Cobb suggested. "It's pretty scarifying, isn't it?"

David looked into his craggy, weathered face. "We've got to do something about it."

"I told you, son, there's nothing we can do."

"I want to check that out for myself."

Cobb almost smiled. "You don't believe me?"

"You're telling me the truth . . . as you see it," David said. "So was Lilienthal when he said that nobody would ever be able to make an airplane that can fly. The Wright brothers found a way."

"And you think you can find a way to stop the catastrophe?"

"I want to try."

"It's already started, you know. It was starting thirty years ago."

"I know. But I've still got to try."

Cobb sank back into the yielding warmth of the couch. "What do you propose doing? All the computer studies in the world aren't going to change the basic data, you know."

"Then we've got to find new inputs, new concepts, now courses of action."

"Where?"

"On Earth. I've got to go there, to see for myself. . . ."

Raising a bony hand, Cobb silenced him. "No. You can't leave the colony."

"But I . . ."

"You cannot leave the colony, David. There is no way that I can let you go."

"I'm old enough to take care of myself!"

"You're a babe in the woods, son. But leaving that aside, you're not *legally* free to leave the colony."

"I know," David said. "I'm not a legal citizen of any Earthside nation. But I can become a citizen of the World Government. All I have to do is fill out a simple form. . . ."

"She told you that?"

"Evelyn? Yes."

"Well, she's right. It's true enough," Cobb admitted. "But that doesn't solve your problem. You see, as far as the Island One Corporation is concerned, you are . . . well, you're sort of property. They own you."

"*Own* me?"

Cobb spread his hands. "The corporation owns your services. Legally, you're chattel—just like the workers who come up here for a five-year contract job. They're not free to leave, either."

"That's just a technicality," David said.

"But it's a technicality that I'm going to insist on observing," said Cobb. "I don't want you going down to Earth. There's nothing there for you except heartbreak and danger. You stay here, where you belong."

David jumped to his feet. "You can't make me stay here! I'm not your slave!"

"I can make you stay here, son. And legally . . . well, you may not be a slave, but you're certainly not free to go where you want to."

"That's criminal!"

"I'm only trying to protect you, David," Cobb said, leaning back on the couch to be able to look up at his face. "The corporation has sunk a bundle of money into you. The Board wouldn't like you running off to risk your very valuable hide. The scientific staff would have a fit! Their prize experiment, getting away from them? They'd sit on you even if I didn't."

"You can't do this to me!" David shouted. "I'll appeal to the World Government! I'll get Evelyn to run the story in all the news media on Earth!"

With a rueful shake of his head, Cobb said, "You won't get the Hall woman to do anything. She's gone."

"Gone?" David's knees seemed to sag.

I hate to sandbag you, boy, but that's just what I have to do. "She took off a few hours ago, on the morning shuttle. I'm still trying to figure out how she managed it."

"You threw her out of the colony!"

"No, I didn't," Cobb said. "I wanted her to stay here. Last place I want her to be is back on Earth. But she must have had forged credentials all set for herself. She got away slick as a whistle."

"You sent her away!"

"I didn't!" Cobb insisted, his own voice rising.

"I don't believe you!" David yelled. "You threw her out and you're holding me here! You sent her away from me because she was starting to open my eyes to what you're doing, and the Board, and the whole rotten situation!"

Your eyes are being opened, all right, Cobb thought wearily. *But why does it always have to come with so much pain?*

"Listen to me, son," he said. "I didn't . . ."

"No! I'm finished listening to you! I'm going to get out of here . . . out of this prison!"

Cobb rose slowly to his feet. He realized that his hands were trembling slightly. "David, you know that you can't leave Island One. Even if I wanted to let you go, son, the

116

Board would never permit it. The staff would be up in arms. The money and manpower that have been spent on you . . . you're much too valuable to risk back on Earth. It's too dirty and dangerous down there for you. You would never survive it."

"I'm going!" David shouted. "One way or another, I'm going to Earth!"

He turned and bolted out of the office, leaving Cobb standing there alone, a trembling old man standing in an empty office amid plush, low-slung couches and sculptured chairs and the whisper of fans stirring perfectly conditioned air through the room.

Standing totally alone.

Slowly a smile spread across the old man's seamed features. A sad smile, but a smile, nonetheless.

Good luck, son, he offered silently.

Spent the whole day on the phone, trying to find a job. Nothing doing. There just aren't any jobs for twenty-year-olds who've spent their whole lives on a farm. I can fix machinery, run a business computer, handle animals, even do some veterinary medicine work. But nobody's interested. I don't have the right college credits. They all look at the numbers instead of the person.

The social welfare people have been talking with Mom and Dad, and at least five different political parties have phoned in their taped pitches. I even got one from an outfit that says it's enlisting men to go to Latin America and fight against the guerrillas who're undermining the duly elected governments down there.

I don't know what to do or where to go. I sure don't like the idea of moving off the farm, but we'll have to, before the end of this month.

—The journal of William Palmquist

· CHAPTER 10 ·

They rode along one of the old canals that led off toward the distant Euphrates River. Denny was no stranger to horses, and Bahjat rode as if she'd been born on an Arabian charger, swift as thought, graceful as if she and the sleek white horse were one.

Past groves of olive trees and fields of new green shoots they rode, breathless with the freedom of the wind, the bright, brazen sky like an inverted bowl of hammered gold, the water in the canal beside them shimmering in the sunlight.

Far above them a helicopter droned. Painted in the black and red colors, of the al-Hashimi sheikhdom, it stayed so high that it was merely a speck in the sky, unnoticed by the two riders below. The helicopter's pilot watched them through electro-optically boosted binoculars fitted onto his helmet. To him, the scene made little sense. The sheikh's daughter was riding madly in the heat of the day along an old canal path, with the *Ah-reesh* interloper struggling to keep up with her. They had just passed the Grove of Ashes and were now skirting the pitiful farms of the peasants. The canal was a muddy gray-brown ditch, useful but ugly.

Denny urged his mount onward, and the horse responded eagerly. But still Bahjat stayed ahead of him, her thick black hair streaming over her shoulders. She glanced back at him and laughed.

Then suddenly she cut away from the canal path, heading up past the edge of one of the cultivated fields, toward the ruins of some old stone buildings set on a slight rise of the flat ground. Denny followed her.

Bahjat reined in under the cool shadow of a massive

stone arch. It was the only part of the building still intact.
The walls on either side of it had crumbled. Denny
brought his horse to a snorting, rearing halt on the other
side of the arch.

"He wants to keep on running," Bahjat called to him.
"He is not ready to rest yet."

"Well, I am," Denny said, swinging his leg over the
creaking saddle and stepping gratefully onto solid ground.

"You ride well," Bahjat said, leading her mount by the
reins.

"Not as well as you."

"Oh, Sinbad and I are old friends. We have ridden together for years." The horse tossed its head, as if it
agreed with what Bahjat was saying.

"Sinbad," Denny said. "You like names from *The
Thousand and One Nights.*"

"Oh, yes," Bahjat answered. "And of all the names in
the tales, I like the name of Scheherazade best."

He grinned at her. "You're not the only one. One of
those PRU crazies calls herself Scheherazade."

"Really?" Bahjat turned slightly away from him.

"She's probably the one who ordered my assassination,"
he said.

"Oh, no," she answered immediately. "I wouldn't think
that of her. How could she want to kill such a man? She
was probably very upset when she learned that her friends
decided to attack you."

Denny made a sour face. "I can imagine."

They tied the horses near a sparse growth of grass and
took the saddles and bags off them. Denny saw that the
ground was sandy, dry. Hardly anything grew from it.
But there was a gnarled old tree in full leaf that had
pushed its way out of one of the crumbling old stone
walls. They took their saddlebags there and sat in the
tree's shade.

Bahjat unpacked sandwiches and iced tea and they ate
a leisurely lunch. Once Denny thought he heard the
thrumming whisper of a distant helicopter, but otherwise
they might be a million miles out in the desert, so alone
were they.

He looked at the sandwich he was munching, then at
Bahjat, and he laughed.

Her dark eyes asked him why.

"Look at this," he said, holding up his wrist. "I can phone any library in the world and get a computer to read poetry to us, right?"

"Yes," she said hesitantly, not understanding.

"So," he said, tapping the wrist communicator, "a book of verses underneath the bough"—he pointed upward to the tree—"a loaf of bread, a jug of wine . . ."

"Omar al Khayyám," Bahjat said. "He was a Persian, and he died in disgrace. A drunkard."

"He was one helluva poet."

With a teasing smile, Bahjat said, "We are not drinking wine."

"So what? The important part is, '. . . and Thou, singing beside me in the wilderness . . .' "

She shook her head. "I cannot sing. My voice is not good for singing."

"Every word you speak is a song, Bahjat. Every time I see your face, your smile, it's the grandest love song that's ever been sung."

She cast her eyes downward, as if she were blushing the way a properly reared Moslem lady should. But he could see her smiling. He reached out and pulled her to him and she came willingly, happily, clinging to him with all the passion that he felt rising in his own body.

Their lovemaking was eager, yet unhurried. Denny explored every curve, every texture of her supple young body: the sweep of her throat, the lithe firmness of her thighs, the softness of her breasts, the nearly invisible down on the curve of her back, the warmth, the trembling, yielding, insistent wonder of her. Her hands, her fingertips, her tongue were finding every nerve that sparked and burned beneath his skin.

The sun was casting long shadows across the ruins when Denny sat up at last. Grinning, he turned back to look at Bahjat, who smiled up at him.

"Your father's not going to like me very much."

She closed her eyes slowly and said, "He did not like you from the first."

"I had that feeling."

"But we have been one person since the first, my beautiful *Ah-reesh*. Our blood is intermingled. That is what my father hated."

"You mean the transfusion."

She nodded, eyes still closed. "The physician said you would die from loss of blood. There was no time. Your blood type was the same as mine. It was foreordained."

"You saved my life twice."

"Once, twice, a hundred times. . . ." She smiled. "Your life is my own, dear one. I knew it from the moment I first saw you, when Hamoud brought you into the car."

"And when I first saw your face," Denny said, "with the moonlight on it . . . I was already in love with you then."

"That is good."

"But what about your father? He doesn't even know that I'm out of the house."

"He is too busy with his work to watch us all the time. The guards can be bribed. One of them is in love with Irene, the Greek servant. It was easy to get him to visit her for a half-hour instead of watching you."

"But he wants to send you away—to Island One."

"I will not go," she answered simply.

"And why is he keeping me a prisoner in the house? Why won't he let me out?"

"To protect you from the PRU assassins," she said. Then, with a growing smile, "And to keep you locked away from his daughter, who is madly in love with you!"

Al-Hashimi was in his mobile office, a giant land cruiser propelled by hydrogen-fueled engines. The interior of the cruiser did not resemble a business office. The sheikh lounged on a small mountain of soft pillows, dressed in his tribal robes. Through the heavily tinted windows of the cruiser he could see row upon row of microwave antennas, thin metal poles poking skyward that drank in the microwave energy beamed down from the Solar Power Satellites.

It was a cosmic irony that the Arab nations, once so rich in oil, were still in the forefront of energy production. The Western nations had expected Saudi and Hashimite power to dwindle and disappear as the oil beneath their deserts was consumed. The greedy industrial nations waited for the collapse of Arab power, looked forward to their revenge on the upstart followers of Islam.

But, blessings be on the heads of their fathers, the Arabs were wise enough to realize that their deserts were the ideal places to build solar-power farms. Using the immense wealth generated by their oil sales, the Arabs invested heavily in Island One and the Solar Power Satellites that the space colony built.

And Allah's empty deserts were more useful than the godless Westerners had ever dreamed. What better place to put the rectenna farms that received the energy from the satellites? Intense beams of microwave energy could not be aimed into the heart of a city, or even into farmlands. Europe was squeezed tight for space. No one wanted an ugly, perhaps dangerous, rectenna farm near their home, their city, their farm, their resort.

The Westerners feared the invisible microwave beams, just as they had feared the nuclear power plants that could have saved them from the energy shortages of the previous century. But there were vast, empty spaces in North Africa, in Arabia, in Iraq, and the Pahlevi empire of Iran. Strangely enough, it was the Israelis who provided much of the high technology and skilled engineering manpower that converted these empty spaces into the energy centers that fed Europe from Ireland to the Urals.

Al-Hashimi smiled as he watched the latest reports rolling in on the communicator screen that was built into the wall of the cruiser. The Scandinavian rectenna farm was shut down again. Environmentalists blamed the influx of energy from the satellites for unbalancing the Arctic ecology and causing the floods that had destroyed farmlands farther to the South.

He touched a button on the small keyboard at his side and the viewscreen showed him the media coverage of the Scandinavian fiasco. He laughed aloud.

"Why must they always refer to every ecology as 'delicate'?" he asked his visitor, who sat silently on cushions facing the sheikh.

The visitor wore the dark uniform and checkered turban of an al-Hashimi chauffeur. He nodded but said nothing. He knew a rhetorical question when he heard one.

"Now they prattle of the 'delicate ecology' of the northern tundra and glacier fields. When we were building the rectenna farms here, it was the 'delicate ecology' of the desert. Hah!"

The young man stirred slightly.

"Look at it," al-Hashimi commanded, gesturing toward

the cruiser windows and the antennas blurring past them. "What ecology? The desert is empty. It holds nothing in it that any sane man would want. We have been using this rectenna farm for five years now, and what has been hurt? A few snakes killed. A few vultures singed because they were too stupid to fly out of the beam."

"But the radiation can be dangerous," the young man said, "if you remain in it long enough."

Al-Hashimi arched an eyebrow at him. "Afraid, Hamoud? You?"

"No." *A Kurd can be as brave as any Arab,* thought Hamoud.

With a thin smile, al-Hashimi said, "There is nothing to fear. Even though some of the beam might leak slightly off the edges of the rectenna farm, this van is very well shielded. We ride in perfect safety."

"And comfort," Hamoud added, to show what he thought of the sheikh's luxury.

"You are an ascetic," said al-Hashimi.

Hamoud shook his head. "I am not accustomed to such delights. For a chauffeur, life is . . . less comfortable."

Laughing, al-Hashimi said, "You mean the head of the PRU does not have his little luxuries?"

"Revolutions are not made by luxuries," Hamoud said dourly.

"I suppose a revolutionary should suffer for his cause. It's part of his image."

Hamoud said nothing.

"And this woman among you . . . this Scheherazade . . . is she an ascetic, also?"

His face impassive, Hamoud replied, "She is a symbol, little else. I am the leader of the PRU in this part of the world."

"Of course," al-Hashimi said.

"My followers in the PRU are afraid of you," Hamoud said. "They fear that by taking your money and your help, we are putting ourselves into a trap."

Al-Hashimi's voice went brittle. "Your followers think that a Hashimite sheikh, a descendant of the son of the Prophet, would break his sworn word? Would befoul the sacredness of hospitality?"

"They are young and uneducated," Hamoud said, "and hungry."

"And frightened?"

"Yes, often. But they do what I tell them to, in spite of their fear."

"Then they are brave."

Hamoud nodded gravely.

"Why do they fight against the World Government?" al-Hashimi asked.

"Because they do not wish to be ruled by foreigners. For myself, I want an independent Kurdistan, free from all foreign rule."

"And why did you try to murder the architect who is building the Caliph's palace?"

"As a symbol of our resistance to the World Government, of course."

"No other reason?"

"No."

"You are not angered by the construction of the palace?"

"It makes no difference. But by killing the foreigner who directs the construction, we tell the World Government that we will resist their dictatorship."

"You are a fool," al-Hashimi snapped.

Hamoud swallowed the anger that rose hot in his throat and asked calmly, "How so?"

"Acts of political terrorism are foolish," said the sheikh. "They accomplish nothing, except to bring a team of World Police flying in from Messina."

"They are symbolic."

"Symbolic!" Al-Hashimi looked as if he were going to spit. "If you must strike, strike where it does some good!"

Hamoud gave him a surly stare.

"I have kept the foreigner in my own house and told the World Police that our local police have the situation in hand. You will leave the architect alone. If you do not, the World Government will descend on you despite my protection, and you and your followers will be crushed utterly. Your ashes will be scattered to the winds."

"But why do you keep the architect? Surely his wound has healed enough . . ."

"My daughter is infatuated with him, and I want him where I can watch them both carefully."

Hamoud nodded. *Not carefully enough,* he knew. *Bahjat is clever enough to get her way.*

Al-Hashimi was asking, "I still do not understand what she was doing in the *suq* at that time of the evening."

"I am only her chauffeur," Hamoud said. "She told me to drive into the *suq,* and I did as I was told." *She had the same reaction as you did,* he added silently, *when she heard we were going to assassinate the architect. Even before she met him, she was concerned about his safety.*

The sheikh muttered, "I must get her to Island One. That is the only way to save her."

"And my people must strike against the World Government in some manner. A revolutionary movement either strides forward or it collapses."

"Then strike somewhere else, not in Baghdad."

"We will need transport. And guns. And explosives."

Al-Hashimi nodded curtly. "Very well. I will see that you get them. But leave Baghdad in peace."

Leave your daughter, you mean, Hamoud thought. He laughed to himself. *But she will leave you, O Sheikh, and follow me. She will leave the architect for me, as well.*

"Go now." Al-Hashimi waved at the door. "My assistant will make the arrangements for the things you need."

Slowly, just deliberately enough to avoid making it an obvious insult, Hamoud got to his feet. He bowed slightly, then went to door that led out of the compartment. He swayed slightly as the cruiser rounded a curve in the road, but the knowing smile on his lips stayed in place.

I will get the transport and the arms we need, he said to himself. *And Bahjat will come with me.*

Once Hamoud had shut the compartment door behind him, al-Hashimi touched his keyboard.

The face of his latest blonde secretary filled the screen. "Sir," she said with a curious smile on her face, "we have a report from the surveillance helicopter."

He closed his eyes. "What is it?"

"Your daughter did leave the house—with the Canadian architect."

"I see."

The secretary read the pilot's full report, including his carefully phrased statement about the length of time Bahjat and McCormick had stayed out of sight beneath the tree in the solitude of the ruins. When al-Hashimi opened his eyes, he saw that his secretary looked amused. *I shall enjoy wiping that smirk from your face,* he thought.

"That is the complete report?" he asked.

"Yes," she said.

He nodded. "Send the chauffeur, Hamoud, back in here to me."

The screen went blank. Almost instantly, Hamoud stepped back into the compartment and sank into a cross-legged squat before the sheikh.

"I have had a change of plan," said al-Hashimi.

"Yes?"

"You will assassinate the architect. It must be made to look accidental . . . perhaps like a robbery attempt, as you first tried. There is to be no hint of political significance in his death."

Hamoud nodded and suppressed a smile.

"But he is to die—as quickly as it can be done. I want him dead!"

New Gold, New Conquistadores, No Natives

About 0.002% of the mass of the Earth is orbiting the Sun in the form of meteoric material. This may not seem astounding at first glance, except for the fact that almost all of that matter is in bodies a few hundred meters in diameter or smaller, and the total mass is 10^{18} tons. To get at this material, there is no requirement for underground or pit mining, no waste-disposal problems, no need to pay outrageous prices for energy. . . . The access to valuable resources is fundamentally simple—once the problem of access to space is solved economically. . . .

Generally, terrestrial miners are happy to find concentrations of one to ten percent of the material they are seeking distributed in useless rock. In the asteroid belt . . . we can find concentrations of useful elements as high as ninety percent. . . .

Economic value of a 100-meter-diameter rock of nickel-iron composition is $1.5 billion plus, based on 3.8 million tons iron, 360,000 tons nickel, and 84 tons platinum. The value of the platinum alone is $32,250,000. In a single carbonaceous chondrite [asteroid] of the same size, the value of [its] gold would be $15, 250,000.

—*Foundation Report*,
The Foundation, Saint Paul, Minnesota,
1 January 1978

• CHAPTER 11 •

David sat alone at the desk in his one-room home, fingering the keyboard of his computer terminal like a concert pianist working his way through an intricate Chopin nocturne.

He kept wondering about Evelyn. If she had left the colony on her own, how had she managed it? And why hadn't she contacted David to let him know she was going? *Maybe she couldn't,* he rationalized. *Or there wasn't time.*

"This colony is a trap," he muttered to himself. "A prison. But they can't keep me locked up here forever."

But his fingers kept working, as if they had a life of their own, coolly tapping the computer's stored memory of data. As the hours drifted by, David reviewed the data on file about Island One's sale of energy to the nations of Earth. He checked the dossiers of the members of the Board of Directors, and ran cross-correlations for conflicts of interest—both political and financial.

It was late at night when David finally turned off the terminal and leaned back dazedly in his chair. His head swam.

It was all there. The whole picture. Hidden, distorted in places, cloudy in other spots. But the general outline was clear enough.

Island One Corporation, Limited, and its parent multinational corporations weren't merely the victims of the coming apocalypse. They were helping to cause it.

They're at war, David told himself. *At war against the World Government. At war against the human race.*

It was all so logical. A struggle for existence. A battle for survival. The multinationals against the World Government. Profits versus need. The rich against the poor.

130

And we're on their side, David realized. *Island One is part of the corporations. Dr. Cobb is helping them.*

Ecological warfare. It was a tenuous thread, but David tracked down the absurd weather conditions that had afflicted key areas of the world. Always they led to the weakening of the World Government. Frequently they led to the strengthening of the corporations, as the recent flooding in Scandinavia had wiped out the state-owned rectenna complex and forced the Norse to buy their energy from the North African complex of Island One Corporation.

And the war was escalating. Typhoid in India: Was it the result of the typhoons that had destroyed so much of their overcrowded cities, or were the bacilli manufactured right here in Island One? *In the same biochemistry laboratory that had manufactured the nutrients that kept me alive prenatally?* David shuddered with horror.

An outbreak of a new and as yet unidentified strain of pneumonia was killing people by the dozens in the Soviet Union. A mutated virus from Island One?

They're killing people!

"It's a three-way battle," David mumbled to himself, sagging in the chair and staring at the blank computer screen. He imagined he could still see the graphs and curves as hazy, indistinct afterimages, negatives, white on black.

"The World Government is trying to force the corporations to use their profits for developing the poor nations. The corporations are trying to get rid of the World Government. And then there are those revolutionaries: *El Libertador* and the Peoples' Revolutionary Underground. If the corporations pull all those guerrillas together . . . the ecological war will turn into a bloodbath, all over the world."

Wearily, he got up from the chair.

One thing is certain, he realized. *I've got to get to Messina and inform the World Government about this. It's not just a matter of me trying to run away from the colony now. It's a question of saving Earth from the apocalypse.*

The counselor at the unemployment office told me today that there are openings for farmers up in the Island One colony, in space. I filled out an application form; there was nothing else available.

Talked it over with Mom and Dad at supper. They're not crazy about me going all the way to L4, but they both said if I got picked and I wanted to go, it would be okay with them. I could see how hard it was for them to say it, though.

Damn, I'm sick of seeing Mom with tears in her eyes all the time, and Dad looking sick-scared. If the weather had only been a little better. If the power company hadn't been on everybody's backs to sell out . . .

Anyway, Dad said he figured him and Mom could make out okay in the retirement village. They're kind of young for it, but there's no place else to go, not with the kind of money they've got. They both hate the whole idea, though, and I don't blame them.

I probably won't get picked for Island One. Too many other people trying to get in. But if I do get picked . . . what about Mom and Dad? Can I leave them?

—The journal of William Palmquist

• CHAPTER 12 •

Ascension Island is little more than the cinder cone of an extinct volcano sticking its head up above the warm waters of the South Atlantic Ocean. Much of the island resembles the slag-blackened, boulder-strewn surface of the Moon. Even the beaches are rocky, more than sandy.

It is an isolated place, nearly ten degrees south of the equator, almost equally distant from South America and Africa. The nearest piece of dry land is St. Helena, the even smaller rock where the British exiled Napoleon.

At the end of the runway farthest from Ascension's airport terminal building, two planes were parked in the high summer sun. Ground power carts converted sunlight into electricity for the planes' air conditioning and lights. Neither plane bore markings of any kind, except for enigmatic serial numbers stenciled on their tails. One plane was painted white and sky-blue: it was a twin-engined supersonic jet, big enough to hold an important executive and a staff of six in considerable comfort, in addition to two pilots. The other plane was a much larger four-engine subsonic jet, in green-and-yellow jungle camouflage stripes.

Emanuel De Paolo sat tensely at the curved desk in his private quarters of the supersonic jet. The compartment was very plush; even the walls were thickly carpeted. But it was tiny, barely large enough to squeeze six people around the plastic-veneered desk. Not that it mattered. There would be only two men at this meeting.

The Director of the World Government peered through one of the minuscule oval windows at the mammoth military jet parked alongside his own plane. *Military camouflage,* he thought. *How unoriginal he is. He will probably be wearing a khaki uniform and a baseball cap.*

134

De Paolo's aide let himself into the compartment with no noise at all except the click of the hatch lock.

"His people just called. They have agreed to have him come to your plane. He will be here in five minutes."

The Director nodded at his Ethiopian assistant. "So the diplomats have settled the protocol. A first step."

The aide smiled, white teeth against dark skin. "The precedent was set a long time ago: this is a World Government territory; therefore, you are the host; therefore, he should come to see you. But dinner will be aboard *his* plane, and you must go to him for that."

De Paolo shrugged. "Trivia," he muttered.

The aide withdrew and the old man waited alone. *How far has each of us traveled for this meeting? Sixty-five-hundred kilometers? Seven thousand? What would the diplomats have done if there were no spot almost exactly equidistant between Messina and Buenos Aires?*

A soft rap on the door. Before De Paolo could do anything more than look up, the aide opened the door and announced, "Colonel Cesar Villanova, Your Excellency."

De Paolo got to his feet, feeling each of his eighty-odd years in the stiffness of his back and legs.

Villanova stepped into the cramped compartment cautiously, glancing around himself like a cat pushed into strange surroundings.

He was not at all like what De Paolo had expected. Tall, but with the sturdy build of a working man. An outthrust spade of a nose, high-arched like that of an Andean Indian. His hands looked hard and calloused, but his voice was a soft, almost girlish, tenor.

"I am honored, Señor Director," he said in Spanish accented by high mountains and cattle pastures.

This one is no city dweller, De Paolo realized.

"You honor me," the old man said. "It was very kind of you to agree to this meeting with so little hesitation."

Villanova gave a barely perceptible nod. His eyes were a clear, light gray. His hair a thick mop of iron-gray. He wore a uniform, but it was jungle-green and neatly pressed.

"Please, be seated." De Paolo gestured to the cushioned plastic chairs. "Uh . . . my protocol advisors are a bit mystified as to the proper term of address for you. We know you were a colonel in the Chilean Army until a few years ago. But now . . . ? Have you taken a title as head of the new government of Argentina?"

Villanova shook his head and answered softly, "I am not an administrator, Excellency, merely a soldier. I will not make Bolívar's pitiable mistake."

"But you call yourself after his title."

"My only conceit." He smiled slightly, almost as if embarrassed. "The only title I desire is that of *El Libertador*."

"I see."

Villanova nodded again.

"Would you care for something to drink? To eat?"

"No, thank you."

De Paolo considered the man for a moment. *His dossier says he is fifty-two, but he looks younger than that.*

"I would like to know," Villanova said, "the purpose of this meeting. My advisors told me that you had requested the meeting personally." He smiled, ironically this time. "Several of my friends warned me not to come. They fear a trap of some kind."

De Paolo smiled back. "A very elaborate trap," he said. "I wish to ensnare your heart."

El Libertador's eyebrows rose.

"I wanted to meet you in person, to invite you with my own lips and heart to join the World Government."

"But that is impossible."

"How so? You are the leader of a great nation. Without exception, every nation in the world belongs to the World Government. Why must Argentina be different? I invite your government to rejoin us, as your predecessor did."

Villanova said quietly, "One of the reasons for our overthrow of the previous government of Argentina was that it took orders from Messina."

"Orders? Come, now . . ."

"And paid taxes to the World Government. Heavy taxes, which should have remained at home to help our poor."

"But you pay lower taxes to the World Government than you spent on your military budget back before we initiated the disarmament."

Villanova shook his head. "That was years ago. The taxes we paid to you were paid now, this year. The children who are starving are starving *now*."

"But we send food to needy nations. We have programs . . ."

"Your programs do not reach the people. They make the rich richer, while the poor go hungry. Why do you think the people of Argentina, of other nations all around the world, are ready to join *El Libertador?* Because they love the World Government and are happy with it?"

De Paolo thought a moment, then said slowly, "Why don't you join us, then, and take charge of our programs for the needy?"

Villanova jerked his head back and gasped as if he had received an electric shock. "That . . . that is a very generous offer."

"It is sincerely made," De Paolo said.

"But I am a soldier, not an administrator. I would be lost behind a desk."

"You are a *leader*," De Paolo urged. "Others can do the desk work. You can direct them."

For a long moment Villanova said nothing. But then, "And who would direct me?"

De Paolo shrugged. "The World Council, of course."

"The same faceless men who direct the World Government now. The same ones who allow villages to starve and cities to fester into hellholes."

"We are trying . . ."

"And failing."

"We would not fail if we had your cooperation," De Paolo said, his voice rising, "and the cooperation of those who support you."

"Support me? I have no supporters, except the poor, the starving."

Waving a hand in midair, De Paolo countered, "Come now, *señor*. Is it a coincidence that the drought which brought ruin to Argentina's cattle-raising district has disappeared since you set up your new government? Is it a coincidence that the reservoirs of drinking water for Santiago have been found to contain such a high bacterial count that the Chilean capital must now *buy* its drinking water from Argentina?"

Villanova hesitated. "What are you saying? What do you accuse me of?"

"The multinational corporations have been tampering with the weather on your behalf—poisoning water reservoirs, spreading diseases—all to *cause* the hunger and poverty that you capitalize on to ride to victory and power!"

"Untrue!" Villanova said. But it was the soft answer of a man who was unsure of himself.

"The storms in India, the floods in Sweden, the rioting and epidemics . . . and all over the world, revolutionaries and guerrillas carry your picture and demonstrate against the World Government."

"Mother of God, am I responsible for the weather?"

"Someone is!"

"I have never heard of such a thing."

De Paolo could feel the pulse throbbing angrily in his ears. "Then you are either a liar or a fool. The corporations have been tampering with the weather and using ecological warfare all around the world to weaken the World Government. You are their beneficiary. You are the one they are helping."

"Me? It is your World Government that feeds the corporations and starves the poor."

"Nonsense!"

"Truth! Who makes the profits from grain shipments? Who sells medicines around the world? Why are all the Solar Power Satellites beaming their energy to the nations of the North?"

Forcing himself to regain his composure, De Paolo said, "We are trying to bring the corporations under our control. But their power is enormous. And we have evidence that they are helping you and other revolutionary movements, such as the PRU."

"I swear I know nothing of that," Villanova said.

"Then prove it."

"How?"

"Let Argentina rejoin the World Government. Work with us instead of against us."

"I cannot. My own supporters would turn against me."

"Then we must crush you."

El Libertador's nostrils flared. "Try to. If your tired old men of the Council have the courage to try, they will discover that the hungry poor can fight. We have nothing left to lose. We know that death is near. Attack Argentina and you will ignite all of Latin America, I promise you. All of the Southern Hemisphere!"

De Paolo realized what his pent-up anger had made him say. *Fool! Fool! All these years of self-control thrown away on an adventurer.*

"I was not speaking of war," he backtracked. "None of us wishes to bring death and destruction. I am pleading with you to see the world as it really exists. Why do you think that the corporations are aiding you?"

"I have no evidence that they are."

"They are," De Paolo insisted. "They know that by helping you they weaken the World Government. By fomenting revolutionary movements, they can destroy the World Government. And what will be left in the ruins? A shattered world, split into hundreds of separate nations, each of them too weak and too proud to be anything but separate. What will be the most powerful force in that world? The corporations! They will rule the world. Your petty national governments will be no match for them."

"That sounds like the paranoid dreams of . . ." Villanova hesitated.

"Yes, yes, finish it—of an old man. That's what you meant to say. But it is not paranoia. It is the truth. They are using you. And once they have achieved their goal— once they have destroyed the World Government—they will sweep you away like a fallen leaf."

"They can try."

"They will succeed—*if* there is anything left in the world when my government falls. We are struggling to preserve order, to preserve stability and peace. If they succeed in tearing down the World Government, the chaos that results will destroy everything—everything!"

"No," Villanova said softly. "The people will remain. The land. The fields. The people will endure no matter what happens."

"But how many of them?" De Paolo insisted, forcing the words out despite the tightness in his chest. "Or, rather, how few? Billions will die. *Billions!*"

Villanova got to his feet and stood at his full height, his head hardly a centimeter below the compartment's plastic ceiling panels.

"I do not think that this meeting will accomplish anything except further recriminations. With your permission . . ."

"Go!" De Paolo snapped as the pain spread within him.

"Go and play your egoistic games of power and glory. You think you are aiding the people. You are helping to kill them."

El Libertador turned and stepped out of the compartment. Before the door could close, De Paolo's aide put his head in.

His jaw dropped open in shock. "Sir!"

De Paolo lay back in his chair, gasping, gray-faced. A sullen hot pain was smoldering in his chest.

The aide came to the desk and punched the communicator button. "Get the physician in here immediately!"

I've been accepted for Island One! On a trial basis, at least. They didn't take long making up their minds. The counselor who called said they handle all applications by computer, and they process them overnight in most cases.

They want to send me to their test and training center in Texas. I've got a week to make up my mind. But I've already made it up. Sure, it'll be tough on Mom and Dad, but I'm not going to spend the rest of my life stuck here and then get thrown out on the slop pile like they did. I'm going into space.

It's Island One or bust!

—The journal of William Palmquist

• CHAPTER 13 •

Leaning back in his desk chair, David stared sullenly at the computer's readout screen. Instead of the data about passengers who had confirmed reservations on the next shuttle rocket leaving for Earth, the viewscreen showed the image of Dr. Cobb.

"David, this is a tape," the old man was saying. "I know you're trying to break into the computer reservations system and wangle yourself a seat on one of the Earthbound shuttles. I've had the computer programmed to respond to your intrusions with this tape. You're staying here, son. I'm sorry, but that's the way it's got to be. I've got every possible input to the computer blocked. There's no way you can tamper . . ."

With a sour grimace, David touched the keyboard's OFF button. The viewscreen instantly went blank. Cobb's voice was cut off in mid-word.

It was the fourth time he had tried to worm his way into the shuttle's passenger list. He had used a false name at first. Then he had tried inserting his own identification records into the place of a confirmed passenger and "bumping" the real passenger off the flight. Neither worked. Nor did his latest, more subtle attempts to get at the computer's basic programming and alter it.

Each time his efforts had resulted in Cobb's taped message. The old man's face looked faintly amused, as if he knew he had won a battle of wits with his young protégé.

You may have won a few battles, David thought, *but you're not going to win the war. I'll get out of this jailhouse yet.*

There were other rockets that regularly left Island One's spacecraft docks. The smaller, more spartan lunar shuttles

142

that ferried men and equipment between the colony and the mines on the Moon's *Oceanus Procellarum*. Like the colony itself, the mines were the property of the Island One Corporation. But on the other "shore" of that dark, solid-rock lunar ocean was the underground community of Selene—a free and independent nation, a staunch member of the World Government.

David grinned to himself. "You may have the Earth-bound shuttles covered," he muttered to Cobb, "but I'll just take the long way around to where I want to go."

David activated the computer again and asked for the passenger lists for the next few ferry runs. The viewscreen flickered momentarily and then cleared to show Cobb's face. The old man's grin seemed bigger, somehow.

"David, this is a tape. I know you're trying . . ."

"Some things never change, thank God," Evelyn said as the taxi swung around the mounted Guardsmen in their splendid, silly uniforms of scarlet with the polished swords and red-tailed helmets of gold. Mounted on clattering black horses, they were jouncing toward Buckingham Palace. The usual crowds of camera-laden tourists were already packed in their places, waiting to catch the Changing of the Guard.

"You didn't like Island One, then?"

The man sitting in the taxicab beside Evelyn had been introduced to her as Wilbur St. George. He was obviously an Australian, despite his Savile Row tweeds and his careful diction. He had the ruddy-cheeked outdoor look of an Aussie, the blustering, unguarded way of speaking, the informality that was just short of impoliteness.

"I liked it very much," Evelyn answered. "I only left because the story I uncovered was too big to miss, and they'd never allow me to tell it from up there. Still, it's good to be home."

St. George shifted slightly in the cab's back seat. He was a large man, past fifty, Evelyn judged, and had to work hard to keep from going fat. "I wanted to talk with you without anyone interrupting us," he said. "Thought a taxi ride through London would do the trick nicely. I don't get to see much of this city, y'know."

Studying the man's face, Evelyn thought, *High blood pressure, too, I'll warrant.*

"Mr. Beardsley told me that you were one of the owners of International News," she said.

"Good man, Beardsley. . . . Ah, there's the King's house now."

Evelyn barely glanced at Buckingham Palace. "Mr. Beardsley said I'd have to speak with you before writing up any of the stories I've brought back with me from Island One."

"That's right. That's what I wanted to talk to you about."

"What do you want to know?"

He shrugged good-naturedly. "What did you find out?"

Evelyn hesitated a moment, then began telling St. George about the empty, unoccupied Cylinder B of Island One. She mentioned all the laboratory and industrial work she had seen. She did not mention David Adams—not one word about him, his story, his background, or the genetic engineering that had created him.

"Anything else?" St. George asked, staring out the window as they passed the Tower and Tower Bridge.

"Anything else?" Evelyn echoed. "There's a huge conspiracy going on up there! They're going to go right on selling us energy from *their* satellites at *their* prices! And they've got that entire empty cylinder, big enough to house a million people—empty, unused, *waiting!*"

"Waiting for what?" St. George asked, his eyes suddenly focused on her, gun-metal gray.

"That's what I'm trying to find out."

St. George shook his head. "Not much to show for a month's work, is it? More than a month, when you count the training they put you through. I've seen your expense accounts, y'know."

"They're keeping something from us," Evelyn said. "Something's going on up there and . . ."

St. George made a clucking sound of disgust. "Rumors. Insinuations. Paranoid plots. Where are the facts? Where are the hard facts?"

"I've got photographs of that empty cylinder."

"I've seen them. What of it?"

"But . . ."

"Hear me out," St. George commanded. "This matter of the empty cylinder. I'm sure that if you had asked Dr. Cobb about it, he would have explained it perfectly well."

"His explanation would have been a smooth one, I agree."

"So? What do you have? Nothing—certainly not a news story."

Evelyn was too stunned to reply.

"You didn't even find out about that boy who was cooked up inside some genetics laboratory or other," St. George grumbled.

"You know about that?"

He made a sour face. "My dear Ms. Hall, it appears to me that you've spent a good deal of International News' time and money for little more than an exotic vacation. I hope you enjoyed yourself."

"*Enjoyed* myself?"

"That's right. Because you're fired. As of this moment you no longer work for International News. Go on back to the office and pick up your severance check. It will be waiting for you."

The cab pulled up to the curb of the narrow, bumpy street in front of a pub called Prospect of Whitby. Evelyn had heard of it since childhood, one of the oldest pubs in London, but she had never been able to afford it.

St. George ducked out of the cab and immediately slammed the door, leaving Evelyn inside. To the driver he commanded, "Take her back to the International News building."

He turned and headed inside the pub without paying the cab driver a penny.

When the going gets tough, the tough get going.

David had read that somewhere. As he pedaled his electrobike along the winding forest trail, deliberately keeping the motor off and forcing himself to work for every meter of progress, he kept repeating that phrase to himself.

A doe, startled by his sudden appearance around a bend in the trail, froze for a moment and stared off at him with huge, liquid, brown eyes, then bounded off through the underbrush.

That's the way, David thought. *Get away while you can.*

There was no way for him to get aboard an Earthbound shuttle. Cobb had outsmarted him there. Even the baggage and freight the shuttles carried were minutely inspected,

since the rockets landed at spaceports that belonged to the
World Government and not to the Corporation.

He couldn't get into a lunar ferry, either. Cobb had
anticipated that move, too. *But,* David thought as he
pedaled, *they don't inspect the freight that the ferries
carry.* Both ends of the lunar run were owned by the
Island One Corporation. There was nothing to smuggle
back and forth from the colony to the barren desolation
of the lunar mines—nothing that Dr. Cobb gave a damn
about, at least.

He had worked his way up to the crest of a ridge and
was now coasting down the dirt trail, heading out of the
woods and toward the grazing area where small flocks of
sheep and goats dotted the grasslands.

David clicked on his implanted communicator and
queried the computer files for information about the
ferries' cargo holds. As he coasted downslope he consciously relaxed the tension in his leg muscles.

And grunted with disappointment. The ferries had no
cargo holds. Individual cargo pods were clipped onto the
ferries' outer framework, riding along like barnacles on a
ship's hull. The cargo pods were sealed, but a stowaway
would have to hold his breath for two days as the ferry
coasted the quarter-million miles between Island One and
the Moon. It would be a cold ride, too: a couple of hundred degrees below zero, cold enough to solidify air . . .
and a human body.

Zooming to the bottom of the downslope, David pumped
his bike faster and faster, scattering a bleating knot of
sheep that had strayed onto the trail. A dog yapped behind
him as the wind plastered his thin shirt against his chest
and sent his hair flying.

A few hundred degrees below zero and no air, he repeated to himself. *At least Dr. Cobb won't be expecting
me to try that route!*

It took David nearly a week to prepare his sarcophagus.

He worked by night in the basement of an electronics
shop in the village nearest his home. The shop sold omni-
phonic sound systems and the new three-dimensional television sets to Island One's residents. It was a simple matter
to get past the electronic locks and turn the shop's basement storeroom into a work area.

COLONY

Using his knowledge of the computer's credit systems, David had acquired a cylindrical freight pod, an astronaut's pressure suit, several tanks of oxygen, and a pair of electricity-generating fuel cells.

He carefully went about his usual routines of study and exercise during the day. He showed up punctually for his regular medical tests and examinations, assuming that Dr. Cobb was watching him—at least intermittently.

He hardly slept at all. *I'll have plenty of time to sleep on the ride to the Moon,* he thought. *A couple of days— or eternity.*

It had been simple to break into the computerized inventory systems that handled all the colony's goods and "liberate" the items he needed. David had learned to jiggle the computer systems when he had been first old enough to send Christmas presents. All his young friends had received extravagant gifts: whole tape libraries, a gossamer-winged soarplane, new clothes from Earth—all from a ten-year-old with no credit rating.

His only mistake had been to send Dr. Cobb a professional-sized astronomical telescope. Cobb blew the whistle on the young Santa Claus and David's delighted friends had to return their "gifts."

Where are those pals now? David asked himself as he studied the specifications of the fuel cells he had just carried into the basement storeroom. One by one his friends had drifted out of his life. He still saw them, some of them often. But they were leading their own lives now, and the old days of childhood and teen-aged camaraderie were gone. *They were out dating and getting married while I was being tested by the biomedics.* David shook his head. His only real friend, these days, was the computer. Even Dr. Cobb had turned against him.

Evelyn was right, he thought. *I am alone up here.*

He put the specification sheet down and surveyed the booty he had laid out on the storeroom floor: the open cargo pod, a two-meter-long gray plastic cylinder lined with a thin layer of foam insulation; the spacesuit, with its bulbous, clear plastic helmet; the bulky green oxygen tanks; and the squat, square, featureless, white fuel cells.

Ten kilos of junk to fit into a five-kilo box. It was too much. He couldn't fit it all into the cargo pod—not if he wanted to put himself into it, too.

He spent most of the night going over his calculations: oxygen consumed per hour, heat leakage through the pod's insulation, electric power required for heating the suit and keeping the air pumps working.

The numbers swam up at him through a haze of exhaustion. David yawned and squinted at the computer's screen, trying to see different numbers, better ones. But the little red-glowing digits wouldn't change.

It won't fit.

Tiredly, he slumped back onto the plastic chair set against the storage shelves and stared at the uncompromising numbers. *Go home and go to sleep,* he told himself. *You're not going to change things by staying up all night and ...*

Sleep.

He remembered one of the tests the biomedics had put him through as a teen-ager—something about controlling his autonomic nervous system and decreasing his base metabolic rate. What had those doctors been joking about? *Hindus . . . yogis,* David recalled. *Transcendental meditation, programmed into a computer!*

He remembered it clearly now, suddenly wide awake. They had plugged him into a sort of EEG machine, but instead of recording the electrical signals of his brain's activity, this machine superimposed the wave-state of a brain in deep, deep sleep. A trance. David remembered going out like a light almost as soon as they had put the electrodes onto his head. Later they had told him that he had slept for six hours, hardly breathing, and his heartbeat had slowed to less than thirty per minute.

Packing all his scattered equipment into the proper boxes, David put the gear onto shelves in the rear of the storeroom. He dragged the cargo pod over to the rear shelves and left it lying there on the floor. No one had bothered his stuff in several nights; no one had questioned it being there. Storerooms always accumulated junk that no one paid attention to.

David rode his electrobike back to his home, the motor purring at full throttle all the way through the dark, winding trails.

Once home, he pored through the computer files for hours until he tracked down the TM test program that the biomedics had used on him years earlier. It was all there:

the technique, the computer program, the test results. *If I can ride to the Moon in that kind of a TM trance, I wouldn't need as much oxygen or heat. I could fit everything I need into the cargo pod.*

Glancing up from his desk, David saw that daylight had broken. He went to his bed, clicked on his implanted communicator, and plugged into the trance-inducing program. It was still set for a six-hour duration.

For a moment he wondered if his implant would work as well as the electrodes they had stuck to his scalp.

But an instant later he was deeply asleep, barely breathing, as still as death.

Mom and Dad drove me to Browerville and we said our good-byes right there in front of Sanderson's Hardware Store while the bus driver waited for me to get aboard. Mom was real good, no tears or anything. That made me feel worse than if she'd blubbered all over me.

I'm dictating this in the airport here at Twin Cities. It's an old airport; they don't let anything big fly out of here because of all the houses and factories crowding in all around it. My plane's gonna be an hour or more late because of the goddamned rain.

But my next stop is sunny Texas!

—The journal of William Palmquist

• CHAPTER 14 •

Jamil al-Hashimi detested the scenes he would have to face. But as he paced the office on the first floor of his Baghdad home, he knew that there was no way to avoid the confrontations.

First he would have to get the architect out of his house. That should be easy. But then he would have to deal with Bahjat, and that would be painful, at the very least.

He puffed intently on a cigarette set into a long, slim ivory holder. Smoking was a vice that he indulged in only in private, and even then only when he was very tense. *I'm doing it more and more often,* he realized. *As the game becomes more dangerous and reaches its critical stages, I lapse back into childish weakness.*

Angrily, he pulled the half-finished cigarette from its holder and stubbed it out in the silver-inlaid ashtray on his desk. There were four other cigarette butts already in it.

Fool! al-Hashimi railed at himself. *Weakling.*

The phone rang. He reached across the desk and flipped the VOICE ONLY switch.

"Sir, Mr. McCormick is here."

"One moment," al-Hashimi said.

He went to the wall and turned the air blower up to maximum. As it hummingly sucked up the smoke hanging in the air, he took a can of air freshener from the cabinet nearby and sprayed a sweet rose scent through the room. Then he turned the air fans down to normal and returned to his desk.

"Send him in," al-Hashimi said into the phone's grille.

As the sheikh sat himself in the tall, plushly tooled chair

152

behind his massive desk, Dennis McCormick came into the office and closed the heavy wooden door behind him. His red-bearded face had a strange expression on it. He sniffed and frowned at the cloying rose scent.

A pistol lay in the top drawer of al-Hashimi's desk. Another rested in a hidden compartment built into the right arm of his chair. The sheikh restrained his impulse to take one of them and shoot the defiler on the spot.

"You asked to see me?" McCormick said, walking casually to the chair set before the desk. His nose twitched again.

I commanded your presence here, al-Hashimi thought. But he kept his face impassive and gestured to the chair before the infidel could sit in it uninvited.

McCormick looked completely healed of his wound. His face had a healthy glow to it. His red hair curled boyishly over his forehead and covered his chin with a neat little beard. He seemed relaxed and comfortable.

"You have enjoyed your stay in my house?" al-Hashimi asked, his voice flat and calm.

"Your hospitality has been more than generous."

"Your wound has healed."

"Not completely," he answered, "but almost so."

"And your work on the palace? It goes well?"

Dennis waggled one hand, almost like an Arab. "It's a bit sticky, directing the crew by picturephone. But they've finished both towers and we're laying the foundation for the central building now."

"Very good," said the sheikh. "I am pleased."

McCormick smiled at him.

"You have met my daughter, haven't you?"

The smile faded. "Yes," he admitted. "I have."

Al-Hashimi very carefully placed both his hands palms down on the desktop. "Mr. McCormick, hospitality imposes certain duties and obligations on a host. But there are also duties and obligations that the guest must observe."

The architect looked troubled. "I haven't been as good a guest as you have been a host."

"I instructed my daughter to stay away from you. She disobeyed me. But you are a man, and you knew my wishes. The responsibility was yours."

"I love your daughter, sir."

Al-Hashimi said nothing.

"And she loves me."

"She is a child, and a female child. She has no right to disregard my commands."

"I want to marry her," McCormick went on. "I've wanted to speak to you about it, but Bahjat said to wait."

The dog is actually smiling about it!

"So I'm glad that you've brought it out into the open. Believe me, I don't like sneaking around behind your back."

"Enough!" Al-Hashimi slammed his hands against the desktop.

McCormick jumped as if it was he who had been slapped.

"There is no possibility under the Sun and Moon and stars that this illicit filth of yours can be justified by marriage. None! My daughter is the descendant of sheikhs, of warriors, and caliphs who trace their lineage back to the Son of the Prophet and even beyond that! She will not share her blood with an unknown, non-believing foreigner who cannot even control his passions well enough to observe the obligations of a guest."

"But we love each other," McCormick insisted.

"Nonsense."

"There's no way that you can stop us."

"You will leave this house. She will be sent to Island One, where she should have gone weeks ago."

"We can still meet—no matter where you send her, anywhere on Earth or beyond it. If she goes there, I'll go, too."

Al-Hashimi held the reply on his tongue in check.

Comprehension dawned on the red-bearded one. "Ah, I see. Once I'm out of your house I won't live long enough to go to her."

The sheikh said, "I am not threatening you."

"But you kept me here for my safety. You told me that the thugs who tried to kill me would try again if I left your protection."

"I have found those who were responsible. I have dealt with them. You need not fear for your safety any longer."

"Needn't I?"

"I am not an assassin," al-Hashimi snapped. "If I wanted to kill you, I would do it here, now, myself." *It is no sin to lie to an infidel who has defiled your daughter.*

McCormick rose slowly from his chair. "I'll take you at your word, then. But you must take me at mine. I love your daughter and I want to marry her. No matter where you send her, I'll go after her."

"I would advise against such foolishness," al-Hashimi said quietly, like a cobra rustling inside its reed basket.

"There's nothing you can do to stop me, short of killing me."

Al-Hashimi made himself smile. "You are a romantic fool, Architect. I can make you penniless with a single phone call. I can have you arrested and thrown into jail for months. You would be surprised at the amount of evidence our police can find when they want to: narcotics, counterfeit money, anti-government propaganda, illegal weapons. . . . You could stay in jail for years."

"It won't work," McCormick said with a shake of his head. He turned and went to the door.

The sheikh watched him go and noted that he closed the door very carefully, without slamming it. *He may be a romantic, but he knows how to control his temper.*

It was after the evening meal that Bahjat stormed into his office.

Al-Hashimi looked up from the viewscreen of his computer terminal. With the touch of a finger he blanked the screen: the comparison of the cost of causing the ruinous rains in North America against the profits to be forthcoming from the Minnesota rectenna farm winked off.

For the first time in years, he looked at his daughter with fresh eyes. *Yes, she is a woman now, a very beautiful woman. And a very angry one.*

Bahjat's dark eyes were fiery, and her tiny frame radiated furious energy.

"You've sent him away!"

"Of course."

"To be murdered!"

"He is perfectly safe. I have dealt with the would-be assassins."

"You have?"

"Yes."

For an instant she seemed confused, standing there before his desk. How many times she had interrupted his work and climbed up into his lap! But not for years now.

155

Al-Hashimi realized that for the past several years their meetings had grown rarer, and when they did speak to each other, it was usually to argue about her latest escapades. *Sending her to Western schools was a mistake. I should have listened to her mother and sent her to the university here, where women are properly taught.*

"Father, don't send him away. I . . ."

"You love him. I know. And he loves you and wishes to marry you."

"He told you that?" Her face lit up.

"Yes. And I told him that he was a fool. You are going to Island One, and I have already seen to it that he will not be permitted to follow you."

"You can't!"

"I already have."

"I won't go, Father. I want to be with him."

Al-Hashimi shook his head. "That cannot be. He is an ungrateful goat. I know that you have made love with him."

She took the accusation without flinching. "You've been spying on me."

"I have tried to protect you."

"From love?"

"From lusting monkeys who would despoil you."

"You're too late for that."

"I know."

"You were too late a year ago," Bahjat said, her face a coppery mask of cold fury.

Al-Hashimi stared back at her. "A year ago?" he repeated dully.

"In Paris," Bahjat said, twisting the knife, "the City of Romance."

"Impossible! Irene was with you every moment."

"Not *every* moment."

The wicked smile on his daughter's face convinced al-Hashimi that she was telling the truth. It was the same smile he himself wore when he had hit an enemy in a particularly painful spot.

"And since then?"

Bahjat shrugged.

So the Architect was not her first, nor her second, most likely. Al-Hashimi sank back in his desk chair and let his hands drop into his lap. *Irene was probably having her own*

*romance when she should have been guarding my daugh-
ter. We shall see how much she enjoys being guarded by
some of the hungry tribesmen up in the hills. That should
make her suitably penitent. If she lives through it.*

Bahjat broke his silent planning. "Don't be angry with
him, please, Father. It wasn't his fault. I bribed the servants to let me be with him."

"Is there no one in my own household I can trust? Not
even my own daughter?"

"I have always been an obedient daughter, except . . ."

"You have been a slut!" al-Hashimi exploded, all the
anger in him boiling over. "A whore parading herself from
bed to bed, man to man, behind my back! You don't deserve the name you bear! You have betrayed me and
dragged our name into the filth of the gutter!"

"Our proud name!" she spat back, never taking a backward step. "We live in splendor while the people go hungry.
You serve the World Government that keeps our own
people from being free. You direct a mighty corporation
that sells energy to the rich and lets the poor die in the
streets. Money is more important to you than honor, and
power is more important than money!"

"We are a family of sheikhs!" al-Hashimi raged. "It is
our duty to rule others!"

"Sheikhs?" Bahjat laughed. "City sheikhs. Money sheikhs.
The only time you travel the Bedouin's trail is when you
are comfortably ensconced in your travel van. A sheikh?
A corporation sheikh is what you are."

"I am a sheikh who shares control of the space colony
at Island One, and that is where you are going. Tomorrow.
With no further delays. Your latest lover, he of the red
beard, will not be able to follow you there, I promise."

Bahjat looked at him, a level gaze that locked onto his
eyes and penetrated to his heart.

"If I go to Island One," she asked, "will you promise
that he won't be harmed?"

"A man must bargain with his own daughter?"

"I will do as you wish if you promise that you will not
hurt him."

Al-Hashimi hesitated. Hunching forward in his chair, he
reached for the ivory cigarette holder, then put it down
again. "It was the Peoples' Revolutionary Underground

that tried to kill him. I am not responsible for their actions."

"I can deal with the PRU," Bahjat said evenly.

He looked up at her. "You?"

"Of course."

"What do you mean?"

She seemed to stand taller, straighter. "You have heard of Scheherazade? I am she."

"You . . . are Scheherazade!" Al-Hashimi lifted his head to the heavens. "No . . . no, it cannot be! Not my own daughter!"

She came around the desk and knelt at his feet. "It is true, Father. But . . . if you spare the Architect, Scheherazade will disappear. I will become your obedient daughter once again."

Looking down at her, his innards on fire, al-Hashimi gasped, "But you . . . with those PRU terrorists . . . not just one of them, but a *leader!* How could you? Why?"

Bahjat smiled sadly. "Perhaps I was angry with you for ignoring me and sending me away to school."

"Oh, no . . . no." He cradled her elfin face in his hands. "But you could have been killed. Half the police in Europe and the Middle East are trying to find you. The World Army . . ."

"I am safe now," she said, resting her head on his lap. "Scheherazade no longer exists. She has given her life for the life of the Architect."

He stroked her lustrous black hair. "It is for your own good, you will see. I am not being cruel to you."

"I understand, Father."

He saw that her eyes were dry. "I am going to Island One myself soon," he said. "You will enjoy living there. In a few weeks, a month at most, you will have forgotten all about this Architect."

"Perhaps," she said softly.

He lifted her chin toward him and, bending down, kissed her on the forehead. Bahjat held both his hands in her tiny ones for a moment, then got up and walked wordlessly out of the office.

For a long moment al-Hashimi sat at his desk and stared at the door that had closed between them. Then he reached for his phone.

He made three calls.

The first was to his household majordomo, to make arrangements for Bahjat's departure the following morning.

"And I want her bedroom guarded tonight. Windows and doors. She is in terrible danger, and if she leaves during this night it will be on your head. Reliable men, do you understand me? Not the bribe-takers who watched the foreigner."

His second call was to Hamoud, in his quarters over the garage. His sullen, dark face appeared on the viewscreen and al-Hashimi said tersely, "Instructions. The red-bearded one is not to be harmed as long as he is in the city. But he will try to get to the airport tomorrow. Let it happen after the plane with my daughter departs."

Hamoud's heavy brows rose. "Your daughter is leaving Baghdad?"

"Yes. And as soon as she does, the Architect leaves, too. By another gate."

"I understand," said Hamoud.

Al-Hashimi snapped off the phone and leaned back in his cushioned chair. *Now for the final call,* he thought. *My unfaithful servant, the girl Irene, and a punishment that will fit her crime.*

Bahjat could not sleep. She lay on her waterbed, covered only by the sheerest silk coverlet, and stared into the darkness. She kept seeing Denny's face, hearing his voice.

Good-bye, my Ah-reesh, she thought, *I will never forget you. Never.*

A sudden rap on her window made her sit up. It came again, a single, sharp tap on the glass.

Wrapping the coverlet around her like a sarong, Bahjat went to the window and swung it wide. A stocky, dark form was crouching on the balcony outside.

"Hamoud!" she whispered. "What are you doing?"

He moved swiftly to her and ducked inside the shadows of the room. "Your father has gone insane. His guards dragged Irene out of the house an hour ago. He's given orders that you're to be taken to the airport tomorrow. . . ."

"Yes. I am going to Island One."

Hamoud went on, "And he has ordered the assassination of your Architect."

Bahjat froze inside, but only for an instant.

159

"Can you help me get out of the house? Now? This minute?"

"Yes," Hamoud said. In the darkness, she couldn't see his grim smile of victory.

Upward Bound Study Says Youths Benefit

Impoverished Students Found to Be More Likely to Attend College If They Take Part in Program

An evaluation of Upward Bound, the $44-million-a-year federal project to motivate impoverished high school students, indicates that the program has been successful in raising aspirations and getting participants to go on to post-secondary education in greater numbers than non-participants.

Upward Bound began as a key element in the anti-poverty campaign in 1965 and has spent $446.8 million since then to provide tutoring, cultural enrichment, counseling, and other aid to youngsters whose potential was jeopardized by inadequate academic preparation and lack of motivation.

An estimated 82 percent of the 194,337 participants have been blacks, Hispanics, Asian-Americans, and American Indians. . . .

An apparent irony of the program is that the raised education expectations of the participants make them more likely than their non-participant counterparts to end up dissatisfied with their high school preparation, lack of family finances, and inadequate financial aid. . . .

—The New York Times,
11 December 1977

· CHAPTER 15 ·

Manhattan gave the impression of being still livable, by day. Old steam-powered buses wheezed up and down the major avenues, with people hanging onto their windows and tail decks. Their blue and gray paint was faded and covered with graffiti, of course. Cabs had long since disappeared from the city, and private cars were almost nonexistent, although National Guard halftracks clanked through the noisy, crowded streets constantly.

The street traffic was mostly bikes, of the muscle-powered variety. It was easy enough to steal an electro-bike, but the sky-high cost of electricity made it impossible for most Manhattan folks to keep one going after the battery ran down.

Long before the first energy shortages, Manhattan had started to die. Slowly at first, and then faster and faster, the city had collapsed. Families with the money to do so moved to the suburbs. Businesses followed them. The poor remained in the city. In fact, poor rural families from the South, the West, even from Puerto Rico, poured into the city. Again and again the cycle turned, as the taxpaying rich left and the needy poor stayed.

And multiplied.

By the turn of the twenty-first century, whole industries had left New York. The stock exchanges had gone, followed by the publishing industry and advertising, and then even the garment district emptied out and turned Seventh Avenue into a ghost town, inhabited by short-lived winos and sharp-toothed rats. Home-sized computers and picture-telephones killed New York. With them, you could live wherever you wanted to and still communicate

162

instantly with anyone, anywhere in the nation. Commuting died. Communications killed the big cities.

Around the world, from São Paolo to Tokyo, from Los Angeles to Calcutta, the cities were dying. There was no longer any reason to live in them. Those who could moved away into the hinterlands. Those who were too poor to get away remained and tried to scratch out some sort of living in the growing piles of garbage and disease.

Only in those rare cities where the population *had* to remain—such as national capitals—or *wanted* to—such as San Francisco, Florence, Nairobi—did the community retain its population, prosperity, and safety.

Manhattan looked bustling and important by day. The terror of the night was lifted. Merchants' musclemen cleaned the streets and removed the bodies that had accumulated during the darkness. They rolled up the bulletproof shields that covered shop-front doors and windows. Peddlers set up their wares on the sidewalks, and the colorful pushcarts of fruits and vegetables appeared at curbsides again.

Leo looked rather prosperous as he shouldered his way through the bustling crowds along Fifth Avenue. The sky was gray with smoke from the city-owned electric power plants. They burned coal, the only fuel they could afford, and their soot filters hadn't worked right within the span of Leo's memory.

The shops along the Avenue carried the necessities of life: food, clothing, and very little else. Live models posed in the store windows. Labor was cheap. Gaunt, wary-eyed kids watched them and envied their glamorous lives. The raucous loudspeakers of discount stores blared their eternal bleat about final, final sales and prices you'll never see this low again.

Dressed in a conservative cream-colored business suit, complete with shirt and scarf, Leo made his way up the Avenue. The crowd was multihued. Clothing was colorful, and so were the people's skin tones. Browns predominated: the light, slightly oily tan of Hispanics, the chocolates and coffees of blacks, the bamboo-yellow-brown of Asians. There were very few whites, and hardly anyone with the deep, purplish African black of Leo's own hide.

Leo strode purposefully through the gawkers and shoppers, the pickpockets and hustlers. His imposing bulk created a bow wave of pedestrians who automatically streamed out of his way. He looked like a huge icebreaker plowing through a choppy sea.

He found the street he was looking for, turned the corner, and headed up the block. Out of the corner of his eye he briefly spotted skinny, quick-moving Lacey in the crowd across the street. Fade and JoJo were nearby, too, he knew. Leo never traveled alone.

The address he was seeking turned out to be a boarded-up shop that had once sold coffee from all around the world. Now it looked abandoned. The plastiboards covering its windows had a dozen layers of advertising posters on them. The latest one—A VOTE FOR DIAZ IS A VOTE FOR HIGHER FOOD ALLOTMENTS—was at least a year out of date. The doorway stank of urine. A grimy body lay curled in the litter of the entrance. It was impossible to tell its age or sex underneath the filthy rags it was wrapped in.

The hallway inside the door was dirty, narrow, and dark. Leo climbed the stairs at the end of the hall, one hand on the rickety railing. The stairs creaked under his weight. The back room that he went straight to was as filthy as the rest of the place, but in addition to a grease-stained formica-topped table and a single wooden kitchen chair, the room boasted a wall-spanning row of shining new metal and plastic electronic consoles. Glassy lenses peered out of the machinery; they all seemed to be staring at Leo.

A slim, dark-skinned man with shiny, long black ringlets welcomed Leo in a high, singsong voice. He identified himself as "Raja."

Sitting massively in the ancient wooden chair, Leo said, "Before the conference starts, I want to talk with Garrison."

Raja looked startled. "I don't know . . ."

Without moving from the chair, Leo said, "Put me through to Garrison or I'll put you through the fuckin' wall."

Raja whirled and started working the machines. There was a hum of electrical power and suddenly T. Hunter Garrison seemed to appear at the end of the worn, grease-filmed table.

Despite himself, Leo was impressed with the three-dimensional solidity of the hologram. Garrison was sitting in a fancy kind of chair, looking annoyed. Golden sunlight bathed the air around him and glinted off his bald head.

"Just what do you want, Greer?" the old man snapped. "I've gone to a helluva lot of trouble to set up this conference for you. What more do you want out of me?"

Leo leaned forward and planted a tree-sized forearm on the tabletop. "You're gonna go through a lot more trouble before this is over. We both are."

"So?" Garrison's voice was a testy crackle.

"So before I really stick my neck into this noose, I want to know where I'm gonna get my stuff from."

"What stuff?"

"The steroids and hormones—all the goods I need to live."

Garrison made an impatient wave of his hands. "You'll get them! From the same place the World Government was getting them for you. Who do you think they bought them from?"

"I want to know where the source is, man," Leo insisted. "Otherwise, it's no game."

Garrison huffed at him. "What's the matter? Don't you trust me?"

"No," Leo said, a slow smile growing. "Not any more'n you trust me."

"Hah! If it wasn't for me you'd still be . . ."

"Never mind. Where's the stuff made? I gotta know before I go one step further."

With a sour face, Garrison said, "One of my corporate research labs, a biochemistry laboratory, up the Hudson a few miles from the city. In Westchester County someplace. Near Croton."

"I'm going to check that out," Leo said.

"Go ahead and check it! Listen, don't think you've got me hung up by the balls.. This whole business of yours doesn't mean a rat's asshole to me."

"Sure, I know." Leo said. "That's why you're buying us the goods."

Garrison made an abrupt motion with his left hand and his image vanished.

Leo leaned back in his chair thoughtfully. *Gotta check out that lab. Can't let him cut off my supplies.*

Raja was standing beside a six-foot-high console covered with gauges and knobs. "The conference is scheduled to begin in a few minutes." He asked, his voice high-pitched with nervousness, "Will you be ready?"

"Sure, man," Leo said. "I'm ready for anything."

With a relieved sigh, Raja turned back to his equipment and fidgeted with the various controls. Leo knew that most of what he was doing was sheer tension-caused busywork. But finally he cast an eye on the digital clock, gave a sigh, and leaned heavily on a single large red button.

Instantly the table was filled with eleven other seated figures, as real and solid as if they were actually in the room, rather than scattered around eleven different cities hundreds or even thousands of miles apart.

Raja made a nervous little bow and scuttled out of the room, actually moving through the holographic images of two of the people "sitting" nearest the door. Leo let the others babble while he listened to the door clicking shut and heard Raja's footsteps receding down the hall stairs.

Then he turned to the others at the table. Four of them were women. Two—one man and one woman—were white. They had all been checked on and vouched for, but Leo found himself distrusting the two of them.

"My name is Leo," he said loudly enough to make them stop their chatter and look at him. "And I want to ask you a question."

One of the black women asked smilingly, "What question?"

"How many blacks in the U.S.? How many Hispanics, Chicanos, Orientals, and Indians?"

"Lots and lots," somebody said. The others laughed.

Leo did not. "Together, we outnumber the white-asses by a ton. How come *they* runnin' the country and we're not?"

For a moment, no one spoke. Then a chunky, brown-faced young man said, "The whities got the Army, man. They got guns. They're organized."

"Right!" Leo snapped. "They're *organized!* That's their secret. It's about time we got organized, too. Instead of a dozen different movements in a dozen different cities— PRU here, Panthers there, Latinos someplace else—we gotta organize and work together.'

"We gotta, huh?" said one of the blacks. "Who says?"

"I say. And I say we can get all the help we want from the PRU and others."

"Big shit."

"You bet it is," Leo said. "What's your name, brother?"

"My name? I ain't givin' you my name. Jus' call me Cleveland."

"Okay, Cleveland. How you suppose we got all this fancy communications gear? Just fall out of the sky? We got *friends*, man—powerful friends. What we need is organization, workin' together. We can beat Whitey. It's *our* country; we just gotta take it."

One of the women said, "Most of the Army is black . . . or brown."

"Fuckin' National Guard ain't. And they back up the white-ass cops."

"We can get 'em," Leo said. "We can beat 'em if we work together."

T. Hunter Garrison sat in his powerchair and watched the dawning looks of interest and ambition on the faces of the men and women listening to Leo.

From the windows of his penthouse, high above the smog of coal-burning Houston, he could see all the way to Clear Lake and to the smudged horizon that showed where Galveston lay.

His craggy face was grinning broadly as he watched the miniature holographic images of the twelve underground leaders. They were no bigger than dolls sitting around a dollhouse table, in the three-dimensional picture that hovered in midair in front of Garrison's eyes.

"Mean-looking bunch, aren't they?" Garrison said.

"I don't know," said Arlene Lee, standing behind the powerchair. "That one on the end, with the Apache headband—he looks kind of rugged."

She was a tall, lusciously billowing redhead, with the fresh, smiling good looks of a cheerleader. She was variously Garrison's private secretary, bodyguard, courier, confidante, and hatchet-wielder.

"Get me another beer," Garrison said, his eyes never leaving the animated discussion that was heating up around Leo's conference table.

Arlene disappeared behind a row of potted plants for a few minutes. From the outside, Garrison Tower looked like any other international-style skyscraper in Houston: a few floors taller than all the rest, of course; a much larger expanse of solar energy panels set along the outside walls that were high enough to be above the smog level, and all around the helicopter pad on the roof. But Garrison's living quarters on the topmost floor of the Tower were a comfortable mixture of efficiency and ease: walls paneled in real wood, bear-skin rugs and animal hides on the tiled floors, all the modern conveniences hidden behind mirrors or cabinet doors.

Arlene brought Garrison his beer and leaned over the back of his chair, twirling the few strands of hair remaining on his head with one carefully manicured finger. He looked across the room to the mirror facing them and silently admired her cleavage.

"They're not very bright, are they?" she said.

"What?"

"These kids who call themselves revolutionaries," Arlene said. "They can't think very far. Why haven't they thought about working together before this?"

Garrison snorted. "Don't learn much about cooperation in the gutter. This big black buck—calls himself Leo—he's got more brains than the rest of 'em put together. He's already got a lot of the New York street gangs working together."

"He looks kinda familiar, doesn't he?"

"Should," Garrison said. "Used to be a major-league football player, over in Dallas."

"How on earth did he ever go from football to being a street fighter?"

Garrison smiled grimly. "Long story. Look it up in the files if you want to. Man of honor, conscience. Wanted to make the world better for his fellow niggers. Then he discovered power. It's the worst drug of them all."

Arlene shook her head, letting her long red hair sweep across the old man's bald head. "You oughtta know about that, honey."

He grinned up at her. "Power's an aphrodisiac, eh?"

With her Texas cheerleader's smile, Arlene replied, "It shore is, honey. It shore is."

Cleveland was grumbling, "So what's all this shit about workin' together? Whaddaya want us t'do, send ya a telegram every Saturday?"

"No," Leo said in a deep, rumbling purr. "I want us to

shake the white-ass power structure to its roots. I want to do something so powerful, so spectacular, that they'll be *glad* to give us control of the country, just to get us off their backs."

"*Jesu Christo!* Whaddaya mean, man?"

Leo smiled slowly and leaned forward in his groaning chair. "Any of you people ever hear 'bout a military action called the Tet Offensive?"

It's hot in Texas! The sun just melts you down. It even bakes the ground 'til it's so hard you couldn't grow anything on it except sagebrush. At least, that's what some of the other students told me.

I talked with Mom and Dad on the phone tonight to tell them I got here okay. They're moving off the farm next week and going to the housing project.

They say the classes here will be pretty rough, but the teachers are good. There's an awful lot I don't know. Guess I've been pretty dumb about a lot of things. But I'm going to make up for it now.

The students are all terrific kids. We spent the first day here going through psychological tests; they screen us for compatibility and such. And there's one girl, Ruth Oppenheimer, who's really a knockout. Very special. She's from California. I think she's Jewish. . . .

—The journal of William Palmquist

• CHAPTER 16 •

David sat on the lopsided plastic chair in the electronic shop's storeroom and stared into the open cargo pod.

It does look like a coffin, he realized.

He had arranged the spacesuit inside the pod to see how much room his own body would take. Crammed in around it were two green oxygen tanks and, at its feet, a single fuel cell. He had lined the pod with extra plastic insulation, as well.

The numbers on the computer terminal that rested on a shelf beside him said that he would have enough oxygen and heat to stay alive for the two-day journey to the Moon—barely—if he remained under the electronically induced TM trance.

"To sleep," David murmured, "perchance to dream."

He had already labeled the outside of the cargo pod with a stencil that identified its contents as MISC. ELECTRONICS SPARES. All the proper code numbers were set in place with orange Day-Glo paint. All he had to do was get into the spacesuit, lie down inside the pod, and run the TM program through his implanted communicator. He had already altered the programming so that it would run for forty-eight hours, instead of six.

All the numbers checked out. Everything was ready. Still he sat in the chair, unmoving.

In his mind's eye he could see the pod being clipped to the ungainly lunar ferry, a gangle of squat metal pods and sharp-angled supporting beams. He saw the ferry push away from its Island One dock and float out silently into the deathly cold vacuum of space. And he saw himself inside the cargo pod, eyes closed, deep in a trance. The oxygen flow stopped. The fuel cell broke down. He froze into a solid brick, an ice sculpture, delicate white crystals rimming his eyelashes, the hairs of his nostrils. His flesh turned brittle blue-white and he was dead, alone, drifting naked through the empty, infinite cold. Forever.

David shook his head. *Stop delaying!* he said to himself.

Slowly, telling himself he could always call it off at the last minute, David donned the pressure suit. Kneeling in its cumbersome bulk, he connected its air-feeder hoses to the oxygen tanks. The helmet visor was still open, though, and he continued to breath room air. *Time enough for the tanks later.*

Step by methodical step, he went through the routine just as he had planned it, until finally he was stretched out inside the pod, clumsily sealing the cover over his face. It was absolutely dark inside. He clicked his communicator on and ordered a freight pickup first thing in the morning.

Then he tried to relax and doze off naturally. If he did, he never realized it. And if he dreamed, he kept any memory of it out of his conscious mind.

The next thing David sensed were muffled voices around him. Then he heard the whine of an electric motor as the pod was hoisted up and carried to a waiting truck. It was dumped onto the truck bed with a spine-jarring bang.

It was like being totally blind and almost completely deaf. The only information David got from the outside world was through his sense of touch. The truck rattled off to the spaceport docking area, down at the Endcap. More hoisting, swinging, thumping. Voices calling back and forth. Motors straining. The whirr of boltguns attaching the pod to the ferry's outer framework.

And then nothing. Silence. For hours. Silence and cold.

David knew the cargo pod was secured to the ferry, which in turn was moored to its dock out at the end of the colony's main cylinder. The big solar mirrors kept the ambient temperature in the dock area from going below zero, but not by much. It was cold.

Not as cold as it'll get after we push off, David knew.

He checked through his communicator to make certain that the ferry's takeoff was still on schedule. It was. *Less than an hour to go.*

The time stretched out agonizingly. David fought against

sleep now, as his body perversely wanted to drowse. *No, you mustn't! You've got to be awake to put yourself into the TM trance as soon as the ferry leaves the dock; otherwise, you'll freeze to death in your sleep!*

He felt hungry, too, and realized that he hadn't eaten in nearly twenty-four hours. Too excited then. Too late now. There was a water tube inside his helmet, and the suit's relief tube would take care of urination. For the rest, sleep and wait. *But wait before you sleep.*

He felt, rather than heard, the ship coming alive around him. Humming vibrations. The thump of hatches slamming. And then a jolt, gentle enough, but surprising, nonetheless. They were on their way.

And the cold began. Teeth chattering, David called for the computer program that would put him into the trance.

What if the altered programming doesn't work? I never had a chance to test it for the full forty-eight hours!

That was the last thought he remembered having.

"David Adams?"

David roused himself from sleep and focused blearily on the man leaning over him.

"Huh? What is it?"

Then he realized he was no longer in the cargo pod. The room around him was strange: small, low-ceilinged, bare metal support beams hanging starkly overhead.

"You *are* David Adams, aren't you?"

"Uh ... what did you say?"

The man wore the pastel-green smock of a medic.

"Welcome to the Moon, Mr. Adams," he said, "although I must admit that you sure picked the hard way to get here."

David lifted his head off the examination table. "The Moon? I made it?"

The medic grinned and nodded. He was a sallow-faced man with a drooping, sandy-colored moustache. "You made it. How do you feel?"

Sitting up slowly, David answered, "A little stiff. Awfully hungry."

"I should think so." The medic helped him down off the table and over to a chair. "Be careful walking. The gravity's only one-sixth of what you're accustomed to."

"I've lived in low-gee environments," David said. But he sat down carefully, nonetheless.

"Sure," said the medic. He picked up a plastic pitcher from the desk nearby and took a mug in his other hand. He poured a steaming stream of coffee. David watched fascinated at how slowly the coffee poured from the pitcher to the cup.

"Try this for a warmer. I'll order some food for you."

"Thanks," David said, grasping the mug gratefully in both hands. Its heat felt good.

Punching out an order on the phone keyboard, the medic said, without looking at David, "You're in a helluva lot of trouble, you know."

"I guess I am." He hadn't thought much further than getting away from Island One. But now that he was at the lunar mines, he was still under the jurisdiction of the Corporation—still within Dr. Cobb's grasp.

Well, I've come a quarter-million miles. About one more thousand and I'm in Selene, David thought. *But how do I get there?*

The medic ducked out of the low-ceilinged room for a moment and came back in bearing a tray of hot food. David attacked it eagerly. It was chicken, vegetables, hot bread, and fresh fruit. No different from the food in Island One. *Must be grown in the colony,* he realized.

While he ate, the medic asked David endless questions about the trance state they had found him in when they opened his cargo pod.

"Scared the hell out of everybody," he said. "We thought you were dead at first."

"I was worried that I would be," David admitted.

"How did you do it?"

David explained and the medic tapped out furious notes on his desk computer terminal. "I'm going to look this up. Might be a way to transport injured miners back to the hospital at L4. . . ."

As David mopped up the last drops of juice in the bottom of his fruit cup, a slightly plump young woman in a bright yellow jumpsuit appeared at the doorway.

"David Adams." It was a statement, not a question. She wore a silver star pasted onto her I.D. badge. Security, David knew.

He handed the tray to the medic and got to his feet. "That's me, all right."

"Follow me, please," she said. She was rather pleasant-looking, with a round face, short-cropped hair the color of mahogany, and eyes to match. She was unarmed, but as they stepped out into the corridor, David saw two very large uniformed guards who fell in behind him.

David didn't know if it was the low lunar gravity or his long sleep in the pod that made his legs feel wobbly. The presence of the guards behind him, their boots drumming at his heels, didn't improve his spirits. And the corridor they were walking through was low, narrow, and claustrophobic. It was dimly lit, as well, with bare fluorescent tubes spaced too far apart.

"Where are you taking me?" he asked the girl.

"Security chief wants to talk to you. Seems that Dr. Cobb has been burning the ether between here and Island One."

"I'll bet," David muttered.

There were doors on both sides of the corridor, and other people were walking busily back and forth. Through the closed doors David could hear the clatter of typing and the electronic singsong of computers. Somebody laughed loudly as they passed the doors. David wondered what the joke was.

Finally they reached a door labeled SECURITY: M. JEFFERS.

The woman rapped on the door twice. A gruff voice answered, "Send him in here."

She turned to David with a rueful little smile. "Into the lion's den, Mr. Adams."

He opened the door and stepped in.

It was tidy little office, even though the low ceiling seemed to crowd in on David. Jeffers sat behind a gray metal desk, its top scrupulously uncluttered, puffing on a blackened pipe and giving David a cold stare. He was a big man, the kind who could intimidate others with his size. Iron-gray hair, cut to within a flat centimeter of his scalp. Hawk nose. Square chin. Ice-blue eyes. Big, gnarled hands.

Another man was standing off to one side of the desk, in front of a row of old-fashioned filing cabinets.

The second man was also big, broad-shouldered enough

to crowd a room this size, barrel-chested, and so heavily muscled that he seemed to be bursting out of his coveralls. And he was furious. His eyes glared at David. His breathing was in rapid, angry snorts. His heavy hands clenched and unclenched.

"You're David Adams," said Jeffers.

"Yes."

"Just what Cobb said," the other man snapped. "He's nothing but a snot-nosed runaway kid."

"Easy, Pete." Jeffers raised the hand holding his pipe. The other man glared, but he shut his mouth.

"Why did you come here?" Jeffers asked David.

"I want to go to Selene," David said. "I wanted to get out of Island One."

"So you had to stow away aboard one of our ferries?" the other man said, his voice barely lower than a roar. "If you had died, do you know what would've happened to our insurance rates? This isn't some goddamned joke!"

"I risked my life to get here," David said. "I'm not joking."

"The hell, you're not." Turning to Jeffers, he added, "I say we ship him back the same way he came here."

"Now, Pete, you know . . ."

"I'm going to Selene," David insisted. "You people have no authority to detain me."

The man looked back at David. "No authority! You little bastard, who the hell do you think you are?"

"Who the hell are you?" David snapped back angrily. "I don't have to take insults from anyone."

The man took a short, swift step toward David and swung his right fist into David's face. David had spent years in gyms, learning every martial art from Aikido to the Marquis of Queensberry. But he was caught completely by surprise, and the lower gravity of the Moon made his blocking arm overreact.

He missed the block and the fist connected with David's jaw. He felt nothing, but suddenly he was off his feet, banging into the door behind him in the slow motion of the Moon's one-sixth gravity. He slid down, knees buckling, and landed on the seat of his pants.

"For Chrissakes!" Jeffers was coming around his desk. He grabbed Pete by the shoulder and pulled him away from David. "He's only a kid. What the hell do you think you're doing?"

Pete shook free of the security man's grasp. "I've got twenty-six men and women out there who risk their god-damned necks every day, and this little squirt prances in here and thinks he can order us around!"

David got to his feet. There was blood in his mouth. It tasted hot, salty-sweet.

Jeffers pushed Pete toward the door. David stepped aside, fingering his jaw, feeling an upwelling of anger as he stared into Pete's berserk eyes.

Calm down, David told himself. *Remember, they've still got those guards outside. Wait until you can get him one-on-one*. But something inside him was howling for revenge.

Closing the door behind the mining foreman, Jeffers turned back to David.

"Need a doc?"

David shook his head. His jaw ached, but he refused to touch it again.

"All your teeth okay?"

"I'm not hurt," David answered.

"Okay. Pete's a hothead; a good foreman, though. He gets sore at anything—or anybody—that interrupts the mining work."

David said nothing.

"Dr. Cobb told me I should make you call him as soon as you were conscious again."

"All right," David said, sounding sullen even to himself. He went to the only other chair in the tiny room, a sling of webbing draped across a fragile-looking aluminum frame. He sat down facing the phone screen as Jeffers touched buttons on the keyboard.

The viewscreen glowed and Dr. Cobb's craggy face took form on it.

"So you ran away," Cobb said without preamble.

"I had to," David said. "I had to get away from the colony for a while."

"You took quite a chance, going the way you did."

"You didn't leave me any alternative."

Cobb pursed his lips, then said, "Enjoy the ride?"

Running his tongue along his teeth before he answered, David finally said, "It was restful."

"I should think so. Well, what do you want to do now?"

"What do you mean?"

Cobb's shaggy eyebrows rose and fell in a shrug that was mostly off-camera. "You're at the mining complex. Do you want to stay a few days and see how the other half lives?"

Surprised at the offer, David said, "Yes, maybe that would be best."

"Don't go getting any ideas," Cobb warned. "You're to stay strictly at the mines. No excursions to Selene or anywhere else. Jeffers, you there?"

With the touch of a fingertip, Jeffers widened the phone's camera angle to include himself. "Yes, sir."

"Keep this young adventurer away from the rockets. He's just foolish enough to steal a ballistics lobber and smear his valuable brains all over Selene's landing grid."

Jeffers nodded and smiled. "Will do, chief. Otherwise, can he have complete freedom of the base?"

"If you think that's reasonable," Cobb replied.

Jeffers glanced at David. "I think it'll be okay. I'll assign a security guard to show him around the place."

"Good." Looking back toward David, Cobb said, "So go ahead and have your fling. But I'll expect you back here by the end of the week. Understood?"

"Understood." David forced himself not to wince at the pain from the lump growing on his jaw.

It took less than a day to see everything that David wanted to see in the mining complex. There were fewer than a hundred people at the base. Most of them were miners operating the bulldozers that scooped up the lunar soil and placed it in the mass accelerator that catapulted the compressed soil and flung it completely off the Moon, to sail out into space, where it was eventually retrieved by a mass catcher hanging in orbit and then shipped to Island One's smelting plants and factories.

David watched the miners at work. At least they had to pull on astronaut-type pressure suits and clamber up into the cabs of their mammoth, nuclear-powered bulldozers. They actually worked the gears and levers that scooped up the hard-packed lunar soil. They worked outside, out on the surface of the Ocean of Storms.

"I'd like to go outside and ride on one of those tractors," David told his security guard.

The guard said, "I'll have to ask the boss."

They phoned Jeffers from the observation dome where they had been watching the mining operation. After some hesitation, Jeffers said, "You'll have to ask Pete Grady if it's okay with him. He's the foreman, and he gets pretty annoyed at anything that bothers the work."

Pete Grady, David thought. *That's his name.*

The guard was unwilling to bother Grady during a working shift. The man's reputation for sudden anger was well known throughout the mining complex.

"I'll speak to him tonight at dinner," he told David.

David nodded and let the guard usher him to his make-shift quarters: a coffin-sized room barely larger than the pod he had ridden in on. The guard promised once again to speak to Grady, then left David alone in his cubbyhole room.

As soon as the door shut behind the guard, David clicked on his communicator. He heard the singsong beeping of the mining complex's non-vocal computer, and he instructed it to connect him with the main computer at Island One.

It took several tries to get into Pete Grady's personnel file, but David finally hit on the right sequence of numbers for the key to unlock the computer's records. Ever since childhood he had thrilled with forbidden pleasure whenever he had mastered the computer's reluctance to tell him what he wanted to know. It was much better than stealing cookies.

After an hour's study of the readout that flashed across the viewscreen set into the wall of his bunk, David sent a phone message to Grady. The mine foreman wasn't in his quarters, so David ordered the computer to leave the message on Grady's screen:

Mr. Grady,

I hope you're still not angry at me for sneaking in here the way I did. Honestly, I didn't think it would mess up your mining work. [*"Your" mining work: appeal to his vanity.*] It was the only way I could get here. I've been watching the mining operations all day, and it's so fascinating that I think maybe I'd like to become a mining engineer someday myself—if I could make the grade, that is. I realize how tough it must be. I'd really like to see the pit operation up close, if it's all right with you. But if it's too risky for you to show me, if it would hurt your work or put you in any danger, I'll understand. [*Challenge his machismo.*] Thanks for listening, and no hard feelings.

Which was a patent lie. But all David thought about as he whistled down the cramped corridor toward dinner was the possibility of getting his hands on one of those huge nuclear-powered tractors.

David awoke to a blinking red light on his viewscreen, which meant there was a message for him. Sleepily, he sat up in the narrow bunk and banged his head against the ceiling. He hunched down a bit and touched the message button.

Pete Grady's intense, tight-lipped face appeared on the screen. "Okay, kid," he said, "if you want to see what real work is like, you be at the tractor airlock at oh-eight-hundred, exactly. I'm not going to wait one minute for you, so be on time."

The numbers in the lower corner of the screen showed that Grady had sent the message a few minutes after midnight. Touching the TIME button under the screen, David saw it was 0645. Plenty of time to have a good breakfast and get to the airlock to meet the mine foreman.

He reached the airlock ten minutes early, after a full breakfast of juice, eggs, sausages, waffles, muffins, jam, and coffee. His security guard, a different man from the day before, had watched sourly as David ate.

"Don't they feed you guys back at Island One?"

"Sure," David said between gulps. "But you people eat a lot better than we do." *And this might be my last meal for a while*, he added silently. *Maybe my last meal, period.*

The airlock was set into the curving wall of a dome that poked up above the lunar surface. Most of the dome's worn, scarred cement floor was filled by rows of the huge, massive tractors. Their heavy caterpillar tread cleats had gouged deep tracks into the floor. *Dinosaur footprints*, David thought, remembering the paleontology tapes he had studied.

The airlock itself looked like the heavy chrome-steel door to a giant bank vault. Twenty men could have walked through it arm in arm and still have room for a half-dozen more rows of twenty, one on top of the other.

"You'd better get suited up," Grady said by way of greeting. He seemed almost disappointed that David had shown up.

He pointed to a row of lockers off to one side of the airlock. David saw that there were empty pressure suits of various bright colors hanging on racks in front of each locker, with their bubble helmets suspended on hooks just above them. The suits had names stenciled on their chests.

"Not those!" Grady snapped. "Can't you see they belong to people? The white ones, down at the end."

Is he always angry? David wondered. *Or is it just me?*

He went quickly down to the end of the row and stepped into the open back of a white suit. The security guard helped to seal the seams as David pulled the helmet down and attached it to the metal neck yoke.

"I'll wait for you here," the guard said as David clumped back toward the airlock.

Grady was in a garish green suit, perched up in the cab of the yellow tractor nearest the airlock hatch. David climbed up the metal rungs to the cab clumsily in his heavy boots and sat next to the foreman. He waved a farewell to the guard, who seemed too embarrassed to wave back.

"Took you long enough," Grady muttered. "Get into this life-support pack." He jabbed a gloved finger toward the white metal backpack resting between their seats.

"Isn't the cabin pressurized?" David asked as he struggled to get his arms through the pack's harness.

"Hell, no," Grady answered. "You think we spend all day sitting up here like chauffeurs? We gotta get out of the cab and get our gloves dirty—ten, twenty times a day. Can't spend all day depressurizing the damned cab every time we gotta get out."

"I see." David had been counting on it. "But these tanks behind the seats here, they're a spare supply of air, aren't they?"

"Yeah, yeah. Now, get your visor down and let's get moving."

David said, "I can't seem to connect the hoses."

With an exasperated grunt, Grady grabbed the air lines from David's backpack and plugged them into the fittings in his suit's collar. "There. Want me to wipe your nose for you, too?"

"Thanks," David said, ignoring the sarcasm. He checked the gauges on his suit's wrist and slid his visor down and sealed it shut. "I'm all set."

Grady did the same and started up the tractor's heavy electric motors. They were nuclear-powered, rather than battery-fed. Each tractor had its own miniature isotope power system buried deep in its guts behind heavy lead shielding.

Grady started working the tractor's steering levers. David watched him carefully as the foreman snapped commands into the radio microphone inside his helmet. The airlock's inner hatch swung ponderously open and the tractor lurched forward into the dark, gaping hole beyond the hatch. The airlock was a huge metal womb. Once the inner hatch shut and the pumps started evacuating the chamber, there was no light except the dim red glow from the tractor's control panel.

David looked at Grady's face, glowering in the sullen red light. *What if you kill him?* he asked himself. And answered, *He won't die. At the most, he'll be unconscious for a few moments and embarrassed afterward. It'll serve him right.*

The airlock chamber was emptied of air at last, and the outer hatch started to swing open. David glanced at the dials on the tractor's control panel. The digital clock showed exactly 0800. Then he looked up at the airless surface of the Moon.

Utter desolation. As far as the eye could see, nothing but emptiness, bare, dead stone. A flat, slightly rolling plain pitted by thousands—no, millions—of craters, some no bigger than a finger-poke. A black-and-gray world set into a dead-black sky studded with stars. A weary, *old* world without air, without water, exposed to billions of years of grinding erosion from infalling meteors. Off on the left were a few tired-looking hills, worn smooth by eons of meteoric sandpapering that had slumped them down into soft, curving lumps of rock. They looked as if they had been made of wax and left in the sun to melt.

Yet it was breathtaking. Open, empty space, with no

one to clutter it. Out as far as the horizon, no sign of the works of man. And silent. The only sounds David could hear were the faint electrical hums of the tractor and his own steady whisper of breath.

David had never seen a horizon before, except in pictures. *It really looks like the edge of the world.* Beyond it was nothing but the emptiness of space and the solemn, unblinking stars.

Then Grady jinked the tractor around to the right and David could see the mines. As they approached the open pit, David began to realize how small it was. *The farmlands inside the colony are bigger than that.*

It was merely an open pit, dug down a few meters from the surface. Two tractors with bulldozer blades on their snouts were pushing mounds of dirt toward a potbellied ore carrier that was hooked behind a third tractor.

"Is that . . . it?" David asked.

Grady's chuckle rattled in his helmet earphones. "That's it, kid. All the material for your nice fancy colony comes from that hole in the Moon."

David looked at the foreman. He was actually smiling. He looked relaxed, even happy. *I wonder if he changes like this every time he goes through the airlock?*

The tension and anger that he had shown inside the base just weren't there anymore.

They rumbled up to the edge of the pit and before David knew it, they were heading down the packed-dirt ramp into the mining area.

"The material to build Island One in the first place," Grady said, "came from a pit just about this size . . . over on the other side of the dome. The mass accelerator's on that side, too."

"I know," David said. "I saw it yesterday, from the control booth."

"Yeah. Well, now we're going over to take a look at the sites for new pits. Got a survey team coming out in"— he glanced at the dashboard clock—"twelve minutes. . . ."

He chattered on like a tour guide. *Damn it!* David thought. *Why couldn't you have stayed rotten and angry? It would've made things a lot easier for me.*

Grady guided their tractor up the incline at the far side of the pit and they were surrounded by barren emptiness again. It was like being at sea: nothing but horizon in every direction, and the dark sky overhead.

He stopped the tractor.

"Want to get out and walk around? Plant your footprints on the Moon?"

He started to slide out from under the controls, and David moved over into his seat.

"No, dummy, go out your own side," Grady said, half-turning toward David.

He was crouched over, framed by the open hatch, one booted foot on the topmost rung of the ladder, the other on the hatch's sill. David leaned across, and grabbed him under the armpits.

"Hey! What the hell . . ."

In the light lunar gravity it was easy to lift him off his feet entirely, even from a sitting position. David yanked him free of the tractor and then gave a slight push and let him go. Grady's green-suited figure flailed for what seemed like an eternity before it hit the ground, boots first, and kicked up a lazy cloud of dust. He tumbled backward, over his life-support pack, and came up in a spraddle-legged sitting position.

"You goddamned son-of-a-bitch!" roared in David's earphones. "What the hell do you think you're doing? I'm gonna break every goddamned bone in your goddamned body. . . ."

He was clambering to his feet. David sat himself solidly in the driver's seat and grabbed the control levers. He tromped on the power pedal and the tractor lurched forward.

"Come back here, you bastard!"

Leaning partway out of the cab to look back at the foreman, David saw the green pressure suit dwindling behind him. Grady was literally hopping up and down in a fury, waving both arms heavenward and screaming with frustrated anger.

"Grady, what's going on?" a third voice asked. The control center, back at the base. "What's your problem?"

But all Grady could utter was a roaring string of profanities.

"Grady, where are you? What's wrong?"

"I'll kill the stupid son-of-a-bitch! I'll tear you apart, Adams! I'll skin you alive!"

David leaned back in the driver's seat. He smiled. *That's better. That's more like the Pete Grady I've grown to know and love.*

In a few minutes, other voices crackled over the communications net.

"He stole the tractor?"

"Where the hell does he think he's going with it?"

"The only other place he can go is Selene."

David nodded. *Right on, friend.*

"Selene? He can't make it there. It's more than a thousand klicks!"

"He's got air enough . . . maybe."

"Yeah, but there're no navigation aids between here and Selene. Nobody makes the trip on the surface. He'll be dead-lost in a couple of hours."

"Good," Grady's voice snapped. "I hope the little bastard chokes on his own juices out there. I only wish we had some buzzards to feed his body to."

The anomalous weather conditions over most of the Northern Hemisphere this past winter and spring have been caused by a reversal of the usual polar low that predominates the Arctic airflow under normal conditions. A rather static high-pressure system has replaced the normal polar low, causing a consequent shift in the Northern Hemisphere jet streams and resulting in anomalous wind patterns and storm tracks in the troposphere. Thus, we have had extensive flooding in the North American Midwest and on the Scandinavian peninsula, with drought conditions spread generally at lower latitudes.

If these anomalous conditions have been triggered by human intervention, the deliberate weather modifications must have been made on a scale so massive that the International Weather Services' computers cannot predict the end of the chain of interlinked anomalies. In layman's terms, the weather may settle down to its normal pattern in a matter of weeks, or months, or years—or not at all. We simply do not have enough information to make valid predictions.

> —Dr. R. Copeland III, Chief
> Coordinator, International
> Weather Services, in testimony
> to the World Government *ad hoc*
> committee on disaster relief,
> 22 June 2008

• CHAPTER 17 •

Hamoud stood on the rooftop and looked out over the city. Basra had once been a busy, bustling port, back in the days when oil exports had brought so much gold into Iraq.

But now the port was hardly used. Most of the piers lay rotting under the high summer sun. The old oil refinery's towers, crumbling from neglect, stood like blackened ruins against the sky. Only two freighters, tired and rust-stained, were in the harbor, taking on loads of dates and wool. *The same cargoes that Sinbad took with him,* Hamoud thought bitterly.

The oil was gone and so was the gold that it had brought. Where had the gold disappeared to? Into the coffers of men like Sheikh al-Hashimi. Into the hands of foreigners who now came back to build tourist centers so that the rich Westerners could come and smile at the wretched, backward Arabs.

Hamoud's fists clenched. *To them we are all Arabs. Kurds, Pakistanis, Lebanese, Saudis, Hashimites—all Arabs. Camel drivers and rug merchants. That is how they see us.*

Hardly anything moved in the drowsing, sun-baked afternoon. But Hamoud peered into the bright sky and waited. Beside him, Bahjat paced nervously, almost frantically.

It had been simple to smuggle her out of her father's house and then return to his own quarters so that suspicion fell on others. Al-Hashimi turned Baghdad upside down searching for her, but Hamoud had gotten her safely off to Shiraz, across the Iranian border, before the dawn had broken. Then the sheikh had summoned him and

188

asked—actually *asked*, rather than ordered—Hamoud to use his PRU contacts to find her. He seemed to know that she was Scheherazade, although he never mentioned the fact outright.

"There it is." The pilot poked at Denny's shoulder, then pointed.

Denny followed his arm and saw a spread of ruins across the bare desert floor. "Babylon?" he yelled over the helicopter's whirring rotors.

"Babylon!" the pilot shouted back, grinning toothily.

"Can you take it lower?"

"We haven't much fuel to spare if you want to make it to Basra without stopping."

Still he swooped down and Denny studied the crumbling pillars and scattered stones of one of the seven wonders of the ancient world. Babylon lay sprawled in the engulfing sands like the bleached bones of a prehistoric monster.

I'll bring you back to life, Denny promised the dead stones. *I'll make them come from all around the world to stare in awe at you again.*

Mentally, he laid out plans for the temple *here,* and the colonnaded walkways *there,* with the palace and the hanging gardens at the end. . . .

The helicopter rose like a leaf in a swirl of wind and angled away from the ruins, heading south. Denny leaned against his shoulder harness for a last look at Babylon, then settled back in his seat.

Bahjat had reached him by phone, breathless and urgent. Her instructions were specific. Rent a car and drive north to Mosul. Don't try to use the airport at Baghdad; it's being watched. In Mosul, find a teacher at the university named Professor as-Said. He will help you to take the next leg of the journey. And she had hung up before he could say a word.

The professor turned out to be a young, bearded, fiery-eyed mathematician who regarded Denny with great suspicion, if not distaste. Denny had heard that the university was hotbed of PRU radicalism, and he thought that as-Said might well be one of the revolutionaries. Why would Bahjat have anything to do with him?

PRU or not, the professor drove Denny to a private

helicopter pad out in the hills and packed him aboard the red-and-white chopper he was now flying southward to Basra. To Bahjat.

Briefly he thought about his work on the Caliph's palace back in Baghdad. It would grind to a halt with him not there. *So what?* Bahjat was more important, all-important. The work could wait. He would fly her to Messina and ask to be taken off the Baghdad project for personal reasons. When they saw her in Messina, they would understand.

How will I do Babylon if her father's still sore at us? Grinning, he answered, *Who cares? As long as Bahjat is with me, who cares what we do or where? We've got the whole world!*

Bahjat and Hamoud stood on the rooftop as the sun sank behind the western hills.

"You have heard nothing of Irene?" she asked.

"Nothing. She is not important. You are."

"But she is my friend."

"There are no *friends* among us," he hissed. "Friendship is a luxury we cannot afford."

Bahjat's shoulders slumped. "That is a cruel way to live."

"You would prefer to remain in your father's house?" Hamoud asked.

Snapping an angry stare at him, Bahjat countered, "Would you prefer that I were sent to Island One?"

He shrugged. "Perhaps it was a mistake to refuse to go there."

"What do you mean?"

"It might be a good thing to have an agent inside the space colony. Think of what we could accomplish if we could destroy it."

"Destroy it? But why?"

"Why not? Isn't it a symbol of the corporations and the power of the rich? By destroying it we could show how powerful we are."

Bahjat looked away from him, back out toward the reddening sky. "His helicopter is late."

Inwardly, Hamoud grimaced. *Waiting for her lover, like a dog in heat. But soon she will have no one but me, and me alone.*

"Are you sure our people in Mosul . . ."

"As-Said is very reliable," Hamoud said. "How do you think he keeps his university post? And his neck?" *He is reliable in two things,* he added silently. *Mathematics and time bombs.*

Bahjat shuddered from a sudden breeze sweeping out of the distant hills. She wrapped her arms around herself.

At last a silvery speck appeared in the deepening violet of the sky.

"Is that him?" Bahjat cried.

Hamoud nodded. "It must be."

Red and white lights winking at them, the helicopter slowly came closer. It was slanting slightly sideways, like a charger cantering. Hamoud knew that the pilot must be fighting a stiff crosswind.

He is a good pilot, Hamoud thought. *But sacrifices must be made for the cause. She would never believe me if one of my own men was not destroyed in the crash.*

The helicopter grew and took form. They could hear the distant whirring thrum of its blades as it approached the landing pad near the docks.

And then it blossomed into flame: a bright flare, and almost before the eyes could register its flash, a heavy, dark flower of smoke and flames bloomed out where the helicopter had been.

Hamoud heard Bahjat's strangled "No!" just before the thunderclap of the explosion reached them.

She stood there rooted into immobility as the blazing remains of the helicopter twisted crazily down into the dusty earth, spattering chunks of fiery debris like sooty fireballs as it fell.

"No . . ." Bahjat repeated, sobbing. "No . . . no . . ."

Hamoud kept his hands rigidly at his sides, his face utterly impassive.

The helicopter hit the ground with a noise like a junk-yard collapsing. A fuel tank ruptured and exploded into a fresh sheet of flame.

"I killed him," she said in a tortured whisper. "It's my fault, mine. . . ."

"No," Hamoud answered. "Your father killed him. He must have given up on using him to find you."

Bahjat looked up at him, her eyes red, her face twisted in agony. "My father. Yes, it was him. He hated Dennis."

Hamoud said nothing.

"And now I hate him!" Bahjat snarled, fury replacing pain. She raised her fists to the sky. "I will avenge him! I'll make the whole world pay for this murder!"

Turning back to Hamoud, she said, "We *will* destroy Island One. You and I, together."

Talked with Mom and Dad tonight. Their apartment looks awfully small, but they said they liked it okay. Probably lying to keep me from worrying about them.

We're having exams already. They don't waste any time here. I haven't told Mom and Dad about Ruth yet. Hell, I haven't even told Ruth how I feel about her. Too much studying to do!

—The journal of William Palmquist

• CHAPTER 18 •

Driving the tractor across the Ocean of Storms was like taking a cruise across the featureless expanse of a heaving, tossing sea, except that the Moon's "ocean" was made of rock. But it had waves frozen into its solid surface, undulating rolls of hills and vales, craters that made the tractor rock as the treads negotiated their slippery sides, long stretches of vast emptiness that lulled David to sleep.

Like a watery ocean, *Oceanus Procellarum* had no guideposts, no signs to give directions. It would have been easy to get totally lost. Not even the stars could be counted on for navigation, because the Moon's north pole pointed in a direction very different from Polaris, the pole star of Earth.

But David had the communicator implanted in his head, and through it he could "talk" directly with the navigation satellites that orbited high above the Moon's rocky wastelands.

If the ballistic rockets can navigate by satellite, so can I, he told himself.

He was certain that he was pointed in the right direction to reach Selene, on the far shore of the Ocean of Storms' thousand-kilometer-wide expanse. *But will I have enough air to make it?* His computer-aided calculations said he would—just barely. There was no food, of course. David's breakfast would have to last him for the next few days.

Thirty-six hours, he estimated. The suit's meager supply of bottled water would have to last that long.

The one thing David hadn't foreseen was his need for sleep. Driving himself across the empty, monotonous desolation was endless boredom. He found himself drifting to sleep. *Stay alert!* he commanded himself. *You can sleep when you get to Selene. Besides, you just spent two days snoozing.* But the urge to nod off was a relentless seduction.

The tractor had no automatic-drive or guidance systems. David had to control it every minute. There were enough boulders and craters strewn across the broad expanse of the lunar desert to make even a moment's inattention dangerous. Once, twice, he drowsed, then snapped awake when the tractor lurched into the steep downslopes of sharp-edged young craterlets.

The third time he dozed at the controls, the tractor grazed a rock the size of David's house back on Island One. One tread ground against the rock and started climbing its smooth face, making the tractor tilt crazily.

David awoke sliding out of his seat, heading out of the open hatchway. Still not instinctively familiar with the controls, he tried to stop the tractor where it was, but the massive machine ground onward, motors whining, tilting over on the one tread that still spun on the dusty ground.

If it goes over on its side, I'll be smashed under it, he realized.

But as if it had a stubborn will of its own, the tractor clambered over the rock and dropped ponderously back onto both treads. Under a full Earth gravity the jolt would have snapped David's spine. Even in the Moon's gentle pull, his head cracked painfully against the padded back of his helmet.

Awash with sweat, gasping in fear of the danger he had just passed, David brought the tractor to a stop. *All right, I'll get some sleep.* But now he couldn't close his eyes; he was too wrought-up from the near disaster he had just come through.

He pushed on. Hours later he stopped the tractor, when he could no longer force his eyes to stay open, and took a brief nap. Then onward again. He sipped water from the tube inside his helmet, checked the dwindling supply of air in his tanks, and tried to find radio broadcasts that would help to keep him awake. Absolutely nothing. The radio frequencies were as dead and empty as the landscape. The only broadcasts he could bring in were the coded signals of the navigation satellites.

No music, no news. But no chatter from pursuers, either. And no warnings of impending solar flares, which could bake a man with a lethal dose of radiation unless he got into an underground shelter quickly. The nearest underground shelter, David estimated, was at Selene.

He sang to himself. He talked to the computer that single-mindedly told him nothing except the correct heading to reach the underground lunar nation. He sipped water from the tube very sparingly, but still found that it ran dry. And he had more than four hundred kilometers to go.

"Twenty klicks an hour in this beast," he said aloud to himself. "That means another twenty hours or so. Not bad. Less than a day, not counting sleep time." It was much slower than he had expected.

He wished he could rub his burning eyes, or scratch one of the thousands of itches that plagued his body. But there was no way to open his suit, not if he wanted to live. Hunger was a pain in his gut now, a gnawing hollowness that refused to be ignored. His back hurt from sitting in the seat for so many hours. His legs were cramping. His arms ached.

And the air was starting to taste bad. That's what frightened him—when he realized that the air he was breathing had an acid, metallic tang to it. *The tanks are running out!*

The navigational satellite told him that Selene was less than three hundred kilometers away. But looking out through his fogged helmet visor, David couldn't tell if he were near Selene or just over the horizon from the mining complex. It all looked alike: rocks, craters, dusty, barren soil, the sudden sharp horizon that cut like a knife across the soft black velvet of space. But he couldn't see stars in that blackness. Couldn't even see the Earth.

Visor's fogged. Or is my vision going? Craning his neck, David licked at the inside of his visor with his tongue, hoping for moisture. The plastiglass was cold and dry. *It's me. Everything's going blurry.*

He had to sleep. Yet he dared not waste the time. Time meant air. Every breath he took brought him one gasp closer to the end. If the air ran out before he reached Selene, he would die. There was no time for sleeping, even though he risked crashing the tractor against a rock or tumbling it down a crater.

He drove on. Groggy, mouth caked as dry and dusty

as the waterless plain all around him, eyes blurring and burning, body so fatigued that it moved only by force of will, pain wracking every motion, every muscle contraction, every flexing of arms or legs.

That's good, David told himself. *Pain is good. Keeps you awake. Keeps you alive.*

"What can I say," he croaked to himself, "brave admiral say . . . Except sail on, sail on and on . . ."

He closed his eyes for what seemed like a second and when he reopened them the tractor was rearing up the raised lip of a sizable crater, its treads grinding on the loose rubble and stones. Slowly, painfully, David backed the cumbersome machine down away from the crater and started trundling around its rim.

When he got past it and could see the horizon again, his heart leaped. The huge blue-and-white ball of Earth hung low on the horizon, alive and more beautiful than anything that David had ever seen.

Except for the small concrete dome studded with observation windows that humped low on the ground a scant few hundred meters ahead of him. It was painted in red-and-white candy stripes—the colors of the lunar nation, Selene.

Everything went hazy after that. David remembered yelling into his suit microphone, his voice sounding strangely cracked, hoarse, hysterical. A hatch in the dome opened; other tractors came out toward him. He recalled the unforgettable sweetness of air from a fresh tank, and then darkness. He blacked out.

The only other memory of his rescue was of the moment when they finally took his helmet off and started to unseal his suit, inside the dome. Someone said, "God, but he smells ripe!"

BOOK THREE

July, 2008 A.D.

WORLD POPULATION:
7.27 BILLION

For Immediate Release

MESSINA: The World Government revealed today that Director Emanuel De Paolo suffered a mild heart attack, "several days ago." He is confined to his quarters, where a team of medical experts is at his bedside. No precise date of the heart seizure was given.

Dr. Lorenzo Matriglione, one of Europe's leading cardiologists, told a hastily assembled press conference this morning that there is no cause for serious alarm. "Director De Paolo's condition is quite good. He is resting comfortably. His attack was more in the nature of a cardiac insufficiency than an infarction."

Among the worldwide team of leading medical experts who flew into Messina during the past week was Dr. Michael Rovin, of the Massachusetts Institute of Technology's School of Bionics and Medical Prostheses.

"It doesn't look to me as if the Director will require an artificial heart or even a temporary auxiliary pump," Dr. Rovin said.

But other medical leaders around the world expressed concern about the head of the World Government. His advanced age was the chief reason for their fears. . . .

—International News press release,
1 July 2008

· CHAPTER 19 ·

It took nearly a month for David to get away from Selene.

A month of enforced idleness. A month of waiting. And questions. And negotiations. Legally, he was a stateless person. Technically, he was the chattel property of the Island One Corporation and had run away from an unexpired labor contract. But he applied for World citizenship, denied that he was legally competent when the contract had been signed (five years earlier), and asked the government of Selene for asylum until the World Government granted him citizenship.

He spent his days wandering the crowded corridors and public rooms of Selene. Inside of a few hours he had seen all he wanted to see of the cramped, crowded underground community. Almost fifty thousand people crowded into a few cubic kilometers of space, and most of that space was taken up by sickly looking underground farms and huge machinery. One place looked very much like another to David: colorless, grim, crowded. But the citizens of Selene boasted of their gardens and the wide-open spaces, up on the surface.

David had seen enough of *that*.

Finally, David found himself talking to a white-haired Russian named Leonov. He had been one of the founders of Selene, a hero of the Lunar Revolution, one of the rebels who had turned the American and Russian lunar colonies into a unified, independent nation.

The skin of Leonov's face seemed to sag, as if the flesh beneath it were melting away with age. But his white hair still flopped boyishly over his forehead, and his Arctic-blue eyes were bright and alert. He had been the head of government in Selene for several years, but now he played the role of revered elder statesman. Despite his age, he seemed lively to David. His voice boomed an echoing basso. The lines on his face were as much from laughter as from years. His hands were mobile, expressive—the only time they were still was when he was lighting a long, thin white cigarette.

He listened for almost a full day to David's story, hardly saying a word, just chain-smoking and nodding.

At last he closed his eyes and murmured, "It appears to me that we have a golden opportunity here to pass the buck, as my American friends say. We should let you go on to Messina and let the World Government worry about you."

David felt as if a weight had been taken off his back. "That's fine! Wonderful . . ."

"But"—Leonov raised a warning finger—"it is not up to me to decide. We must speak with the chief administrator."

David spent another empty day wandering through Selene's underground plazas and corridors before Leonov phoned and asked him to appear at the chief administrator's office the following morning.

The office was hardly impressive: just a small room with a couple of couches and a computer terminal in it. The floor was live grass, and the fluorescent light tubes set into the bare rock of the ceiling had a slightly reddish tinge to them.

The chief administrator was a short, waspish, black former American named Franklin D. Colt. He shook David's hand in a firm grip while studying his face with probing tawny eyes. It was like being watched by a lion, David felt.

They sat down—Leonov perfectly relaxed, David so tense that he perched on the front two centimeters of the couch beside the old man. Colt sprawled lazily on the couch facing them.

After David gave a brief review of his problem, Leonov said, "We should let him go to Messina, as he desires. This is not our problem. It is not up to us to decide if he is a World citizen or the legal chattel of Island One."

Colt's voice was sharp, hard-edged. "The corporations won't like it if we don't return their property to them."

Leonov shrugged. "You forget that I was born into a socialist society, my friend. The corporations may rule much of Earth and all of Island One. Even Mother Russia has made accommodation with them. But I have not. In the foolishness of my second childhood, I even hope for the advent of true Communism someday."

Colt broke into a grin. "You don't think that we ought to let the Island One Corporation muscle us around?"

"Are we an independent nation and a member of the World Government, or are we lackeys of the capitalists?"

The chief administrator glanced at David. "Never did think much of those corporate labor contracts—too close to slave-holding."

"It's important that I get to Messina," David said. "I have vital information for the Director of the World Government about the corporations and their intentions."

"Tired of living in paradise?" Colt asked.

"I'm tired of living in a fool's paradise," David answered.

With a sardonic grin, Colt said, "Well, then, you ought to go to Earth, all right. Messina's a good place to start. But you ought to go farther than that."

"Farther? Where?"

"Out into the hills in Sicily, where they still have blood feuds and use wooden plows to clear the rocks out of their fields. Go to the South Sahara, where the land's been totally depopulated by starvation. Or India, where they cart the dead away every morning, but they leave the garbage on the sidewalks. Or to some of the big American cities, where I was born, where they've got the poor people penned up in the rotting downtown sections while anybody with any money at all lives out in the suburbs. It's a beautiful world. You'll love it."

David stared at him. "But . . . if it's so horrible back there, why don't you try to do something about it?"

Leonov sighed and Colt laughed bitterly. "We did do something about it. We stopped them from having a nuclear war and we helped create the World Government. It would've been better if we'd let them blow themselves to hell and gotten it over with."

Sailing under a cobalt-blue sky dotted with happy puffs of cumulus clouds, Bahjat felt her body relaxing under the

warmth of the Mediterranean sun and the languid rhythm
of the schooner's rising and dipping as it plowed through
the deep sea swells.

But her mind could not relax. Each time she closed
her eyes she saw the helicopter exploding, burning fragments hurled across the sky, murdering her love, ending
her life before it had really had its chance to begin.

She had not slept in the month since Dennis' death,
except when she drugged herself into unconsciousness.
And even then her frenzied dreams were of death and
burning and mutilation.

But the dying man in her dreams was her father.

Hamoud had hidden her and for many weeks she had
been a fugitive from her father's armies of searchers. Long
accustomed to underground adventures as Scheherazade,
the much-publicized rebel, Bahjat found that it was very
different when she had no safe refuge to return to. Her
father's fine house and its servants were more dangerous
to her than a breathlessly hot, windowless room under the
roof of some pitiful laborer's hut. She couldn't even use
her credit numbers to get into a hotel or restaurant.

Despite her pain she smiled at herself. *It isn't so romantic when you are forced to be a full-time fugitive.* But
as she leaned against the smooth polished wood of the
schooner's mast, she knew that she would suffer any trial,
face any danger, pay any price to avenge the murder of
the man who loved her.

Looking out on the rolling, heaving sea, she marveled
at how straight and absolute the horizon was. No mist or
cloud confused the division between sea and sky. *You are
either the one thing or the other,* Bahjat told herself. *For
too long I've played at being a revolutionary. Hamoud was
right. I can't destroy the privileged class while I remain one
of the privileged myself.*

Hunted in every street, at every pier, in every shop,
Bahjat could not stay long in Basra. It was impossible to
get a boat there, Hamoud had told her. Together they
slipped out of the city in a truckload of felt, driven by one
of the young PRU men. Nearly smothering under the piles
of itchy, choking, dust-filled felt, Bahjat felt Hamoud's
hands on her body, his mouth against her skin. She did
not struggle, did not resist. Even when he told her in
elaborate, husky-voiced detail what he wanted her to do,

she simply listened and obeyed. It was only her body he was using. If it gave him pleasure, it was a small price to pay for his help.

But she had to concentrate on the ugly, hot stickiness all around her to keep her mind from memories of Dennis.

They got to the port city of Tripoli, in old Lebanon, and bribed a freight schooner's captain into taking on a passenger. Hamoud had decided that they should travel across the Mediterranean separately, for better security.

The sail-driven freighter had a crew of three men, plus a computer that handled most of the sail adjustments. With almost no need for fuel of any kind, running quietly and without pollution, the sailing freighters traded economy for time. Merchants who placed orders well in advance could halve their transport costs by having the goods delivered under sail.

The two under-officers left Bahjat alone. They seemed more interested in each other than in a woman. The captain, a crafty-eyed, solidly built Turk with a jewel set into one of his front teeth, had invited Bahjat to share his quarters the first night after they had left Tripoli. She declined. He came to her compartment later that night, calmly unlocking the door, smiling at her in her bunk.

The light over her bunk flicked on and he was staring into the muzzle of an automatic, held rock-steady by this little *houri*. The gun itself made the captain hesitate. But when he saw that there was a silencer on it, he turned without a word and left her compartment.

She knows guns, was his first thought. His second was, *Someone is probably offering a reward for her. I must find out who once we reach Naples.*

Bahjat was unmolested from then on. Now she stood on the main deck, leaning wearily against the solid strength of the creaking mast, and looked out at the emptiness of sea and sky.

It is all a desert, she thought. *The entire world is a desert, as empty as my soul.*

She refused to cry. Instead, she thought of how she would help Hamoud to destroy Island One.

NEWSFLASH***NEWSFLASH***NEWSFLASH***

PRETORIA: South African rebels, aided by covert military assistance from the Latin American revolutionary movement led by *El Libertador,* have claimed complete victory in their lightning-fast uprising against the Union of South Africa.

South Africa's ruling government called for a cease-fire and agreed to the rebels' terms for turning over the powers of government to a racially mixed junta made up of leaders in the underground movement.

It was rumored that *El Libertador* himself is in South Africa, although other rumors claim that he is still in Argentina, which fell to his revolutionary forces only two months ago.

The World Government seems stunned by the swiftness of the rebels' takeover in Africa's southernmost nation. Military opinion in Messina appears divided: some of the generals are demanding a counterattack to restore the ousted government, while others fear that such an action would plunge the entire African continent into war and destroy the authority of the World Government.

The rebels have already announced their intention to secede from the World Government, a move that . . .

• CHAPTER 20 •

David had finally left Selene's crowded, stifling underground warrens and sailed to Space Station Alpha on the regular lunar liner, a bulbous, plushly outfitted craft that carried tourists up to the lunar nation twice each month. David was given a first-class cabin all to himself. His luggage consisted of a single change of clothes—a blue jumpsuit with red piping, in the style popular in Selene—and a wallet full of identification tapes and personal introductions from Leonov to Emanuel De Paolo.

The two-day journey from Selene to Space Station Alpha, which orbited only a few hundred kilometers above the Earth, was a forty-eight-hour-long party for the ship's passengers. They were tourists, most of them, and they had paid extravagant prices for extravagant entertainment. There were dances, games, gambling, and gourmet meals going on constantly. And almost anything else the passengers wanted was available, as well. The non-rotating zero-gravity section of the liner was a favorite playground. Zero-gee sex was the main topic of conversation all through the ship.

David wandered through these strange pastimes. His dancing was graceful, but free-form. He ate prodigiously and carefully noted all the foods that were totally new to him: beefsteak, rice, watermelon, venison, duck. Of them all, he like duck the best. In the dim, red-lit "Brave New World" room of the zero-gee section, David found several willing partners to share the warm, scented, steamy intimacy of a padded zero-gravity love nest. Most of the girls his own age had never been in zero-gee before. They were eager to learn about it.

But every time David returned to his cabin, no matter

208

how tired he felt, he turned on the viewscreen that showed him the approaching blue-and-white sphere of Earth. *It's real,* he said to himself. *I'm really going there.*

Briefly, he wondered what had happened to Evelyn. He had tried phoning her at International News several times when he was in Selene, but they said she was no longer employed there and they would give no number where she could be reached. Even a computer search of the entire London phone directory failed to turn up a number for her. There had been one up until a few weeks earlier. But it had since been disconnected.

Many of the passengers stayed at Space Station Alpha to continue their vacations. It was the oldest continuously inhabited man-made structure in space. Every schoolchild had grown up with photos of its bicycle-wheel structure staring out of textbooks and viewscreens.

But David couldn't leave Alpha fast enough. He stopped long enough only to stare briefly through one of the long curving windows in the station's transfer terminal. Earth was a huge expanse spread before his eyes, blotting out everything else, close enough to touch. David could see individual white clouds parading across the dazzling blue oceans. Smears of brown and green suddenly took shape and he recognized the massive bulge of Africa's horn, the Arabian peninsula, and even the boot shape of Italy.

Eager as a child, he clutched his small travel bag and pushed his way through the milling, chattering tourists, following the lighted signs and arrows along the walls that led him to the dock where the Earthbound shuttle waited.

It took only a few minutes to get past the customs inspectors and the automatic equipment that checked his ticket code and searched him and his bag for weapons. Then a smiling stewardess ushered him to the shuttle's hatch. He ducked through and let an equally smiling steward lead him to his seat.

There were no windows in the passenger section, but each seat had a viewscreen built into its back. David strapped himself in, inspected the choices of entertainment channels, and opted for a real-time view from the shuttle's own television cameras.

A heavy, wheezing Oriental man eased himself slowly into the aisle seat next to David. Muttering in Japanese, he buckled the safety harness over his rotund middle and promptly closed his eyes. Folding his chubby hands over his paunch, he let his head nod forward. David counted five chins, then turned back to his viewscreen.

The shuttle's takeoff was so gentle that if the steward hadn't announced it, David wouldn't have noticed. He flicked the picture to the rear television camera and saw the steel girders of the spacecraft dock dwindling slowly. In a few minutes the entire Station Alpha was visible, a set of wheels within wheels, rotating slowly against the starry sky.

David flicked back to the view of Earth. It was changing now, sliding before his eyes as the shuttle started its long, arcing orbit around the gleaming blue-and-white planet.

The cabin speakers played their standard safety tapes. Passengers were cautioned not to leave their seats without the aid of a steward or stewardess; Garrison Aerospace Lines took no responsibility for passengers who injured themselves in zero gravity if they ignored safety precautions.

Then the captain's voice came over the speakers and his square-jawed, gray-templed face appeared on all the viewscreens.

"We'll be establishing a low Earth orbit in about half an hour, and we will initiate our reentry maneuver just west of the Isthmus of Panama. You should get a good look at Central America on your screens before we slide the reentry shields over the camera ports. We should arrive in the World Capital on time. The weather in Messina is gorgeous. . . ."

David stopped listening and looked around at the other passengers. Most of them seemed to be businessmen, probably returning from Island One. Space Station Alpha was a transfer point for most traffic to and from Earth. He recognized a few tourists from his own flight, including one of his zero-gee companions. There were several other passengers who were neither lunar tourists nor businessmen: people his own age.

The captain ended his talk and the view of Earth came on again. David watched it intently.

He never noticed that several of the younger passengers were getting up from their seats and floating along the shuttle's central aisle. There were six of them: three went back toward the galley at the rear of the shuttle, and then

210

a few minutes later three more went forward, toward the cockpit.

Bahjat had marveled at Hamoud's slipshod ideas of planning. She had been forced to locate five comrades who had experienced zero gravity before, because Hamoud hadn't even thought of that problem. Like herself, none of the others came from the poor, hungry masses. They were children of wealthy families who fought in the PRU because it was the right thing to do.

Hamoud himself could not go with them. He had never been in space and the hijacking was too important to trust to someone who might suddenly become sick at his first taste of weightlessness.

And it had been Bahjat who had hit upon the best landing place for the stolen shuttle: Argentina. The PRU would land in *El Libertador*'s backyard and ask for asylum. He could hardly refuse fellow revolutionaries.

Bahjat had to do her work quietly, carefully, subtly. Hamoud—code-named Tiger—was in charge, and he would never admit that Scheherazade did his brainwork for him.

Her main worry had been that she might be picked up by the police at the spaceport in Anguillara, just outside Rome. Her picture and identity codes had been broadcast all over the world by her father. The corporations and the World Government were both looking for her. But the Italian police, tall and impeccably handsome in their long blue cloaks and fashionable moustaches, totally ignored her as she went from the train station to the spaceport and bought her ticket for the shuttle to Alpha. The *carabinieri* seemed much more interested in strutting and being admired than in looking for diminutive runaway Arab women who scuttled through train stations with shawls over their heads. Bahjat gave Hamoud credit for selecting Italy as their new base of operations.

Now she unbuckled the straps of her seat harness and lifted lightly out of her chair. She had an aisle seat so that her freedom of action would not be restricted. Holding her makeup kit in one hand, she started floating down the aisle toward the galley and the toilets at the tail end of the passenger compartment.

A steward quickly started down the aisle toward her,

propelling himself by pushing off the handgrips set into the sides of each seat. His feet never touched the Velcro-matted floor.

"You shouldn't try to move around without help, Miss," he said, his admonishing tone lightened by the broad smile on his ruddy face. He was a redhead. *Like Dennis.* But his accent was different. Australian? It didn't matter. *You are alive and he is dead,* Bahjat thought, an acid bitterness rising in her throat.

"I must go to the restroom," she said.

He took her by the arm and made certain that her slippered feet were in solid contact with the floor. Bahjat let him lead her to the rear of the shuttle, knowing that Marco was already in a restroom, putting together his weaponry. And the third one in her task group, Reynaud, was standing in the galley chatting with the two stewardesses as they waited for the microwave ovens to heat the passengers' snacks.

Once in the restroom, with the door clicked shut, Bahjat took the spraycans from her toiletries bag. It had been a simple matter to drain the cans of hairspray and replenish them with knockout gas. No customs inspector or detection equipment could spot the difference.

The gas was non-lethal, Hamoud had assured her, although she knew that a person with a bad heart or certain allergies could die from it. She looked at herself in the mirror over the tiny metal sink and shrugged. *We are not responsible for their health.*

She glanced at her watch. Forty-five seconds to go. The face in the mirror looked tense. The eyes were dark and ringed from sleeplessness.

They will begin to pay back for your death, my beloved, she said silently. Looking down at her wrist again, *They will begin . . . now!*

Bahjat opened the restroom door just as Marco came out of the other toilet. His swarthy, ringlet-framed face was strained and tense, but he held a spraycan in each white-knuckled hand. Reynaud, who boasted of having ice water in his veins, was telling a joke to the steward while the two stewardesses listened and laughed. All according to plan.

Bahjat glanced up the aisle. The other passengers were

talking or reading or dozing, all except the blond, athletic-looking one who had been staring at his viewscreen ever since takeoff. *He could be troublesome*, Bahjat thought, *if he decides to be a hero*. The others all looked like stupid sheep.

The three men of the other task group started unbuckling their seat harnesses. Their action station was at the cockpit.

The steward's back was to them, but one of the stewardesses, still giggling at Reynaud's off-color jokes, noticed the passengers getting out of their seats and gestured toward the steward.

He turned and sighed wearily, "They never learn, do they?"

Bahjat stepped in front of him, blocking his access to the aisle. "Don't move," she said, her voice low but clear.

"I've got to . . ." Awareness dawned on his face. "What do you think you're . . ."

Bahjat sprayed a cloud of the knockout gas in his face. His knees gave out and his eyes rolled up. Reynaud grabbed him and pushed him back inside the galley where the passengers couldn't see.

The two stewardesses were white with shock. But silent.

"Do as you're told," Bahjat hissed at them, "and no one will be hurt. Above all, be quiet, stay calm. If you make a fuss, we will all be killed."

They stared wide-eyed at her, then at Reynaud, who smiled carelessly and gave a nonchalant Gallic shrug, and finally at Marco, who glowered at them.

"Call your captain on the intercom," Bahjat commanded. "Tell him the steward has collapsed and you need him back here to help you."

The taller of the two women was closest to the intercom. She hesitated a moment, but when Marco took a single growling step toward her, she unhooked the phone and spoke into it very quickly.

Bahjat saw that her three cohorts were now standing by the cockpit door, trying to look as if they were casually enjoying weightlessness. Their weapons were also spraycans, tucked into their jacket pockets.

The cockpit door slid open and the captain stepped

through. One of the hijackers grabbed him immediately while the other two ducked inside the cockpit.

David heard an angry voice and looked up just in time to see the captain scuffle briefly with a much younger man. Then the young man sprayed something from a can into the captain's face and the astronaut sagged weightlessly.

"What's going on?" David asked. The Japanese businessman beside him slumbered on.

"Please remain in your seats," a man's voice called over the intercom. "You are in no danger as long as you stay seated."

Twisting around in his chair, David looked back toward the galley. Three passengers were standing there, staring taut-faced up at the cockpit door. The steward and stewardesses were nowhere in sight.

He turned to look into the cockpit, too, and saw a gangling, raw-boned youngster come out grinning. He made a circle with his fingers. His other hand held a spraycan.

"What's happening?" a woman's voice asked.

"Is something . . ."

The intercom drowned out their questions. "This is Second Officer Donaldson speaking. Our ship has been taken over by members of the Peoples' Revolutionary Underground. They say that if we do what they tell us, no one will be hurt. But if we don't cooperate, they'll kill us all."

The cabin erupted in shouts and screams. Every passenger was talking, shouting, gesticulating—all except David and the fat businessman snoring beside him.

"Be quiet!"

It was a woman's voice, and it didn't need the intercom. She strode up the aisle, brandishing a pair of spraycans as if they were hand grenades.

Maybe they are, he thought.

"You will be quiet and stay where you are," the woman was saying. "This ship will not land at Messina, but you will all be brought down to Earth safely—*if you do as you are told!"*

David saw that she was beautiful, young, a lithe, petite, dark-skinned girl with a fierce-yet-fragile little cat's face.

But crazy. *You can't hijack a space shuttle. You'll kill everyone aboard. The captain's already down, either dead or unconscious. In another few minutes we'll be starting reentry. . . .*

David began to unbuckle his seat harness. He wasn't certain of what he was going to do once he got up, but he knew he couldn't just sit there.

The cat-faced girl whirled to face him. "Stay in your seat!"

"Now, wait, you can't just fly this shuttle . . ."

"Sit down!" Her eyes were wide and flashing. She held one of the cans up, as if to menace him with it.

"But I'm trying to explain . . ."

The can hissed at him. David saw a misty spray, felt it tingling on his face, and slumped back into his seat, unconscious.

AMANDA PARSONS: But the Moon is such a *bore!* I mean, after you've put your footprints into the dust of the *mare* or whatever they call it and climbed one or two of those old hills and gone over to see the Apollo monument, what do you have? An underground rabbit's nest that's overcrowded and understaffed. Our subscribers aren't interested in Selene.

Even Space Station Alpha is getting old-hat. *Everybody's* been there. There's nothing new about it. Even in zero gravity, there are only so many permutations the human body is capable of, after all.

We need something *different* and exciting for our travel features. You can't go anywhere on Earth without being hounded by beggars or running into a plague or terrorists of one sort or another. Why not a piece about Island One? I mean, you went to all the expense of sending a reporter up there and maybe she got herself fired when she came back, but why can't we . . .

WILBUR ST. GEORGE: Amanda, it won't work. She is fired, and she's going to stay fired. And forget about doing any features on Island One. That's final!

—Transcript of London–Sydney
phone conversation,
routine surveillance by
corporate telephone monitors,
2 August 2008

CHAPTER 21

Evelyn's apartment was a mess. *That's what happens in a one-room flat,* she explained to herself. *There's no place to hide the chaos while you tidy up.*

She had pulled a shapeless robe around her body and was rummaging, barefoot, through the cabinets above her sink, searching for a tin of tea. The sofa bed was open and thoroughly rumpled. Her mouth still tasted of toothpaste.

"It can't all be gone," she muttered to herself.

But the cabinet was not so heavily stocked that a tin of tea could be hiding behind something else. In the weeks since St. George had fired her from International News, no other news outfit would take her on. She couldn't even sell freelance pieces to the media. Evelyn's cupboard and her bank balance had both dwindled rapidly and were heading for exhaustion.

For the tenth time that morning she wondered if she should try to phone David again, now that she had the phone service restored. Of course, since now she was paying the phone bills herself, instead of charging them to International, she had to count the pennies there, too.

"Picturephone rates aren't expensive," she told the image in the mirror above her dressing table.

You've fallen in love with him, you silly girl.

"No," she answered herself aloud. "That's not it at all."

You're behaving like a moonstruck calf.

"I don't love him. He doesn't care a whit about me. I hate him!"

Then why haven't you tried to sell his story to one of the scandal shows? They'd snap it up in a second.

"Don't be too sure that I won't, old girl. I could use the money, even if they won't give me a credit line."

But he's so sweet. How could you do that to him?

"Why shouldn't I?"

He's so handsome, so kind and gentle.

"He never calls me! He won't answer my calls!"

How can he? That horrible old man, Dr. Cobb, is keeping him a prisoner up there. He'd call you if he could.

The teakettle's whistle broke into her dialogue.

Evelyn frowned at it. "You can jolly well whistle 'til you're dry. There's no tea. I've nothing to put into the water."

As she crossed the room to turn off the range, the phone chimed. Evelyn lifted the kettle off the burner, which automatically shut itself off once the weight was removed. Then she put the kettle down beside the burner and threw herself across the rumpled bed to reach for the phone.

She touched the VOICE ONLY button and lay prone on the bed as the phone's small viewscreen formed a picture of Sir Charles Norcross. He was handsome enough to be an entertainment star, or perhaps Prime Minister. *He'll be that someday,* Evelyn thought. Aristocratic, almost haughty face. But a hint of deviltry in his twinkling blue eyes. Neat little moustache starting to turn gray, but the rest of his hair was a rich, full golden blond.

"Evelyn, dear, are you there? The screen's blank. They haven't turned off your phone again, have they?"

"I'm not decent, darling," she said.

"Really? I can be over in five minutes."

"And risk your career for an unemployed scandal monger? Hardly."

Sir Charles smiled. "It would be almost worth it, with you. I've lusted after your body since you first interviewed me."

"Yes, so you told me at the time. Well . . . my body is going to part company with my soul if I don't get an assignment soon."

"International's blacklisted you, have they?"

Nodding, "Very thoroughly."

"I'd be glad to help you," Sir Charles said. "We could . . . uh . . . work on my biography. I'll tell you the whole, long, boring story of my life."

"And we'll write it on your bedroom ceiling? Hardly."

"Your scruples are too high," Sir Charles said, pretending to frown. "You'd never get far in politics."

"You will, though."

"I certainly shall," he said.

"Good. Perhaps by the time you're Prime Minister you can open an inquiry into why the promising young journalist Evelyn Hall starved to death in her Paddington flat."

"Is it that bad?"

"It's getting rather grim."

Sir Charles ran a forefinger along his moustache. "I . . . uh . . . have some rather touchy news for you. If I recall correctly, you had asked me about the legal status of a young man you interviewed while you were in Island One. David Adams, wasn't it?"

Evelyn pulled herself up to a sitting position. "Yes. David Adams."

Hesitating for a moment, as if he were glancing over his shoulder to see if anyone were watching him, Sir Charles went on: "It's very hush-hush just at the moment, but apparently there's been a hijacking. A space shuttle bound for Messina from Space Station Alpha has been pirated away by the Peoples' Revolutionary Underground."

"You can't keep news like that quiet."

"Oh, I expect not," Sir Charles admitted. "Even the present Government knows better than that. The PRU shall be crowing about it all over the world any minute now. But I thought you'd be interested to know that listed among the passengers is one David Adams. He was inbound from Selene, and he gave his place of residence as Island One."

Evelyn could feel her pulse throbbing in her ears. "He's here!"

"He's hijacked," Sir Charles said. "We're not certain where he is. The shuttle was originally destined for Messina."

"I've got to go there!"

He shook his head. "Can't. World Government security authorities have cordoned off the entire World Capital area. The nearest you could fly to is Naples."

"Naples, then!"

"I believe I hate this Adams chap," Sir Charles said. Then, "Can you afford the fare?"

Her stomach felt hollow, quivery. "Somehow. I've still got a credit account that's not overdrawn *too* badly."

Sir Charles raised his eyebrows slightly. "I'll have my office arrange a flight and book you a hotel room in Naples."

"I couldn't . . ."

"Of course you can. And you shall." He smiled ruefully. "Pity I have so much work to do here. Ah, well, I understand it's beastly hot there this time of year."

"Are you insane? Have you no wisdom at all? No foresight?"

El Libertador paced angrily up and down the parqueted floor of the ornate old ballroom. Portraits of uniformed generals, old men in ancient stiff-necked suits, and ladies pale and languid graced the walls of the high-ceilinged room. Three chandeliers, dripping crystal, caught the sunlight that streamed in from the spacious windows at the room's far end.

Through the windows there was nothing to be seen but endless grassland stretching out to a horizon broken by the hazy, mirage-like shimmering images of mountain peaks.

Bahjat felt grimy and foolish. She had not bathed or changed her dress in the thirty-six hours since boarding the shuttle at Space Station Alpha. Her fellow hijackers were off in another wing of this "guesthouse" far out on the pampas of Argentina. The local police at the Buenos Aires airport had not taken their gift of the space shuttle graciously. She had expected that. But *El Libertador* would be pleased, she had thought. Even Hamoud had agreed that the Latin American revolutionary would welcome her and her hostages.

But instead he was angry. Furious. He paced the long, splendid room, red-faced, his lean, tall frame radiating displeasure.

He is the same age as my father, she thought. Somehow, that unsettled her.

At least he was dressed no better than she: wrinkled khaki fatigues, not even as good as her own silk blouse, skirt, and slippers. She sat in one of the stiff-backed chairs of real wood that were set along the paneled wall and watched the old man pace, his boots clicking solidly against the flooring.

Finally he stopped. Standing close enough to Bahjat for her to see that his eyes were weary, bloodshot, he shook his head.

"Why didn't the PRU contact me beforehand? How dare you drop this shipload of hostages into my lap without a warning, without even asking. . . ."

His voice trailed off. He sighed. "I should control my temper," he said more gently. "I have just returned from South Africa. You may have heard that the revolution there has succeeded."

"Yes," Bahjat said, genuinely pleased. "It was wonderful news."

"Attained at the cost of nearly a hundred World Government troops killed. That is . . . less than wonderful."

"But they were defending an evil regime."

"They were following their orders," *El Libertador* said. "Three days ago they were an unknown, faceless contingent of World Army troops. Now they are martyrs, and the whole world is crying for vengeance for them."

Bahjat said nothing.

The old man dropped wearily to the chair next to hers. "You see, we cannot afford to antagonize the World Government so strongly. If they mobilize their army against us . . ."

"But their army is small," Bahjat said. "We can raise ten times their number."

"Their army consists of professional troops. They have mobility and firepower. We have numbers and enthusiasm —cannon fodder."

"We will fight until we win."

"More likely we would fight until we were all killed. Why did you hijack a space shuttle? What possible good can it do?"

"To show the weakness of the World Government," Bahjat answered, not trusting him with her real motive. "To force them to pay ransom for the hostages—those fat businessmen and tourists."

"And you brought them here because you thought I would protect you?"

"Yes."

"But I could not even protect myself if the World Army invaded Argentina."

"But you are a revolutionary!"

"Yes," he said, his back straightening. "But not a terrorist. Not a hijacker."

"Our goals are the same," Bahjat said, "even if our tactics differ."

"Are they?" *El Libertador* mused. "I wonder."

"You are the inspiration to us all. Everyone in the PRU looks up to you."

He gazed at her for a long time. "Are you serious?"

"Of course."

"The PRU would follow my leadership?"

"All around the world, you are our symbol of resistance to the World Government. If you want to lead us, we will follow."

The old man's eyes took on a faraway look. "Back when the World Government was first formed," he said in a voice so low that Bahjat wondered if she were meant to hear it, "we were officers in the Chilean Army. How we supported De Paolo then! The new World Government would end all our woes, give the land back to the people, drive out the foreign corporations. But they never did that. Things got worse instead of better."

"We can fight them," Bahjat said.

"Fight against whom? Tourists? Merchants? Robbing banks? Hijacking space shuttles? What kind of fighting is that?"

"We do what we can," Bahjat answered, feeling almost as if she were talking to her father.

El Libertador shook his head. "No, my dear. The battle is against the governments, the leaders, the decision-makers who think only of themselves and not of the people."

"The rich," Bahjat said.

"Not the rich," he snapped. "Those who serve the rich, and themselves, without caring about the poor."

"What can we do?" she asked.

"Were you serious when you said the PRU would follow my leadership?"

"Yes," Bahjat said eagerly. "You could mold all our separate struggles into one grand, worldwide effort. We could fight against the oppressors all over the world, united, coordinated."

"Very well, then," *El Libertador* said. "The first thing we must do is to return the passengers from the shuttle—and the machine itself. We do not make war on tourists and workers."

"But . . ."

"You have made your point. You have shown that the World Government cannot protect its citizens from the PRU. You have gained worldwide publicity. Now is the time to be generous."

Still Bahjat hesitated.

El Libertador leaned toward her, smiling slightly. "The world loves a romantic bandit, a Robin Hood or Pancho Villa—as long as innocent people do not get hurt. Don't turn world opinion against you by holding those captives too long."

She looked into his strong gray eyes for a moment and decided that she had no choice. His mind was made up, and he had the power to enforce his decision. "I understand," Bahjat said. "Will you . . . can you arrange for their release?"

He nodded. "I will see what can be done."

"The World Government will demand that you turn us over to them," she pointed out.

"That I will not do, of course. It is the price they must pay. They can have the hostages and the spacecraft, but not the PRU . . . revolutionaries."

He was going to say "terrorists," Bahjat knew. She nodded. She trusted this old man—up to a point.

When David awoke he was still in the shuttle, strapped into his seat. His head thundered with pain. The fat Japanese was gone from the next seat. All the passengers were gone. No one was in the shuttle, except for a soldier in an olive drab uniform slouching up at the front hatch, by the door to the cockpit.

We've landed, David thought through the throbbing in his head. *But . . .*

Then it hit him. *I'm on Earth!* Everything else fled from his thoughts.

He tried to get up, but the seat harness cut into his shoulders. Impatiently, he unsnapped it and got to his feet. His head roared and his legs felt watery. For a moment he leaned against the seat in front of him. The guard eyed him and hooked a thumb around the butt of the holstered gun at his hip.

David thought dimly that he had taken quite a dose of gas to produce this strong a headache. After several deep breaths he thought about the zen masters and yogis who could make pain disappear through an effort of will. He concentrated on dissolving the pain, but that only made his head feel worse. *It doesn't work without the computer helping you,* he realized.

He stepped out into the empty aisle and headed for the open hatch. The air smelled strange, and there were odd buzzing noises coming from outside. *Or is it inside my head?*

"Alto!" snapped the guard. *"Se siente!"*

David did not understand Spanish. He clicked his communicator to get a translation from the nearest computer. But there was no response. He tried again.

Nothing.

There's no computer here! David was shocked to think that human beings could live anywhere without at least a terminal that connected to a time-shared computer somewhere within range of an implanted communicator.

The thought staggered him. All his life he had been able to use Island One's intricate network of interlinked computers as an extra memory, an immediate encyclopedia of information that was available to him, inside his head, with the speed of light. Even on the Moon he could tap into the computers and the tiny simpleminded electronic "brains" of the navigation satellites. But here on Earth he was blanked out. It was like suddenly becoming blind, or having all the libraries of the world closed to you. It was like suffering an amputation, a lobotomy.

"Se siente!" the guard repeated, gesturing with his left hand while his right gripped the pistol in its holster.

Numbly, David slumped into the nearest seat. The guard shouted to somebody outside the hatch, then returned his gaze to David. For the first time, David realized it must be night out there; the ship's overhead light panels were glowing and the slim slice of outdoors he could see through the open hatch was dark.

He tried to lean back and sleep, but his headache pounded away at him. *I finally get to Earth,* he groused, *and they won't let me see anything.*

He only realized he had dozed off when a touch on his shoulder startled him awake. The girl was standing over him, the one who had knocked him out.

"You have returned to the living," she said in International English. A slight smile played along her lips.

David started to nod, but the headache made him wince.

"You are in pain?" she asked.

"Hell, yes," he said. "Thanks to you."

She looked concerned. "You shouldn't have tried to resist. I warned you to stay seated."

"I've never been hijacked before."

"Come," she said, extending her hand to him. "We will find something for your headache."

He took her hand and got up from the seat. She led him past the guard and they walked down the metal stairs that extended from the hatch to the ground.

David stopped at the bottom of the stairs and looked around. The sky was a soft blue-black. It glowed. The stars twinkled gently, not the harsh, unblinking pinpoints of Island One. There were fewer of them, but they formed the shapes he knew from books: the Hunter, the Ship, the Southern Cross. He even saw the soft nebulosity of Magellan's Clouds.

All around him stretched open fields. It was too dark to see if they were cultivated or not. A house bulked darkly against the gentle night sky, a few of its windows bright with light.

But it was the sounds and the smells that hit David hardest. Crickets chirruping. The scent of warm earth and grass and living things. A breeze touched his face, cool and strangely fluctuating, dying away for a moment and then returning stronger than before.

"It's still untamed," he said aloud. "It's not controlled at all! It never will be tamed, not completely!"

Bahjat tugged at his arm. "Come up to the hacienda. They have aspirin there."

"No . . ." David took a few steps away from the spacecraft, feeling the soil against his boots. "No, I want to see this. I want to watch the Sun come up."

She laughed. "That won't be for hours."

"I don't care."

In the starlight he could barely make out the expression on her face. But her voice sounded stern, suspicious. "It would be foolish to try to run away. There are no other buildings for a hundred kilometers or more."

"Where's the Moon?" David asked, turning around in a complete circle.

"It rises in an hour or so."

"Oh. And that bright one over there," he said and pointed, "that must be Island One."

She studied him. *Either he is in shock from the gas, or he's trying to lull me into letting him escape.*

"You can't stay out here all night," she said. "The others are . . ."

"Why not?" he asked simply.

"The others are all inside the hacienda."

"So? They've all been on Earth before. I haven't. It's beautiful!"

"You were born in Selene?" she asked.

David shook his head. The headache was already easing. "Island One. I've spent my whole life in Island One—until a few weeks ago."

"You really must come inside," she insisted.

"I don't want to. I've spent my whole *life* inside!"

Bahjat had no weapons with her. *He is much bigger than I, and in good shape.* She considered the odds for a moment, then shrugged to herself. *I can always scream for the guards. And there is no place for him to run to. He can't very well hide on this empty plain.*

"Very well," she said. "Come with me to the house for a few seconds, and then we can walk out here and watch the Moon rise."

It happened much more slowly than on Island One, of course. David and Bahjat sat on the sweet-smelling grass and watched the Moon's nearly imperceptible rising. He was too lost in the newness of Earth to speak. But Bahjat found herself talking endlessly, as if she had to justify herself, apologize to him, explain it all.

". . . it may be hard, dangerous, even cruel. But we can't let the World Government dictate to us. We must have freedom!"

"But the World Government isn't a dictatorship," he answered, his eyes still on the slowly rising Moon. *It really does look like a face! I'll be damned!*

"They take taxes from us and give us nothing in return," Bahjat said. "They turn everything into a gray sameness. Why should Arabs dress like Europeans, who dress like Americans, who dress like Chinese?"

"That's why you hijacked the shuttle—because you don't like the clothes you wear?"

"You're being sarcastic."

Taking his attention from the skies, David admitted, "Yes. But you're not being very realistic. World Government taxes are lower than the armament budgets that Iraq and the other nations had back before the World Government came into existence."

"If our taxes are lower, why are there more poor people now than ever before? Why are people starving in the streets?"

"Because there are more people," David countered. "What's the world population now? Over seven billion? As long as you keep your birth rate so high, you're going to be heading for disaster."

"I am speaking of dying people," Bahjat said. "Mothers, babies, old people—starving to death, all over the world!"

"But that's not the World Government's fault."

"Of course it is! Who else?"

"The people who are having all those babies. The people who are maintaining such a high birth rate."

"They are ignorant and frightened," Bahjat said.

"Then educate them," said David. "And feed them. Stop wasting your time hijacking space shuttles and holding people hostage."

"We *can't* feed them. The rich nations hold their wealth to themselves. The corporations run them, and the World Government, too."

David shook his head. "I've seen all the pertinent data. I know the projections. There isn't enough food in the world to feed many more people. There just isn't. Even if you reduced everyone to a subsistence diet, it wouldn't be enough to go around—not for seven billion and more. Starvation is inevitable."

"No. That can't be true. We won't let it be true!"

The Moon had completely topped the horizon. It was nearly full, and in its soft light David could see her face. She was beautiful, truly beautiful, despite the fear and anger in her expression.

"Wishing won't make it so," he said as gently as he

could. "There's no way to avoid the coming disaster. It's already too late to stop it from happening."

"That's inhuman," she said. *"You're inhuman!"*

Bahjat scrambled to her feet and stomped off back toward the hacienda.

David watched her for a moment, then turned back and looked at the Moon. It was grinning at him, lopsidedly.

Bahjat awoke with the Sun, stretched sleepily, and looked around her bedroom. For a few moments she could not recall where she was or why she was in this strange place. The room was small, but comfortable. The drapes on the windows were opened enough for the morning light to come streaming through.

She climbed out of the too-soft, too-high bed and looked at herself in the full-length mirror hanging on the back of the door. All her life she had wanted the voluptuous body of a film star. Instead, she was slim, small, narrow in the hips, and taut of bosom. Not a good body for making babies, the older women of the house had said when they thought she couldn't hear them.

A metal shower stall stood in one corner of the room, obviously put in long after the hacienda's original construction. Bare pipes led from the stall and disappeared through rough holes in the wall.

Heading for the shower, Bahjat passed the window and glanced outside. *He's still out there!* She stepped to the window, staying behind the half-opened drapes. *The idiot must have slept out there all night.* He was lying on his back with his hands behind his head. Despite herself, Bahjat smiled. *He slept through his first sunrise.* Then she thought, *He's probably never heard of dew, of course, or frost. He's probably caught a cold. Or pneumonia. How stupid, staying out there all night!*

By the time she had finished her shower and dressed, in the same blouse and skirt, Bahjat had decided to go outside and see if he were all right.

But as she went down the broad, bare wood stairs that led to the hacienda's main floor, one of the soldiers, an officer, smiled at her and said, *"El Libertador* wishes to speak with you urgently."

Bahjat dropped all other thoughts and followed the officer to the ballroom, where she had first met *El Liber-*

tador. The room was empty. The portraits, the chandeliers, and the stiff-backed chairs were lined against the paneled walls. But no person waited for her.

"Where . . ."

The officer smiled again and touched a button on a panel set into the wall near the doorway.

One section of the paneling slid up, revealing a blank viewscreen. Bahjat watched as he pulled up a chair facing the screen, bowed slightly to her, and then left the ballroom. He closed the door quietly behind himself.

Abruptly, the screen began to glow. Then *El Libertador* took on solid, three-dimensional form. It was as if an alcove had been cut into the ballroom, and he was sitting in it, at a battered old gray metal desk. The wall behind him was a faded pale green. Bahjat could see cracks in it.

He may have holographic communications equipment, she thought, *but he certainly doesn't live in splendor.*

The man didn't look quite so old now. *He must have had a good night's sleep. Yet he is awake and active so early. From the light in his room, it isn't even dawn yet, wherever he is.*

"I hope I haven't taken you from your sleep," he said courteously.

"No. I arose with the Sun," Bahjat answered.

El Libertador allowed himself to smile. "That is a luxury I cannot afford, not when I must confer with governments and media reporters all around the world."

Bahjat said nothing.

"I have arranged for the release of the hostages," he said. "My men will take care of their transport to Buenos Aires, where the World Government will take them."

"I see."

"The media are filled with stories of Scheherazade and her daring symbolic struggle against the World Government." He put a slight stress on the word *symbolic*.

"Then we have achieved our primary objective." Suddenly Bahjat felt weary of the entire business. It was all foolishness, vanity, a hopeless battle against inevitable defeat. Seven billion people! Who could help them? How could anyone?

El Libertador was saying, "If your primary objective was publicity, you have accomplished it beyond your fondest dreams. You have even helped me to accomplish a goal of my own."

She caught the expectant look on his face. "What is that?"

"I have negotiated an . . . arrangement, an understanding, with the World Government. In return for the release of your hostages, they have agreed to . . . uh . . . 'overlook' the battle in South Africa in which their own troops were killed."

"How sweet," Bahjat said, letting the irony show on her face. "We get publicity and you are saved from invasion by the World Army."

El Libertador pursed his thin lips. "You are not pleased?"

"As you say," she replied, "we gained much publicity."

He hesitated, then asked, "Are you still willing to follow my orders? Still willing to turn your scattered efforts into a united worldwide battle?"

"Yes."

"Even at a high personal cost to yourself?"

A cold fear clutched at her heart. "What do you mean?" Bahjat asked.

"The understanding I have worked out with the World Government . . . the deal for returning the hostages in exchange for their overlooking the incident at Johannesburg . . ."

"Yes? What?"

"I negotiated it with a World Government councilman named Sheikh Jamil al-Hashimi. He added two further conditions to the agreement."

Bahjat waited in icy silence to hear the conditions, knowing what one of them would be.

El Libertador explained, "The first condition is that the passenger David Adams, a contract laborer from Island One, must be returned there."

Nodding, Bahjat felt a tiny spark of hope kindle inside her, even though she knew it was foolish.

"And the second condition?" she asked.

"Sheikh al-Hashimi said that his daughter was among the passengers aboard the shuttle, traveling incognito. He expects her to be returned to him. As far as he is concerned, Scheherazade is dead. But he wants his daughter back. Otherwise, the World Army will attack Argentina."

The spark died in blackness. "So I am the price that must be paid."

El Libertador shrugged helplessly. "I cannot afford to fight an organized war against the World Government. Guerrilla warfare is one thing . . . pitched battles . . . not now."

"I see."

Sadly, he continued. "Please do not try to leave the hacienda. My soldiers are under orders to keep you in strict custody until we can turn you over to your father."

5 August 2008

GENERAL ORDER 08-441

From: Dir. De Paolo
TO: Adm. Johnson, CINCNAV
    Gen. Bulachev, CINCARM
    Mshl. Peng, CINCAIR
Subject: Counterstrike against Argentina

Although negotiations with the Argentinian Government show promise of reaching a satisfactory conclusion, it may still be necessary to make a show of force before that government surrenders hostages taken by the Peoples' Revolutionary Underground when they hijacked a space shuttle.

Therefore, I require immediate estimates as to the time it will take to: (a) mobilize, (b) deploy, and (c) commit the following forces against key Argentinian military, industrial, commercial, and/or population centers:

1. Air forces only, for non-nuclear strikes at some or all of the above centers;

2. Combined air/sea forces, aimed at blockading Argentinian ports and interdicting rail and road lines;

3. Joint air/land/sea forces, which will seize and hold selected areas of Argentinian territory.

    --Dictated but not signed by the Director, E. De Paolo

• CHAPTER 22 •

David sat with his back against a sturdy tree, letting the afternoon sun soak his body with warmth. A steady breeze blew across the flat, almost featureless land. It was almost treeless, as well; the only trees were the few near the hacienda. Gray clouds were building up on the horizon, where the mountains floated in mist, their blue-white snowcaps seemingly in midair, unconnected with the rest of the world.

But he paid scant attention to the scenery. He was watching the hacienda and the people who came in and out of it. Most of them were soldiers in olive drab uniforms.

I wanted to get to the World Government at Messina, and I end up at some revolutionary hideout in Argentina, David said to himself. *A ten-thousand-kilometer error in navigation.*

He had purposely stayed away from the other passengers, who huddled and bleated together like sheep. They ate when they were told to and tried not to look fearful. They gossiped and invented rumors. David knew that if he found a chance to escape, he'd have to be free of the others in order to seize the opportunity; otherwise, they would get in his way.

And he knew how to escape. That was simple. There were autos, and, better yet, several electrobikes parked in front of the hacienda. Only one soldier lounged in the doorway to watch over them, and he seemed more interested in smoking endless cigarettes and chatting with the women hostages than in staying alert.

But where to go? *That's the stopper.* He had no idea of where they were in relation to any reasonable destination.

His computer link was still silent, and that frightened him down at his deepest level of being. *I'm alone,* he thought, *alone in a world filled with more than seven billion people.* None of them would tell him what he needed to know; none of them could link with his mind and feed him directly the data on geography, political affiliations, road maps, weather conditions, food availability—all the million details he would need before he could even try to escape.

Running away blindly was out of the question. It would be foolhardy and could only end in death or recapture.

Then he saw Bahjat walking slowly from the hacienda out toward the empty grassland that stretched off in every direction. A pair of soldiers followed her, carbines slung over their shoulders.

She rates a bodyguard, David thought. *Why? Who would she be in danger from? The passengers? Or is she a prisoner now?*

He had seen two of the other hijackers walking around the grounds earlier in the day. No soldiers trailed after them. *So they're not prisoners. Maybe it's a sort of honor guard. She's their leader.*

But she looked unhappy. That incredibly beautiful face had sadness etched into it.

Something's happened to her. She knows . . .

David sat up straighter. *She knows a lot!* he realized. *She knows everything I need to know to get out of here. There's a computer inside that pretty head that carries all the information I need.*

Suddenly David felt like a tawny lion, lying in the tall yellowing grass, watching his prey with patient cunning.

Bahjat strolled slowly, aimlessly, staring straight ahead and seeing nothing. David watched and waited. The Sun swung westward, the slate-gray clouds slid in behind it, and the wind picked up. David ignored the chill and growing dampness in the air. He ignored the gnawing hunger in the pit of his stomach. He had stayed out all night, then missed breakfast and lunch to study the house, the guards, the soldiers' routine of patrolling the area, the cars, and the bikes.

Finally Bahjat turned back toward the house after walking so far off that she and her guards had dwindled to specks, almost lost in the broad, flat landscape. Thunder grumbled far off, and a flicker of lightning danced at the corner of his vision. But David kept his attention on the girl and her guards.

He smiled to himself, grimly. *What could be more poetic than kidnapping the kidnapper?*

The trio ambled slowly back toward the hacienda, heading for the main entrance, with the cars and bikes parked in front of it. The guard up at the doorway was still smoking away, chatting with somebody inside the doorway rather than looking out at the parking area.

David got up slowly, not wanting to attract attention to himself, and glided noiselessly behind the two guards as they unhurriedly followed Bahjat. The carbines were still slung over their shoulders. One of them had an automatic pistol holstered at his hip.

More lightning snaked out of the clouds off to the West, and a hollow boom of thunder rolled across the plain. The guards looked skyward and muttered to each other in Spanish.

Then one of them switched to International English for Bahjat's benefit. "It will rain soon."

"And hard," his partner agreed, also in English. "At least we will be inside the house instead of getting wet."

"I wouldn't mind getting wet with *her*. I would even protect her from the elements by covering her with my body."

"And get a lightning bolt up your ass!"

They laughed.

David covered the final twenty meters between himself and the guards like a lion dashing at its prey. He hit the one with the pistol first, a solid edge-of-the-hand chop on the back of his neck. He fell forward.

The other guard spun around, unslinging the carbine from his shoulder as he moved, his mouth wide open, all the teeth showing, his eyes round with shock. He couldn't have been more than eighteen or nineteen, David saw as he launched a kick at his midsection.

The soldier folded with a gasping puff of breath exploding out of him. David jerked the carbine away from him with both hands and rapped him viciously across the temple with the barrel of the gun. He sprawled on the grass and lay still.

For an instant David couldn't believe it had been so easy. *Surprise is always the best weapon*, he remembered his martial arts instructor telling him. *Always do the unexpected.* The wiry Okinawan would be pleased with his pupil's performance.

As Bahjat turned to see what the scuffling noise had been, David bent to scoop up the other carbine. Slinging it over his shoulder, he jerked the pistol out of its holster. The guard at the doorway still had his back turned. David could see that he was talking with one of the stewardesses. Bahjat watched him wordlessly.

Tucking the pistol into his waistband, he gestured at her with the carbine. "Into the nearest car," he hissed. She hesitated. "The car!" he whispered savagely. "Get into it and get it started."

She went to the nearest auto and pulled the driver's door open. "Do you have the key?" she whispered back.

David glanced at the guard at the door, then back to Bahjat. "What key? It's not locked."

"The ignition key. You need a key to start the engine."

There were no autos on Island One, and the electrobikes were started with the flick of a toggle switch. Not knowing whether he could believe her or not, David stood alongside the car in a rising panic of indecision.

"The bikes, too?" The guard was taking the butt of a dying cigarette from his mouth with thumb and forefinger. He would turn and flick it out into the parking area's paved surface as he had done with all the others, David knew.

"Of course," Bahjat answered.

Is she telling the truth? What can I do if she's not?

But Bahjat was already moving past him. "I can get the bike started by hot-wiring it," she said. "It's simple."

Lightning streaked across the sky and David winced, waiting for the roar of thunder. Bahjat trotted to the nearest electrobike and bent over its motor. The guard turned to look up at the sky. The thunder exploded overhead just as the guard stiffened in surprise, the cigarette butt a burning red ember in the gloomy shadows of the hacienda's doorway.

With a glance over his shoulder, David saw that the other two soldiers were still flat-unconscious. But the one up at the doorway was cocking his gun and coming down the stone steps toward them. The stewardess was still inside the doorway, watching, frozen.

David had fired guns only on practice ranges as part of the testing that the biomedics constantly put him through. He aimed high, felt with his thumb that the safety catch was off, and squeezed the trigger. The gun blasted and bucked in his hands. Spurts of dust and stone chips exploded from the lintel above the doorway.

Like any well-trained soldier, the guard dove for cover at the base of the steps, flat onto his stomach.

"It's started!" Bahjat yelled. "Come!"

She was astride the bike. David fired another burst, into the ground well in front of the guard this time, then leaped for the bike's saddle extension. The second carbine banged against his spine.

The doorway guard was trying hard to melt into the cement paving he lay on. His gun was in his hands, but he was face down, making himself as small a target as possible.

Bahjat put the bike into gear and they lurched off with a whining screech of the electric motor. "The cars and the other bikes!" she yelled over her shoulder. "Shoot them up!"

"What?" Lightning and an immediate clap of thunder. The world flashed and shook. Huge raindrops spattered down.

"Shoot the cars and bikes—so they can't follow us!" Bahjat hollered over the thunder's roar.

It was suddenly dark. The rain swept over everything, soaking them both, making it impossible to see more than a few meters ahead. David leaned back slightly, the carbine at his hip, and blasted away at the vehicles in the parking area. The roar deafened him; the gun kicked and shook as if it wanted to be free of his hands. Bahjat swung the bike back across the row of cars and David fell off, thudding onto his back into a muddy puddle.

He got to his feet snarling and fired at the parked cars. A hydrogen fuel tank exploded, sending up a mushroom of hot orange flame. Then another. He couldn't see the guard, couldn't see Bahjat and the bike. He stood there, blazing away with the carbine, watching bikes topple over, tires shred, seeing chunks of cars shatter and fly as the bullets ripped through them, feeling the heat of the flames on his face and the cold of the rain sluicing down his back.

The gun stuttered to silence. Bahjat was a couple of

meters away, the single headlamp of the bike almost lost in the windy rainswept darkness.

"Come!" she called. "Quickly!"

David threw away the empty carbine and swung a leg over the bike's saddle. "Let's get out of here!" he said as they zoomed off into the dark, drenching storm.

NEWSFLASH***NEWSFLASH***NEWSFLASH***

BUENOS AIRES: The Argentinian Government announced this afternoon that all of the passengers aboard the hijacked space shuttle will be returned to their homes.

The hijackers' leader, known only by her romantic code name of "Scheherazade," escaped from the government security center in which she and her fellow hijackers were being detained. Sources at World Government headquarters in Messina had reported earlier that Scheherazade had been killed during the hijacking.

Meanwhile, reaction among world leaders to the Argentinian decision to grant the other hijackers political asylum was decidedly hostile. . . .

—International News release,
6 August 2008

• CHAPTER 23 •

T. Hunter Garrison stretched his knobby limbs and let the steaming-hot water cover him up to his chin. Sweat broke out across his bald head and trickled down into his eyes. One of the Oriental girls in the huge tub with him noticed this and carefully wiped a single finger across his brows. She smiled at him and he grinned back. The other girl was standing in the tub, reaching up to the shelves of oils and perfumes over Garrison's head.

Arlene came into the room, making the steam swirl as she pulled up a wooden bench and sat at the edge of the sunken pool.

"This is going to wilt my dress," she said, smoothing the skirt that barely covered her suntanned thighs.

"Then take it off and jump in," Garrison said. "Got plenty room in here."

"I wish I had the time," Arlene answered.

"How do you like my new pearl divers? Hashimoto sent them over as a gift for being rescued from the hijackers."

Arlene eyed the girls. "They're lovely."

"They can hold their breath for five minutes at a shot," Garrison said. "Do their best work underwater."

"I bet."

"Ever try baton twirling underwater?"

Pushing at her thick red hair, Arlene said, "Is that what they do?"

Garrison grinned wickedly. "Among other things."

"Listen, I've talked with Steinmetz in Rio . . ."

"Where's that boy?"

"No sign of him," Arlene said.

"Dammit, he can't have disappeared off the face of the world!" Garrison splashed angrily and the two Japanese

242

girls jerked away from him. Sitting up in the tub, he frowned at Arlene. "Now listen . . . that kid can't have got very far on a goddamn motor scooter."

"It's a big country down there."

"Bullshit!"

"And he's with this PRU girl, calls herself Scheher azade," Arlene went on. "There seems to be some doubt as to whether she grabbed him as a hostage or he grabbed her. He did all the shooting, looks like."

"I don't give a good hootin' damn who did what to who. Or with which. I want that kid! He's my property, by damn, and I want him back. Cobb's been burnin' up the air about him. He says he needs him back in Island One."

Arlene shook her head and the steam-wilted curls slid down over her eyes again. "If she's helping him . . . or if he's her hostage—well, she knows every underground hide-out, every guerrilla terrorist from there to . . ."

Garrison thought a minute. "In that case, I want her too."

"It's not easy."

"You tell Stienmetz he's fired. Whoever's his second down there in Rio, make him first. Get Steinmetz up here. I'm gonna make an example of him. And get every one of our people in South America lookin' for the two of them. I want 'em both."

"It's like looking for a pair of ants in a jungle," Arlene said.

"You want the same treatment Steinmetz is gonna get?"

"No!"

"Then do what I tell you."

She got to her feet. He had to crane his neck to see her long, long legs, the curve of her ample body, her flustered face.

"Where you goin'?" he asked.

"To make the calls you just told me to make."

"There's a phone over there." He pointed through the soaking steam. "Call from here." Grinning again, he went on, "And peel off those clothes while you're phoning. I want you to get into this tub when you're finished and see how long these girls can hold their breath underwater."

Arlene looked at him, the smallest hint of a frown tugging at the corners of her mouth.

"Don't get sassy," Garrison told her. "Let these girls do a good job on you and I'll show you what else Hashimoto sent. He remembered you, too."

"Did he?"

Garrison nodded. The two "pearl divers" smiled and nodded, standing hip-deep in the scented, steaming water. They had been instructed to do whatever they were told and not to speak a word in any language unless commanded to do so.

Arlene's lips curved slightly upward. "You're a dirty ol' man, you know?"

"Why shore," Garrison admitted genially. "But at my age, just about the only fun I get's from watching. And you're an exhibitionist anyway. You love it."

Arlene said nothing.

"Tell me the truth," Garrison said, just the slightest ring of iron in his gravelly voice. "You love showing yourself off, don't you?"

Still she didn't answer.

"Don't you."

"Sure I do, honey," Arlene said at last, unbuttoning her blouse. "I love every minute of it."

Kowie Boweto and Chiu Chan Liu could not have been more different and still belong to the same biological species.

Boweto was big, hulking, with a broad black brow that beetled over tiny, darting, suspicious eyes. His normal expression was a scowl. His first instinct was always to attack a problem head-on.

Liu would have been a philosopher, a sage, a Mandarin in earlier times. He was slight, quiet, almost an ascetic. He kept his tempers, his passions, his pleasures carefully veiled behind an expressionless face.

They were sitting in Liu's suite at the World Government headquarters in Messina. The room had only the slightest Chinese aura about it: a silk painting on one wall, a precious vase in a corner. Otherwise, like all the suites in the headquarters building, it was furnished in Western contemporary chromes, plastics, and glass.

"But he's recovering from the heart attack," Boweto was saying. He sat heavily in a plastic webchair, a mug of dark beer on the low table before him.

Liu was sitting stiff-backed on a plush-covered stool at the end of the table, a thimble-sized glass of apricot wine at his elbow.

"He is more than eighty years old," the Chinese said softly. "He cannot last much longer."

Boweto shrugged. "So then the Legislature will elect a new Director."

Liu inclined his head a bare centimeter. "Have you given any thought to who the candidates may be?"

The African's eyes narrowed. "Some."

"It might be . . . useful," Liu said gently, "if we discussed the possible candidates and agreed on one person. If such an agreement could be reached between us, surely we could convince the bulk of the African and Asian delegates in the Legislature to vote for that person, and he would certainly become the next Director."

Boweto took a long, thoughtful pull on his beer. "Who do you see as the most likely candidates?" he asked.

Liu permitted himself a slight smile. "I think that neither Williams nor Malekoff has a chance. The Legislature would fear a reopening of ancient Cold War wounds if they elected either an American or a Russian."

"Maybe," Boweto said. "What about al-Hashimi?"

"I don't believe that he is interested in the Directorship, although I may be wrong. Should he make a bid for election, I think it will be merely a ploy—a move to gain concessions from others in return for backing their candidate."

"Andersen?"

"He is an able administrator. He would have the European bloc voting for him, and probably the American votes as well, so long as Williams does not seek the post. He is respected and even liked by many in the Legislature."

"But you don't want to see him get the job," Boweto said. It was not a question.

"I have another candidate in mind."

"Who?"

"You, of course."

Boweto's eyes flashed. *How easily his heart shows on his face,* Liu thought.

"You would accept the responsibility?" the Chinese asked.

"Would the Asian bloc vote for me?" Boweto countered.

"I would do my best to have it so."

Boweto reached for his beer again. "Well, I'd have to think about it, of course. This is something I haven't even thought of until just now." But his face was shouting, *Yes, yes, yes!*

After putting the nearly empty mug back on the table, Boweto said, "That's all in the future. What are we going to do about the problems that face us today? This *El Libertador* . . ."

"Al-Hashimi has negotiated the release of the shuttle hostages," Liu said. "He is handling the problem."

"But *El Libertador* was behind the overthrow in South Africa. And the leader of those PRU hijackers got away. He must have let her escape. And he's granting political asylum to the others!"

"That is not important," Liu said. "These petty rebellions are of little consequence. We must concentrate our efforts on making certain that the Directorship passes from De Paolo's infirm, aged hands into the hands of a strong, capable leader. *Then* it will be possible for us to deal with rebels and revolutionaries."

Boweto scowled, then smiled. "I suppose you're right," he said.

They drove grimly through the cold rainstorm, bumping along the narrow road, soaked to the skin, ears ringing with the booming peals of thunder, landscape strobe-lit by the snake-tongued flicks of lightning that threw everything into sharp blue-white glare for an instant and then disappeared into blackness once again.

David could feel Bahjat shivering as she drove the electrobike. After a few kilometers he told her to pull over to the road's shoulder. It was raining so hard they could barely see beyond the bike's headlamp rim.

"We've got to find some shelter," he yelled over the crashing thunder.

Her hair was plastered down over her face. Water dripped from her nose, her chin. Her clothes were stuck to her body, molding every curve, outlining her navel, her nipples, her ribs.

"There is no shelter near here," she hollered back. "And we mustn't stop. They'll catch up with us."

"Not in this storm," David yelled.

"We can't stop," she insisted.

"Then at least let me drive."

He took over the handlebars and she clung to him, shivering, teeth chattering, as he leaned forward to peer through the solid sheets of rain.

It was terrifying and exhilarating. David had read about storms, had seen tapes of hurricanes and tornadoes. But this was real. He could feel the stinging cold of the rain-drops lashing him, forcing him to close his eyes to slits. The thunder was overpowering, awesome, earthshaking. The lightning seared every nerve in his body as it split the darkness.

No wonder our ancestors worshipped them, David thought. *Lightning and thunder. They reduce you to insignificance. I'm an ant, a bacterium, a molecule scuttling across the landscape. Theirs is the power to terrify you into worship. The power and the beauty. Gods, visible gods. So much bigger and more powerful than we are!*

Then the more pragmatic part of his mind wondered if the lightning wouldn't be drawn to them, on this broad, flat, treeless pampa.

We ought to stop and lie down alongside the shoulder of the road, he thought, *and keep this metal bike a good distance away from us.*

But instead he drove on, with Bahjat shuddering behind him.

The rain ended at last and the clouds scudded past, revealing a crystalline, star-filled night sky. David knew that the bike's batteries wouldn't go all night without recharging, so he began to look for a town, a village, a solitary house in the darkness. Nothing. Only darkness from horizon to horizon.

It was almost dawn when they saw a shack on a little rise far up off the road. In the gray early light David turned the bike off the paved road and they started bouncing across the grass up toward the shack's sagging wooden door.

The battery chose that moment to give out, and David had to pedal—teeth clenched, legs straining—the rest of the way to the shack.

"Bring . . . the bike inside," Bahjat said, her voice terribly weary, her face gray with exhaustion. "Don't let them . . . see it . . . from the air."

It was an old *vaquero* line shack, where the cattleman's

riders could shelter themselves overnight in the days before helicopters and electrobikes. Apparently now it was still used by occasional campers, because the wooden one-room structure was still standing, unpainted but weatherproofed. There were four bunks inside and even some canned food on the shelves above the sink. The shack had been built over a well; the sink had an old-fashioned manual pump standing at its side.

Bahjat was trembling uncontrollably and she started to cough as soon as she lay down on the bunk.

"You've caught a cold," David said, putting a hand to her forehead. It was hot. "Maybe worse."

"And you?" she asked between coughs.

"I'm all right," he replied.

"We can't stay here for long."

"You can't travel if you're sick."

"Yes . . . I can."

David went to the stock of canned foods. Most of them were self-heating. He pulled the tops off two cans of soup and one of meat stew. They started sizzling immediately. Sitting on the edge of her bunk, he helped Bahjat drink the soup directly from the can. There were no dishes, no utensils, no glassware.

And no medicines.

"The road . . ." Bahjat said. "We can hitch a ride. . . . There must be trucks. . . ."

"With two-way radios and full descriptions of us from the police, or army, or whatever," David said. He helped her eat part of the stew, and her coughing abated. He finished the stew himself, despite her feeble warnings that he would catch her germs by eating from the same can. Then he drank his soup, filled two of the cans with clear, cold water from the pump, and left them both beside Bahjat.

"Get some sleep," he said. "That's what I'm going to do."

"I'm cold," she said.

David scanned the cabin carefully. There were no blankets, not even sheets. The sun coming through the window was warm, but the sunlight wouldn't reach the bunk, which was built into the wall and couldn't be moved. So he undressed her and laid her still-damp clothes in the square of sunlight on the planks of the floor. Then he undressed himself and went back to her.

Like a baby sparrow, he thought, looking at her nude body, *frail and beautiful.*

He stretched out beside her and took her in his arms. She curled into his body, still shivering slightly. He held her tightly, then started rubbing her bare back and buttocks with his hands. She coughed a few times, then fell asleep. He did, too, with his last waking thought the realization that exhaustion is a stronger force than passion.

The sound of an engine awoke David. His eyes flicked open and he was instantly awake, alert. The wooden slats of the ceiling. Bahjat nestled in his arms. And a heavy internal combustion engine droning toward their cabin. Not an electrobike. Not a helicopter. A truck, maybe.

Carefully, he disengaged his arms from the sleeping girl. Her breathing was heavy, rasping, almost a wheeze. The sunlight had moved across the floor from where he had laid their clothes. But they were dry now.

David quickly draped Bahjat's skirt and blouse over her naked body, then scooped up his own pants and shirt and pulled them on.

Through the cabin's window he could see the road arrowing straight out to the horizon. A big tractor-trailer rig was puffing along the highway, the sign painted on its white flanks proclaiming that it carried DON QUIXOTE CERVESA in its refrigerated innards.

No way to get to the road and flag it down, David told himself. *Probably a mistake to even try. But she needs a doctor, or at least a pharmaceutical dispenser.*

He glanced back toward the bunk. Bahjat was sitting up. One arm shielding her breasts, the hand gripping her opposite shoulder, as if she were posing for a painting.

But David saw the dark circles beneath her eyes. She coughed and it sounded painful.

"We mustn't stay here," she said.

"I know."

"There will be other trucks."

"But they'll radio the police, won't they?"

She tried to smile. "Let me tell you how a properly trained guerrilla hitches a ride on a truck."

Crouched along the edge of the highway, David waited tensely. A dozen times he thought he heard the sound of a truck motor. Each time it was only his eager imagination.

Once a helicopter flew overhead and David hid himself and the bike under the tall yellowish grass by the roadside. The copter apparently saw nothing; it fluttered away without even circling the area.

Finally, he really did hear a truck approaching. Looking back, he saw Bahjat atop the shack's roof; she waved once to him and disappeared. David wheeled the bike onto the highway and left it there, on its side.

"I hope this works," he muttered, his hand moving to the butt of the pistol he had tucked in his waistband. That was their only alternative if this truck didn't stop.

He dashed back toward the cabin and saw Bahjat running toward him. He picked her up off her feet and raced toward the road again. She tried to protest, but her words turned into coughing.

They hunched down along the shoulder of the highway a dozen meters back from where the bike lay.

The truck huffed to a stop and the two drivers climbed languidly down from their cab to stare at the bike. They looked at each other and shrugged. Then they scanned the landscape. David and Bahjat hugged the ground.

The taller of the two drivers scratched his head and said something in Spanish. It sounded like a question and had the word *terroristas* in it.

The shorter man laughed and gestured toward the truck. His partner shook his head and said something about *policia*. The shorter man spat on the ground.

"Policia! Pah!"

After a few more exchanges, they set the bike up on its wheels and rolled it around to the rear of the truck. The taller man seemed much more reluctant than his partner, who happily punched the combination code on the trailer's tail-door lock. David watched his fingers carefully.

Grunting, they lifted the bike off the pavement and pushed it inside the trailer. Then they slammed the big double doors shut and headed back for the cab. David yanked Bahjat by one arm, scuttling up to the rear of the trailer. She cupped her free hand over her mouth and bent over double. He tapped out the same code on the combination lock's buttons, and the tail door popped open.

The truck was starting to move as he boosted Bahjat up inside it. He had to run to catch up, grab the frame of the open door, and swing himself up inside the dark interior.

Slowly, carefully, he shut the door. The lock clicked and they were plunged into darkness.

It took a few moments for their eyes to adjust to the gloom. The truck's interior was stacked high with see-through plastic crates of furniture.

"Too bad it's all in crates," David said over the hum of the engine and tires. "We've got a comfortable house full of sofas and chairs in here."

Bahjat's voice was a croupy whisper. "It's fine," she said. "We are safe . . . for the time being."

She collapsed into David's arms.

Many people reacted to the Solar Power Satellites the way they had reacted a generation earlier to nuclear energy—with their glands instead of their brains. The rioting in Delhi when the first Solar Power Satellite rectenna farm was opened up near the Indian capital was typical of the hysteria that greeted the Solar Power Satellites in many places. Somebody put out the rumor that the microwave radiation from the satellite was being beamed directly into the city at night, for the purpose of sterilizing the women!

You'd think the idiots would welcome some form of painless birth control, with famine victims piling up like autumn leaves all over India, and plagues sweeping the country, too. But, no. They rioted instead. Killed hundreds. Smashed up the rectenna farm so badly that the local power company went broke. No skin off *our* noses; we just aimed the satellite at North Africa, where they were taking in power to sell to Europe. And India remained poor and needy.

The Indian Government wouldn't move an inch; coming to the aid of the power company would've been political suicide. Even when the World Government tried to intervene, its people were beaten, threatened, and one or two of them were kidnapped and murdered. Gruesomely.

All because of a stupid rumor. . . .

> —Cyrus S. Cobb,
> Tapes for an unauthorized
> autobiography

• CHAPTER 24 •

The quickest, easiest, and most reasonable route out of the Argentinian interior lay eastward, toward the country's long coastline, where there were cities and seaports and airfields from which you could head north to Brazil and ultimately to the United States, or across the Atlantic to Africa or Europe.

So David and Bahjat headed westward, deeper into the hinterlands, toward the rugged mountains that separated Argentina from Chile.

At first they had no choice. They hunkered down among the crates of furniture in the back of the tractor-trailer they had sneaked into and rode where the truck took them. Bahjat was weak and feverish; she slept most of the time.

The truck finally stopped in Santa Rosa. David held a hand over the sleeping Bahjat's mouth to muffle any cough as the two truck drivers swung the rear doors open and hauled the bike out. David glimpsed a narrow street of cracked blacktop, with weeds springing up amid the ancient paving. Dingy, dilapidated two-story buildings of stucco or cement. *We're not at the trucking terminal,* he knew.

He eased the door open and saw the drivers wheel the bike into a *cantina* on the street corner. Through the grime-streaked *cantina* window he saw them greet a small, dark-skinned, rat-faced man. The taller of the two drivers stayed at the bar, with the bike propped up against the wall beside him, while the other driver disappeared into a back room with the dealer. He came out a few moments later, beaming happily, and ordered drinks for everyone—there were six tired-looking men in the bar, and they all accepted a free drink smilingly.

254

David took Bahjat out of the truck and helped her to walk to the *cantina*. She was very weak. He had to hold her up.

"Where . . . what are you doing?"

"Are you strong enough to make a phone call to your friends in the PRU?" he asked. The few meters between the truck and the *cantina* seemed like a kilometer. No one was on the street; it was early afternoon. A dog yapped in an alley somewhere, but otherwise everything was still.

"Yes," she answered weakly. "But, how?"

"Ssh! Leave it to me."

When they stepped through the *cantina*'s ancient swinging doors, everything inside stopped. No one moved. Talk ended in mid-word. All eyes focused on them.

David helped Bahjat across the bare plank floor and went straight to the dealer, who was again sitting at a table near the rear wall.

"I want to talk to you about a stolen electrobike," he said.

The dealer looked perplexed. Out of the corner of his eye, David could see the two truck drivers at the bar. They looked terrified.

"In there," said David, nodding toward the door that led into the back room.

The dealer got up from his table and led them into the back room. It was tiny. The bare plaster walls were covered with graffiti and crude drawings. But there was a shiny new picturephone on the chipped, lopsided table, as David had hoped there would be.

Easing Bahjat into one of the chairs, David turned to the dealer, who stood close to the door. David hooked a thumb into his waistband, next to the butt of the automatic, and smiled at the little man.

"You can keep the bike. All we want is to use your phone for a few minutes, and then, perhaps, to arrange for some transportation."

He could see the dealer's mind working. "Of course, sir," the man said in good English. "You may use the phone freely. But transportation—that can be expensive."

David nodded. "I understand."

Bahjat tried to get through to Hamoud at their hideout villa above Naples, but he was too cautious to answer an unexpected call. Instead, through a circuitous route that went to a PRU phone in Cuba, then to a second phone in Mexico, and finally—by satellite relay—to Naples, the call eventually went through. Even then Hamoud would not speak directly, but had a young woman appear on the screen.

Coughing, face flushed, voice weak, Bahjat arranged for a credit transfer from the Italian bank they were using to the local outlet in Santa Rosa. The dealer mentioned a sum, Bahjat offered half of it, and they finally agreed on three-quarters. The Italian woman disappeared from the screen for a few moments, then came back and okayed the transfer. She cut off the connection abruptly.

The dealer poured drinks for them both and sent a runner out to the local automated bank outlet. The transfer would go through in minutes: computer-to-computer transactions worked with electronic speed as long as no human beings got in the way.

"The lady needs a doctor," the dealer said as they waited for the messenger to return.

"Yes," David agreed. "Can we find one here?"

The rat-faced man shrugged. "Once, Santa Rosa had an entire street of doctors. But our town is dying. All the jobs have gone, and the doctors have gone with them. We have one man, but he is out at the emergency station up in the hills; they have plague there. You don't want to go there. Too dangerous. Plague."

"Then where can we get her some medical attention?"

"I will arrange it," the dealer said. "For no additional fee," he added proudly.

Bahjat smiled at him. "We agreed to more than you expected?" she asked, her voice barely audible.

The man smiled back. "Money is no consideration when it comes to the well-being of such a beautiful young lady."

The messenger burst into the tiny room then, grinning hugely. He pulled a wad of International dollars from one pocket of his skintight jeans, then yanked an equally thick handful of bills from the other.

"Ah," the dealer sighed. "International dollars, too. They are worth much more than Argentinian *pesos.*"

His friendship assured, the dealer made a few phone calls and then personally drove Bahjat and David, in a dust-covered old station wagon that hummed with well-oiled power, to Santa Rosa's rugged little airstrip. A small twin-turboprop plane was waiting for them, with a silver-haired pilot already at the controls, warming up the engines.

David and the dealer helped Bahjat into the plane. Then the dark-faced little man made a small bow to David.

"*Vaya con dios,*" he said over the growl of the engines. "There will be a doctor waiting for you when you land. And be assured, my phone is not tapped by the police."

David shook his offered hand, thinking to himself, *I'm thanking a criminal for doing illegal things.* Then he clambered into the plane and helped Bahjat buckle on her safety harness.

They took off with a roar, the plane shaking and quivering so much that David half-expected to see pieces rattling loose and falling away. But it all held together.

They sat side by side behind the pilot, a talkative, round-faced, smiling man with strong, steady hands and an obvious paunch. The co-pilot's seat was empty.

"I am flying ever since I was big enough to see over the control yoke and out the windscreen," he said happily over the muffled roar of the engines. "Fly everywhere. You pay, I fly. Sometimes I fly for no pay, like when earthquakes come and people need help—food, medicines, you know."

David looked at Bahjat, in the seat beside him. She seemed to be asleep. Her face was still flushed, her body roasting with fever.

"Where are we heading for?" David asked the pilot.

"Peru. Nobody looking for you there."

"Peru," David repeated. In his mind he saw Incas and conquistadores, golden temples set high in inaccessible mountains.

"Ever been there before?"

"No," David said.

"High mountains. Some people have trouble with the breathing because the air is thin. I flew opium up there back in the Nineties."

"Smuggling?"

"That's what the *policia* called it," he said with a slight shrug. "Somebody fly the stuff in from China or someplace and they process it up in the mountains. Had big factories up there in those days. Then somebody'd fly it north, to the *gringos*. I never flew that leg of it. Too dangerous. Those crazy *gringos*, they shoot you down with SAM's when you try to cross their border."

"Surface-to-Air Missiles?"

"*Si*. It was a big business then, the drugs. Lots of money for everybody. That was before the World Government came in and closed it all down."

David nodded.

"They had big factories up in the mountains. Plenty of work for everybody—even fliers, like me. Goddamned World Government ruined it all. Put everybody out of work."

He chattered on for hours as they flew northwestward. The ground below them changed from grassland to forest, from forest to matted jungle, and finally to high, craggy mountains. David could see snow on many of the peaks. But no signs of roads, towns, habitation.

"This is the tough part," the pilot said, just as cheery as ever. "We fly low enough to get under the radars back where we started. But here in the mountains, in this season, you must fly higher—or say hello to the angels. Is she buckled in well?"

David checked Bahjat's seat harness and then his own. The plane started bouncing around in the strong mountain air currents. The bare, jagged rock walls looked awfully close.

"Have no fears," the pilot called as the plane lurched. "I have flown these mountains for longer than your years. They are my friends."

A sudden drop made David glad his stomach was empty. Bahjat stirred and moaned in her sleep.

He said he'd have a doctor waiting for us, David repeated to himself for the hundredth time. *He promised.*

"Oh-oh!"

David looked at the pilot, who was half-turned in his seat. "What's wrong?"

The pilot pointed out the right side of the plane. David saw three swept-wing fighters cruising off their wingtip. David stared at the insignia on the fighters: the sky-blue globe of the World Government. And on their raked-back tails, a stylized sunburst of gold. *The ancient Inca symbol. They're Peruvians.*

The pilot had slipped on his earphones and was muttering into his throat mike in the clipped jargon of professional airmen.

Turning back toward David, he said, "They want us to land at their World Government airfield. They know the two of you are aboard."

"That man back in Santa Rosa," David said.

"There must be a large reward out for you. He is very trustworthy until money is available."

"What will they do if we don't follow their instructions?"

The pilot was no longer smiling. "They will shoot us down. Their leader says they carry both missiles and laser guns, so unless we can fly faster than light, we have no chance to outrun them."

"Not much of a choice."

The smile returned a little. "Not to fear, *amigo*. I know these mountains; they don't. I'll get you down safely. It won't be where you are expected, but it won't be at their damned airfield, either. They can kiss my ass before I'll let them get their hands on my plane!"

"But they have missiles and . . ."

The pilot waved a carefree hand. "I have this." He tapped an index finger against his temple. "And these." He pointed downward. *"Cojones,"* he explained.

For fifteen minutes they flew along with the fighters, as straight and level as the tricky mountain winds would allow. The sleek supersonic jets had to throttle back constantly to stay close to the little turboprop. The pilot was back on the radio, chatting with the fighter pilots in Spanish, explaining that he was going as fast as he could.

"I'm not a rocketship, you know!" he yelled in English, for David's benefit, as he eased his throttle back slowly.

Then came an argument over altitude. The mountains were still rising, growing higher and higher in front of them. The fighter pilots wanted to climb as far above the peaks as possible. David's pilot shook his head and explained that his poor, tired little aircraft was already straining at its ceiling, and it could not climb any higher without stalling and crashing.

Soon they were maneuvering around snow-crusted peaks, flying in and out among the mountains. Below them was a hazy sea of clouds and mist, but up at this height the thin air was clear.

And then quite suddenly the pilot slammed his throttles forward, pulled a heavy left turn, and banked so steeply that David saw nothing but rock hurtling past his window. Engines roaring, the plane dove into the clouds and within an instant they were shrouded in gray mist, flying totally blind.

David wanted to yell, but his throat was constricted.

The pilot yanked the earphones from his head and smiled back at David. "Have no fears. I have the radar." He tapped the tiny orange screen in the center of his control panel. It was jagged with return echoes from the mountains on all sides of them.

But you're not looking at it! David screamed silently.

"They have radar, too," the pilot said, still over his shoulder, "but they will be too frightened to take their very fast, shiny new aircraft down here to make love with the rocks. I know these mountains. I could fly through them blindfolded and kiss each one as I went by."

David nodded and tried to smile.

After a bouncing, shuddering, ear-popping ride that seemed hours long, they dropped out below the cloud deck and David could see broad Alpine meadows sloping away beneath them. Sunlight slanted through the heavy gray clouds overhead. The grasslands looked bare and brown, treeless, strewn with boulders.

The pilot had no time for talking now. He ran the plane in low over a level patch of withered grass, circled the area once, then dropped wheels and flaps and flared down to a bouncing, dust-raising landing.

He never switched off the engines, just reached back and opened the hatch alongside David.

"Okay, you're safe now."

"Safe? Where are we?"

"About fifty kilometers from Ciudad Nuevo—that is where your friends are waiting for you."

"But how will we get there?"

"I don't know! And maybe your friends have already been picked up by the *policia*. You will be safer here for a few days."

"What do you mean? There's nothing here!"

"There's an Indian village over that hill. You can stay there for a while."

"But . . ."

"No time! I must get back to an airstrip where I can get some fuel before the shit-eating *policia* catch up with me. Go! Quickly!"

With barely a chance to think, David unstrapped Bahjat from her seat and lifted her out of the plane. The pilot gunned the engines, spraying them with a miniature hurricane of dust and pebbles as David held Bahjat in his arms.

The plane roared bumpily across the sloping meadow and lifted into the cloud-heavy sky. In a few minutes it disappeared into the gray clouds and even the sound of its engines was lost. David stood alone in the empty wilderness with the sick, unconscious girl.

It happened!

I went over to Ruth's dorm room to work on the electronics project we're doing together and her two roommates were both out for the afternoon, and, well, instead of the project we wound up in bed. She's wonderful. It was her first time, too.

I told her I want to marry her and I love her and she just giggled and said we shouldn't even think about marriage for a long time yet. Her family's Jewish, but they're not strict or anything, so they wouldn't mind her marrying me. But if we ever had any children, they'd be Jewish, she said. I don't really understand that; it doesn't seem to have anything to do with which church they're brought up in. They'd be Jewish even if we raised them as Lutherans. That's what Ruth told me.

Anyway, I'm going to work harder than ever on these damned classroom studies. Ruth's so bright that she's sure to pass the tests and go on to Island One, and I'm not going to let her go up there without me.

—The journal of William Palmquist

• CHAPTER 25 •

Let's face it, old girl, you've got to be a masochist.

Evelyn was sitting in the Vesuvio Bar, where the decorations consisted of three-dimensional holographic views of past eruptions of Mount Vesuvius. Turn one way and you could see red-hot lava crushing a village beneath its inexorable flow; turn another and you were treated to the sight of stones the size of schoolhouses being hurled from the volcano's fiery cone.

Evelyn ignored all the views as she sipped her drink in the darkened, noisy bar. Most of the crowd was Italian, Neapolitans who preferred singing to talking and arguing to singing. The bartenders argued with the waiters, the waiters argued with the customers, and the customers argued with each other—all at the top of their lungs, accompanied by more eloquent gestures than a symphony conductor ever got to make. *You could have your eye put out simply discussing the weather,* Evelyn thought.

But she sat at the bar in a cone of silence. All the noise and action around her canceled itself out. She was lost in her own thoughts.

They've landed in Argentina. If I fly there, will they still be there by the time I arrive? Will the Argentinians allow me to see David? Or interview the PRU hijackers? And how will I get there? Borrow the money from Charles? He'll expect payment.

She didn't mind Sir Charles' bisexuality. What he did with others was no concern of hers. But the man was a masochist, and he turned Evelyn off with his hot-breathed demands for punishment. *Two masochists can't have fun together,* she thought. Even though her masochism was strictly confined to her chosen profession. *You've got to be*

264

*a masochist to stick to journalism. There's no other ex-
planation.*

"May I buy you a drink?"

Startled, Evelyn looked up to see a thick-necked, swarthy
young man standing next to her stool. He didn't look quite
Italian, even though he was dressed in the same casual
slacks and sleeveless shirt as everyone else in the bar.

"I was just about to leave," she said.

He rested a hand on her wrist, gently, lightly, but it was
enough to keep her from getting up.

"You are the English reporter who wants to interview
the hijackers, are you not?"

His accent isn't Italian. "What makes you think . . ."

"We have been watching you for the past several days.
Please. We mean you no harm. Have a drink with me.
Perhaps we can help you." He signaled to the bartender,
who was loudly debating the eventual fate of the hijackers
with two of the waiters.

"Another of the same for the lady, and I will have iced
coffee."

Glaring disapprovingly at him, the bartender reached
for a pair of glasses.

"You're an Arab," Evelyn said.

"Kurdish. You may call me Hamoud. I already know
your name. It is Evelyn Hall."

"Yes."

"And you wish to interview Scheherazade and the
others."

"Yes."

Hamoud nodded. "I will take you to them."

"To Argentina?"

"She is no longer in Argentina. She and one of the passengers have escaped from the false revolutionary *El
Libertador.*"

"Which other passenger?" Evelyn asked, feeling her
heart race. "Where are they?"

"They are heading north. The man she is with apparently did not want to return to his home. He is from Island
One, I believe."

Reaching for her drink, Evelyn asked, "And you are
going to meet them somewhere?"

"Eventually. Are you willing to come with us to meet
her?"

"Yes!"

"You will have to do exactly as I tell you, and live with us. Not a word to anyone outside until I allow it."

She nodded eagerly. "All right."

"You will be in danger. And if you try to trick us, the PRU will destroy you."

"I know," she said. "I understand." *A masochist's dream come true.*

Jamil al-Hashimi felt as tense as a coiled panther as the helicopter fought its way through a stiff, gusty wind to land atop the Garrison Tower. The city of Houston sprawled beneath its smoggy blanket as far as the eye could see in every direction. The riches that had once come from cattle and then from oil were now flowing into Houston from space, where the Solar Power Satellites were converting sunlight into incredible wealth.

But why hasn't Garrison shared his wealth with his city? al-Hashimi wondered. *Why does he allow them to continue burning coal? Cancerous stuff!*

The copter touched down on the pad and its engines whined down to a lower pitch and shut off. The sheikh's aide, clothed in *dishdashi* and turban, opened the passenger compartment's hatch.

"Stay here," al-Hashimi told him. "Do not go outside the aircraft. I shall not be long."

Al-Hashimi stepped out of the air-conditioned cool of the helicopter into the muggy blaze of a Texas afternoon. He wore a European-style business suit, woven from a fabric that gave far more ventilation than traditional Arab robes. Still he sweated. The wind on this rooftop was as humid as in a swamp. Al-Hashimi frowned with displeasure.

Squinting against the sun's glare, he saw that a tall, leggy, very American-looking woman was standing at the edge of the helicopter landing circle waiting for him. Two stone-faced men stood a few paces behind her.

"Sheikh al-Hashimi," the woman said, with a slight Texas twang to her American English, "welcome to Houston."

She extended her hand. He touched it briefly. *Americans,* he sniffed to himself, *all informality and no manners.* This woman was taller than he was, very attractive in a show-girl kind of way: thick, long red hair, strong white teeth, full bosom and hips.

"I'm Arlene Lee," she said, her voice rising half a note at the end of the statement. "Mr. Garrison asked me to meet you and bring you down to his office."

"Very kind of Mr. Garrison to provide such a lovely welcome for me."

"Why, thank you! You're very sweet."

Sweet! Al-Hashimi fumed.

He allowed her to lead him to the elevator and they descended two flights. The doors slid open onto a single room that spanned the entire floor of the building.

It was part office, part Western ranchhouse living room, part garden. Impressive modern desks of real wood stood nearest the elevator where the sheikh stood. To his left was a row of blue-gray communications consoles that seemed intricate enough to reach any corner of the Solar System. Arlene guided the sheikh past the desks, into an area of pine-paneled walls, animal-skin rugs, and hide-covered chairs. A long redwood table was heaped with dishes of food, bottles of refreshments, and a glowing copper *ghoum-ghoum* surrounded by silver-inlaid cups.

"Would you care for something to eat or drink?" Arlene asked, gesturing toward the waiting feast.

Al-Hashimi checked his first impulse to refuse. "Some coffee, perhaps," he said, inclining his head slightly toward the copper vat. "It *is* Arabic-style coffee, is it not?"

"Oh, sure," Arlene answered offhandedly.

She poured him a cup and he sipped the strong, hot brew.

"Where is Mr. Garrison?"

"He'll be here directly, I'm sure. He knew your helicopter had landed."

"In my land," al-Hashimi said without a smile, "it is often the custom to make a visitor wait to impress upon him that he is inferior in importance to the host."

"Oh, that's not it at all!" she said, looking genuinely shocked at the idea.

" 'Course it is!" Garrison snapped.

Al-Hashimi turned to see the old man cruising down a lane between exotic shrubbery in the garden area of the immense room. Garrison rode his chair up to the sheikh and grinned crookedly at him.

"Mr. Garrison," al-Hashimi said.

"Sheikh al-Hashimi," replied Garrison.

"It is kind of you to receive me on such short notice," al-Hashimi said, feeling anything but grateful.

"Ya got me curious," said Garrison, his voice a corduroy-rough wheeze. "What's so hell-fired important that we couldn't talk on the phone about it?"

Al-Hashimi glanced at Arlene. "I wanted to speak to you personally, in private."

Garrison said, "I got no secrets from my right-hand lady, here."

"But I do." Al-Hashimi tried to control his temper. *This old man is toying with me. He knows I need his help.*

"I'll leave," Arlene said. "Y'all call me when you want me."

"No," Garrison snapped, and for an instant al-Hashimi tensed, ready to stalk out of the place and go back to his waiting helicopter.

But Garrison went on. "I got a better idea. You come with me, Sheikh. Arlene, you stay here and get back t'work on those travel arrangements."

Garrison pivoted his powerchair and started off back into the greenery. Al-Hashimi, seething, had no choice but to follow him.

He doesn't really need that chair, the sheikh thought. *He's old but he's not crippled. It's merely an excuse for remaining seated, for humiliating me, for showing me who is master in this house and who is supplicant.*

"Gonna let you see something that only six other people in the world've seen," Garrison said. "And two of 'em are dead!" He chuckled and coughed.

"I wanted to speak with you about finding this escaped hijacker," al-Hashimi said, following the powered chair through rows of exotic ferns and flowering shrubs.

"This Scheherazade girl? The one who's run out from under *El Libertador*'s nose with one of my people?"

"Yes. Scheherazade, she calls herself."

They reached a moss-covered wall. Garrison snapped his bony fingers and a door slid open, revealing another elevator cab. He drove the chair into the elevator and spun himself around to face forward. Al-Hashimi stepped in beside him and the door slid silently shut.

"She's your daughter, ain't she." It was no question.

The elevator was dropping rapidly. Al-Hashimi's innards felt hollow and weak.

"Yes," he said. "You know that."

"And you want her back."

"Alive and unharmed."

"Why would I want to see her harmed?" Garrison asked.

The elevator was whistling, plummeting down. A part of al-Hashimi's mind asked, *How far down will we go? Surely we must have reached the basement level of this tower!*

Uneasily, he answered Garrison, "Scheherazade is a revolutionary, a guerrilla. She seeks to destroy the established order—our corporations, as well as the World Government."

"But she's your daughter and you want to protect her, eh?"

"Of course."

The elevator slowed at last and came to a heavy, knee-bending stop.

Garrison chuckled. "That's why I stay in this chair, sonny. My old legs can't take the ride this baby gives. I was down here when you landed; that's why I was a little late greetin' you. Came down an hour before you were expected and just plain lost track of the time."

The elevator door was open, revealing a short blank corridor of gray cement. A single fluorescent overhead tube lit the bare floor. A gleaming steel door, looking almost like a bank vault, was set into the end of the corridor.

"Well, don't worry," Garrison said. "I've already got my people lookin' for the kid with her—piece of my property, that young man is. Cobb let him sneak away from Island One and I want him back, all in one piece. We'll get your daughter back, too, at the same time."

"Also undamaged."

They were at the steel door. Garrison stopped his chair and twisted slightly to look up at al-Hashimi.

"Haven't you figured out yet that these fire-eatin' kids are our best allies? They can't hurt us. Sure, they'll destroy some property and kill some people, but how's that gonna really hurt us? They kidnap our people. So what? We pay 'em ransoms and get the people back. Good way of funnelin' money to the little hell-raisers without the goddamned World Government catchin' wise."

"I understand all that. I have used local PRU groups to good effect against the World Government myself. But if they gain too much power . . ."

"They won't," Garrison said flatly. "They can't. Everything they do is counterproductive. Oh, they'll be fine, helpin' to pull down the World Government. But they'll never be able to run the show. They've already made a pass at workin' with *El Libertador,* but that's not goin' to work. He'll expect them to follow orders, to be patient, to lie low. . . . They'll never go for that."

"You're certain?"

"Yep. But enough politics," Garrison said. "Took you down here to see something special." He leaned forward in his chair and pressed his palm against the I.D. plate set into the steel door's center. The plate glowed red for a flicker, then turned bright blue. Garrison sat back in the chair and the heavy door swung inward.

"C'mon in," he said over his shoulder as he wheeled through the open doorway. The area beyond was dimly lit.

Al-Hashimi stepped through. It was a fairly small room, cool and very dry. A soft carpeting muffled his footsteps.

"Stand right where y'are," Garrison called from a little distance away. His voice seemed to be swallowed up by the darkness, as if the room were acoustically insulated to prevent any possibility of echoes.

A single beam of light lanced down from high overhead. It revealed a picture, a painting, al-Hashimi saw. Stepping closer toward it . . .

"That's the da Vinci Madonna and Child!"

Garrison chuckled in the shadows behind him.

Another light clicked on, and al-Hashimi turned to see a small statue of an aged woman: unmistakably Rodin. A third light: Chagall. A fourth: a tiny pair of gold chariots resting on a velvet pad. Al-Hashimi stepped over to inspect them. There was no glass case over them; he could pick them up in his hand.

"These are from ancient Babylon," he said, his voice a hollow whisper.

'That's right. Not far from Baghdad, as the jet flies."

Al-Hashimi straightened up. He could see Garrison's face etched by the overhead lights.

"But these were stolen from the Baghdad Museum some ten or twelve years ago," the sheikh said.

"Yep. Sure were." Garrison cackled and more lights came on: Brueghel, Picasso, Donatello, old Chinese silk paintings, ultra-modern electronic sculpture, oils, bronzes, drawings, rocks shaped and painted by unknown primitive hands.

"All stolen!" Garrison wheezed. "Every one of 'em! Stolen from their owners, right out from under their noses. That Hunsberger there : . . the abstract . . . got that one while it was on its way to the White House!" He bent over, laughing so hard that he was suddenly racked with coughing.

The entire ceiling was glowing with light panels now and al-Hashimi could see that at one end of the fairly small room stood a complete stained-glass window from some European cathedral. At the other end was an incredibly intricate tile mosaic wall behind a life-sized golden statue of a seated Buddha.

"Every piece in here was stolen," Garrison said, controlling his voice so he wouldn't cough again.

Al-Hashimi stroked his trim beard, not knowing whether he should feel anger, awe, or disgust.

"Listen," Garrison said, his voice suddenly hard. "When you've got all the money you can ever spend, when you can *buy* anything or anybody you want, what's left? Only the priceless things—the things that nobody would sell, ever. That's what I do for fun. I steal art treasures. That's my hobby."

"You have them stolen for you."

"Same thing," he said with an impatient wave of his hand. "Important thing is, I take 'em away from people who'd never sell 'em to me. Priceless art objects. Hah! Let 'em stay priceless. I could offer a hundred million apiece for each and every item you see here, but it's more fun to steal 'em. Break their hearts. Those stuffed pigeons think they can hold onto something that *I* want! Not for sale at any price, eh? Good!"

Al-Hashimi looked slowly around the room.

"Take a good look! You're only the seventh man ever inside this room. And the last one on Earth to see this. It's all going up to Island One with me, real soon now."

"How soon?"

"A few weeks. We all take off before everything falls apart. There's gonna be blood in the streets around here.

271

We've gotta be safely up in Island One before the shootin' starts."

"And my daughter?"

"We'll get her and bring her up there with us," Garrison said, silently adding, *If we can.*

If [M.I.T. astronomer Tom] McCord is right, there are hundreds of millions of billions of tons of nickel-iron alloy in the asteroid belt. The economic potential of this storehouse of metal, in the event mankind conquers and industrializes space, is staggering.

—Dr. Clark R. Chapman,
The Inner Planets,
Scribner's, 1977

• CHAPTER 26 •

David walked up the slope of the hill the pilot had pointed to, trudging up the sparse, scrawny brownish grass slowly, carefully, carrying Bahjat in his arms the way a man would carry a child. She didn't stir or open her eyes. He would have thought she was dead, except for the heat of her fever that penetrated his thin shirt.

It's good heat, he told himself. *Fever means the body is fighting the invading microbes. There'll be a doctor in the village. We'll get there soon.*

The sun dipped below the cloud deck, but its slanting rays brought no warmth. The hilly gray and brown landscape seemed barren and dreary. And cold. David realized he was puffing; he couldn't get enough air into his lungs. His head started to spin. Looking down at Bahjat, so small and frail in his arms, he wondered why she felt so heavy. His legs were like lead weights. His arms and back ached.

But he pushed on, up the hillside. *Another hundred meters,* he urged himself. *You've been through worse than this. Only seventy-five meters, more likely. Count them off. Each stride . . . one . . . two . . .*

He lost track of time and distance. The whole world, the entire universe, narrowed down to that one goal, the crest of that tired hill, and the tuft of browning shrubbery that topped it. David's body moved like an automaton. He ignored the pain and weariness in every muscle and simply moved ahead, step by plodding step.

And when he finally reached the crest of the hill, he stumbled and nearly collapsed. The village that the pilot had spoken of lay far below, nestled among hillsides. A half-dozen stone huts. A thin whisper of smoke rose lazily from a hole in the roof of the largest hut. A couple of tiny

274

children sat in the dirt outside another. A dog howled from somewhere.

It was a scene straight out of the Neolithic: a primitive village, as far from civilization in years as in kilometers.

Feeling as if he were striding back into the Stone Age with each step, David carried Bahjat down the hillside toward the village. As he approached, several dogs started barking and howling. A dozen or so people came out of the huts and formed a mute, staring line, gaping at him and the burden he carried.

They're not savages, David thought. They wore trousers and loose shirts and blankets of colorful reds and blues thrown across their shoulders. He could see no weapons among them.

More people came out of the huts and clustered with the others until there were about three dozen in all. The adult men—fifteen of them, David counted—stepped forward to form a line in front of the women and children. One of the youngsters—it was hard to tell if it was a boy or a girl because they all had the same clothing and bowl-shaped haircuts—peeked out from between the legs of one of the men. A woman—its mother?—yanked the child back where it belonged. No one said a word or made a sound.

David stopped a few paces in front of the unsmiling men. He held Bahjat out in his leaden arms.

"She's sick," he said. "She needs a doctor."

They didn't answer. They were stocky men, broad-shouldered and barrel-chested. Their faces had the high cheekbones and strongly arched noses of old Incas.

"She is sick," David repeated, wishing he spoke Spanish. "Do you have a doctor? Medicine?"

The man in the middle of the line said something in a deep-voiced guttural language that David could not understand.

Desperately, he asked, *"Habla español?"*

They were as unmoving as the mountains that surrounded them. A chill wind swept past and David saw that the sun would disappear very soon.

He hoisted Bahjat up in one arm, freeing his right hand to touch his own forehead, then touch hers. The men looked at one another, puzzled. David repeated the action, then gestured toward them.

"Touch her forehead," he said, beckoning to the one who had spoken. "See how hot she is."

Slowly, hesitantly, the man stepped forward. After a few more demonstrations from David, he placed his fingertips on Bahjat's forehead, very gingerly, then quickly drew them back again.

"No," David said, shaking his head, "like this." He placed the palm of his hand on her forehead. His left arm was screaming under her weight.

The man stared grimly at David, then put his hand out again. He placed it on Bahjat's forehead. His eyes widened. Turning, he called back to the others. A short, fat old woman bustled past the line of men, chattering in the same harsh language. She looked sharply at Bahjat, then touched her forehead.

"Ah!" she exclaimed, then said something to the man. Without the slightest sign of fear, she reached up and touched David's cheek. She had to stand on tiptoes to do it. Then she grasped Bahjat's wrist.

She's taking her pulse!

The old woman spoke urgently to the man, who apparently was the village's leader. The other men joined in the debate while the rest of the women and children peered curiously at David.

David could not understand their words, but the tones seemed clear. Most of the men were clearly against the idea of allowing these strangers into their village. The woman pointed to Bahjat and spoke jeeringly. David saw that she was practically toothless. The leader, who seemed to be the oldest man in the group—his thick hair was streaked with gray—said very little.

But when he did speak, the others fell silent. Then he turned to David and, gesturing, led him into the village. The others moved aside and then fell in behind David, the old woman, and the chief.

The huts were cramped and smoky and smelled of human sweat. The floors were smooth-pounded earth; the walls were rough stones. If you sat close enough to the pitiful little fire in the center of a hut, your face and hands could get warm while your back froze. The food was a spicy gruel of vegetables, without any meat at all.

The utensils they used, the pots they cooked in, the decorations they carved in wood or stone or clay were the same that David remembered seeing in texts about the Incas.

These are the mountain people, he realized. *They've been living this way for thousands of years. While the Incas built their empire, while the Spaniards conquered them, while the nation of Peru was created and threw off Spanish rule, while the World Government was coming into being . . . these people have lived the same way, untouched by any of it, for hundreds of generations.*

They had practically nothing, but they shared what they had with David and Bahjat. The old woman was apparently the village healer. She took Bahjat off with another pair of toothless crones to her own hut and began feeding her hot broth made from dried herbs that dangled from pegs set into her walls. For two days Bahjat did not open her eyes, and David hovered outside the hut where they kept her.

He slept in the leader's hut, on a pallet of straw and hides, together with the chief's wife and one child—the little girl who had peeped through her father's legs when David had first stumbled into their village.

At dawn on the third day, the chief roused David by gently shaking his shoulder, and he made it clear with gestures that he wanted David to go with him and two other men. They headed out of the village, each of them carrying three or four long, spindly wooden spears and steel knives in their belts. *A hunting party?* David wondered. *Or are the weapons for me?*

He still had the pistol in his belt, with five cartridges in it. The Indians had shown no interest in it at all.

They walked downslope to the tree line, where huge conifers, bigger than any David had seen on Island One, towered up into the misty sky. It was dark in the woods, cold and gloomy and mysterious. But the men knew exactly what they were doing as they set up simple traps of twine and sticks.

The morning's work over, the chief conferred briefly with his men and then led David deeper into the forest. Feeling uneasy with the chief ahead of him and the two spearmen behind, David trudged along the shadowy, silent trail, unconsciously touching the gun butt every few steps.

The woods thinned out and David saw that they were nearing the edge of an escarpment. Far below them a stream gurgled and splashed downslope. And beside it was a paved road.

The chief pointed to it and then back to David. Then he said something and made a wide, sweeping gesture.

David nodded. "You're saying that this is the way back to civilization. This is the way I should go when we leave your village."

David pointed in the same direction that the chief had. A broad smile broke out on the chief's weather-beaten face.

But instead of heading back toward the village, he led David along the edge of the escarpment, farther along the direction that the road ran.

After nearly a half-hour's walk, David saw it: a huge gouge in the woodlands far below them. Bulldozers and earth-moving equipment were knocking down the trees and ripping up the topsoil, cutting a jagged, raw wound into the land. The stream ran foul and muddy now.

They were so far above the construction crew that the giant trucks and tractors looked like toys. David couldn't even hear the sounds of their engines above the fresh breeze blowing up along the clifftop.

"The road brings civilization," David said. "And it's coming your way."

From the grim shakes of their heads and the way the three Indians stared with clenched jaws at the mammoth construction works, it was clear they had no liking for the approach of civilization.

"There's nothing I can do," David said to them. "It's not me. It's not my fault. I can't stop them."

They didn't understand his words, but they seemed to know what his tone meant. Helpless. They were all helpless.

Slowly they retraced their steps, returned to the forest and found the traps. A half-dozen furry animals had been caught in them. They slaughtered the game quickly and cleanly with their knives—all except one snow-white rabbit, which for some reason they turned loose.

It was dark by the time they returned to the village. The women and children streamed out of the huts to welcome the mighty hunters. David went straight to the hut of the old healer, where Bahjat lay.

The old woman let him in, and David saw that Bahjat

was sitting up, clear-eyed, the fever obviously broken and gone.

"You're well!" David said. "How do you feel?"

"Weak . . . but better than I was."

The toothless healer tugged at David's shirt and jabbered at him. She pointed to the door and made it plain that he was to leave.

"But I just want to talk with her for a minute," David said.

It was no use. The old hag clattered at him and pushed him toward the door. Bahjat smiled and shrugged, then picked up a steaming bowl from beside her pallet and started sipping from it.

"I'll see you tomorrow," David said grudgingly from the doorway, over the healer's white head of hair.

"Tomorrow," answered Bahjat, grinning at him.

David left the hut, his insides churning in a mix of emotions he had never known before. He felt light-headed, dizzy. *It's the altitude and all the day's exertion,* he said to himself at first. But soon he realized it was more than that. Bahjat was going to be all right. The Indians had shown him the road back to civilization. He felt enormously grateful and relieved, happier than he had ever been before. But there was still more to it, something bubbling inside him that he couldn't identify.

It haunted him all through the evening meal of meat chunks and ash-roasted potatoes. David smiled to himself when he tasted the meat: rabbit, one of the staples of Island One. But instead of going to his pallet once the hut's fire had sunk into embers, he stepped outside into the sighing night winds of the mountains.

It was a clear, cold night. David walked through the sleeping village, a borrowed itchy wool blanket wrapped around his shoulders. He stared up at the stars, trying to figure out why he felt the way he did, what was happening inside him. High overhead the unblinking beacon of Island One rode serenely above him.

Slowly, as the stars slid across the bowl of night, David began to understand what his feelings were. He owed Bahjat's life to these people, and his own. They could have refused him, turned him away. He would have died in this mountain wilderness before he could have found help. And Bahjat would have died before him.

What can I do to repay the debt I owe them? David asked himself, looking up at the star-like image of Island One. For a moment he wished he could talk it over with Dr. Cobb; he'd know what to do.

No, he told himself. *I must figure this problem out for myself. No computers can help me. All by myself.*

He spent the night at it, walking around the village's scant perimeter. Twice he noticed the chief had come out of the hut to watch him, never leaving the hut's doorway, never interrupting his walking and thinking as he circled the village again and again.

They had everything they needed, everything they wanted. They lived in harmony and peace with this rugged environment. But soon all of that would be wiped away, carved out of the mountains by civilization's encroaching earth-moving machines. A new town to house the exploding billions of the cities and farms. An airport, an industrial complex. Whatever they were building those few kilometers down the road, they would be building another one in a few years, closer, perhaps right here.

There was nothing David could do to stop that from happening. *But maybe . . .* He looked up at the sky once again. It was turning gray with dawn. Island One had set below the saw-toothed horizon.

Before he left this village, David realized, he had to give them something, something of his own—something that would serve as a symbol, a pledge, to show his gratitude and to leave a promise with them. But what? He had nothing to give, only the clothes on his back, his boots, the gun. He would need them all when he returned to the world of cities and rebellion and violence. And the villagers had shown no interest in any of them.

Then it struck him. A gift that had no real value at all, but which was deeply symbolic. As the sun rose and began tinting the snowy peaks, David knew what he had to do.

He slept the morning away, and then he went to see Bahjat. The old healer let him into the hut, but squatted inside the doorway, watching them both.

Bahjat was thinner than before, the bones of her face sharper. But her eyes were clear,

He spent the afternoon with her. The old woman let Bahjat get up and walk around the village with David. Four young girls followed them at a respectful distance.

"I think I'll be able to travel by tomorrow. My legs feel strong. I'm just a little light-headed."

David said, "That's the altitude. We must be two thousand meters above sea level, at least."

"Where are we?" she asked. "What happened? I remember the truck, and then a plane . . ."

David began telling her about being intercepted by the Peruvian jet fighters, and how the pilot left them stranded here in the mountains.

"But the Indians have taken good care of us, and they showed me a road that must lead to a town sooner or later. The pilot said we were about fifty kilometers from Ciudad Nuevo, and if your friends are still there . . ."

"You took me with you? When you could have left me for the police to pick up and gotten away by yourself?"

Surprised, David said, "Yes, I suppose I did."

"Don't you realize that if I make contact with the PRU, they will consider you to be our prisoner?"

He shrugged. "I never thought of that."

The next morning the chief led David out of his hut as soon as they had finished their clay bowls of grainy gruel. The whole village seemed to know that their visitors were leaving. The old healer led Bahjat out of her hut, and as the two of them met in the village's central open area, everyone else clustered about them.

Silently, solemnly, the chief presented them each with red and blue blankets.

"They're beautiful," Bahjat said as she accepted hers. "Where do they get them?"

"Maybe they keep sheep someplace farther up in the mountains," David said. "Or they trade pelts for them."

Others came forward and presented them with sacks of grain and small, ornately decorated eating bowls.

"For our journey," Bahjat said.

David nodded, remembering the gift that he had decided to give. He stepped toward the chief and pointed to the knife in the man's twine belt.

A frown crossed the chief's face, but slowly he pulled the knife from its leather sheath and handed it to David. The whole village was silent, watching.

David went back to the small pile of treasures they had given him and took the little bowl in his left hand. Then, with the knife in his right hand, he made a swift slash across the meaty back of his forearm. It wasn't deep, but it stung and quickly started dripping blood.

The villagers gasped. Bahjat's mouth fell open. David handed the knife back to the chief and then put the bowl beneath the cut. Several drops of blood spattered into it. He handed the bowl to the chief.

"It's the only thing I have to offer," David said, "for now."

The chief was clearly moved. He held the bowl in one outstretched hand, the bloody knife in the other. He raised them both and turned for the whole village to see. A murmur of approval went up.

"You're still bleeding," Bahjat whispered.

"It'll stop in a minute," David said. "I've got a very strong clotting factor."

And then he realized what the chief was going to do. The silver-haired man, looking as solemn and strong as the mountains themselves, put the cup to his lips and drank David's blood.

"*Inshallah!*" Bahjat said softly.

Then the chief deftly cut his own arm and let the blood drip into the bowl. He handed it back to David.

"You're not going to . . ." Bahjat's voice choked off as David drank the chief's blood.

The villagers shouted. The chief raised his hand and rested it solidly on David's shoulder. He said not a word; none was needed. They simply stood there for a long moment while the whole village watched and the mountain winds sighed and moaned above them.

At last the chief stepped back. David picked up the food and blankets, and he and Bahjat started on their way. The chief sent two men to lead them through the forest and down to the road. He himself retired to his hut, too moved to make the short journey himself.

By the time the sun was high, David and Bahjat were trudging down the paved highway, alone again. They had skirted the construction site, choosing instead to find the town where they had a chance of linking up with a local PRU group.

"But what was that ceremony all about?" Bahjat was asking.

"I wanted to give them something to show how grateful we were for their kindness to us." David's arm throbbed slightly, but the bleeding had long since dried up. "They saved our lives, after all."

"Yes, but . . . blood?"

"That's all I had. And it has a deep meaning for them. I think we've been officially adopted as members of their tribe."

"You have," Bahjat said. "They ignored me."

Grinning at her, he said, "We could go back and repeat the ceremony for you. I'm sure they'd be very glad . . ."

"Never mind!"

They walked along the empty highway for a while, under the warming afternoon sun. Then Bahjat asked, "How did you get me to the village if I was unconscious when the plane landed up there?"

"I carried you," David said absently. He was still thinking about the villagers and what he could do to help them.

"You carried me? All the way to the village?"

"It wasn't far."

"And then you stayed there while I was sick for two more days and nights?"

David nodded.

"Why did you stay with me?"

"You were sick. I couldn't leave you."

She stopped and grabbed at his arm. "But don't you realize that we're enemies? I hijacked your space shuttle. You want to go to Messina; that's the last place in the world that I want to be. When we reach the town I'm going to contact my friends and you'll be our prisoner, our hostage."

Tapping the gun at his waist, David said, "Maybe you'll be my prisoner."

Bahjat shook her head. "You couldn't get very far without my help."

"And you would have been in a police hospital in Argentina without my help," he countered.

"So you expect me to be grateful."

"I expect you . . ." David stopped, took a deep breath, and then began walking again. "Look," he said, "can't we just be friends and leave the politics aside?"

"That's impossible," Bahjat said firmly.

"Well, impossible or not, we'd better give it a try. We're

283

going to be walking down this road together for a long time, it seems to me. And if your friends in Ciudad Nuevo aren't any better than the people we've contacted so far, we may be on the road even longer."

Bahjat said nothing. David kept on walking and she stayed alongside him. After a while he began singing a song she had never heard before. She tried to frown at him, but she found herself smiling back, instead.

FOR YOUR EYES ONLY

28 August 2008

To: Dr. Cyrus S. Cobb
From: Mr. T. Hunter Garrison
Subject: Operation Proxy

Phase I of the operation is now essentially complete, and Phase II will be initiated shortly. As you know, Phase II will escalate very quickly and reach its planned objectives in less than three months. At that time, the evacuation phase of the operation will begin. All preparations aboard Island One must be finished, therefore, within sixty calendar days of receipt of this memorandum. DESTROY AFTER READING!

• CHAPTER 27 •

T. Hunter Garrison sat in the sweltering hot greenhouse at the far end of his quarters atop the Garrison Tower and watched the holographic cross-country conference. The hologram screen in the greenhouse was full-sized. It gave the illusion that the greenhouse was cut in half: where Garrison sat was a hot, humid tropical garden filled with orchids, ferns, lianas; where Leo and the other rebels sat was a crazy-quilt conference table, with a different background behind each of the two dozen guerrillas.

Garrison leaned forward in his powerchair's enfolding softness, his bald head glistening as he watched the revolutionaries arguing. He wore only a sweat-soaked terrycloth robe of royal blue. No one else was in the greenhouse with him.

He had plugged in to every one of Leo's conferences since the first one several months earlier. He had listened to every detail of their planned nationwide uprising. It was doomed to fail, of course, but Leo had the right idea—strike hard and don't count the costs.

The time to strike was very near. Garrison had been supplying arms to the guerrillas in each of twenty-four cities all summer long. It looked like an impressive arsenal to them, but the old man knew exactly how far it would take them.

"We're gonna tear it all down, man," said the bushy-haired youth from Los Angeles. "They'll think an earthquake hit 'em."

"The question is, when?" Leo said calmly.

"We're ready to go."

"So're we!"

286

Most of the men and women around the electronically created conference table nodded enthusiastically.

"Hey, there's still somethin' botherin' me about this whole operation," said the woman who headed the Kansas City rebels. She wore turquoise and beads and a circlet around her head, but to Garrison she looked more black than red.

"What is it?" asked Leo.

"Well . . . we're gonna hit the streets and start shootin' up everything, okay. But we know we can't hold out against the Army. They can bomb the shit outta us, gas us, hit us with tanks, planes, ever'thing. And they'll have the World Government backin' 'em up, too, with more troops. So what's the good of all this? Lotta brothers an' sisters gonna get killed. For what?"

"I know," Leo said. "We've hassled this out a thousand times."

"Make it a thousand and one," she said, unsmiling.

Leo nodded ponderously. "We gotta show the nation, the people, the *world,* that we're willin' to fight for what's ours. Eighty percent of this country's black or brown or yellow. An' we got eighty percent of the unemployment, the hungries, the sick. *They* got the big piece of the pie—the white-asses. We're gonna show 'em we want our fair share."

The woman gave a small shrug.

"By strikin' at the same time all across the country," Leo went on, "we'll show 'em that we're organized. They got to take our demands seriously. We ain't no little bunch of street hustlers cryin' in the welfare line."

"Yeah, but when they bring in the Army . . ."

"We're gonna show 'em that not even the fuckin' Army can protect them from us. Sure, they'll beat us back *after* we strike. But by then it'll be too late for Mr. Average White-ass Citizen. He's gonna be hurt! We're gonna hit him and hit him hard!" Leo thumped a fist on the table. "Every city in this country's gonna be a burnin' mess by the time we get through."

"Don't sound like much to mo," the Kansas City woman said, "considerin' all the deads we gonna get."

"Yeah. An' the Tet Offensive was called a defeat for the Viet Cong. But they won the war, baby."

"Ten years later."

Leo smiled. "Not ten. Less than ten."

"What bugs me," another man blurted out, "is where all the guns are comin' from."

"Yeah. Who's bein' so good to us?"

"Or settin' us up for a trap?"

"No trap," Leo said. "The weapons are from people who want to help us."

"Who? And why?"

"I can't tell you that. Besides, you're better off not knowin'."

"You know who, though?"

"Damn' right."

Garrison grinned to himself. Several of them around the conference table had tried to trace the arms shipments back to their sources. But they were amateurs at cloak-and-daggering. They knew their way around city streets, but how could they match the skills and power of the giant corporations?

"Okay, okay," Leo was saying. "We still got the big question: When do we strike?"

"Sooner the better; can't keep these guns hidden forever."

"We're ready to go now."

"A couple days, at most."

"Okay," Leo said. "It's Monday. We strike on . . . Thursday, at noon, Eastern Time."

"Nine A.M. out here," said the Los Angeles lad.

"Hey, Thursday's Thanksgiving Day!"

Leo chuckled. "Yeah, so it is. Good. Catch 'em with their turkeys."

They all laughed.

"Any objections?"

No one spoke.

"Then it's noon, Eastern Time, this Thursday. Good luck."

The three-dimensional picture on Garrison's holoscreen fell to pieces as, one by one, the twenty-four individual segments winked off. But Leo's image remained at the far end of the otherwise blank screen, sitting alone, his shining black face lost in thought.

He's their leader, all right, Garrison thought. *One of these days we'll have to let him die—after he's done what we need him to do.*

Leo turned and looked into the camera. He seemed to be

staring straight at Garrison. The old man's fingers quivered over his armrest keyboard, ready to turn off the picture.

"Garrison, you watchin' me?"

The old man was not surprised to hear Leo speak to him. He tapped a button on his keyboard to transmit his image.

"I'm watching you, Greer."

Leo grunted. "Thought so."

"You seem to have become a national leader," Garrison said.

"Fuckin' right, I am."

With an impatient snort, Garrison said, "You can drop the gutter language now, Greer. I'm not impressed by it."

"Yeah, I guess so. But maybe the gutter's got me hooked, Garrison. I *am* Leo now. Greer's dead—or at least he's sleepin' pretty fuckin' hard."

"The gutter hasn't hooked you. You're hooked on power."

"Same's you, man."

Garrison considered a moment. "That's right, boy. Same as me. Power. That's where it's at."

"Damn' right," Leo said. "You taught me that years ago, back when I was playin' football. You didn't own franchises; you owned leagues."

"I still do," Garrison said.

"How come you're helpin' us so much?" Leo asked, his voice hardening. "Think we'll kill ourselves off?"

"Most likely."

"We won't, you know. Lots of us will die, but there's an awful lot of us, man. We're gonna tear the guts outta every big city in your U.S. of A."

"Go right ahead."

Leo's eyes narrowed. "What's in this for you? Why you helpin' us?"

"That's my business. You just go ahead and do what you think you've got to do. Let me worry about my white ass."

"You gonna neutron-bomb us, aint'cha? Kill everybody in the cities but save the buildings. Once we start the uprisin', boom!"

Garrison shook his head. "No neutron bombs. The World Government dismantled the last of them years ago.

I'm not going to try to stop you. Go ahead and start slaughtering the whites. See how far you get."

"You're white, man. You're gonna be part of the massacre."

"We'll see about that . . . boy."

"Yeah," Leo said, his voice a jungle cat's rumble now. "We'll see."

His image faded and the screen went blank.

Garrison stared at the empty screen for a moment, then stabbed at the keyboard again. "Arlene," he called, "we go Tuesday."

"Tomorrow?"

"Is tomorrow Tuesday?"

"Yes."

"Then get with it! Tell Cobb, and tell him yourself. Speak directly to him. Tell him to have Cylinder B ready for us. Is my whole art collection ready to go?"

"Has been for a week."

"Send it now, tonight. And get word to the other Board members. We meet here tomorrow at noon and go straight to the colony; no stopover at Alpha or anywhere else. Whoever isn't here at noon will have to make his own arrangements."

"Some of the Board won't be able to get here by noon tomorrow," Arlene's voice answered. "Sheikh al-Hashimi is all the way over . . ."

"You tell him and the others to get their asses up to Island One tomorrow. The shit hits the fan Thursday!"

BOOK FOUR

November, 2008 A.D.

WORLD POPULATION:
7.33 BILLION

Mankind cannot afford to wait for change to occur spontaneously and fortunately. Rather, man must initiate on his own changes of necessary but tolerable magnitude in time to avert intolerable massive [and destructive] change. A strategy for such change can be evolved only in the spirit of truly global cooperation, shaped in free partnership by the world's diverse regional communities and guided by a rational master plan for long-term organized growth. All our computer simulations have shown quite clearly that this is the only sensible and feasible approach to avoid major repeated and untimely global catastrophes and that the time that can be wasted before developing a global world system is running out. *Clearly, the only alternatives are division and conflict, hate and destruction.*

—Mesarovic and Pestel,
Mankind at the Turning Point,
The Second Club of Rome Report,
Reader's Digest Press, 1974

• CHAPTER 28 •

As the airliner circled the gray-brown smog dome over New York City, David thought of the ironies of his past three months.

It had taken him a couple of days to travel the quarter-million-mile distances between Island One and the Moon, and from the Moon to Earth. But it had taken more than three months to cover slightly more than five thousand miles from Argentina to New York. And still he was an ocean away from his original destination.

He grinned to himself ruefully. *I was closer to Messina at Space Station Alpha than I am now.*

Traveling through the emptiness of space had been easy. But making headway on Earth, where David was a fugitive —that was very difficult.

Technically, he was also a prisoner. He stayed with Bahjat as she contacted a seemingly inexhaustible succession of PRU rebels. Most of them were as young as David and she herself, but a surprising number were older. One thing many of them had in common: they were poor. Penniless, most of them. Hungry, hollow-eyed, and angry.

They lied and stole, bartered for horses here and a boat there, forged credentials for the pair of them, shared their dingy homes and even darker hideouts—caves, cellars, church lofts, stables. They were all ready to help the renowned Scheherazade and her prisoner from Island One.

Some of the guerrillas were financially well off, enough to keep Bahjat supplied with enough money to survive.

"Why are they revolutionaries?" David would ask her. "What are they rebeling against?"

"They are like me," Bahjat would inevitably reply. "They fight against injustice."

David wondered.

He was hardly ever alone with her. But when he was, contrary to her chosen name, Scheherazade became a listener, not a talker. She got David to talk about himself, his life, his studies, about Island One. She would sit with him for hours—on a train, on the backs of pack mules, aboard a fisherman's blacked-out night-running boat—and listen to him talk, smiling encouragingly. David knew she was pumping him for information about Island One, but he didn't care. He also knew there was more to it. *She cares about me as an individual,* he thought. *I know she does.*

And he began to care about her.

It was a strange relationship that grew between them: friends, yet opponents; fugitives racing for a goal that neither of them fully comprehended, each hoping to find safety at the end of their journey; each afraid that safety for one meant mortal danger for the other. They lived together week after week, never out of each other's sight, caring for each other, helping each other, trusting each other with life itself—yet they were not lovers. They hadn't even kissed.

They seldom slept without others nearby, usually in the same room. And when they did—out on a hillside trail in Ecuador, in an abandoned gasoline station on a ghost highway in Mexico, in an alley near the docks of Galveston—they were too exhausted to see if their friendship could include physical lovemaking.

But it included something else, something that grew subtly between them. David knew that he could rely on Bahjat. And she knew that she could rely on him. They were partners. *Maybe that's more important than being lovers,* David thought. *It's certainly more unusual.*

They aimed for New York, on the telephoned instructions of the PRU leader she called Tiger. David didn't argue. There was a World Government headquarters in New York, near the site of the old United Nations building.

They had traveled by foot from the Indian village in the Peruvian Andes until a friendly truck driver picked them up. Once in a town with communications, Bahjat found PRU friends and helpers. They dyed David's blond hair and the shaggy beard that curled around his face. They darkened his skin. Now he and Bahjat looked like a young Latin American couple, at least superficially.

The two of them rode on horseback, on pack mules, in a stolen sailboat, in fishing smacks, on trains and buses, and even once in a stolen limousine. They went through Ecuador, by sea to Panama, across the crumbled and useless canal, through steaming jungles into Mexico, and finally—with forged credentials—past the heavily armed immigration and customs inspectors at the Rio Grande.

Through it all, David watched the people of Earth, his kinfolk, watched and learned.

He learned that hunger was not only painful, but it could affect the way you thought. It could teach you to hate.

In Panama he learned that World Government officials could be bribed; in Galveston he learned that agents of the multinational corporations couldn't be.

In New Orleans, David learned that he could trust no one, not even professed revolutionaries.

The leader of the PRU cell there was older than most, a broad-shouldered former longshoreman, over thirty, who mumbled about the battle that he was preparing for—an uprising that would involve not merely the whole city of New Orleans, but many other cities, as well.

His name was Brandy, and his face had been broken and scarred in hundreds of dockside fights. He drank hard, smoked continuously, and talked too much. But when he looked at Bahjat, David quickly noticed, he stopped talking and his face grew thoughtful, scheming.

After an all-night session of drinking, planning, and smoking, Brandy decided that he and his two closest aides would sell David to the Garrison Corporation. He calmly announced this to David as they sat in a smoke-filled, beer-smelling upstairs room over a street-corner church near the old quarter of New Orleans.

Brandy's two aides were in the room with Bahjat and David and their leader. They grinned at David's shocked surprise.

"We'll keep you with us," Brandy told Scheherazade. "We'll have a lot of fun with you."

With a strength David didn't realize was in him, he picked the closest man up off the floor and hurled him through the flimsy door that led to the stairs. It splintered and he went crashing down the steps. The second man lunged at David with a knife, but he never got close. David shattered his breastbone with a karate kick.

He whirled to deal with Brandy and saw that the leader was on his knees, doubled over and holding his crotch, vomiting with pain. Bahjat stood over him, tiny fists clenched, teeth bared.

Bahjat wanted to run then, but with newfound cunning David used the knife he picked up from the grimy floor to convince Brandy that he should phone a bank and set aside a sizable credit account for Mr. and Mrs. Able. As the point of the knife touched his eyelid, Brandy agreed.

Then they ran—as far as an all-night computerized bank terminal, where they had the entire amount of credit transferred to them as a cashier's check made out to cash.

Then they walked into the best hotel in New Orleans, registered as Señor and Señora Pizarro, and, with Bahjat speaking nothing but Spanish, were wafted up to their suite by a real, live, uniformed bellman.

The room clerk shook his head as they went to the elevator. *Another pair of scruffy-looking Spicks,* he grumbled to himself. *Where the hell do they get the money? I can't afford to stay here!*

The hotel room had two beds. David let Bahjat luxuriate in the shower as he paced the thick carpeting, wondering what to do about her. She came out with a towel wrapped modestly around her petite body. David showered very quickly, but by the time he came back into the bedroom, also towel-wrapped, she was already in the farther bed with her back turned to him.

He sat on the edge of her bed. Without turning toward him, Bahjat said, "Please, David . . . I know what you want. I can't . . . I just can't."

He sat on the edge of the bed for a long while, then got up, leaned over, kissed her bare shoulder, and went to the other bed. Despite his expectations, he fell asleep almost immediately.

The next morning, Mr. and Mrs. Pizarro bought a pair of airline tickets for New York, after Bahjat had a long phone conversation with Naples.

"Tiger is heading for New York," she told David. "We are to meet him there."

David nodded. Tiger was guiding her. They would meet in New York and she would turn David over to the PRU leader. *You don't make love with your prisoners, I guess,* he thought bitterly.

Evelyn sat in the sun on the balcony of her hotel room. Barbados was a beautiful island, rich with lush tropical greenery that climbed the rugged mountains and filled the air with an exotic, pungent scent. The sky was a flaming orange, the sea glittering in the high sun. Breakers softly rolled up onto the white sand beach off in the distance.

But the city surrounding the hotel festered like an open sore in the hot sun. Hollow-cheeked children played list-lessly in the streets and the rubble-strewn open lot across the street, where tourists had once parked their rental cars. There were no tourists now. The whole island was sinking into bottomless poverty. No jobs, except the pathetically few makework projects put in by the World Government. Plenty of hunger, though. And lots of babies. *Like Hamelin's rats,* Evelyn thought. *Babies everywhere.*

Gaunt-faced, bloat-bellied babies. Not one of them looked healthy.

With a toss of her head, Evelyn tried to dismiss the troubles of Barbados from her mind. *You've got the inside track on the biggest story of the century,* she reminded herself briefly. *This is no time to go squishy and senti-mental, old girl.*

Hamoud had been keeping in contact with Scheherazade through intermediaries. And David was with the PRU woman. They were leading everyone a merry chase. They had gotten as far as New Orleans, but that was the last Hamoud had heard from her. He was out now, trying to reestablish contact.

In the meantime, Evelyn was learning how the Peoples' Revolutionary Underground worked. Hamoud had not let her out of his sight for more than a few hours since he had picked her up at that bar in Naples months earlier. But this meant that *he* was constantly under Evelyn's scrutiny, too.

She had quickly discovered what he really wanted: fame. Notoriety. Publicity. He wanted the headlines that Scheherazade got. Now he had his own personal media specialist, his own publicist. And his own one-woman harem. Evelyn realized that his male ego could only really be satisfied in bed.

At least he's inventive, she thought, grimacing. *A few more weeks and I'll be able to start a new career—training call girls.*

Hamoud thought of himself as domineering, but Evelyn had learned long ago that the way to truly rule a male is to let him think you're totally submissive. So she gritted her teeth and gave him the anal pleasures he desired, and anything else, besides. She learned a lot about how to use furniture, especially chairs that were solid enough to hold their thrusting, contorting bodies. One thing she insisted on: cleanliness. They showered before they fucked— Evelyn couldn't think of what they did as lovemaking. Hamoud seemed to enjoy having her soap his body and make panting noises over his penis.

He talked in bed. Never very much. He was not a man given to many words. But Evelyn learned enough, bit by bit, to start to piece together the big picture of the PRU. Within a couple of weeks she had learned enough to decipher what he was saying over the phones, no matter how guardedly he spoke.

She wasn't surprised when she learned that much of the PRU's financing came from the multinational corporations. It made sense. Both the guerrillas and the big corporations wanted to pull down the World Government.

Digging deeper, she began to learn just which corporations were involved. The names were kept very secret, but Island One Corporation kept popping up, and more than once she heard names such as al-Hashimi and Garrison. *T. Hunter Garrison,* her reporter's memory told her, *of Garrison Enterprises.* And Wilbur St. Damnation George!

Stretched out on the recliner to let the Barbados sun soak her tired body, Evelyn still burned inwardly at the thought of St. George. No wonder he had fired her from International News. She had been sent to Island One to snoop on Cobb, she realized now, and had come back instead with a story that the Board would never allow to be published.

The door to the hotel room opened and clicked shut. Evelyn sat up in the recliner and saw Hamoud standing in the middle of the room, the usual scowl on his dark, brooding face.

She got to her feet and walked in from the balcony.

"That's a new swimsuit," he said.

"It's not for swimming; it's too fragile. Fall off in a minute."

He seemed unmoved. "Where did you get it?"

"In one of the shops. It was dirt-cheap."

"When?"

"A few days ago." Evelyn made herself smile. She shrugged out of the halter. "Do you like it better topless?"

Hamoud smiled tightly. "It's an improvement."

She pulled the briefs off her hips and stepped out of them. "You prefer nothing at all, don't you?"

"We don't have time," he said. "We are leaving inside of an hour."

"Oh? What's happened? Where are we going?"

He shook his head. "Too many questions."

Stepping close enough to him so that her nipples brushed his open shirt, she murmured, "We have *some* time, don't we?"

He laid his heavy hands on her hips. "No time for a shower."

Running a fingertip across his stubbly chin, she said, "But we could do it *in* the shower. It's very nice in there. You'd like it."

With a grunt, Hamoud slid an arm around her waist and headed for the bathroom.

As Evelyn bent to turn the taps in the tub, she asked, "Will my clothes be all right for where we're going? I don't have anything except a few summer frocks and such."

"You'll need a coat in New York. We'll get it there."

She frowned to herself. *So it's New York. That's where we'll meet them.* She had the answer she wanted. But now she still had to go through with the damned shower she had promised him.

Sitting comfortably in the airliner, wearing clothes that had been stolen in Mexico City and carrying I.D. cards that had been forged in Galveston, his beard neatly trimmed, his hair and skin dark, David sat back and waited for the plane to land. He was wolf-lean now, the easy sleekness of Island One burned away by months of hunger and danger. Wolf-alert, too. He had learned how to sleep lightly.

He thought for a moment of Evelyn. *She wanted me to see the real world,* he recalled, looking down at his brown-stained hands. They were toughened, calloused. *I wonder if she's seen half of what I have.*

Bahjat was sitting beside him, drowsing. She looked so fragile, vulnerable. Her long black hair cascaded over her slim shoulders. Her full lips were slightly parted.

But we're enemies, David reminded himself. *Once we get to New York she'll turn me over to her PRU friends. And I'll make a break for the World Government offices.*

Their months of closeness, of sharing mutual danger, sharing their lives and facing death together—all that was over. *That's why she didn't want to make love with me last night,* he told himself.

And that was why he did, he knew.

The plane finally touched down after a long delay of circling over the smog dome that hovered over New York. David shuffled along with the murmuring crowd exiting the airliner, with Bahjat directly behind him. She had warned him that other PRU people would be stationed inside the terminal building, watching him to make certain he didn't try to run away.

As they stepped out of the access tube and into the terminal building's gate area, David deliberately reached for Bahjat's hand. She let him hold it.

Except for the seventy-odd passengers from their own flight, David saw no other travelers walking through the littered, filthy terminal. A few planes were parked outside the cracked, grease-stained windows, but they seemed unattended, lifeless.

"I remember the old days," a passenger slightly ahead of David was loudly complaining. "Why, back then, this place'd be a madhouse the day before Thanksgiving. A regular madhouse!"

"It's nicer now," his diminutive wife said soothingly. "We don't have to fight the crowds."

They had no luggage, so they strolled out of the terminal building—still hand in hand—and across an empty roadway to a huge expanse of a parking lot. It was only half-filled, and many of the cars there were obvious wrecks: rusted, wheels gone, windows smashed in, hoods gaping open.

The sun was a squat red oval glowering impotently near the rooftops across the highway. It brought no warmth. The damp wind off the water cut through David's thin suit.

A wrinkled, gray-haired man stepped out from between parked cars and hailed Bahjat. They chatted briefly in Arabic. He led them to the farthest corner of the vast parking lot, where most of the cars seemed to be in working order. Bahjat let go of David's hand to follow him.

There were armed guards stationed around this part of the lot, David saw, and a brace of dark-faced young men standing beside a battered-looking, sand-brown four-door car. The old man ushered Bahjat into the rear seat of the car and held the door open for David. He stayed outside and waved cheerfully to them as the two youths got into the front seat and drove the car away.

"The driver knows where we're going?" David asked.

"Certainly," said Bahjat.

"Do you?"

"No," she admitted.

Their destination turned out to be an abandoned old building near a large park in Manhattan. David thought he could make out the outlines of letters on the building's facade; they spelled out PLAZA, he thought. They drove past the front, turned the corner, and parked at curbside.

Wordlessly, the two youths escorted Bahjat and David into the hotel through a side entrance. The windows were all boarded up, and the original doors had been replaced by slabs of dented metal. A legal notice of a public auction was pasted on one of the doors, its edges frayed and curled.

Inside, the lobby was bustling with people hustling purposefully back and forth. Voices hummed. Everyone seemed to be armed either with a pistol on the hip or a rifle slung over the shoulder. Men and women. Some had both pistol and rifle.

The hotel lobby smelled of mildew. The carpeting and draperies looked gray with years of dust. The few pieces of furniture left inside were covered with sooty sheets.

"What's going on here?" David asked. "It looks like an army headquarters."

"We just got here ourselves," one of the youths said.

"Shut up," said the other one, who had done the driving. "Don't answer questions . . . and you"—jabbing a thumb at David's chest—"don't ask."

They walked past a bank of elevators. Most of the doors were open and showed dark, empty shafts. Up the stairs they went, the two youths in the lead, David behind them, and Bahjat following him. The wide, carpeted staircase ended after two flights. They moved on to a set of clanging metal fire stairs built into a bare, echoing well of gray cement. There was just enough light from the sinking sun to let them pick their way around the garbage and broken junk that had accumulated on the stairs. David saw bugs scuttling in the refuse and wondered what else lived inside the ancient hotel's walls.

After six more flights, they moved into a corridor. It, too, smelled of mildew, and urine. The youths stopped before a pair of adjoining doors and handed Bahjat two keys.

"We have our people on this floor, and the Americans have the lower floors filled with their own troops. If he gives you any trouble, just shout."

Bahjat told them she understood, and they left.

"Something big is about to happen," David said as soon as they had closed the fire door behind them.

"Did you notice," Bahjat asked, "that all the men and women down in the lobby were blacks?"

"Not all of them," David said.

"There were some Latin types among them," she agreed, "but not one white."

David thought a moment. "You're right—not one white person among them. What do you think they're up to?"

"Whatever it is," Bahjat said as she unlocked one of the doors, "it will happen soon."

The two rooms were joined by a single door between them. They looked at both of them in the last sullen light of the sinking sun.

"Which room would you prefer?" Bahjat asked. "The red one or the blue one?"

The tattered decorations in each room were the same, except for their color. Each room had a large bed, a drawerless dresser, and a doorless closet. David pulled down the single sheet over the bed in the blue room; there was nothing beneath it but a bare mattress. He walked into the red room and saw that it had a cracked mirror over its dresser. In the blue room, a square patch of slightly cleaner wall showed where a mirror had once been.

He stood in the doorway that connected the two rooms. Bahjat was in the red one.

"I suppose," he said, "you ought to take the room with the mirror."

She smiled. "You are gracious, as always."

"And you are kind, as always."

She went into the bathroom of the red room.

"Ah," she called, "they have put in soap and tissues. Towels . . . even shaving things, for you."

"I'll take them back to my room."

She came out with a shaving kit in her hands. "But no makeup. Men never think of that."

"You use makeup?" David pretended surprise.

Bahjat grinned at him. "You've seen me without make-up."

"And you looked just as beautiful as you do when you're wearing it."

"And you look very handsome in your beard. Perhaps you should keep it."

He scratched at his chin. 'We're being gracious to each other, aren't we?"

"Yes." She looked up at him, almost shyly. "That was the first time you ever told me that you think I am beautiful."

"Really? All this time . . ."

"Yes," she said, "all this time."

"Well, you are beautiful, Bahjat, very beautiful."

"Thank you."

He didn't know what to say next. Then he heard himself asking, "What happens tomorrow?"

Bahjat gave a small shrug. "Either Tiger meets us here, or we go to wherever he is."

"And what are they going to do with me?"

"I don't know. It hasn't been decided."

"What will you do?"

Just a shake of her head. "Whatever I must."

"No matter what it is?"

"No matter what."

With a gesture toward the door that led into the corridor, "Are you going to lock me in?"

"Must I?"

"Doesn't make much difference," David said, walking slowly over to the bed in the blue room. "I can kick it down whenever I want to." He sat on the bed. It sagged and gave off a musty odor.

Bahjat went as far as the doorway between the two rooms and leaned tiredly against the jamb. "Don't talk foolishly. You can't escape."

"There's a World Government headquarters not too far from here," David said. "It's not Messina, but it'll do."

"I see," she said.

"You've known all along that I wanted to get to Messina," he said. "I haven't kept any secrets from you."

"Yes . . . but I had thought that . . . after being together all this time, after seeing all the hunger and injustice that we've seen together . . ."

"That I'd join your revolution?"

She nodded.

"Blow up bridges and shoot people? Rob banks and hijack space shuttles? What good does that do? It doesn't put any food on the tables of the poor."

"How can it?" Bahjat snapped. "After we overthrow the oppressors . . . after we have demolished the World Government, then . . ."

"When? All you'll have done is to destroy a form of government. You won't change the way people live. You won't open up any new gold mines. You won't have manna falling out of the skies."

"You understand nothing!" Her eyes were blazing.

"I know more than you think!" David shouted back at her. "All this nonsense with guns and killing, overthrowing governments. It's nonsense! It's worse than nonsense—it's playing right into the hands of the people you want to overthrow."

305

She advanced toward him, fists at her sides. "What do you know about it? All your life you've lived in a sheltered paradise, like some rare animal that's preened and petted and fed because it's too stupid to survive in the real world outside its cage."

He grabbed her and pulled her down on the bed beside him. She tried to knee him, but he took the blow on his hip and rolled his body on top of hers. He had her arms pinned on the musty bedclothes. She stared up at him. Her eyes showed no fright at all, nor anger.

He kissed her, covered her mouth with his, and let go of her arms and took her lovely, fragile, hauntingly beautiful face in both his hands and held her as if she were the most precious, most delicate, most wondrous treasure in the world.

Her hands slid over his shoulders and clutched at the tangle of his long hair. He could feel her breathing—hard, wracking gasps of sudden passion.

Their clothes disappeared as if by magic. He celebrated the lean, lithe suppleness of her naked body, her golden, tawny skin smooth and warm and yielding. He entered her effortlessly, two warm, glistening bodies joining, hearts racing, limbs thrashing, and suddenly he spasmed as her back arched and they pulsed together for a long, agonizing, ecstatic instant of flame.

They lay side by side, suddenly quiet, unmoving.

Then Bahjat giggled.

"What's funny?"

"I was wondering if you wanted me to lock you in your room."

He laughed and turned toward her. "I told you I could kick the door down."

"Can you kick down the door twice?" she asked.

"I can try."

This time it was slower, gentler, but the heat was the same, the passion stronger. David felt her hands on his body, her fingernails tracing light, delicate lines that sent shivers through him. He sucked at her nipples, then felt them rise as he felt himself rising, too.

"Not yet," she whispered. "Wait . . . just a . . ."

"Soon," he said, tracing lines of his own across her abdomen and down between her thighs. "Soon."

She uttered a long, keening sigh and he grasped her by the hips and pulled her onto him. She shuddered and convulsed as he closed his eyes and saw stars bursting everywhere.

They slept. When David awoke it was black night outside. He left the bed quietly, almost tripping over his own bunched-up clothing on the floor. He found the bathroom in the dark and then padded softly to the room's only window. The city was a blacked-out cemetery, silent and still. No streetlamps in sight, but there was a glow far off in the distance.

Everything closes down tight for the hours of darkness, David realized. *The streets are empty at night.*

He went back to the bed where Bahjat lay. *Dawn. I'll go at dawn.*

"My sultan has come back to me?" she whispered dreamily.

"I never left you," David said to her.

"But you will soon, won't you?"

"Yes."

"Then let us make good use of the few hours we have remaining."

The Moon slowly rose and threw a soft, sad light into the musty old room. For once, Bahjat was speaking, talking into the moonlit shadows, telling David of herself, her childhood, her mother's death, her father's stern love.

"He was like a hawk . . . an eagle," she said as she lay beside David, "proud and fierce, ready to tear to shreds anyone who threatened me."

"And he kept you in the eagle's nest," David said.

"Until he sent me to Europe," she replied. "He thought I would be safe there, with a chaperone and his own agents always watching me. But I fooled them all and became Scheherazade."

"He never knew?"

"He never acted as if he knew. But he knows now."

"And Hamoud, this Tiger you've been talking with—is that where you met him, in Europe?"

She laughed softly. "Hamoud had never been outside of Baghdad when I first met him. He thinks he is the fearless leader, but it has been my brain that directed him."

"But how did you become a revolutionary? How did it start?"

He felt her tense slightly. "It was a game, a daring game. There were exciting people in Europe . . . in Paris and Florence and Milan. Then I went to Rome and fell in love with a beautiful Italian. He was a revolutionary, a very wise and dashing older man. He must have been thirty, at least. His father had been a revolutionary, and his grandfather had been a Communist resisting the Fascists."

"So you became a revolutionary, too."

"Not because he was," Bahjat said. "I do not echo others just because they are men and I am merely a woman. My father would like me to behave that way, but I am not any man's ornament."

"Of course not."

"Giovanni taught me—he showed me how spoiled I was, how the poor lived in wretchedness. He opened my eyes."

"So you joined his battle."

"Yes. But it was still a game to me, a glorious game. I was Scheherazade. I *wanted* my father to find out about me, I think."

"It's not a game anymore, though."

"No, not anymore." And she told him about Dennis, about how the architect was murdered by her father . . . because of her.

"So now I will destroy everything of his that I can," she said, her voice as cold and hard as steel. "Everything."

"Including yourself?"

"That doesn't matter. I don't care."

"But I care," David said. Then he realized. "Last night . . . in New Orleans . . . you were thinking about the architect, weren't you?"

"Yes." Her voice was barely audible.

"You still love him?"

"Yes."

"But he's dead," David said. "You can't spend your

whole life among the dead. You belong with the living; you're much too wonderful to throw your life away."

She turned toward him and put a soft hand on his cheek. "You are a dear man, David. You don't belong here, in this blood and squalor. You should return to your Island One."

"Not without you."

For a long moment she didn't answer.

"Come back with me," he urged.

"You don't understand."

"Do you love Hamoud, then?" he asked.

"Heaven forbid!"

"Do you think," David asked, his throat going dry as the words formed themselves, "that you might love me?"

"I . . ." She hesitated, then fell silent.

"I love you, Bahjat. I love you with all my heart."

She was silent for so long that David wondered if he should have told her. *I do love her,* he marveled. *I've been a fool not to see it sooner.*

And then he realized that she was crying, sobbing quietly in the darkness.

"I'm sorry," he said quickly. "I didn't mean . . ."

"No," she answered. "I don't know why I'm crying. I shouldn't be such a weakling."

She slid her arms around his neck and clung to him. They made love again and fell asleep in each other's embrace. The sky outside paled to a silvery-gray. Dawn became full daylight and the sun climbed toward its zenith while they slept peacefully.

They were awakened by the sound of gunfire.

Memorandum
From: R. Pascual, Philadelphia Field
      Office
To: J. Collins, Director of Field
    Operations
Subject: PRU urban activities
Date: 26 November 2008

My recommendations for full alert
status of all field offices, and notifi-
cation of the National Guard of an
impending emergency, have been ignored
both by the Philadelphia Field Office
and by your assistants. I have strong
evidence that a general urban uprising
is being planned by PRU units all across
the Nation, timed to begin very soon.
After the Thanksgiving weekend, I re-
spectfully request a personal discussion
of this matter with you. It is of the
utmost urgency, I am certain.

• CHAPTER 29 •

It was the best gun Lacey had ever seen in his life. Sleek, deadly black gleaming metal, the stock fit into the curve of his hand as if it had been made specially for him. The short barrel ended in a blunt recoil suppressor. The banana-curved magazine clip held a full hundred rounds.

Chop down trees with this baby.

Lacey was sitting in the back of an old pickup truck waiting for noon to strike on the big insurance company clock a few blocks downtown. He grinned nervously at Fade and JoJo, sitting with him among the lettuce leaves and other scraps on the truck bed floor. The pickup was a rolling fruit and vegetable stand every day of the week. Except this day.

They were parked in front of the old, grim, stone-faced Armory. *Lots more guns in there*, Lacey remembered Leo telling them. *And trucks and armored cars, too.*

"When that fuckin' clock gonna ring?" JoJo grumbled.

None of the boys had a watch. Lacey had thought they should steal a few, to time their attack better, but Leo had said no. "No tipoffs, no chances. You get caught shoplifting' or muggin' you gonna miss all the fun."

Fade jittered nervously and licked his lips. "Maybe they got wise. Maybe they ain't gonna ring it."

"They'll ring," Lacey said, trying to sound disgusted with their fidgeting. "Don' worry 'bout it. They gonna ring and we're gonna start shootin'. Jes' keep your ass tight when those guys inside start shootin' back."

They hunched inside the pickup truck in silence. The

312

streets were empty outside. Quiet, except for the chilly wind blowing paper and trash along the cracked sidewalk.

"Won't be long now," Lacey promised.

"How we know the other guys where they supposed t' be?" JoJo demanded.

"We're here, ain't we? So they're there."

"You hope."

The first chime of the bell's noontime gong boomed out like the voice of God. For an instant the three youths froze. Lacey felt his mouth go dry.

Swallowing hard, he croaked, "Le's go!"

He led them out of the truck, jumping onto the pavement hard enough to shock his sneaker-shod feet. Without a backward glance he raced up the front steps of the Armory. He could hear Fade and JoJo clanking along behind him, ammo belts and grenades jouncing as they ran.

Take the front gate. That was their mission, their first objective.

The gate was a high iron grill. Beyond it, in dim shadow, was the entrance to the Armory building. No one stood at the gate. From all outward appearances, the Armory was empty and unguarded. But Lacey knew better. They might be asleep in there, but they were inside. Lots of National Guardsmen, on long-term duty as backup for the New York Police Department.

The gate was padlocked. Lacey skidded to a halt a few meters in front of it and fired a burst from his assault rifle. Inside the stonework arch the roar was deafening. Ricochets and chips of metal flew everywhere. Lacey felt something sting his cheek. But the chain parted and clattered to the ground. They pushed the gate inward on its rusty, creaking hinges.

"C'mon!"

Fade was through the gate first and he heaved a grenade at the inner door, a solid steel slab set into the stone facade. The concussion knocked all three of them to the ground, but as Lacey looked up he saw the door was sagging open. Turning, he saw a dozen more lean black kids racing toward them from across the avenue. Each of them had an assault rifle in his hands.

"Tol' you they was there!" Lacey yelled to JoJo.

They dashed inside the blown-open door and found themselves in a little entryway. A wooden partition had been set up on one side. A fat guy in Army khaki was down on all fours on the other side of the partition. *Musta been knocked groggy by th' blast,* Lacey thought.

Fade rounded the partition and squirted a burst at the Guardsman, point-blank. The bullets lifted him off the floor and slammed him against the stone wall, a bloody mess.

The other kids were pouring in now and running up the stairs to the barracks area where the Guardsmen slept. Lacey heard shots from up there and the muffled *crump* of a grenade.

Remembering the floor plan of the Armory that had been drilled into him, Lacey headed down the main corridor toward the right and kicked open the door to the Motor Pool garage. Once it had been an auditorium, and the neighborhood kids had played basketball in there, years earlier. Even before that it had housed a free tennis clinic for schoolkids. Now it held four rows of armored cars and trucks.

"Get th' side door," Lacey commanded.

JoJo sprinted off toward the big garage doors. Another team of kids waited on the street beyond it. They had no guns, there just weren't enough to go around, but they could drive the vehicles once they got inside.

A burst of machine-gun fire knocked JoJo off his feet. His body went skidding along the cement floor, suddenly slick with blood.

"Muthafucker!" Fade screamed at the Guardsman who had popped up from inside one of the armored cars.

Fade fired at him but the bullets whined harmlessly off the armor plate that protected the gunner, striking sparks as they hit. The gunner swung his twin-barreled machine guns around toward Fade, who ducked behind a truck as the heavy slugs started tearing up the concrete floor and slamming into the truck itself.

Lacey doubled over and half-ran, half-crawled between two rows of vehicles, moving off to one side of the armored car. When he got close enough he yanked a grenade off the belt slung around his thin shoulder and tossed it, just like sinking a basketball from midcourt.

The deadly black egg arched up and into the open hatch where the gunner was firing. Lacey could even see the startled look on his white face as the grenade clunked down at his feet. Then a shattering roar and a boiling billow of smoke.

Fade was trying to slap a new clip into his rifle, blubbering incoherently as he fumbled with it, his face streaming tears.

"Th' door!" Lacey yelled, heading back the way they had come in. "Get the fuckin' door!"

"JoJo . . ."

"Never mind! He's dead, man! Get th' door!"

Fade tottered off as Lacey planted himself at the corridor that led back to the main entrance. If the other guys were forced back downstairs by the Guardsmen up there, his job was to hold the garage until the drivers could get all the trucks and armored cars out.

Wasn't supposed to be no white-ass in those armored cars, Lacey raged to himself. *Sonofabitch musta been some kinda freak, workin' when he supposed to be upstairs.*

In his command headquarters in the basement of the Plaza, Leo followed the progress of his battle through a double row of seventy-two picturephones. Operators bent over each viewscreen, relaying orders or jotting down situation reports as they came in. Leo paced up and down the aisle between the phones, grabbing handsets to talk to his lieutenants whenever he thought it was needed.

It was going much better than he had hoped. The City had been caught completely asleep. All but two of the National Guard Armories were in their hands. Most of the police precinct stations had been taken or demolished. The Mayor's residence had been captured and then burned to the ground when the guerrillas realized that the Mayor and his wife were not there. No one knew where they were.

The complex of City buildings downtown was a tougher nut. Police headquarters was a fortress and the cops were fighting back. Somebody had been bright enough to send out radio calls for help. But, watching the phone screens intently, Leo saw that all the bridges and tunnels connecting Manhattan with the rest of the city were either blocked or held by his troops.

Okay, he thought. *We can hold Manhattan for a couple days. 'Til the food runs out. Then we split, let the Regular Army come in. Gonna be hell to pay when they do. Anybody with a black face is gonna get smeared. But they won't have much to come back to, that's for sure.*

He paced down the aisle, head swiveling to see all the picture screens. Scenes from hell were playing on each of them.

The Forty-Second Street Library was roaring with flames, fifty-foot-high sheets of fire flaring up from the shattered roof, smoke billowing black and thick. Somebody had blown the head off one of the stone lions in front of the Fifth Avenue entrance. The statue lay there headless, blackened, surrounded by a sea of stone fragments.

Crowds of stunned, panicked people ran through the streets, screaming, scrabbling, looking for a place of safety. There were none. Guerrillas shot it out with policemen and the National Guard on the sidewalks, in the streets, across the pathetic browning hillocks of Central Park. Black youths kicked in windows, burned buses, smashed furniture and threw it out of apartment house windows.

The World Government offices at the old UN Plaza were already gutted and smoking. Somebody had clobbered the place with Molotov cocktails.

In one or two spots blacks were shooting at other blacks. The street gangs that Leo had welded together into a single strike force were already coming apart, old grudges flaring into violence as the expected resistance from the whiteasses crumbled much earlier than they had thought it would. *They're gonna be unstoppable tonight,* Leo thought. *Wouldn't want to be a white broad tonight.* From their hotel window, David and Bahjat watched the brief flurry of fighting that broke out on Fifth Avenue. A lone police cruiser, its siren screaming, had careened up the Avenue, chased by four other cars. It swerved out of control, jumped the curb, and smashed into the corner of a store building. Two police officers staggered out of the wreck as the other cars pulled up onto the sidewalk around them. Nearly a dozen youths popped out of the cars. One threw something into the smashed police cruiser and it burst into flames. Both the policemen were knocked down by the blast, their clothing suddenly afire. The others formed a circle around them and watched them burn.

Bahjat put her hands over her ears. David pulled her close to him. Still she could hear the screams. And David could not take his eyes away from the scene.

I am not going to cry and I am not going to run, Karen Bradford told herself as she cradled her carbine and crouched behind the steel railing.

Indistinguishable from the other National Guard troopers in her olive drab fatigues and plastic helmet, Karen felt every nerve in her body winding up tight.

Waiting is the worst part, she told herself. *They warned up about that in training. The waiting is worse than anything else.*

Ten meters in front of her Joey DiNardo squatted, hunched over, peering out from under his helmet down along the length of the bridge.

He turned and grinned at her over his shoulder. "How ya doin', Blondie?"

"I'm okay. You just watch what you're supposed to watch," Karen snapped.

There were four women in the squad. Weekend soldiers. National Guard. They weren't even supposed to be working on the holidays. But the call came early in the afternoon and by two P.M. they were in uniform, in the trucks, and getting briefed by the sergeant about how the shit had hit the fan.

"We're holdin' Queens and fightin' for Brooklyn," the sarge told them. "Looks like they got Manhattan to themselves."

An on duty unit had counterattacked and taken the Fifty-Ninth Street Bridge away from the black rebels. Karen's unit was assigned to hold the bridge, because the Guardsmen who had taken it were too decimated from the bloody battle to hang on without help.

"Nobody moves over the bridge in either direction," the sergeant ordered, "unless it's Army or National Guard."

So now they crouched and waited tensely. Karen wished

she had something more than a carbine with a single clip of thirty rounds in it. Max and Gerry had the heavy machine gun. The sergeant kept the grenades in their locked crates inside the truck. *I'll tell ya when we need 'em,* he had growled. *Ain't none o' you fuckups gonna blow up the Queensboro Bridge 'less I tell ya to.*

Nothing was happening. They had heard a few shots earlier in the afternoon, seen some smoke. But now as Karen slid tiredly down and planted her slim rump on the cold cement paving, she could hear or see nothing unusual.

Except that the city was absolutely still. No cars on the bridge. The cablecar to Roosevelt Island wasn't moving from its terminal down on the street. No subway trains rumbling across the bridge. No traffic in the streets, not even pedestrians.

It was as if the city were empty. Row after row of massive, silent buildings, their windows staring out blindly. Like a big fairy castle that stretched on for miles.

Karen was staring down at the water of the East River, almost hypnotized into dozing by its endless steady flow, when DiNardo said, "They're up on the top level!"

"Keep it down," the sergeant snapped.

"But I can hear 'em up there! Somebody's drivin' a car up there! I can hear it!"

"There's a couple of squads on the upper level," the sergeant said. "You just worry about this level, shitface. Do your job and keep your mouth shut."

DiNardo shook his head unhappily.

An armored car came trundling up the access ramp onto the bridge's main roadway.

"That's what it was," Karen said. "That's what you heard." She grinned at DiNardo with relief.

It was a big, blocky, armored personnel carrier, with a turret-mounted set of twin machine guns up on the top. The driver's cab was armored all around, with only slits or electro-optical periscopes for him to see through. A big white five-pointed star was painted on top of the hood against the sandy-brown body paint.

The armored carrier pulled to a stop in front of the squad's parked truck. Karen could hear its brakes grind and the muffled whine of its turbine engine spin down into silence.

The sergeant got to his feet and walked over to the armored car. "What the fuck is goin' on? We been here . . ."

The blast from the twin machine guns cut him in half. Blood and flesh spattered Karen's face. She heard somebody screaming—herself—and every weapon in the squad went off.

Karen saw the twin machine guns slowly swing past her as bullets whined and zipped off the turret's armor. For an instant she was staring into their two hollow eyes. Then they swung past her and opened up on the truck. It exploded into flames.

Men were leaping out of the back of the armored car. Not soldiers, not Guards, but kids. Black kids. Firing automatic rifles and assault guns.

Joey DiNardo snapped back from the railing, a bloody punched-in hole where his face should have been. A grenade went off somewhere and Karen could hear the heavy machine gun behind her firing in rapid, jerky bursts. Sparks glanced off the armored car, but some of the black kids were flung off their feet like boneless dolls.

She couldn't see for the smoke and the tears. Her ears rang numbly. Her gun was empty; she realized she'd been holding the trigger down for some seconds, but nothing was happening. Ducking low, keeping the railing between herself and the twanging, buzzing bullets, she crawled back toward Max and Gerry.

Who were dead. The machine gun was a twisted wreck. Suddenly Karen realized the noise had stopped. She looked over her shoulder and a handful of wide-eyed kids were staring at her, smoking guns in their hands.

One of them snicked the bolt of his rifle back.

"Wait a min," said the skinny, pimply kid next to him. He was lighter than the others, Puerto Rican, maybe.

He stepped up to Karen and used the muzzle of his assault rifle to lift the helmet off her head. It clattered to the blood-streaked pavement and her yellow hair caught the sunlight.

"I tol' you she was a chick." He grinned.

Karen went for the knife in her boot, but they grabbed her, pinned her arms painfully back, and ripped the shirt off her in one swift, fierce, terrifying surge. She didn't start screaming until they spread her legs and slashed the pants from her hips.

Kiril Malekoff strode along the covered rampway that connected the fortieth level of the European wing of the World Government headquarters towers with the fortieth level of the African wing. Outside, beyond the heavily tinted glass that arched over the rampway, the brazen Sicilian sun bleached the city and hills bone-white. But inside the climate-controlled building the temperature was always crisply cool, the humidity efficiently low.

Malekoff paid no attention to temperature or humidity as he barged past startled secretaries and scurrying aides. But when he burst into Kowie Boweto's inner office, he suddenly felt oppressively hot and uncomfortable.

"How can you work in this swampy atmosphere?" he demanded, slamming the heavy wooden door shut behind him.

Boweto looked up from the viewscreen on his desk, where a startled secretary was trying to tell him that Malekoff was heading his way.

"How can you enjoy sub-freezing temperatures?" he countered. "And snow?"

"We do not enjoy them; we endure them." Malekoff plopped his lanky frame into a chair in front of Boweto's wide, impeccably clean mahogany desk.

Boweto leaned back in his zebra-skinned swivel chair. His broad, heavy-boned face showed neither annoyance nor surprise. "You are upset. The uprisings in America?"

"Of course! What else?"

"It's Williams' problem, not ours . . . not yet," Boweto said. "I believe the American Government has asked the Canadian Army for help."

"What about the Mexicans?"

Boweto shook his head. "The Yankees are afraid that their brown-skinned neighbors to the South would side with the rebels against the whites. No Mexicans. In fact, a large portion of the American Army has been rushed to reinforce their border with Mexico."

"While their cities burn to the ground! God!"

Shrugging, Boweto said, "Think of it as a unique experiment in urban redevelopment."

"How can you be so calm about it! What if this is the beginning of a worldwide PRU movement? What if such rebellions break out in Europe? Or Africa?"

"Surely you're not afraid that Soviet citizens will openly rebel against their government?" Boweto asked, smiling slightly.

Malekoff's shaggy red brows contracted. "It isn't totally beyond possibility. But it's Eastern Europe . . . Germany . . . suppose it breaks out there? It could start here, for God's sake—right here in Messina! This is all directed by the PRU against the World Government, you realize. Against us!"

"I know," Boweto said.

"And De Paolo sits on his bed, more dead than alive."

"Has anyone told him about this crisis?"

"I doubt it," Malekoff said gloomily. "They are all afraid of killing him."

"But if we must take action . . . if the crisis spreads beyond North America . . ."

"We'll be paralyzed. The Director must approve all inter-regional actions."

"We could appoint an Acting Director," Boweto said, poker-faced.

Malekoff threw his hands up. "Even *that* would have to be approved by the Director! We are hamstrung!"

Boweto said nothing for a long moment. Malekoff, fidgeting, rummaged through his pockets until he found a silver cigarette case and lighter.

"I didn't know you partook of the vice."

"Only in private," Malekoff said, puffing a long, light brown cigarette to life. He blew out a cloud of smoke. "And under extreme stress."

Boweto nodded sympathetically. "We shall have to tell him, no matter how great a shock it is to him."

"His staff won't let anyone near him," Malekoff said.

"We will have to force his staff to give way. The government of the world cannot remain hamstrung, as you put it, because of one sick old man."

"It *will* kill him, you know," Malekoff said.

Boweto shrugged.

Malekoff puffed furiously on his cigarette.

"Let me handle it," Boweto said at last.

The World Government promises a wonderful future in which all men are brothers. But the hungry people of the world cannot wait for tomorrow. They are starving today. Already the oppressed masses in the United States are rising to seize what is rightfully theirs.

Four-fifths of the world's people are hungry, sick, uneducated, without hope. They are desperate. They do not want a World Government. They want food, land, work. They are willing to fight for these elementary needs.

We do not need a World Government, a huge bureaucratic barrier that protects the rich from the poor. We need smaller governments, individual nations that are responsive to the cries of their people.

The poor of the United States are in arms. The poor of other nations will rise, also. If it takes bloodshed to break free of the World Government, so be it. The poor have nothing to lose.

> —*El Libertador,* televised speech
> broadcast worldwide by satellite,
> 27 November 2008

· CHAPTER 30 ·

Deep underground, more than a hundred meters below the crumbling old Pentagon's basement arcade, the real nerve center of the American military machine pulsed with intense electronic energy.

Since the advent of the World Government and the strategic disarmament that followed, no national military force possessed nuclear or biological weapons, nor lethal chemical weapons. Armies were reduced to border patrols and internal peace-keeping functions. War was outlawed and the means for waging mega-death wars had been confiscated by the World Government.

But this still left a panoply of weapons that would have gladdened the heart of any fighting man from Genghis Khan to George S. Patton: rifles, machine guns, cannons, tanks, pistols, bayonets, jet bombers, napalm, swift patrol boats, helicopters, tactical rocket launchers, armor-piercing heavy lasers, sonic janglers, strobe lights that could induce epileptic fits . . . a long, long list of weapons.

But the most useful, most necessary tool of the military was communications. Instant electronic links told the assembled generals and colonels (and the dazed, bemused admirals among them) what was happening and where.

The contiguous forty-eight states were spread out on a huge electronic map, winking with lights and coded situation reports. The map was so big that the tallest man in the underground Situation Center—a very junior colonel from Mississippi who had starred on the West Point basketball team—was no bigger than the yellow-glowing area that represented Los Angeles.

Much of the map glowed red, for danger. All the cities

of the Northeast, from Boston to Cincinnati, were in red. Chicago was completely dark; nobody knew what had happened there. Communications had ceased hours earlier. Even the "absolutely secure" satellite communications link had gone off the air.

"I told them," a one-star general kept muttering to the grim-faced men and women who scurried across the huge floor of the Situation Center. "My intelligence reports warned that this was coming. But they wouldn't pay any attention to me." Nobody was paying attention to him now.

Hawaii, Alaska, Samoa, and Puerto Rico were on smaller maps on another wall. The first three appeared trouble-free. The rebellion had not spread to any of them. But Puerto Rico had already been abandoned, earlier in the day, its garrison flown to New Jersey, the island left to fend for itself until order was restored on the mainland.

The situation was worst in the big old cities of the Northeast, although Los Angeles was a tangle of conflicting reports and St. Louis, Denver, Atlanta, and Houston were all in flames. Phoenix had been overrun by an avalanche of howling mobs that had wiped out the retirement centers inside of an hour or two. Dallas-Fort Worth was holding its own, with the Texas Rangers—reinforced by the heavily armed local citizenry—counterattacking street by street.

Miami was strangely quiet, as was a good deal of the South.

"Damned niggers control the cities there, anyway," said one of the admirals, who had nothing to do except watch the progress of the land battles.

"Yeah, and they'll take in the refugees who get away from the cities under attack," said the colonel from Intelligence. "The blacks will take care of their own. We'll have a reverse Underground Railroad running a couple of days from now."

Some cities seemed totally free of disturbances. Minneapolis reported nearly total calm, except for a few skirmishes near the airport. An unexpected early autumn blizzard might have saved the entire upper tier of Midwestern states. San Francisco was unaffected, also, except for a peaceful rally—spontaneous, its organizers claimed—to show support for the embattled minority groups around the nation.

But Boston, New York, Philadelphia, Detroit, Cleveland, Pittsburgh, Indianapolis—all the dying, decaying, old industrial cities—were the scene of heavy fighting. Washington itself was under siege, although soldiers and marines from the bases that ringed the nation's capital were now counterattacking and clearing the streets. Too late to save the White House from its second burning; too late to prevent the murders of most of the Congressmen and Senators who had remained in town for the holiday. But the military situation in Washington was definitely improving.

"New York is the key," said the Chief of the Combined Staffs, a four-star general who wore all his ribbons on his tunic every day. It was no different now. While others scurried about the Situation Center in shirtsleeves (even rolled-up shirtsleeves!), the Chief kept his tunic buttoned properly and his sleeves creased.

"Remember your textbooks, gentlemen?" The Chief smiled grimly at the ashen-faced generals and colonels. "Remember how Marshal Zhukov let the Germans grind themselves to a bloody stump in the streets of Stalingrad while he built up his forces for a massive counterattack outside the city? How he surrounded von Paulitz's army and annihilated it? Well, that's what we're going to do with New York."

"But, sir . . . that would take a couple of days, wouldn't it? The rebels could kill a lot of innocent citizens in the city by then."

"This is war, man!" the Chief boomed. "We're not here to ransom hostages."

"Maybe we could do something, though," suggested an Air Force general. "Smother the city with gas, rattle them with nerve janglers. Tactical Air Command could hit them, show the citizens of the city that we haven't abandoned them, give the rebels enough grief to prevent a general bloodbath during the night."

The Chief shrugged. "See what you can do about it," he said, an odd little smile playing across his lips. "Perhaps it's a good idea to keep the enemy off balance during the night. In the meantime, we'll be pulling a noose of men and armor around New York City."

The Air Force general was already on the phone, sending out orders in an urgent whisper.

"I want those rebels in the palm of my hand," the Chief of the Combined Staffs was saying. "I want to sew them up in a trap so tight that none of them can escape. None of them!" He held out his hand and slowly squeezed the fingers together into a white-knuckled fist.

"What about the other cities, sir?"

"Local forces will have to take care of them. The Canadians are already sending troops across the border. Let them tackle Chicago; that'll be enough action for them. If the locals can't handle their own problems, let them appeal to the World Government for help. But we, gentlemen, are going to recapture New York without anybody else's help. Just we few. We precious few."

He lifted his face to the map and smiled.

"Go check on the Holland Tunnel, I said." Leo's face in the tiny phonescreen seemed tense, angry, weary.

Lacey was sitting at a phone desk on the balcony level of Grand Central Station. The wide expanse of the station's main floor, where the flea market was usually open for business twenty-four hours a day, was packed with scared, shocked, homeless people. Black and white and brown, men and women and children, the station's main floor was wall-to-wall huddled humanity.

"Hey, man," Lacey complained, "I just come up here from downtown. Now I gotta go back? I'm tired, man. Been heavy all damn' day."

"You see me restin'?" Leo snapped. "We all tired, monkey. But we still got work t'do."

"Shit."

"Yeah, I know." Leo's stern expression softened a bit. "You want some fun. Lotta cunts out there waitin' for the conquerin' hero. Well, go check out the tunnel for me. Make sure they can hold it if the white-asses try comin'

327

back that way durin' the night. Then you can go fuck anything that moves, far's I care."

Lacey grinned. "Now you talkin'!"

With the darkness came the screams. David and Bahjat heard them, screams of pain and terror that seemed to echo up and down the streets of the concrete canyons near their hotel room. They strained to see what was happening, but the shadows beyond their window obscured everything except an occasional running figure.

"The spoils of battle," David muttered.

Bahjat said nothing.

"Look," he told her, "if you think you'll be safer here with your comrades, then you can stay. But I've got to go. And I want you to come with me."

She shook her head. "Not unless you know where you are going and how to get there."

"You'll take your chances here?"

"Yes."

He went to the door and actually grasped the tarnished, grime-slickened knob. Then he turned back.

"The hell, you're staying here. You're coming with me, whether you like it or not."

Bahjat's eyes widened. "You speak as if I were your prisoner."

"No. But you're coming with me. I'm not going to leave you alone here." He stepped toward her.

Bahjat pulled a flat little pistol from the shoulderbag that rested on the dusty night table beside the bed.

"You won't use that gun on me," David said, advancing to within a hand's span of her. "And I can't let you stay here with these madmen. It's too dangerous."

"I won't go with you."

He reached out and took the gun from her hand and tucked it into his belt. Then he grabbed her by the shoulders, kissed her soundly, and lifted her off her feet.

"I've carried you before; I can do it again."

"Put me down!" Bahjat said, struggling against him.

Instead, he hoisted her over his shoulder, fireman-style. "Listen to me, woman. I'm bigger and much stronger than you . . . and more stubborn, too."

"You'll never get anywhere carrying me like a load of straw!" Bahjat started to laugh, despite herself. "Don't be so silly."

"You're coming with me," David said, heading for the door, "either on your feet, or as a load of straw. Take your pick."

"Put me down!"

"You'll come with me?"

"Yes."

He slid her off his shoulder and stood her on her feet. "You mean it?"

Bahjat eyed him for a silent moment. Then another scream split the night, definitely a woman's scream. She shuddered.

"If they catch us . . ."

"It's better than sitting here waiting for them."

"You're wrong."

"I can't stay here and do nothing," David said.

With the tiniest shake of her head, she said, "Well, come on, then."

They crept into the darkened hallway and groped down the stairs toward the light of the hotel's lobby. Scores of people were there, they saw from the stairs: young men and women with guns slung over their shoulders, slumped on the floor in weary clumps, talking low and earnestly. Bodies were laid out in neat rows across the far end of the lobby. The smell of tobacco, sweat, marijuana, and fear hung in the misty air.

But David saw something else.

"Look," he whispered to Bahjat as they huddled on the shadowy stairs, "up there on the mezzanine. Isn't that a phone desk?"

She nodded silently.

"I wonder if it's still working."

"Are you going to call for a taxicab?" she whispered.

Wordlessly, David got to his feet and headed up the half flight of stairs toward the mezzanine. Bahjat walked at his side.

It's okay, he told himself. *Nobody's paying any attention to us. We're both brown enough to pass muster. Be-*

329

sides, she's the famous Scheherazade—one of them, one of their heroes. Still his knees shook.

The phone did work and David quickly made contact with the automated computerized services directory. While Bahjat stood at the mezzanine's rail and watched the staircase and lobby, David scanned the city's maps for some open route of escape: streets, subway tubes, sewers, utility tunnels.

That's it! he realized as the map of the various utility tunnels appeared on the phone's compact screen. He asked the computer for a close-up of the Fifth Avenue and Central Park South area. The computer—accustomed for years to accepting commands in oral English or Spanish from a populace that was largely illiterate—obliged with electronic speed and precision.

Within minutes David had all the information he needed. He clicked off the phone and went to Bahjat.

"All right. I know how to get out of here and where to go."

She arched a questioning eyebrow.

"There's a marina full of small boats out on the Hudson River, west of here. We can get to them underground, through the telephone cable tunnels."

"The boats have probably been destroyed," Bahjat said.

"Maybe, but even if they have been, we can still find a place to hide for a couple of days. And I'm betting that we'll find more than one boat in sailable condition."

It took hours.

The tunnels had originally been designed to walk through. They had been built large enough for a telephone repairman to stand up inside them and work on the long, snaking cables that carried the city's phone messages. But over the decades more and more lines had been laid in the tunnels, leaving less and less space available for human beings.

David held a flashlight in one hand as he wormed his way through the narrow confines of the tunnel. The cables that rubbed against his back and hung a bare centimeter in front of his eyes were coated with greasy dust, the accumulation of year after year of neglect.

He squeezed through an especially tight place and turned to shine the flashlight back on Bahjat. She squirmed past the knot of sagging cables more easily, but still her face was smeared, her dress blackened with grime.

"Are you certain this is the right direction?" she asked, pausing to catch her breath.

David nodded. "From what the computer maps showed, we ought to be pretty close to the river by now."

The computer had shown neat blue lines on its map, not this black, greasy, foul-smelling tunnel they were in. It had also claimed that there were color-coded directional arrows painted onto the tunnel walls every fifty meters. But the thick layers of grime that caked everything covered up the arrows completely.

"This way," David said, staying in the main tunnel and ignoring a branching one that headed off to their right.

Bahjat followed him.

The flashlight he held in his hand cast a feeble pool of illumination out to a few meters ahead of them. In its reflected light he could see Bahjat's dirt-streaked face close behind him.

"Not the easiest way we've ever traveled, is it?" David asked.

She didn't smile. "It's better than being on the streets."

"Yeah."

Suddenly she clutched at his arm. "I hear something . . . behind us."

David halted. He was stooped over almost double because the cables were strung overhead in this part of the tunnel, making the ceiling claustrophobically low.

A scrabbling sound, from down the tunnel.

"Someone following us?" he whispered.

"Turn off the flashlight."

David clicked it off. The darkness covered them smotheringly. He could feel a dampness, a wet, sour chill that seeped through the tunnel walls. *We must be close to the river.*

The scratching, chittering sound drew closer to them. David couldn't tell if it was coming from behind them or from ahead—or both.

Bahjat screamed. David flicked on the flashlight and

the tunnel was alive with a flurry of gray-brown fur screeching, clattering away in both directions to get out of the sudden glare of the light.

"Rats!" Bahjat gasped, clinging to David.

"The tunnel's full of them."

He could see their red, shining eyes glaring at them from just outside the pale circle of light cast by the flashlight.

"They're ahead of us, too," Bahjat said, her voice high-pitched, shaky.

"But they're afraid of the light."

"For how long?"

"Come on," he said. "There's no point in standing still for them."

He pulled her forward. Shining the flashlight ahead of them, he saw a nearly solid mass of reeking fur break up into hundreds, maybe thousands, of screeching rats. He swung the light back behind him, past Bahjat's terrified face, and another horde of them skittered back into the darkness.

They pushed ahead, a tiny island of light in a dark sea studded with baleful red eyes that inched closer and closer with each step.

The flashlight's getting weaker, David thought. *No,* he told himself, *it's my imagination.* Still he drew the pistol from his belt.

"How much farther must we go?" Bahjat asked.

David considered for half a moment. "We'll take the next ladder up. That ought to be close enough to the river."

The light was definitely weakening. David could see the eyes glaring out of the darkness that was growing tighter and closer around them, hear the rats' chittering, scratching. They were coming closer, getting bolder.

He saw a ladder rising up into the darkness overhead. It was filthy and slippery with slime, but it looked wonderful to them both. Shining the feeble light up its length, David saw that it was going to be a long climb to the street.

Something brushed against his ankle and he jumped backward, bumping into Bahjat, nearly dropping the flashlight.

"Sorry," he mumbled.

Bahjat put a hand on a rung of the ladder.

"Here, take the light with you," David said. "Shine it up ahead so you don't get any unpleasant surprises while you're climbing."

"But you . . ."

"Do it," he said, putting the flashlight into her hand. "I'll be right behind you."

Bahjat's lips were a tight, frightened, bloodless line. She took the light and started up the ladder. David hefted the gun in one hand. Then he grabbed the slippery metal rung and started up after Bahjat.

He looked down into a galaxy of seething red eyes. Slipping the gun into a pocket, he climbed with both hands and stayed right behind Bahjat.

He had to squirm past her when they got to the manhole lid at the top of the ladder. She held the light as he pushed and strained and finally nudged the heavy iron lid up and onto the paving of the street. A few more heaves and he had it slid back far enough for the two of them to squeeze out.

The night air felt good on his face. David took a deep lungful and only then noticed that it was rank with sewage. Between a pair of dilapidated, fire-charred, roofless warehouses he could see the Hudson River sliding by in the waning moonlight, looking oily and rancid and somehow darkly menacing.

I wouldn't want to swim in that, he knew.

Together they picked their way past the rubble that was heaped between the warehouses. Not one window in either building had a shard of glass left in it. The glass was all on the ground, together with garbage, junk, broken machinery, and bones. David saw something the size of a terrier flit from shadow to shadow. *More rats.*

Across the river, the Jersey Palisades were dark. From the water's edge, David looked up and down for some sign of life in the dockside area. Nothing. No lights. No sounds, except the insistent lapping of the water against rotting piers. Everything was still. The night was clear, except for smoke wafting from fires farther downtown.

"Are those the boats?" Bahjat whispered, pointing.

David saw a half-dozen rotting old hulks tied to a pier a few hundred meters down the riverfront from where they stood. Most of them seemed to be settled on the muddy bottom, with just their cabins and masts above the water.

But that one at the end of the pier ...

"Come on," he said, taking Bahjat by the hand. They ran along the crumbling pavement at the water's edge and out along the sagging, creaking dock.

The boat at the end of the pier was an old cabin cruiser. It floated with stately dignity in the bobbing waves of the river. David thought that the heavy-looking bulk under a tarpaulin at the rear of the boat must be a motor.

He stepped down from the pier onto the boat's deck, then turned and held Bahjat's hand as she hopped lightly aboard. The boat swayed in its mooring.

"Do you know how to run a boat like this?" Bahjat asked.

"No," David realized. "I didn't think ..."

Smiling, she said, "It's all right. I can do it."

She led him to the cockpit and started peering at the switches on the paneling alongside the tiny spoked steering wheel.

Suddenly the hatch to the cabin below banged open and the biggest man David had ever seen loomed up in front of them. He was huge, a black mountain of a man with hands the size of footballs.

"What the fuck you doin' on my boat?" Leo roared.

We were at the training center when the fighting broke out in Houston. There were only eleven of us left in the class out of a starting number of sixty.

The training center—the old Johnson complex from back in the days of NASA—wasn't being threatened by the guerrillas. But with fighting going on both in Houston and Galveston, the Corporate officials decided to get us up to Space Station Alpha as quickly as possible.

They didn't give us any choice in the matter. All of a sudden, it was military discipline. The eleven of us were marched out to a waiting shuttle on the airfield and bundled inside. We could see smoke smudging the horizon off in the direction of Houston.

They buttoned us up and off we went, just like that. I sat beside Ruth, at least. Everybody wondered what was happening, and if there was fighting going on back home.

—The journal of William Palmquist

· CHAPTER 31 ·

Emanuel De Paolo's bedroom had been turned into a
cardiac intensive-care unit. It had always been an austere
monk's cell of a room. De Paolo was not a man of pomp
or personal aggrandizement. Now the writing desk bore a
gray metal box of electronics with an oscilloscope screen
in its middle that faithfully traced out the weakened heart-
beats of the World Government's Director. More electronic
consoles blocked out the room's only window. The bed
itself was surrounded with life-support mechanisms, monitors, bottles, and tubes that entered the gray-faced old
man's body.

The Ethiopian stood at the doorway, afraid to go any
farther. The only sounds in the room were the hum of
electronics and the chugging of the little electric motor
that powered the auxiliary blood pump the surgeons had
implanted inside the Director's lower aorta.

De Paolo had responded to none of their treatments.

"He's an old man," they said to each other, quietly,
out of range of their patient's possible hearing.

"What can we expect?" It was a funeral notice.

Boweto had demanded to be allowed in to speak to the
Director. Line by line, the burly African had crumpled the
defenses that De Paolo's staff had thrown around their
chief. Boweto had gotten as far as the Director's personal
residency suite. There the Ethiopian—the last line of de-
fense—had stopped him. Nothing that Boweto could offer
or threaten would budge the Ethiopian: not the urgency
of the situation, the need for immediate decision, Boweto's

importance in the Council, the future of the Ethiopian's career. Nothing. The Ethiopian was immovable.

But the Director had to be told. That much was clear. So the Ethiopian himself reluctantly agreed to carry the news.

He held an official order in his right hand. It required De Paolo's signature. It would be the old man's death warrant, the Ethiopian knew.

De Paolo's eyelids fluttered open as his aide slowly approached the bed.

"I was sleeping," the Director said, "dreaming . . . of my parents." His voice was a fading whisper. "I haven't thought of them in years . . . decades . . ."

The Ethiopian stood uncertainly by the bed.

De Paolo asked, "What time of day is it?"

"Early in the morning, sir," he whispered back, "just past dawn."

De Paolo's eyes flickered with their old intensity for a moment. "You have been up all night, haven't you? What is happening? What's wrong?"

The oscilloscope across the narrow room showed his heartbeat quickening, the peaks spiking where they should be smoothly rounded.

"A rebellion," the aide whispered. "The Peoples' Revolutionary Underground."

"Where?"

"In America . . . most of the major cities."

"Open fighting?"

Nodding, "Yes. Fighting in the streets. The American Government can't handle the situation alone. There have even been reports of mutiny within the American Army's ranks."

"Santa Maria!"

"We must be prepared to act. . . . The Council has drafted an order authorizing the World Army to intervene. It requires your signature."

"Have the Americans asked for our help?"

The monitoring equipment screeched out a high-pitched electronic whistle. De Paolo's pulse, breathing, heart rate were all moving into dangerously high areas. The auxiliary pump inside him was beating away at maximum.

"Not yet," the aide replied. "They have asked for help from the Canadians, but they have not yet requested anything from the World Government."

De Paolo was beginning to gasp. The door to the bedroom was flung open by an angry-looking woman doctor.

"The Council wants standby authority for intervention," the aide said.

The doctor bustled a few steps into the room, but De Paolo raised a frail hand to halt her. "In a moment, *señora*. In a moment."

"A moment may be too late," she snapped.

Ignoring her, De Paolo asked his aide, "Who on the Council wants my authority?"

"Boweto. Malekoff and Liu are supporting him."

"And Williams, the American?"

"He disagrees."

"Of course. No one wants foreign troops on their own soil, no matter what their problems are."

Now comes the difficult part, the aide thought. "Sir, I'm afraid that I must agree with Boweto and the others. The Council must have the authority to act, even though you are incapacitated."

De Paolo's face contorted in a spasm of pain. "Or . . . dead?" he gasped.

The doctor made a rush toward him. The Ethiopian could not trust his voice. Tears blurred his eyes.

"You are right, my son, as usual," De Paolo said as the doctor pressed a hypodermic spraygun to his emaciated arm. "Give me the document."

It was clipped to a writing board. The Ethiopian took the pen from the board and placed it in De Paolo's free hand. The old man signed in a wavering, weak scrawl, then let his head sink back on the foam pillow.

"It is finished," he whispered. He closed his eyes. The monitors all began to keen a funeral dirge.

The doctor pushed the Ethiopian away from the bed and yelled into the communicator built into the wall, "Resuscitation team! Quick!"

Knowing that it was all pointless, the aide walked out of the bedroom with the signed document on the clipboard weighing down his arm. In the little library adjoining the bedroom, the resuscitation team raced past him, wheeling their useless machinery at a breakneck pace.

The aide entered the sitting room, where early morning sunlight streamed in on Boweto and several of the Director's inner staff people.

"Here," he said, handing the signed authorization to Boweto.

One of the women, her face reflecting the agony the Ethiopian felt, asked, "Is he . . . did . . ."

"He has died," the Ethiopian said. Turning to Boweto, who was trying to make himself look sympathetic, he added, "The Council will have to elect a new Director . . . and approve a new staff for him."

Without another word he walked across the sitting room and stepped out onto the balcony. Behind him he could hear sobbing, not just from the women. Fifty floors below the city was beginning to awaken, to begin a new day.

His own eyes blurred again. With a final, deep breath of the clear, wine-sweet Sicilian air, the aide swung a long leg over the balcony's parapet and let himself drop into eternity.

"Here they come again."

Lacey almost laughed. The Holland Tunnel was starting to smell like a garbage dump. Bodies were heaped all over the place. White-asses, mostly. All night long the dudes from Jersey had been trying to push their way through the tunnel and get back into Manhattan. All they had done was get themselves slaughtered.

Lacey and his handful of blacks were holding the Manhattan end of the tunnel, at the entrance. They had set up a barricade of overturned cars and trucks and placed their machine guns and automatic rifles behind the barricade.

The white-asses had come at them in bits and pieces. Civilians, mostly. Some National Guard, in their green uniforms and helmets. They came in cars; a few times they tried ramming the barricade with trucks. All they did was make the barricade bigger, heavier, harder to get past.

Standing between a pair of overturned cars, Lacey looked back over his shoulder at the silent, moonlit night out in the Manhattan streets. He had sent a team of younger kids out to hunt down some ammo so they'd be set if the Jersey white-asses tried again. They'd been out for more than an hour now.

Since then, it had all been quiet. Until now.

"Here they come again."

Lacey could hear the rumbling, clinking noise of slow-moving trucks coming through the tunnel.

He didn't notice the faint, faint whisper of very high-flying jet bombers. In the moonlight, their contrails left beautiful fine white lines scratched across the cloudless sky.

"Mutha-fuck! Looka that!"

The white-asses were coming at them with huge orange-painted snowplows, bulldozers, earth-movers, one after another. Lacey saw the first two, so big that they could barely inch through the tunnel side by side. Behind them were more. Like army tanks. Their massive, thick steel scraper plates jutted out ahead of them like a boxer's probing fist. The first volley of gunfire spattered harmlessly off their shields.

They seemed to be aiming straight at Lacey. He swallowed hard and yelled, "Save the ammo! Get up on th' walkway an' hit 'em from the side!"

The tunnel rang with gunfire. The acrid smell of cordite burned in his nostrils. Lacey saw there were soldiers lying on top of the 'dozer cabs, firing back at them. A pair of kids sprinted out onto the walkway where bored Port Authority cops used to watch cars speeding through the tunnel. They picked off one of the soldiers and threw a brace of Molotov cocktails at the nearest 'dozer.

Flaming naphtha spread over the bulldozer's cab. Lacey could hear the driver's screams pitched high over the echoing shooting. But the 'dozer kept coming, flames and all.

It crashed into the barricade just as the snowplow alongside it hit the other end of the piled-up trucks and cars. Everything started sliding slowly backward.

"Get back!" Lacey yelled. "Get th' drivers! Th' drivers!"

Kids were being crushed, trapped between the screeching, grinding, slowly moving tangle of vehicles. Lacey blazed away with his automatic rifle, firing from the hip as he backpedaled. It seemed to have no effect at all. The entire monstrous wall of cars and trucks was sliding down on him.

High overhead, the bombers circled the city once and then began to release their dead-black canisters. The metal eggs fell to a predetermined height, then burst in flares of pyrotechnics and sprayed millions of tiny golden slivers that showered downward over Manhattan. Their bomb-bays emptied, the bombers wheeled in perfect formation and headed back toward their bases.

The golden slivers drizzled down out of the clear sky. They coated streets and rooftops, awnings and empty lots, shattered cars, bombed-out buildings, dead bodies lying on the sidewalks. For almost a minute they lay quiescent, a golden powder that glittered in the pale moonlight.

Then each sliver began its programmed reactions. Most of them simply hissed out noxious gases that reacted with the tissues in the human nasal passages to induce severe nausea and dizziness. Other slivers were micro-miniaturized electronic transmitters that broadcast very low-frequency waves that interfered with the electrical impulses of the human nervous system. Anyone within fifty meters of such a nerve jangler would most likely go into a spastic imitation of an epileptic fit. Test subjects had bitten off their tongues and snapped their own bones in convulsions. A few had strangled and several had suffered permanent brain damage.

Lacey and his gang gave way before the inexorable push of the bulldozers and snowplows. The whole makeshift barricade was lifted, shoved, screeching, grinding, groaning up and out of the tunnel's mouth. The youthful blacks scattered as the bulldozers and snowplows began rolling out of the tunnel. But they didn't run far.

Fanning out into an arc, they dropped to their knees or flopped prone on the pavement and began peppering the juggernauts with high-velocity rifle fire that easily shattered windows and killed the drivers. Soldiers riding on top of the cabs or behind them became easy targets for crossfire. The line of tractors started to waver. One after the other, they stumbled out into the plaza and either crashed into buildings or ground to hissing, groaning halts.

The men on foot behind the tractors were firing back, though. They had shotguns, ancient Tommyguns, rifles, pistols—anything they could lay their hands on.

And in the middle of the firefight it started to snow. *Snow?* Lacey wondered as golden slivers filtered slowly down out of the clear sky.

An instant later the plaza was seething with grayish-yellow gas puffing up from the ground, from the tops of cars, from the cabs of the 'dozers. Men were suddenly snapping and jerking like rabid dogs, their guns forgotten, coughing and choking, limbs cracking, bodies spasming.

Lacey wanted to vomit. Everything was going bleary, dizzy. He sank to his knees. *Gotta fight it off!* he screamed at himself. *Got to!* He groped for his assault rifle, gripped it hard. Whatever was making most of the others jerk around like rag dolls wasn't hitting him. He just felt sick, bad in the gut, woozy. He looked around, cold sweat beading his forehead.

Almost everybody else was down. The battle was over. Just about everybody was acting either sick or crazy. There were only a couple of . . .

"Hey, nigger!"

Lacey stumbled as he turned. But as he went down he saw the twin muzzles of a double-barreled shotgun staring at him. He even saw the flash deep inside the barrels as the triggers were pulled.

It was the last thing Lacey ever saw.

"What the fuck you doin' on my boat?" Leo roared.

David yanked the pistol from his pocket and pointed it at the huge black man. It felt foolishly small in his hand.

"We're trying to get away," David said.

"Not on this boat, you don't." Leo took a menacing step toward David. He was so big that he had to crouch to avoid hitting his head on the canvas top that covered the boat's cockpit.

"Wait!' Bahjat snapped. "You are Leo, the head of the PRU unit here in New York."

Leo turned his massive head slightly and looked down at her. "Yeah. Who're you?"

"Scheherazade."

In the darkness it was impossible to read the expression on the black man's face. But his voice softened.

"Scheherazade? You supposed to be at the Plaza. Why didn't you stay there? My people would've taken care of you."

"She's my prisoner," David said. "And so are you."

Leo laughed, a bubbling chuckle that quickly grew into a head-tossing roar. "I'm your prisoner? Yeah? 'Cause you got that little popgun in your hand? Man, you could shoot that thing at me all night and it wouldn't do no good."

"Don't try to bluff me," David said.

Leo's laughter subsided. "Okay. No bluff. But what you gonna do about the two dudes back there who got their guns pointin' at you?"

David glanced quickly over his shoulder and, sure enough, two wiry black youths were pointing rifles at his head.

With a reluctant sigh, David handed the pistol over to Bahjat. "I guess I'm your prisoner again," he said.

"I guess you are." She turned to Leo. "Why are you here instead of at your headquarters? Are you leaving?"

"Got my escape route all planned out," Leo said. "Nice little laboratory upstate a ways. Right on the river. Nobody'd look for PRU guerrillas there."

"When do you leave?"

Leo shrugged massively. "When the white-asses make their counterattack. We can't hold out against the Army; I know that. When they make their move, I make mine."

"You're going to leave your people here to fight and die while you run away?" David asked.

"Damn' right. We can always get more troops. That's easy. But you gotta protect the leaders. Can't replace them."

"But . . ." David spread his arms and gestured at the blacked-out city. "What was the point of all this? The killing, the terror, the destruction . . . what was the point?"

"To show the white-asses that we're gonna get 'em," Leo said. "Show 'em that we can tear this whole country apart if they don't give us what we want."

"It's a revolution," Bahjat said, "a true revolution. What

was the point of Bunker Hill, or Lexington and Concord, in the American Revolution?"

"The *first* American Revolution," Leo corrected. "You just saw the opening shot in the second American Revolution."

David sank down onto one of the boat's plastic-covered benches. "It's all so futile. You kill whites so they'll send in their army to kill blacks."

"Yeah, and when they do, every non-white in the U.S. of A. will hafta pick which side he's gonna be on. And they'll be on our side, all of 'em. Ain't no other choice."

"The American Army itself is mostly non-white, isn't it?" Bahjat asked.

"Yeah. How you think they gonna feel when they get ordered t'wipe out whole city blocks?"

David could feel his head spinning. "It's just blood. Blood, blood, and more blood. There's got to be a better way."

"The tree of liberty must be refreshed from time to time with the blood of tyrants and of patriots," Bahjat said. "Thomas Jefferson wrote that."

Leo added, "He also wrote that *all* men are created equal—not just white-asses."

But David said, "You can't build a better world by destroying the one you have. What will you replace it with?"

Leo grunted. "We'll worry 'bout that when the time comes."

"The time is here," David insisted.

"Hey, look!" called one of the kids at the stern of the boat. "Planes!"

Leo pushed past David and Bahjat to get out from under the canvas top. Bahjat was right behind him. David turned and, leaning an elbow on the gunwale, peered out the side of the boat. Silvery, feather-like contrails were etching across the moonlit sky. David counted five groups of a dozen each: sixty planes.

"Start the motor!" Leo snapped.

"They ain't doin' nothin'," said one of the kids. "They too high."

"Ain't here for our health," Leo muttered. "An' whatever they gonna do, they gonna do it to the city. Get this bucket movin' *now!*"

Within minutes a fine golden dust sprinkled out of the sky, but the boat was racing so fast—bow out of the water —that the dust blew off them as fast as it came down. In a few moments the golden snowfall was over. Leo let the kid at the helm ease back on the throttle.

As they slid past the blacked-out city, they could see the streets choked with gray-green gas. Leo scanned the scene silently with a pair of binoculars. After several long, wordless minutes he handed them to Bahjat. She put them to her eyes, then gasped.

David heard her murmuring in Arabic. "What is it?" he asked.

She gave him the binoculars. David couldn't see much at first, but as he learned to hold the glasses steady in the chugging boat, he started to make out human forms in the swirling tendrils of gas. They were staggering, falling, spasming. Everywhere he looked, in the streets, in the green park area along the riverfront, he saw chaos. People who had huddled on rooftops to be safe from the marauding guerrillas were tearing themselves apart to get away from the gas and whatever else it was that turned them into spastic, gibbering epileptics. He watched someone hurl himself from a roof and fall twenty stories to the street, twitching and screaming all the way down.

David handed the binoculars back to Leo.

The black man lifted his chin a notch and pointed skyward. "An' those are the guys who're tryin' to *help* the white-asses in the city," he said, his voice a deep, rumbling sadness. "They don' mind killin' their own people t'get at us. So don' think we're that mutha-humpin' bad."

The strangest, saddest, gladdest day of my life!

As soon as they assembled us in a meeting room at Space Station Alpha, the instructors told us that we had all just about completed our training for Island One, and we were going to move right on to the colony as soon as they could send a spacecraft to pick us up. No more classes, no more testing. We had made it!

They let us try to reach our homes by picture-phone. I got Mom and Dad okay. There wasn't any fighting in Minnesota—for once the weather was kind to us. Ruth couldn't get through to California for hours; then the Corporation finally put through a special high-priority link. Her parents were okay, but their house had been burned to the ground and they were living in an army barracks.

Three of the class asked permission to go home. They didn't want to go to Island One while their families were in danger. So that left eight of us—out of sixty who started the classes a few months ago.

I talked it over with Ruth, about going to Island One. All of a sudden I found myself telling her we ought to get married so there'd be no problem about us living together in Island One. And she agreed! So we found the chapel down on level one [full Earth gravity] and had the ceremony performed with two of our classmates as witnesses, and with Mom and Dad watching by phone link. We couldn't get through to Ruth's parents, but my folks promised to send them a videotape.

We honeymooned last night on level six [nearly zero gravity—wow!]. Today we head for Island One to start our new life together. Man and wife.

—The journal of William Palmquist

• CHAPTER 32 •

Hamoud paced the white-painted dock impatiently. He wore the clothes the local PRU activists had given him, knee-length pants and a loose shirt with gaudy stripes and numbers splashed across it. An imitation of a sports uniform, the current rage among American youths. He felt ridiculous, but he regarded the costume as necessary camouflage.

Up on the hilltop overlooking the river stood the research laboratory. No one suspected that it was now a PRU headquarters. The lab had been officially closed by Garrison Enterprises, and the staff had been given indefinite leave, with pay. They were all home, nervously locked inside their suburban houses, ready to protect family and property in Nyack, Tarrytown, and Peekskill. Sitting in front of blazing TV screens with shotguns on their laps, they watched with horror as cities flamed and died. They thanked God and Garrison Enterprises that they lived far from downtown. But was it far enough? Each of them wondered.

It was a gray, cloudy day and the wind along the river was damp and chill. Hamoud shivered as he strained his senses, trying to conjure up the expected boat the way a *fakir* entices a cobra from its reed basket.

Bahjat was on the boat, he knew. The radio message he had received during the night had been in code, but it was quite specific. Scheherazade was coming to him, together with the New York leader, Leo. And she was bringing him a gift, a treasure, a prisoner—the man from Island One.

A jewel of inestimable price, this prisoner from the space colony. He knew all about Island One: its workings, its

348

security, its weak points. A gold mine of information. And the research laboratory was an ideal place to extract that information from him. Afterward? Hamoud shrugged to himself. Worthless prisoners don't live long.

Evelyn was staring at the river, too, waiting for the boat to arrive.

She was in one of the laboratory offices, standing at the window and looking out at the gray sky and grayer river. Even the conifers on the other side of the Hudson seemed gray and lifeless under the low, scudding clouds.

Why do I feel like this? Evelyn asked herself. Her hands were knotted into sweaty-palmed fists. Her insides were fluttering. Deep within her she had the feeling that something bad, very bad, was about to happen.

She watched Hamoud pacing the dock like an eager little boy. He had ignored her since they had arrived at the laboratory the night before. Normally dour, often surly, he had been all anticipation since the radio message had come in that Scheherazade was on her way.

He's madly in love with her, Evelyn realized.

Good. She was glad he wanted Scheherazade and not herself. And David was on that boat, too. The premonition of danger, of death, that was hanging over her had to do with David. Somehow she wished he were somewhere else, no matter where, just as long as he could be safely away from Hamoud.

The office she was in was a small one, with little more than a desk, some shelves for tapes, and a chalkboard. Evelyn had slept fitfully for a few hours on the carpeted floor in a sleeping bag that the local PRU kids had provided. Shocking blue. Even more shocking against the lime-green walls and pale gray carpet. It was dusty on the floor, and Evelyn had coughed herself awake every time she had drifted off.

There were color photographs of a woman and two tots in slim metal frames on the desk. The chalkboard was half-filled with indecipherable equations; the other half had been wiped clean with a smeary plastic sponge.

The laboratory's cafeteria was closed, of course, but the locals had brought in bags full of soggy sandwiches and rancid, cold coffee. Evelyn couldn't stomach any of it. She went back to the window and watched Hamoud watching the river.

"So how do you like living in a tropical paradise?" Garrison asked Arlene.

They were on the rooftop of a low, gracefully designed house set in the midst of the lush tropical growth of Cylinder B. Birds chittered and squawked in the sunlight. A narrow, fast stream gushed nearby.

"It's sure different from Texas," Arlene said. "I don't think I'll ever get used to having the ground curve up clear over my head."

"You will, you will," Garrison said. "You're gonna live like a princess up here. Like a goddamned jungle priestess."

She smiled at him.

"I could just sit here an' *look* all day long," Garrison said. "Th' work of a lifetime . . . I'm finally here. I'll spend the rest of my days right here, honey. Safe home at last."

"Dr. Cobb called again a half-hour ago," Arlene said. "Said he needed to talk to you about . . ."

"Let Cobb cool his ass," Garrison snapped. "He's all hot and flustered about the rioting back in the States. Looks like some sympathy riots have busted out in other places, too. Tokyo got hit pretty bad."

"You'll have to speak with him sooner or later," Arlene insisted.

Garrison wheeled his powerchair to face her. "Now don't you take that schoolmarm tone with me, lady!" But he was grinning. "C'mon, let's go back downstairs and see how Houston's makin' out."

Arlene followed him to the elevator doors and they went down the single flight into Garrison's office area. The windows were wide and unglassed. Birds could fly in and out. The lounges and chairs were set along the grass-covered floor as casually as an interior designer could calculate, and the decor looked more Tahitian than Texan.

But in the corner was a ceiling-high smoked glass screen, and behind it the intricate electronic machinery of a holographic video set.

Arlene sat in a rope-webbed chair beside Garrison. Her flowered skirt was slit to the hip and slid away to show her long suntanned legs.

But Garrison was looking at the smoking ruins of Houston, in the three-dimensional viewscreen. The city was a shambles: buildings gutted or blasted out, rubble and dead bodies choking the streets. Even the Garrison Tower had been attacked and its lower floors were charred and blackened, windows gone. An Army tank squatted ponderously in the otherwise empty parking area beneath the Tower, its long cannon drooping slightly downward, as if ashamed of what it had been doing.

"Not's bad as I thought it'd be," Garrison muttered.

He tapped the keyboard on his armrest. New Orleans. Pittsburgh. Los Angeles. St. Louis. Atlanta. Gutted, flattened, blood-soaked. As if earthquakes and tornadoes and hurricanes had all come together at once. But the destructive power of nature could not equal the deliberate calculated deadliness of man. Battles were still raging in Chicago and New York. Garrison watched network news coverage of the street-to-street, house-to-house fighting.

"Lotta dead niggers," he said.

"A lot of dead whites," Arlene added, her voice flat, hard, controlled.

"Yeah, now. But I mean later. After the fightin's over. Next week. Next month. They're gonna have ballparks filled with PRU punks—blacks, Chicanos, PR's, Indians. Gonna get rid of boatloads of 'em."

Arlene stared at her boss. "You had this all figured out, didn't you? Months ago, you had all of this planned."

"Years ago," Garrison said, watching the screen. Canadian jets were divebombing a block of city-built apartment towers on Chicago's South Side.

"But why?" Arlene asked. "How could you do this . . ."

He flicked a glance at her. "Feel sorry for 'em?"

"Sort of."

"Can't make an omelet without breakin' eggs."

"I don't understand," she said. "How is this going to help you? What's all this got to do with protecting Garrison Enterprises or the Island One Corporation?"

Garrison leaned back in his chair and grinned crookedly at her. He broke into a cackling laugh.

"You really haven't put it all together in your head, have you?"

Arlene said, "Tell me about it."

"Look at her." Garrison chuckled. "Sooo curious. Sooo

351

eager to learn what my strategy is. Figger you're gonna take over when I'm gone, honey?"

Arlene's eyes flashed. "What are you talking about?"

"Don't make any plans for my funeral, 'cause I'm gonna outlive most of you."

"You're talking silly." She was all innocent surprise and hurt feelings.

"Sure I am."

"I just want to know how all this is going to help us." She slid off her chair and knelt beside him, turning her ice-blue eyes up toward Garrison's. "I'm just trying to understand how your mind works, that's all."

"I'll bet," he said. Then, "It's a trick the Commies useta use, back in the Cold War days. Stir up as much hell as they could, anywhere and everywhere. Bound to help 'em, one way or another, 'cause they were against the *status quo*. Wherever there was trouble, war, riots, hunger, labor strikes, guerrilla movements, th' goddamn' Commies'd be right here, helpin' the underdog. They didn't believe in any of it. They weren't interested in the underdog . . . they just wanted t' knock off the *overdog* so's they could take over themselves."

Arlene nodded. "And that's what you're doing now."

"The World Government wants t' control markets, prices, tax rates . . . those damn' bureaucrats'll put a stranglehold on everything. All in the name of helpin' the poor countries . . . feedin' the starvin' billions. Well, the more you feed 'em, the more starvin' billions they make. And the less able they are to feed themselves. That's why the World Government's gotta go."

"And they're bad for profits," Arlene added, smiling.

"That too." Garrison smiled back.

She gestured at the viewscreen. Heavy olive-green Army tanks were trundling slowly across the George Washington Bridge. No guerrillas were in sight.

"But all this fighting in the cities, how's this going to get rid of the World Government?"

"It was gonna happen anyway," Garrison said. "Sooner or later the cities were gonna explode. Miracle is they didn't blow up years ago. We just helped 'em blow off the steam that's been buildin' up for years."

"And the World Government . . ."

"Looks bad no matter what happens. If they had moved

fast and sent in their troops to help the U.S. Army, the American people woulda got pissed off about foreign soldiers in their backyards. Most of the World Army's just as black an' brown as these PRU guerrillas . . . blacker. The African troops are blacker than any American nigger. They might not've wanted to shoot up their colored cousins. Even if they did, there'd be lotsa pillaging and raping. Always is when you get foreign troops."

"And that would have stirred up the American people against the World Government."

"Shorely would. Especially with our new media folks stirrin' 'em up."

"But the World Government didn't act. They haven't done a thing . . ."

"Even better," Garrison said. "Now we can blame *them* for sittin' on their fannies while American cities went up in smoke."

"What about De Paolo's death?"

Garrison snorted. "Thirty years too late. Everybody dies. Except me. I'm gonna go on forever. Don't you ever forget that."

Her eyes searched his face. "You really believe that, don't you?"

Laughing, "Why d'you think we're up here in Island One, with all these fancy biology labs? If they can tinker with genes and make a kid who's physically perfect, they can help an old man get young again."

"They can?"

"They will," Garrison said, all traces of humor gone from his voice.

Dr. Cobb welcomed us personally to Island One and spoke to each of us individually for a while. Of course, in the case of Ruth and me, he spoke to the two of us together. He got a priority call through to California and helped us to track down Ruth's parents, who are okay and living with relatives for the time being up near Santa Cruz. L.A. is a mess.

Most of us were pretty scared and glum about the rebellion back home, but Dr. Cobb tried to cheer us up by pointing out that Island One is our home now, and we have a very bright future ahead of us.

He advised Ruth and me—in our private talk with him—to start reading up on the asteroids. He said there were gold mines waiting for us out beyond Mars. And not just gold, but minerals and metals that would be far more valuable and important. I told him I was a farmer, not a miner, but he laughed and asked me if I didn't think miners would need food to eat while they're out there nearly four times farther away from the Sun than we are now.

—The journal of William Palmquist

· CHAPTER 33 ·

Evelyn burst through the double metal doors with the rest of the crowd and headed down the flagstone path that led toward the dock. It was beginning to drizzle and the gray clouds were getting thicker, but no one seemed to mind. Already she could hear the footsteps of the foremost in their group clumping on the wooden stairs that scaled down the riverbank's steep side and connected with the dock.

Evelyn stopped at the top of the stairs. The boat was already tied up at the end of the dock and its passengers were walking slowly up toward the laboratory.

Hamoud was striding alongside a small, slim, dark woman. Scheherazade, Evelyn knew. Hamoud wasn't touching her, but it was obvious that he claimed her for himself. His attitude toward her was something Evelyn hadn't seen in him before: no longer the surly, moody, domineering Moslem male. He was nodding and speaking with her, teeth flashing in a boyish smile, shoulders slightly stooped in deference to her diminutive stature.

But where was David? A huge black man walked behind Hamoud and Scheherazade, so big that the dock seemed to bow under his weight.

And beside him . . . Evelyn stared. It couldn't be David. But it was! Lean, bearded, his face colored a darker brown than she would have thought possible. And his hair was dyed brown, too.

But Evelyn knew that walk, the way his arms swung at his sides. *It has to be him.* He looked up in her direction, and even at that distance she could see that he was indeed David—but changed. His face was haggard, and his eyes

356

had lost their innocent sparkle. He looked straight at Evelyn without showing the slightest sign of recognition.

Then she noticed the two black youths walking behind David, with rifles in their hands, and remembered that David was their prisoner.

David saw her standing up at the top of the stairs and recognized her honey-blonde hair. *Evelyn! What's she doing here?*

He flicked his eyes back toward the massive form of Leo, who had just reached the bottom of the stairs. *Is she a prisoner, too? How'd she get here?* David wondered.

Then he saw Bahjat and her friend, her countryman, her fellow guerrilla, her lover climbing the stairs together, side by side. He looked again at Evelyn. She was staring at him, waiting tensely as he came up the stairs toward her.

If she's a prisoner, would they let her out here to watch us land? Nobody seems to be guarding her, or even looking in her direction. Could she be one of them?

He reached the top step, and she was standing there.

"David?"

"Evelyn," he said.

"It *is* you!"

He reached out his hand and she took it, stepped next to him, and slid her arm around his waist. Up ahead of them, neither Bahjat nor Hamoud saw what they were doing.

"What's happened to you? How are you?" Evelyn asked.

David said, "I was going to ask you the same thing. Are you . . . on their side?"

"A bit," she replied. "I was actually trying to get to you. How did you get away from Island One? What have you been up to all these weeks?"

He laughed. "Believe it or not, I was looking for you."

She clung closer to him and smiled happily. "Tell me all about it."

Nodding, he answered, "It's a long story." *And there are parts of it that I can't tell you,* he realized.

Looking up at the laboratory building, David saw that it was a low, ground-hugging, two-story structure. Strictly efficient, with no decorations marring its sleek, window-walled sides. Flat roof with a yellow windsock drooping

from a short mast. *Helicopter pad up there,* David con-
cluded.

Evelyn chattered about Hamoud and the worldwide
PRU organization as the group went inside the building
and walked into the large, open central area where long
cafeteria tables were set up in perfect rows. Stainless-
steel counters and serving trays, hot plates, coffee-makers,
and grills stood off to one end of the big, two-story-high
area. The entire far wall was a window that looked out on
the drizzling gray landscape of bare trees and a nearly
empty parking lot.

Leo and Hamoud stood off in one corner with Bahjat
between them. The huge black man made the swarthy
Arab look stunted, and Bahjat looked like a waif beside
them. It quickly became apparent that the two men didn't
agree on something or other.

Power struggle? David asked himself as he sat at one of
the tables. Evelyn went off and came back a moment later
with stale sandwiches and tepid, synthetic coffee. David ate
gratefully, but he kept his attention on Leo and the Arab.

"The Arab . . . he's the one they call Tiger?"

"Yes," Evelyn said. "His real name is Hamoud, and
he's Kurdish, not Arab."

*Leo's been the boss in this area, but Hamoud is higher
in whatever internal organization the PRU has,* David
thought. *He thinks he's the boss.*

"Be careful of him," Evelyn said in a low voice. "He
enjoys killing."

David nodded, then turned and counted the others sitting or lounging on their feet in the cafeteria area. *Looks
like more of Hamoud's people here than Leo's. It's going
to be an interesting time.*

Then he noticed that Bahjat had started to do the talking. She spoke more and more, and both men lapsed into
silence.

Despite himself, David grinned. *She's going to be the
boss, after all. I'll be damned.* Somehow, he wasn't surprised.

Their meeting finally broke up as David munched the
soggy sandwiches. Bahjat went off with Hamoud, and
David felt his innards burning. But Leo was heading for
him like a brooding black mountain looming closer and
closer.

"Okay, spaceman, we gonna find you a safe place to stash your ass."

Evelyn got to her feet beside David. "I'll see you later," she said.

David nodded and followed Leo.

Not so bad, David decided after a shower and shave. *Some people on Earth live pretty well*.

The laboratory's upper floor included a few one-room apartments. Whom they had been built for, or why, was a mystery to David. But they were comfortable and fully furnished, with a bathroom full of soaps and shaving gear, a tiny refrigerator/freezer stocked with frozen foods, a microwave cooker, and even a TV set.

A knock sounded at his door. He crossed the carpeted room in four strides and grasped the doorknob. It wouldn't turn. *Locked from the outside*.

"Who is it?" David called.

"Evelyn."

"The door's locked."

A key scraped in the lock and the door swung open. David saw that an Arabic-looking youth held the key. And a carbine. Evelyn was empty-handed.

David reached for his shirt, took it off the bed where he had dropped it, and pulled it on.

Evelyn smiled at him. "I thought you'd want to come down to the cafeteria for dinner. Some of the local people just brought in a whole carload of pizza and beer."

Tucking the shirt inside his pants, David said, "Would you rather eat here? There's food in the freezer. We'd have some privacy."

The guard slammed the door shut without waiting for Evelyn's answer. They heard the rattling of the lock.

She laughed. "I suppose that decides the matter." She was wearing a simple light green dress that showed off her coloring very well. She watched David carefully, as if seeing him for the first time.

"You look more like your old self," she said.

Instinctively, he put a hand to his chin. "Oh, you mean . . . I shaved."

"And your skin and hair are back to their old colors, almost."

"I washed off the tint. No need for a disguise now, I guess."

"You've lost weight, though. You look . . . harder."

"Yes, I suppose I do." He gestured toward a sling-back chair near the window. "Sit down and enjoy the sunset while I pop something into the cooker."

Going toward the chair, Evelyn said, "This is like old times—up in Island One."

"Old times," David echoed.

"A lot has happened since then," Evelyn said.

"Damned right," he agreed fervently.

Turning back toward him, Evelyn said, "Tell me about it. I want to hear all of it."

"Sure," he said, trying to sort out in his mind how much he actually could tell her. Stalling for time, he asked, "But tell me, how did the PRU arrange to make this research laboratory its local headquarters? How well organized are these people? What are they planning to do with us?"

Evelyn sank back into the chair. "I don't know what Hamoud's going to do next. I doubt that he knows himself. Except that it will have to be something bigger, more spectacular, than Leo's urban offensive."

"Bloodier, you mean," David said from the tiny kitchen alcove.

"Most likely," Evelyn said. "He's in love with headlines, Hamoud is, and he feels that Leo and Scheherazade have had all the publicity. He wants his share."

"God help us."

"Exactly. He's a born killer."

"This research lab—it seems to be part of Leo's setup."

"It is," Evelyn replied. "This laboratory has been supplying him with drugs that he needs."

"Narcotics?"

She shook her head. "No. Hormones, steroids. I don't know the chemistry, but apparently he's been using them since his college days to maintain his size and strength. Now he needs them just to live. He'll collapse without them."

"So that's why we're here," David said.

"But there's a fly in the soup. The laboratory has been closed down. And all the drugs that Leo needs have been carefully removed from here. The place has been stripped of everything that Leo needs—deliberately."

David slid two frozen dinners into the microwave cooker and let the door slam shut.

"He's been tricked," he said.

Evelyn nodded. "He's been assassinated. Without those chemicals, he'll die."

Leo stalked down the aisle between the lab benches and advanced on the terrified technician.

"Whaddaya mean, they took it all?"

The technician was a Cuban, almost as tall as Leo, but not even one-third of his girth. His face was long and droopy, like a hound's. His skin was the color of cigar leaf. He had been the PRU agent inside the laboratory for many months.

"They took out most of the medical supplies when they closed the laboratory Wednesday," he said in the unaccented English he had learned at the university. "All the steroids, the adrenocorticals, the whole stock of hormones —all of it."

"Son-of-a-bitch." Leo's fist closed around a section of metal tubing standing on the lab bench at his side. The tubing bent, then cracked. "I gotta have that stuff! Got to!"

"I didn't know," the technician said, his eyes on Leo's massive hand, his voice trembling. "We got orders to ship everything out. It was all sent to Island One. Half the staff is going up there, they told us."

"Island One? They shot my stuff off to Island One?"

"The orders came from Mr. Garrison himself."

"From Houston?"

"No, from Island One. He's up there now."

"That bastard!" Leo swung his tree-trunk-sized arm through the metal-and-glass spiderwork that covered the lab bench. It shattered. The technician hopped backward, away from the spraying shards of glass.

"That mutha-fuckin' bastard!" Leo roared. "You know what'll happen to me in a couple of days if I don't get those steroids? Garrison knows! He set me up! That mutha-fuckin' son-of-a-bitch! He let me do the fightin' for him and then he figured he'd just let me die by turnin' off my supply!"

Bahjat sat in the cafeteria and tried to eat the doughy, spicy pizza. But like the other two dozen men and women there, she was watching the big, wall-sized TV screen and the Slaughter of the Innocents.

The TV cameras were cutting from Los Angeles to New York, stopping briefly at every beleaguered city along the way. The guerrillas were being hammered into a bloody pulp everywhere. The real, organized battles had already ended in most of the cities. Now it was the local police, the National Guard, the regular Army, and hordes of tight-lipped vigilante mobs, their faces stark with hate and anger, rounding up every non-white they could find.

"Suspected guerrillas are marched off to a detention center," the unseen TV commentator said cheerfully as the screen showed lines of black youths city blocks long, hands on their heads, trudging the rubble-filled streets between bayonet-wielding men in uniform and heavily armed tanks and armored cars. The picture cut to the Kansas City Municipal Stadium, filled with blacks of all ages, mothers with babies trailing after them, weary old men sitting with their heads between their knees.

"All across the nation," the commentator went on, "the forces of law and order have reestablished themselves. How many revolutionaries have been killed in the battles is not yet known, although casualties among police, National Guard, and Army units have been very high. Civilians, too, ordinary citizens, have been murdered by the thousands. . . ."

Bahjat got up from the table, left the unappetizing mess in its plastic wrapping, and headed for the room where they had locked up David.

David and Evelyn were sitting together on the soft, wide foam couch, watching the TV set that had been built into the plastic-paneled wall. The Battle of New York was now on the screen. Regular U.S. Army units were grinding through Manhattan, street by bloody street, building by burning building.

Teams of infantrymen were pulling kids out of the doorway of a building where they had been crouching. The soldiers prodded the kids into the middle of the street with their bayoneted carbines. A massive olive-green tank poked its gun barrel toward the building and fired point-blank. The wall exploded and collapsed in a billowing cloud of dust that filled the screen.

"They'll kill everyone in the city," Evelyn said, her voice hushed with shock.

"They're taking some prisoners," David said. "Not many. But they'll want some for interrogation, to find out how this whole thing could have started."

Evelyn stared at him, ignoring the firefight now on the TV screen. "You were there when it began?"

Nodding, "We had just flown into New York. The PRU isn't much on organization, but they have people all over Latin America . . . and in the States, of course."

"And how did you get to the boat?"

David told her in as few words as possible. The TV kept claiming his attention. He realized that they were not showing any scenes in which Army soldiers were hit or killed. *It's not being shown live,* he knew. *The government must be editing every centimeter of the tapes, letting the public see only victories.*

"My God, what you've been through!" Evelyn said.

He turned to her. "You told me to see the world. I've seen some of it."

She reached up and touched his jaw lightly with her fingertips. "And it's changed you. You're not the same person you were on Island One."

"How could I be?"

Her sea-green eyes were searching his. "You're . . . harder, but not bitter, I don't think. You . . . you're like a piece of forged steel now. You've been through the hottest flame and you're stronger for it."

David shook his head. "I don't feel any stronger."

Her hands slipped over his shoulders and twined in the hair on the back of his neck. "You are, though. I can sense it."

As if of their own volition, David's hands went to her waist. She slid closer to him, her body touched his, and he could smell the faint salty tang of her unperfumed skin, feel her breath on his neck.

"We've both come a long way," Evelyn whispered, her voice husky and trembling. "We've found each other, at last."

"It's too late for that, Evelyn," he said.

A hint of pain crossed her face. "No, don't say that. . . ."

He kissed her, gently, because he didn't know what else to do. She clung to him, locking herself against him.

"If you knew what I've been through . . ." Evelyn was nearly sobbing.

David heard something scratching somewhere—a metallic sound, just barely audible over the shooting and explosions flickering across the TV screen. He pulled away slightly from Evelyn and turned to see . . .

Bahjat was standing in the doorway, staring at them, her expression unreadable, a flat mask of self-control that turned her beautiful face into the cold, dead features of a bronze statue.

David started to get up from the couch, but Bahjat turned and swept out of the room. The grinning Arab guard out in the hall pulled the door shut and locked it.

The violence that has swept through the United States and other parts of the world has seared the heart of every man and woman of conscience. I, *El Libertador*, call myself a revolutionary. But the violence in North America's cities has gone beyond revolution. It can lead to nothing but more bloodshed and chaos. I hereby disassociate myself from it, and I urge all true revolutionary movements around the world to disavow such mindless bloodletting tactics.

Let us have a moratorium on violence! Enough of killing! The time for reconciliation has come.

To help bring an end to the violence and terrorism that are increasing in scale throughout the world, I hereby offer to meet with the new leadership of the World Government—anywhere in the world that they may choose—to discuss with them a method of bringing peace to the world and a means to correct the grievances that have caused revolutionary movements to arise everywhere.

It is a choice between peaceful negotiation and world-wide civil war, between reconciliation and chaos. I, *El Libertador*, renounce violence as of this moment. We will strive for peaceful reconciliation.

> —Global broadcast,
> 30 November 2008

• CHAPTER 34 •

As Bahjat strode down the corridor from David's room, blind fury whirled hotly in her mind.

Fool! she raged at herself. *To believe that what he felt and spoke of when we were together in danger would be his real heart. He has known this Englishwoman since before he came to Earth. How could he love an Arab, a guerrilla who holds him prisoner, a woman who has already confessed her other loves to him?*

The cafeteria was empty now, the TV turned off. Bahjat frowned in puzzlement. *Why? Where could they all have gone?*

"Scheherazade . . . there you are."

She turned and saw one of the young black girls who was part of the local PRU structure. She seemed frightened, fighting for breath but calm enough to speak.

"They got a big argument goin'—Leo an' Tiger. Ever'body scattered, don't wanna be in the middle. You better go calm 'em both down."

"Where are they?" Bahjat asked.

The girl pointed off toward a row of offices that led down a corridor away from the cafeteria.

She could hear Leo's booming voice and Hamoud's urgent, hissing sibilants before the words themselves became clear to her.

The two men were in a big office. An ultra-modern curved desk was in the corner by the draperied window. Most of the room was taken up by a circular conference table. But no one was sitting. Leo paced along a wall-long stack of bookshelves like the lion of his namesake. Hamoud stood by the green chalkboard, radiating stubborn anger and looking faintly ridiculous in his mock football uniform.

366

Two of Hamoud's bodyguards stood tensely at the door. Bahjat had to shoulder her way past them.

"I *need* those steroids, man!" Leo was shouting. "Like food! Like air! If I don't get them, I can't keep my body goin'. I'll fall apart. I'll be dead of a heart attack in a couple of days."

Hamoud's bearded face was just as obstinate as ever. "I cannot give you men and guns for a raid on the Kennedy spaceport. It would be madness—especially with the local police and militia already inflamed by *your* attack."

"My people are gettin' themselves killed by the thousands, fightin' *your* fight!" Leo bellowed. "Now I need some help. . . ."

"A suicide mission is stupid!" Hamoud snapped.

"What is going on here?" Bahjat demanded, stepping into the center of the room.

Hamoud gestured angrily toward Leo. "He needs certain drugs."

"To stay alive. Not narcotics. Steroids. Other things, enzymes and stuff, to keep my body goin'. Been livin' off them since I was a teen-ager in college football."

"And he wants us to raid Kennedy spaceport to get them."

Leo's voice contracted, lowered in volume, as he explained to Bahjat, "See, they was makin' the stuff for me here, in this lab. That's why I had this place staked out for my getaway. But Garrison double-crossed me and stashed the stuff at J.F.K."

"Why the spaceport?" Bahjat asked.

" 'Cause he's sending it up to Island One. Maybe it's already gone there. . . . I don't know."

"All the more reason," said Hamoud, "to stay away from the spaceport. It's a trap to catch us."

"I gotta have that stuff!" Leo said.

"Wait," Bahjat said. She asked Leo, "Garrison? The same man who controls Garrison Enterprises?"

Leo nodded.

"And he controls Island One," Hamoud said, "together with four other men."

"Including Sheikh al-Hashimi." She almost said *my father*, but she caught herself at the last moment.

"Including the sheikh," said Hamoud.

"They're living on Island One," Leo said, "all five of 'em."

"All of them?" Bahjat asked. "Including al-Hashimi?"

Hamoud nodded.

Suddenly it all became clear to her. "Then we must go to Island One, also."

"What?"

Leo gaped at her.

"Don't you see?" Bahjat said to them both. "It all fits together perfectly."

Hamoud walked slowly across the room toward her. "What do you mean?"

Bahjat said, "Island One controls all the Solar Power Satellites. Whoever controls Island One controls all the energy being beamed to Earth from those satellites."

Hamoud's eyes widened. "Almost all of Europe depends on that energy."

"And most of North America," added Bahjat, "as well as Japan."

"By destroying Island One we could destroy the whole energy system!" Hamoud exulted.

"We will not destroy it," Bahjat said firmly. "We will capture it, and with it, the five wealthiest and most powerful men in the world. Imagine what hostages they would make!"

"And they've got my steroids up there," Leo said.

"By seizing and holding Island One," Bahjat went on, "we could topple the World Government at a stroke. The revolution will have been won, and a new world order will begin."

"With *us* in command," Hamoud said, his fists clenching.

"Exactly."

"We could take it," Hamoud said, "if we had the transport. But how could we hold it? The World Government could shoot us out of the sky. The laser satellites could destroy us in minutes."

Bahjat smiled at him. "With ten thousand hostages aboard? With T. Hunter Garrison and Sheikh al-Hashimi and all those others? With the control center for the Solar Power Satellites? Would they destroy *that*? They cannot, and they know they cannot."

"We'd have them whipped!" Hamoud said.

Leo added, "An' we could get 'em to turn my people loose."

"We could run the world the right way—our way!" Hamoud said, and he actually smiled at the thought of it.

Bahjat nodded and said nothing.

"But . . ." Leo raised a ponderous hand and pointed toward the ceiling. "How do we get there? They ain't gonna send us no engraved invitations."

"Yes, they will," Bahjat said. "Leave that part to me." Inwardly she smiled. *My father wanted me to go to Island One. Now his repentant daughter will beg his forgiveness and ask to be with him.*

A young Arab burst into the room, wild-eyed, a bluish bruise just visible along his jaw.

"The prisoner . . . the one from the space colony . . . he's escaped!"

NEWSFLASH***NEWSFLASH***NEWSFLASH***

FOR IMMEDIATE RELEASE, INTERRUPT ALL PROGRAMMING AT ONCE

30 November 2008

MESSINA: With unexpected swiftness, the World Government Council has agreed to meet with representatives of the breakaway nations of Argentina, Chile, and South Africa to discuss means of ending the worldwide outbreaks of violence and revolution.

"I will be glad to meet with representatives of the secessionists," said Kowie Boweto, Acting Director of the World Government, "and with *El Libertador* himself."

Rumors in Messina suggest that the meeting place may be literally out of this world—on Island One, the space colony a quarter-million miles from Earth.

"It's a neutral location," said a Council spokesperson who refused to be identified. "We certainly won't be interrupted there by riots or other politically inspired acts of violence."

• CHAPTER 35 •

Within a few moments after Bahjat had stormed out of his room, David whirled to face Evelyn.

"Tell the guard you're leaving," he snapped.

"What?"

"Call him. Now! Tell him you want out."

Looking confused and hurt, Evelyn got up from the couch and went to the door. "Let me out," she said. "I'm leaving."

The guard was still grinning as he swung the door open. David yanked him by the arm, spun him around, and felled him with a solid punch to the jaw.

Evelyn stared, goggle-eyed.

"Do they trust you?" he asked her. "Would you be in trouble with them if they thought you helped me get out of here?"

"Of course I would . . ."

She got no further. He clipped her on the jaw, too, and she fell backward onto the couch.

"If you're smart you'll stay there until the guard wakes up," David muttered, pulling the carbine away from the guard's numb hands. He ducked out into the hall, then pulled the door shut behind him.

There's no way for me to escape and no place for me to escape to, David thought as he padded swiftly down the corridor.

What he needed was information. *Must be a computer system here,* he told himself. *Find an empty office and . . .*

He poked into the first open doors he could find. Another apartment, vacant. A janitor's closet, with sink and mops.

An empty office, with a computer terminal sitting atop

the otherwise bare desk. Its blank gray viewscreen looked like a precious jewel to David. He closed the door and jammed it shut with the carbine. Then, sitting at the desk, he tapped into the computer's data system.

It seemed like only a few minutes, but he knew the time was flying by. The computer flashed information on its screen. It held back no secrets. Whatever David wanted to know, the computer would tell him . . . if he asked the right questions.

It was a medical lab, as he suspected. Most of its work was in manufacturing antitoxins for contagious diseases. Like most modern laboratories, the manufacturing process involved mutated microbes that happily reproduced the antitoxins that the biologists inserted into their genetic structures. But there was a large research section that developed new antitoxins and tested them on live bacterial and virus cultures.

Another sizable section of the laboratory had been devoted to manufacturing steroids and other hormones.

Know thy enemy, David thought as he fished Leo's medical records out of the computer. It took a bit of doing, because he was listed under his real name. David had to ask the computer for a list of clients who were on steroid therapy and check them out by physical description.

ELLIOT GREER, the data file said, glowing in green letters on the viewscreen.

"My God, he's a walking chemistry lab!" David muttered. Adrenocorticals, ACTH, somatotrophic hormones for stimulating growth, thyroid hormones to maintain his metabolic rate, cyclic AMP . . . "Even his dark coloring comes from the drugs," David noted aloud.

And without a steady supply of the drugs, Leo's cardiovascular system would clog and break down in a matter of days—if something else didn't go wrong with his muscular systems first.

He tapped the keyboard's TIME switch. *The guard ought to be up and giving the alarm by now. Got to move.*

David needed speed and stealth. He kept to the shadowiest parts of the corridor, slipping along unnoticed. He heard a hubbub from downstairs, in the cafeteria area, and knew that his "escape" had been discovered.

Skirting along the balcony that ringed the cafeteria, he headed back toward the laboratory area.

If only they haven't cleaned out everything back there, he thought. *They've taken Leo's drugs, but maybe there's a chance that they left what I need.*

The laboratories themselves were vast, confusing tangles of glass and metal piping. David had to stop at each computer terminal he could find to learn exactly where he was and what the equipment around him was supposed to do.

He heard shouts off in the distance, and turned down the lights around him. The computer viewscreen glowed an eerie green, but he couldn't do without the information he sought.

In the back of his mind, he knew what was at stake: not only his life, and Bahjat's and all the others', but Island One. That was what they were after. Maybe they didn't know it themselves yet, but David did. Sooner or later they would realize that Island One was the key to their violent dreams. They were going to try to seize Island One, or destroy it. David knew that he would have to stop them. No one else could.

He was in the deepest end of the toxic disease laboratory when all the overhead lights flared up.

David looked up from the lab bench, got down from the stool he had been using, and walked as slowly and calmly as he could toward the front of the lab.

A half-dozen young blacks burst into the room, with Leo at their head.

"There he is!"

One of the youngsters raised his rifle, but Leo pushed it aside.

"They want him alive," Leo said.

"Thanks," said David, who had his hands up, palms out, to show that he was unarmed.

Leo grunted at him. "Don' thank me, man. Once they start workin' you over, maybe you'd be happier to be dead."

Bahjat sat behind the desk. Hamoud paced nervously in front of it. The office was small, its only window a mere vertical slit in the wall. The air was acrid with electrical tension.

"Destroy him!" Hamoud snapped. "I say we execute him

here and now. He almost slipped away from us once. We cannot afford to have him escape and reveal our location."

Bahjat sat quietly in the chair, trying to remain calm, when in fact her mind was a whirlpool of conflicting emotions.

"We must not kill him," she said. "He is too valuable to us."

"To you, perhaps." Hamoud glowered at her.

"To our plans for capturing Island One," she countered as coolly as she could.

"You two were together for months," Hamoud said. "Don't tell me that you didn't sleep with him."

"I will tell you this. I discovered that he has lived all his life in Island One. He knows every part of the space colony—every leaf of each tree, every dial on each computer terminal. He is a living blueprint of the entire colony."

"And you love him!"

She ignored that. "Island One is a huge, complicated place. To capture it, we will have only as many people as can be fitted into a single space shuttle. We must learn where to strike, where their key control centers are, how to take them. . . ."

"I know." Hamoud stopped his pacing and faced her. "We must have detailed information about every square centimeter of Island One. I know that."

"And we have such information. It is inside his brain. He knows everything about Island One—everything."

"But will he tell us?"

Bahjat suddenly felt as if she were somewhere else, far away, looking down at herself as if she were watching a play or a TV show. She watched herself smile cruelly, and she heard herself say, "Oh, I'm sure we can persuade him. If nothing else works, we can always let him watch as we slice pieces off his English girl friend."

The office had been turned into an efficient little interrogation cell. David sat in the unyielding stiff-backed chair, a strap pinning his arms to his sides and holding him firmly against the chair's back. The overhead lights were off. A single harshly bright lamp was aimed straight into his eyes.

His arms and feet were numb. He had lost track of the time since they'd strapped him into this chair. He couldn't see the walls. The window, if there was one in this room, must have been behind him. His mouth and throat were sandpaper-dry; they hadn't allowed him even a drink of water for a very long time. Yet his bladder was full and ached dully.

For the moment he was alone. The bruise under his eye throbbed painfully. They hadn't used any physical torture on him, but they'd underestimated his own anger and determination. David had fought them when they brought him into this interrogation room. He knocked down several of them before Leo and the others had battered him into unconsciousness. When he woke up, the strap had been tightly fastened around him.

He heard the door open, but he couldn't see anything beyond the glare of the lamp. A single pair of feet stepped lightly toward him.

"You are a very stubborn man." It was Bahjat's voice.

"Thanks," he replied, his voice cracking.

"Here." He could just make out her shadowy form. *She must be standing next to the lamp on the desk,* he thought. Her hands materialized out of the darkness. There was a glass of water in them.

He leaned his head forward and sipped. The water tasted wonderfully sweet and refreshing. Bahjat tilted the glass for him and he gulped it all down.

"You must tell them what they want to know," she said, her voice soft, concerned.

"Why? So they can blow up Island One?"

"No," she said, "not that. We simply want to . . . to occupy the space colony. We don't want to hurt anyone."

"This is your idea, isn't it?"

"Mine . . . and Hamoud's."

He gave a harsh, dry bark of a laugh. "I guess you were right. We can't be political opponents and lovers—not at the same time."

"You don't love me," Bahjat said.

"I did."

"Until you were reunited with your Englishwoman."

"Evelyn? I hardly know her."

"Don't lie," Bahjat said. "You can't protect her."

"She came up to Island One for a couple of weeks."

"And you came to Earth after her."

"And found you."

A long, silent pause. Then; "I saw the two of you together...."

"And I saw you with Hamoud. You've slept with him, haven't you?"

"Before ... it seems like years ago. But not anymore. Not since ... you."

David said urgently, "You mustn't destroy Island One. For God's sake, Bahjat, it's too important!"

Her voice hardened. "That's precisely why we want it. It is important. And we will take it, not destroy it."

"I won't help you," he said.

"Yes, you will. We have sent some of the local volunteers out to find the proper drugs. The small doses we've already used on you haven't been enough. Now we'll be forced to give you massive doses of serum. You will tell us everything we want to know, David. I only hope it doesn't permanently harm you."

"Thanks for your concern."

"Help us, David. Help yourself," she whispered. "When all this is finished we can be together. I promise you."

"I love you, Bahjat," he said, "but I don't trust you."

She stood there feeling the sullen anger in his bleary eyes. He looked gaunt, battered, drained of strength and hope ... yet undefeated.

With a conscious effort, Bahjat clasped her hands behind her back; otherwise, she would be caressing him, soothing his wounds, unstrapping him from that chair and helping him toward freedom.

Not trusting herself to say another word, she abruptly turned and hurried out of the room. *Do not look back at him!* she commanded herself. Yet she did as she opened the door. His head had dropped to his chest. He seemed to be dozing.

Hamoud was out in the corridor. Bright daylight streamed through the windows on the opposite wall, making Bahjat wince and squint after the darkness of the interrogation cell.

"He's not asleep, is he?" Hamoud asked, peering over Bahjat's shoulder as she closed the door. "He mustn't get any sleep."

"He isn't asleep," she lied. "He's just trying to get his eyes out of the lamp's glare."

Hamoud looked pleased. "He's close to cracking. The

kids have found a whole satchel full of scopolamine and other things. Snatched it from the local hospital: We'll pump him so full of it that he'll be bouncing off the ceiling."

"Make certain that you don't kill him before he tells us what we must know," Bahjat said sternly.

"We wouldn't have to do this if you would let us try a little carving on the English. A few screams from her and he would talk."

"No," she said, shaking her head. "That's what I found out from him just now. She didn't help him to escape. And he doesn't care about her." *They are not lovers!*

"But he's the kind who wouldn't let her suffer."

"He is the kind," Bahjat snapped, "who will not tell us anything that will endanger his beloved Island One. Not willingly. Not consciously. Besides . . . I thought you liked the Englishwoman. I thought she was one of yours."

Hamoud shrugged. "There are always others."

With a pained sigh, Bahjat said, "If you have the necessary drugs, use them. But be careful with them!"

"Yes," Hamoud said, grinning, "O mighty Scheherazade. Hearkening and obedience."

"And be certain that you don't kill him," she added.

"Of course not." Hamoud made a low, mocking bow. *Not until after he's talked,* he added silently.

BOOK FIVE

December, 2008 A.D.

WORLD POPULATION:
7.34 BILLION

Island One isn't paradise, but it's close enough! The people are friendly—most of them, anyway. The administration settled us in a nice, roomy apartment in a building close to the farms. And as soon as we've worked up enough credit, we can get a house of our own. Ruth works at a research laboratory and I go to the fields every morning. I'm glad her lab is inside the main cylinder here, because I don't like the idea of her going out every day and getting doses of radiation. We're planning to have children, and I don't care how safe they claim it is—I don't want her taking chances.

The farms are so highly automated that there's not all that much for me to do. I've got lots of spare time. I read a lot more than I was able to back home, and we're both getting involved in lots of civic groups. Following Dr. Cobb's suggestion, I'm studying about the asteroid belt. Looks to me like there's going to be another gold rush out there someday. But when?

Called Mom and Dad and told them to plan to come up here for Christmas. Between the two of us, Ruth and I can afford their fare. Next year we'll invite her parents.

—The journal of William Palmquist

• CHAPTER 36 •

David fought his way through a cold gray blanket of fog that enveloped him completely. He couldn't see, couldn't move, couldn't even feel anything except the chill dampness that seeped through every pore and iced the marrow of his bones.

He could hear, though. Far, far off in the gray blankness that engulfed him he could dimly hear voices. They were saying something important, something about him. Something terribly important.

But it was too cold. *Sleep,* David told himself. *Sleep. Forget everything else and let yourself sleep. You deserve to rest and have some beautiful sleep. You need it after what you've been through.*

After what you've been through. The thought echoed through his mind. It had something to do with what the voices were saying. They were talking about life and death —David's life or death.

He shuddered and moaned. With every ounce of his will he tried to penetrate the all-pervasive fog. Nothing. He was still blind and helpless. Yet . . . he could feel something. A vibration tingling against his spine, the backs of his legs. He could feel his fingers. They were curled around something soft, yet firm.

David slowly realized he was lying in some sort of reclining chair. It had been cranked far down so that it was almost a couch. And the vibration he felt was a kind of muffled roar, the type of bone-shaking thunder that a rocket liftoff would produce.

We're on a shuttle, he suddenly knew. *We're taking off for Island One.*

He still felt horribly cold and could see nothing. The

massive doses of drugs that they had forced into his bloodstream, though, were burning away. His body was recuperating faster than his captors would have believed possible.

David didn't move a muscle. He kept his eyes closed. But his sense of touch told him what he needed to know. The safety harness of a shuttle seat was buckled tightly across his chest. His wrists were taped to the armrests. A cloth sack was over his head; he could feel the fabric against his nose and chin, his ears. His breath wheezed through it. It smelled sweaty.

My own sweat, he realized. *I'm soaked in it. That's why I feel cold. I'm getting rid of the drugs, burning them out of my body.*

The rumbling roar died away. The vibration dwindled to nothingness. David felt his weight disappear and the floating, falling sensation of zero gravity took hold of him. His empty stomach started to heave, but an effort of will made it calm down almost instantly. He relaxed and concentrated on listening.

He could understand the voices now, recognize who was speaking.

"It is foolish to keep him alive," Hamoud was saying in a guarded whisper. "He will be troublesome once we are in Island One."

Leo answered in a purring rumble. "Scheherazade says we're gonna need him up there."

"We have all the information we need from him."

"I dunno. That space colony's a damn' big place. Complicated. We might want t'get more outta him."

"He knows *too much* about Island One," Hamoud hissed. "Once he gets back there, he will be dangerous. He will try to get away, to fight against us."

David nodded inside himself. *I already am.*

"Look," Leo snapped. "Scheherazade says we need th' guy to grab off Island One. Go argue with her about it."

"If you're afraid of her"—David heard a rustling sound; Hamoud was reaching into a pocket or the folds of a robe —"I can give him one more shot of this. She would never know. He will die of a drug overdose, that's all."

David could picture the hypodermic spraygun. He'd seen enough of them when they had him strapped to that chair in the interrogation cell.

"I ain't afraid of nobody," Leo said, "but her way makes more sense than your way."

"She is in love with him," Hamoud grumbled. "She is a woman and thinks with her glands instead of her head."

"Yeah? Well, I think with my head, and I think she makes more sense than you do."

"Bah!"

David heard the clicking snap of a safety harness being unbuckled, then sensed Hamoud's stocky body floating up near him, smelled his scent, his breath. He could *feel* the hard plastic of the hypospray in Hamoud's hands.

A gasp. And Leo said, "Leave him alone, man, or I'll break your fuckin' arm."

Hamoud's presence receded. David could picture Leo's mammoth hands completely swallowing Hamoud's arm. Then he heard the *snap* of brittle plastic being broken.

"You don' look so good," Leo said. "Ever been in zero gravity before?"

"No." Hamoud's voice was a sulking dark cloud.

"Better drag your ass t' one of th' bathrooms and take some pills. You look kinda green."

For several moments David heard nothing. But he sensed Leo's giant form hovering over him.

"Thanks," David said.

"You awake?"

"I heard the whole thing. Thank you."

Leo came closer and whispered. "Keep your mouth shut, white-ass. I didn't do you no favor."

"It's the second time you could have killed me, but didn't."

"Shit . . . I never killed nobody. Givin' orders is one thing, but doin' it yourself . . . well, I never killed anybody."

David tucked that scrap of information into his memory. "You've been in zero gravity before?"

"Jus' once. Long time ago, when I was still playin' football. They sent th' whole team up to Alpha for a publicity stunt. Now you jus' keep quiet an' let 'em think you're still out of it. Hamoud's scared enough of you. If he knows you're awake already, he'll knock you off first chance he gets."

"Thanks again," David said. Then he lay back and grate-

384

fully let sleep wash over him. He was safe for the time being. He felt that a very large lion was guarding him.

Cyrus Cobb scratched irritably at his throat. The damned turtleneck shirt he was wearing felt as if it were strangling him. And the damned diplomats were playing their usual childish games, making everybody else stand there and wait like a bunch of idiotic spear-carriers.

The Director of Island One was standing in the passenger debarkation lounge, a smallish lobby that generally held no more than a few people at a time. Now it was crammed with news reporters, camera crews, curious Island One citizens, security guards (in and out of uniform), V.I.P.'s, and an assortment of bureaucrats from the World Government and from *El Libertador*'s staff.

The lobby area was wall-to-wall people. You couldn't see the bare utilitarian plastic walls or the scuffed floor tiles. The only clear space was the narrow red carpet that one of the advance flunkies from Messina had brought with him.

Briefly, Cobb thought of how much he wanted David to be with him. *He's not dead. They would have found his body by now. He got as far as New York, and he wasn't killed in the fighting. He'll get here eventually. He's got to get home; none of this means a rat's backside unless David comes back here to . . .*

The radio clipped to his earlobe crackled. "They've settled it, Chief. Boweto will come out first, representing the World Government. Then *El Libertador*."

"How'd they come to agree?" Cobb subvocalized into the microphone hidden beneath his turtleneck.

The voice in his ear chuckled. "Their two top negotiators flipped a coin."

"Very intelligent of them—after keeping us waiting half an hour."

"They didn't expect such primitive facilities up here, boss. Thought there'd be two reception lounges so they could arrive simultaneously."

"They should've asked. We told them we had facilities to berth both shuttles at the same time. They never asked about the god-blessed reception lounge. Or the airlock."

Jamil al-Hashimi, standing beside Cobb, listened to the chatter on his own miniaturized radiophone, but his mind was roaming elsewhere. *Bahjat is on her way here at last. But has she really renounced her revolutionary nonsense? She says all the violence has sickened her. But will she try to foment a guerrilla movement here?* He almost laughed. *Ah, well, her childish violence was a reaction against me, according to all the psychologists. Now she wants to be with me, so I suppose she has grown up, at last. I'll have to find a husband for her.* His brows knit into a frown. *That will be our next argument. A husband.*

For the hundredth time in the past half-hour, Cobb wished he hadn't given in to his staff's pleadings and worn such a formal outfit: full turtleneck shirt (that itched); dark conservative suit with lapels, even; boots instead of his comfortable slippers. *Blasted tribal rites,* he grumbled inwardly. *Barbaric.*

But at last the gleaming metal hatch of the inner airlock swung open. The crowd sighed and surged against the velvet ropes that lined the red-carpeted path. Tape recorders whirred and cameras clicked.

Four uniformed World Army soldiers marched out in full regalia, ceremonial swords at their sides and tiny, deadly laser guns clipped to their belts. They arranged themselves on either side of the airlock hatch. Then four civilians stepped through the hatch, two of them women. To Cobb they looked like civil service flunkies.

Finally, Kowie Boweto strode through the open hatch, smiling broadly for the crowd and the cameras. He wore a plain beige suit with open-neck shirt and a large gold medallion hanging from a heavy chain on his broad chest. The crowd broke into applause as Boweto walked confidently up the red carpet and extended his hand to take Cobb's.

Cobb was surprised at how short the man was. Not especially tall himself, just under six feet, Cobb realized that all the pictures he had seen of the World Government's new strong man—even live TV pictures—had been cleverly composed to make Boweto appear much taller than he actually was. *Do all politicians have the Napoleon complex?* Cobb wondered as he exchanged formal greetings with Boweto. *Is that why they become politicians?*

Boweto took his place at Cobb's side as his retinue of followers flowed by them shaking hands with Cobb, al-

Hashimi, and the other Board members. *The reception line,* Cobb thought. *Caesar Augustus must have invented it.*

Then, after the crowd had quieted down a bit, the air-lock hatch closed. Cobb mentally counted off the seconds for the hatch to recycle. At exactly the proper one hundred fifty, the hatch swung open again and four of *El Libertador*'s soldiers stepped through. They wore rough khaki fatigues and plain automatic pistols in black, oil-gleaming holsters.

Right behind them came a fifth man in khaki fatigues, unadorned with insignias of rank. If Cobb hadn't seen *El Libertador*'s photographs, he would not have known that this was the revolutionary leader who had caused the World Government so much trouble.

He was taller than Boweto, though not by much. His graying hair and beard gave him an air of dignity. He took Cobb's hand in a firm, friendly grip. His smile was warming.

"Colonel Villanova," Cobb said.

"Dr. Cobb. Thank you for accepting the responsibility of being the host for this meeting."

"It's my pleasure. I only hope that the meeting is productive." Turning slightly, Cobb said, "May I present the Honorable Councilman Kowie Boweto, Acting Chairman of the World Government Council. Councilman Boweto, Colonel Cesar Villanova . . ."—Cobb departed from the script the bureaucrats had prepared for him—". . . also known, in fact, much better known, as *El Libertador.*"

Boweto almost hid the scowl that came over his face at the mention of Villanova's infamous cognomen. But he forced a smile and took Villanova's hand as the cameras zoomed in for close-ups.

"A pleasure to meet you at last," Boweto said.

"And an honor to meet you, sir," said Villanova.

Cobb thought, *There's enough saccharin in the air to give us all cancer.*

Someone was nudging his shoulder. David snapped awake, felt a momentary surge of panic when he couldn't see, then remembered the sack over his head.

"Are you all right?" It was Evelyn's voice.

He took a deep breath before answering. "Yes," he said. And it was true. His head was clear. He no longer shivered or felt cold. Flexing his slightly numb fingers and toes, he felt strong and well.

"I'm awfully hungry, though," he said.

"I'll get you something."

David felt her move away from him. The shuttle was still coasting in zero gravity. He could hear the faint electrical hum of air-circulation fans and other equipment. No voices near him, though.

Evelyn came back. "I've some hot soup in a squeeze bulb, and a couple of sandwiches."

"Where are we?" he asked.

"In a private space shuttle, one of the al-Hashimi craft, heading for . . ."

"Island One, I know. I mean, where in the shuttle do they have me?"

"You're in the last row of the rear passenger compartment. Everyone else is up forward, going over their plans for taking Island One."

"I told them everything they wanted to know, didn't I?"

"I imagine so. They gave you awfully heavy doses of drugs. We thought you might die."

"Not yet," David said. "Not yet."

"I'm afraid they won't allow me to take the hood off you," Evelyn said, "but I can pull it up a bit."

He felt her hands on his face.

"There. Now I can feed you. They don't trust me, really. They think I helped you to make your break back at the laboratory."

"How many of them are there?"

"Aboard this shuttle? Fifty-two, counting the pilots. Why didn't you run away from the laboratory when you had the chance?"

"And let them take Island One? No. I had other things to do."

"They're going to take Island One, anyway," Evelyn said.

"No one at the colony suspects that this shuttle is a Trojan horse?"

He could sense her shaking her head. "Lord knows what this Scheherazade girl told her father. He's the Sheikh al-Hashimi."

"I know."

"Yes. I suppose you do. It seems that the entire al-

Hashimi empire is riddled with guerrillas who are working for the PRU. She got the spaceport manager to report to her father that she's bringing only two people with her. As far as the sheikh knows, this ship is almost empty. It's his daughter's private yacht."

"He can't be that naïve," David said. "He must suspect something."

"About his daughter?" Evelyn dismissed the idea. "And with his entire organization lying to him? How could he possibly suspect that they're working for her, and not him?"

David thought for a moment. Then, remembering, he asked, "How are you handling the weightlessness? Does it still bother you?"

"Awfully," she replied. "I'll never get accustomed to it."

"You should be lying down in your seat, then."

He sensed her shrug and smile. "I've been assigned to feeding you. It's a very democratic system these PRU people have. Scheherazade gives the orders and everyone else follows them. Except Hamoud—he sulks and grumbles and then pretends they were his own orders."

"But he does what she tells him to."

"Oh, yes. Scheherazade is very clever. She's playing Hamoud against this monstrous big fellow, Leo. Keeps them both on their toes."

He felt the tip of the squeeze bulb's plastic stem against his lips. He sucked on it and felt the warmth of the broth in his mouth. Swallowing, it felt good going down.

David finished the soup. Evelyn fed him the tiny precut sandwiches, one mouthful at a time. Then she gave him a bulb of orange juice.

"Thanks," David said. "That's the best meal I've had since our last dinner together."

"You *are* all right? No aftereffects from the drugs?"

"I think so. They built a pretty strong metabolism into me," David said.

"Thank God."

"How long will it take to get to Island One? When will we land?"

"About another day and a half," Evelyn said. "A bit more than thirty-six hours. All in zero-mucking gravity."

"And then they're going to try to take over the whole colony."

"The solar mirror controls, the power plant, the spacecraft docks—that's what they intend to seize first. And then the V.I.P.'s—as hostages."

"Dr. Cobb?"

"He's small potatoes now. Hunter Garrison is there, and all the other bigwigs who own Island One. And *El Libertador* and the Acting Director of the World Government are holding a peace conference there. The place is teeming with Very Important Hostages."

David said nothing.

She touched his stubbly cheek, then bent over and kissed his lips. "Stop thinking about it," Evelyn told him. "Just stay alive. Don't do anything to antagonize them. Cooperate with them or they'll kill you. Please, David, stay alive."

"I'll stay alive," he answered. "Don't worry about that."

She tugged the hood back down on his chin and left him. David leaned back in his seat, his mind racing.

Thirty-six hours. It won't be enough time. It won't be enough.

It never occurred to any of us that Island One could be seized by a handful of terrorists. Oh, we thought about it and even made contingency plans during some of our security meetings, but it was like the French army in the nineteen-thirties making plans against a German invasion. They knew they had their Maginot Line, and no army could get past it. We knew we were a quarter-million miles from Earth and the nearest terrorist; the reality of our vulnerability never hit us at the gut level, where people really live.

Sheikh al-Hashimi held back a lot of vital information from us, of course. Funny how a man can be so clever in so many ways and so completely blind about his daughter. Same thing—intellectual understanding versus gut feelings.

But there's no doubt about it—if we had taken the possibility of a terrorist takeover seriously, if al-Hashimi had told us all he knew, we could have avoided a lot of deaths.

A lot of deaths.

—Cyrus S. Cobb,
Tapes for an unauthorized
autobiography

· CHAPTER 37 ·

The passenger debarkation lounge was no longer filled with people. The red carpet and velvet ropes had been taken away. At the far end of the lounge were two slightly bored middle-aged customs inspectors, loafing at their counters, waiting for the ship's three passengers to come through the airlock.

A worried-looking little bald man paced from the inspection counters to the airlock hatch and back again, endlessly. He had been there for nearly twenty minutes, waiting for the shuttle to disgorge its only important passenger: the daughter of the sheikh.

The airlock hatch finally swung open and a landing-dock technician stepped through, a strange expression on his face. He stood by the open hatch in his stained, heavy-duty coveralls as a stocky, intense-looking bearded Arab came through the hatch and took up a position beside him.

The bald man felt puzzled. Landing-dock technicians should stay outside, in the landing docks, not in here, where the passengers come through.

Then a beautiful young lady stepped sedately through the open hatch. But she was strangely dressed for the daughter of the sheikh—in a zippered jumpsuit of desert tan, just like the moody-looking Arab's. The jumpsuit looked at least a size too big for her. She had rolled the pants cuffs up and he could see that she wore soft leather boots, good for hiking. A sturdy webbed belt circled her hips and she carried a large black travel kit over her shoulder.

Confused, the bald man glanced from the Arab to the woman. Why would they dress alike?

But there was no mistaking the shiekh's daughter, despite her odd costume. The long black hair, the uplifted chin, the al-Hashimi imperiousness.

"Princess Bahjat!" The bald man bowed, then began babbling, "Your father, the sheikh, asked me to greet you since he is unable to leave due to the political conference that is going on to meet you himself, but he instructed me . . ."

Bahjat swept right past him, heading for the inspection counters. Behind her three more swarthy young men followed.

The two inspectors stood up straighter. The older man tried to hold in his potbelly and smiled at Bahjat as she placed her travel kit on the counter before him.

"May I see your identification, please?" he asked as pleasantly as he could. His partner at the other counter started to ask the same thing—much less pleasantly—of the pimply-faced youth who had reached him first.

Bahjat looked over the lounge area and the inspection counters. "No one else is here?" she asked.

"I was trying to explain to you," the bald man said, "that everyone is tied up with the political conference that has been going on for two days now, and they could not arrange a proper welcome for . . ."

Bahjat silenced him with a wave of her hand. To the customs inspector she said, "My I.D. is in my bag." She started to unzip the black travel kit.

The inspector's smile broadened. *I wonder what kind of clothing she has in there. Would she get sore if I searched it by hand instead of putting it through the X ray?*

Instead of her identification cards, Bahjat pulled a small flat black pistol from the bag. It fit into her hand snugly. The inspector suddenly saw its deadly snout staring at him.

He gasped.

"Not one word," Bahjat said, her voice low and sweet. Now she was doing the smiling. "Come with us."

One of the young men vaulted over the counter and unerringly found the switches that deactivated the TV cameras that monitored the area. Bahjat had been careful to position herself where the inspector's back shielded her gun hand from the camera's view.

A horde of men and women poured through the airlock hatch, more than fifty of them. The bald man stared, uncomprehending. Among them was the biggest man he had ever seen, towering massively above the heads of the others. He barely squeezed through the airlock hatch.

David went through the hatch just behind Leo. A tiny thrill of homecoming tingled through him as he set foot inside the debarkation lounge. He knew every scuff on the tiled floor, every tiny crack in the plastic wall covering.

But he remembered the awful task before him, and the thrill was quickly smothered under that crushing realization.

Evelyn walked alongside Hamoud. *They don't really trust me,* she knew. But she was the only one among them who had actually been in Island One before, except for David, whom they knew they couldn't trust at all.

Bahjat's plan is working well, Evelyn thought. In less than five minutes the landing docks and debarkation lounge had been taken. The dock technicians and the three old men at the inspection counters had been thoroughly bound, gagged, and drugged into unconsciousness. Now the guerrillas were fanning out to their objectives.

The fifty-two of them were split into three groups: Bahjat would lead the team that seized the spacecraft control station; Hamoud would take a larger team to capture the communications and administration buildings; Leo would head the group that took the power plant.

Control the controls. That was Bahjat's scheme. The guerrillas would capture the colony's only spacecraft landing facilities, its internal and external communications systems, and the power plant that provided the colony's heat, light, and electricity. *Then they'll control the colony and everyone in it,* Evelyn knew.

They? she asked herself. *Or we? Whose side are you on, old girl?* With something of a shock, she realized that she really wasn't entirely certain.

As the guerrillas headed toward the escalators that led down to the underground tube trains, David cautiously flicked the switch in his molar that turned on his implanted communicator. A hum buzzed in his ear implant and he heard the computer's flat, non-human voice say, "READY." It was the most exciting sound David had heard in months. *I'm whole again!* he exulted. *I've got my brains back!*

At the head of the downward-trundling escalator, the guerrillas began sorting themselves into three groups. *Assault teams,* David knew. Leo stood at the front of one, Hamoud had a much larger group gathering around him, and Bahjat led a third team, the smallest of them all.

Instinctively, David stayed close to Leo. But Hamoud pointed to him. "You come with me, blond one. Quickly!"

David looked to Leo, who shrugged.

Bahjat worked her way through the milling crowd and spoke with Hamoud, low and swiftly, in Arabic. Hamoud looked flustered and angrily tapped his wristwatch. Glancing at her own watch, Bahjat nodded curtly, then walked quickly to David.

"You will go with Hamoud's team . . . to the communications center."

"So that he can shoot me in the back and say that I tried to escape?"

Her eyes flicked to his, then slid away. "Don't give him any excuses to do so. We have no time for arguments. I will take the Englishwoman with me."

And that was that. Bahjat headed off for the spacecraft control station, Leo took his team down the escalator, and Hamoud's larger gang followed them down toward the trains.

David found himself sandwiched between a pair of unsmiling, Arabic-looking young men who carried heavy, deadly assault rifles in their hands.

They know that Security only checks the cameras here a few times each day, unless there's a disturbance of some kind, David thought. *They know because I told them. They made a Judas out of me.*

Leo's team had farther to go and took the first one-car train at the platform. Hamoud's group stood tensely waiting for a few minutes until the next train arrived.

As they hustled him into the empty car, David turned on his implanted communicator and patched into the Security phone network. Nothing but normal chatter; everything was routine, except for the few special men detailed to stand guard at the political conference going on in the administration building.

Which was exactly where they were heading.

Judas, David repeated to himself. *That's me. But they don't realize how much of a Judas I really am.*

Briefly David thought of alerting the Security force, but he knew it would be a foolish waste. They were totally unprepared to handle assault teams of heavily armed guerrillas. There would be bloodshed, and Hamoud's PRU people were experts at killing. So he sat in the train and listened to it whisk along the smooth, metal-walled tube toward the administration building. The muzzle of a young woman's automatic rifle pointed absently at his chest as she sat beside him with the weapon cradled in her lap.

The assault team boiled out of the train when it pulled into the village where the communications and administration centers were located. Without a word they raced up the steps toward the surface, the clinking of their ammunition belts, the scuffing of their boots on the stairs, the heavy panting of their breath the only sounds they made.

The startled people in the village screamed and scattered as the guerrillas erupted into the sunlight. There were only twenty-five of them, but they looked like an army and moved through the peaceful pedestrian walks of the village with the trained discipline of professional troops.

David ran along with them, the two youths flanking him and Hamoud's stocky figure a few paces ahead as they raced unerringly into the administration building.

In the lobby, one security guard managed to get his pistol out of his holster before a burst of automatic rifle fire cut him down. The other two guards simply gaped, round-eyed and slack-jawed, as the guerrillas poured into the building and sprinted to their preassigned goals. Two of them disarmed the guards, turned them to face the lobby wall, then clubbed them down with rifle butts.

The Landing Control Officer and his ten technicians were already standing at their consoles in the spacecraft control center, hands raised, staring at a dozen gun muzzles.

"But you're crazy," the L.C.O. was saying. "You can't hijack the whole colony. What the hell do you think you're doing?"

The slim dark-haired woman smiled tightly at him. "Do not concern yourself about us. Worry about yourself and your crew. You must do exactly as you are told or we will be forced to shoot you."

"Jesus H. Christ!" the L.C.O. muttered.

Evelyn hung back near the entrance to the hot, tense

little room where the spacecraft were monitored. A part of her memory wondered if the astronaut who had shown her this control center, so many months ago, were out there somewhere in a ship, depending on these technicians to guide him safely back to the colony. *He's a dead man if he needs their help,* she thought.

Scheherazade was saying to the L.C.O., "We will keep three of our people here to watch you. You will shut down all your systems."

"But we can't! There are spacecraft in transit!"

"Send them back to Earth or to the Moon. We have no desire to harm you, but we will not allow any ships to land here. And no ships may leave Island One. Do you understand?"

"Nobody in, nobody out."

Bahjat nodded. "Very good. Remember that."

"But there are people out there in the work pods," the L.C.O. insisted. "We can't leave them there. They've got to be brought back home."

The pistol in Bahjat's hand stayed firmly pointed at his midsection. "Recall them—at once. Close down all the work pods and get them all back here within the hour."

He nodded slowly.

"Be very careful and very cooperative. We all want to live through this, you know."

Cyrus Cobb had seen his guests through a working lunch in the conference room. Now that they had cleared away the crumbs and tableware and were getting down to serious talk, Cobb excused himself and headed for his office. The conference room was on the administration building's top floor; Cobb's office was on the ground floor, three flights below. He ignored the elevator and started down the stairs.

As he rounded the corner to start the second downward flight, a gang of tight-faced men and women burst into view, pounding up the steps toward him with heavy rifles in their hands.

And David was among them.

"What in the name of . . ."

In an instant he was surrounded.

"Keep moving!" shouted a swarthy, sour-faced man. The gang pressed on up the stairs, but David and their leader stayed behind.

"Dr. Cobb . . ." David's face was an agony of guilt, shame, anger.

"You are Cyrus Cobb," the leader said, waving a blue-gray automatic pistol at the man's face.

"Who the blazes are you?" Cobb growled.

"You may call me Tiger. I am the leader of the Peoples' Revolutionary Underground liberation team, and you are my prisoner."

"They're taking over the whole colony," David said, looking miserable. "They've already got the communications center and the spacecraft docks. Another team is taking the power plant."

"And they've got you, too, eh?" Cobb said.

David spread his hands in a gesture of helplessness. His face was bone-thin, haggard, eyes lined and dark, jaw stubbly with several days' worth of prickly blond beard.

"You will take me to your office," Hamoud said to the old man. "I want to see this fabulous surveillance system you have—the nerve center of the colony, I am told."

Cobb suddenly felt every one of his years. His shoulders sagged. But David took him by the arm and held him firmly. He looked at the young man. Something in his eyes . . .

Straightening his spine, Cobb said sharply, "All right—Pussycat. Follow me."

They went down the stairs to the ground floor. Cobb saw the sprawled bodies of the security guards. Blood caked the tiled floor. A pair of guerrillas stood at the main door. Two more lounged on chairs in the lobby, rifles on their laps. They had made no effort to move the men on the floor.

Tight-lipped, an angry fire seething inside him, Cobb led Hamoud and David through his outer office and into his observation chamber.

Hamoud stared goggle-eyed at the hundreds of screens inside the high, domed room. Cobb went to his pedestal and stood beside the high swivel chair. David paced uncertainly between the two of them.

"I can see everything!" Hamoud shouted, whirling around and around. "It's like being God!"

Like being God, David repeated to himself. There was the passenger debarkation area, where they had come in. And on the screen next to it were the spacecraft docks themselves, now disgorging workers brought home from the pods. Villages and forests, lakes and farmlands being tended by yellow-painted machines no bigger than golf carts.

Hamoud turned and saw viewscreens that displayed intricate machinery. And others showed huge vistas of towering green trees, a whole tropical world without a building to be seen. Yet, beside those screens were others that pictured low-slung opulent palaces of the purest white stone and crystal, set into the same tropical greenery. He recognized the markings of Sheikh al-Hashimi on one of the buildings.

"Where is that?" he asked, pointing.

The old man, Cobb, looked more angry than afraid. "In Cylinder B, where the Board members live."

"Sheikh al-Hashimi?"

"Yes. And the others—Garrison, St. George, all five of them."

Hamoud grinned wolfishly. "I shall pay them each a visit. The sheikh was my employer at one time."

"He's not at home," Cobb said dryly. "He's attending the conference with Boweto and *El Libertador*."

Cobb jabbed at the keyboard on his pedestal, and the largest viewscreen, in the center of the wall in front of them, showed the men sitting around the conference table, deep in talk.

"Yes, there is the sheikh," Hamoud said, a warm glow of satisfaction spreading through him. "I shall visit him at the conference . . . and then go and see what these houses of the billionaires are like."

People of the world! Attack units of the People's Revolutionary Underground have seized Island One. The stranglehold of the multinational corporations on the energy coming from space has been broken. No longer will the corporations and their lackies of the World Government keep the price of energy so high that the world's needy cannot afford it. A new day is rising!

We of the PRU present the following non-negotiable demands: (1) all anti-PRU activities must cease immediately, all over the world; (2) the World Government must be disbanded; (3) national governments must open their legislatures to PRU representatives; (4) all multinational corporations must be broken up into smaller, non-monopolistic units, under control of PRU overseers.

Until these demands are met, *no* power from the Solar Power Satellites will be beamed to *any* receiving station on Earth.

Among the prisoners we are holding hostage on Island One are: Kowie Boweto, Acting Director of the World Government; T. Hunter Garrison, of Garrison Enterprises; Sheikh Jamil al-Hashimi . . .

—Broadcast on all communications frequencies from Island One, 7 December 2008

• CHAPTER 38 •

Jamil al-Hashimi was sitting at the conference table as the PRU announcement of their takeover was beamed to Earth on every private and commercial radio, television, and hologram channel.

The conferees knew nothing of what was happening around them. Al-Hashimi was leaning back in his contoured chair, listening to the politely icy discussion among the diplomats. His thoughts drifted to his daughter.

Kowie Boweto seemed bored. His aides were arguing procedures, protocol, agenda. The African looked as if he wanted to cut through all the red tape and speak directly to *El Libertador*. The Latin American appeared unhappy, too, al-Hashimi noticed. He had come here to make agreements, not to argue about seating arrangements.

Bahjat should have arrived by now, al-Hashimi thought. *Will she be angry that I didn't greet her at the landing dock? No matter. I must maintain a firm hand with her. It was my laxity that allowed her to drift away in the first place.*

"Taxation is too complex an issue to be placed on the preliminary agenda," one of the World Government functionaries was saying, his voice a low, polished, smooth drone, carefully calculated not to offend anyone by the slightest inflection or show of emotion. *He will put you to sleep before he'll make you angry,* al-Hashimi murmured to himself.

The Argentinian who was acting as *El Libertador*'s spokesman gave a small shrug. "Perhaps so. But the question of local autonomy . . ."

I could excuse myself and go to the landing dock, al-Hashimi told himself. *Or, better yet, I could go out and*

*meet her at her quarters once she has landed. That way it
will not seem as if I have been waiting for her to make her
arrival . . .*

"No!"

The word was spoken softly, but everything around the
long gleaming table stopped. For a moment the only sound
in the room was the hum of the air-circulation fans hidden
in the ductwork above the ceiling.

All eyes turned to *El Libertador.*

"I say no." His calm gray eyes surveyed the men around
the table, stopped at Boweto. "We are here to come to an
understanding, not to debate how many angels can dance
on the head of a pin."

Boweto broke into a wide, toothy grin. "I agree," he
said, slapping his hand lightly on the tabletop.

"But, sir," the aide next to him said, "these matters are
too important to be approached haphazardly."

Across the table, *El Libertador* said, "Then let us fix an
agenda—now, quickly, without all this mincing and hair-
splitting."

"What do you suggest?" Boweto asked. His aides looked
shocked, aghast that their chief would speak directly to
The Other Side.

"The World Government's decision-making apparatus in
Messina too often ignores the needs, the desires, the
national . . . soul, for lack of a better word, of the individual nations that those decisions affect," said *El Libertador.* "The individual nations must have a stronger voice
in the decision-making process."

Boweto hunched forward in his chair. "Restructuring the
World Legislature—put that on the agenda."

The secretary sitting behind Boweto's shoulder tapped
the computer keyboard sitting on his knee. The aides flanking him sat in stony silence.

"Taxes are important," Boweto said. His grin returned.
"In fact, taxes are the main business of governments."

El Libertador nodded. "Agreed."

"What about the PRU?" asked the one woman in *El
Libertador*'s retinue, a tall, haughty-looking aristocrat with
the chiseled features of Spanish nobility. Her regal bearing
was wildly out of place with the baggy khaki uniform she
wore.

"Yes," said *El Libertador*. "The violence must be

stopped. There must be no further killing. That should be the foremost item on our agenda."

"Very good," said Boweto.

"And trade relations," a World Government aide suggested in a timid voice, "especially those between . . ."

"Not now," Boweto snapped. "But we should discuss the return of Argentina, Chile, and South Africa to the World Government."

El Libertador nodded. "I am not empowered to speak for the governments of those individual nations, of course, but we could work out the conditions under which they would consider rejoining. . . ."

The main door to the conference room opened. Al-Hashimi, sitting closest to the door, turned angrily in his chair. "We gave orders that no disturbances . . ."

The ashen-faced Island One security guard simply stood there in the doorway, his mouth hanging open, the holster at his side open and empty.

Behind him stepped Hamoud, the guard's heavy automatic pistol in his hand. And behind Hamoud were two more raggedly dressed guerrillas carrying gleaming new assault rifles at their hips, almost carelessly.

"Hamoud!" al-Hashimi gasped. "How did you . . ."

"Gentlemen! And ladies!" Hamoud said, his smile an arrogant badge of insolence. "You are the prisoners of the Peoples' Revolutionary Underground. No . . . do not move! Stay in your seats. Don't make my men start shooting. We have captured the entire space colony. You will remain in this room until you are ordered to move. Obey all orders instantly. If you do not, however trivial the order is, you will be shot."

Leo sat heavily on the engineer's little plastic swivel chair. Its back bowed out, its spraddled legs creaked under his weight.

Taking the power plant had been easy. There were no guards; nobody even had a weapon. His dozen PRU troops had just walked in and all the engineers and technicians froze in their places.

"Just relax and keep workin'," Leo had told them. "We ain't gonna hurt nobody, long's you do what you're told."

He had expected massive rumbling machinery and the winking lights of computers flashing everywhere in the power plant building. The computer consoles were there, all right: row after row of them twinkling quietly to themselves. But the long, high-ceilinged, brightly lit room was quiet and cool. No huge turbines shaking the air, no hissing steam or maze of pipes carrying strange coolants and fluids. Just an efficient, clean room with shadowless light panels for a ceiling. No noise except the soft hum of the computers and the padding of men and women in comfortable slippers and spotless white coveralls.

Then why'm I sweatin'? Leo asked himself.

His legs ached and his stomach was twisted into tight knots. *Nerves,* he told himself. *Nothing but nerves.*

He had been all right during the action. Not a qualm, even though he thought he might have to pull the trigger of the assault rifle they had given him. He carried the weapon easily, in one massive hand, handling it like an elongated pistol.

Okay, you didn't have to shoot anybody. It all went down smooth as a virgin's tit. Why the shakes?

He knew. He didn't want to believe it, but he knew. It was starting. His heart was thumping wildly inside him. *If I don't get my stuff soon, my whole body's gonna fall apart.*

William Palmquist raced to the phone and banged the ON button before its first buzz could end. Ruth's normally cheerful round face looked worried.

"You're all right?" they asked simultaneously.

Ordinarily they would have laughed, but he merely nodded as she said, "They recalled us from the lab pod. We thought it was a solar flare or something."

"Worse," he said. "Terrorists have taken over the colony."

"I know." Ruth glanced back over her shoulder. "They have armed PRU guards here at the landing docks."

"You're okay? They haven't bothered you?"

"No. They said they're going to let us all go home, and we should stay in our quarters until they give us further orders."

His head bobbing, "That's what they told us when they made us shut down all the equipment and come in from the farm."

"I'll be home as soon as I can get a train. There's a big

405

mob of people here. Everybody in the pods was recalled at once."

"I'm just glad they didn't make you stay out there. I was going crazy worrying."

"I'm fine, Bill," she said, smiling for him. "We'll be all right, you'll see."

"Sure," he lied, knowing that she was covering up her fears, too.

"You must try to negotiate with them!"

Cesar Villanova smiled bleakly. "I doubt that they would treat me any differently from the rest of you. After all, I have never been one of them."

Boweto got up from his chair and paced the length of the long table. The others around the table were whispering in small, frightened knots of groups or staring off blankly into nothingness, like al-Hashimi.

When Boweto reached the end of the table he turned and said, "You should at least *try* to speak with them. They look up to you. *El Libertador* has been their hero— all around the world."

"Until I agreed to negotiate with you," Villanova said.

Boweto scowled. "You think they've turned against you?"

"Certainly."

"Nonsense! They wouldn't . . ."

The door swung open and all talk stopped. One of the armed guerrillas, a gangling, pale-skinned teen-ager who carried his assault rifle as if he'd been born with it in his arms, called, "Sheikh Jamil al-Hashimi!"

Al-Hashimi got to his feet. "I am he."

The lad brusquely motioned with the rifle for the sheikh to follow him.

Casting a *Who knows?* glance at the others, al-Hashimi went after the boy. Two PRU guards stood just outside the door to the conference room, one of them a girl. Both carried automatic rifles. They closed the door as the teen-ager strode down the corridor without a backward look. Al-Hashimi followed him.

They walked out into the open and crossed a carefully tended lawn, heading for another small, low building of white-painted cement. The village lanes and streets were empty; the normal late-afternoon pedestrian traffic had disappeared.

Inside the smaller building, the boy went directly to an unmarked door and rapped on it. A muffled voice sounded from within and the boy opened the door, then motioned brusquely for al-Hashimi to step through.

He found himself standing at the rear of a strange theater. Ten rows of seats scaled down from where he stood, and each seat had a desk-like console in front of it. Most of the seats were empty, but down at the front two rows, technicians bent over the consoles, their fingers moving across the colored buttons of the desktop keyboards like musicians working out an intricate symphony.

The huge screen that filled the theater's front wall showed an electric map of the world. Al-Hashimi recognized the screen's purpose instantly; he had similar screens in his offices in Baghdad. Glowing green lights along the equator showed where Solar Power Satellites hung in orbit. Huge areas of the map—all of them in the Northern Hemisphere—were color-coded to show how much energy each area was receiving from the Solar Power Satellites.

Already one swatch of territory in the Balkans was glowing red. As al-Hashimi watched, another slice, covering most of Italy, went from cheerful yellow to sickly pink.

They are turning off the Solar Power Satellites, al-Hashimi realized. And he saw PRU guerrillas standing behind the technicians, fingering their guns as the technicians obediently cut off the energy flowing from space to the people of Europe and North America.

All this al-Hashimi took in at a glance as the door clicked shut behind him. And he saw, standing near him on this last, highest row of the theater, his daughter, Bahjat —the guerrilla leader, Scheherazade, dressed in her mannish jumpsuit with a pistol buckled to her hip.

"So, Father," Bahjat said in the shadowy lighting at the back of the theater, "I have come to Island One, as you wished."

In the dim light it was difficult to read the expression on her face.

"Not exactly as I wished," al-Hashimi countered. "But, then, you seldom did what I wanted you to."

"Scheherazade has not finished her work."

He pointed toward the electronic map. "So I see."

"Did you really believe that I would join you here as a faithful little daughter?"

"I had hoped that you would have come to your senses by now."

"As my mother came to her senses."

He felt a pang of surprise flash through him. But no one else was within earshot. They were all many rows down, hunched over their destructive work.

"Your mother was a drunkard and a fool. You know that."

"I know she died of drinking. She drank because she was lonely. She missed you."

"She may have thought she did," al-Hashimi said, steel springs coiling in his chest, "but she lied, even to herself."

"And you killed her."

"She killed herself—with drink, as you said."

"You allowed her to."

"She disgraced herself. I would not allow her to disgrace me."

"You kill everything that stands in your way, don't you?"

He smiled without pleasure. "Scheherazade has no blood on her hands?"

For an instant Bahjat's eyes flared. Then, "I am my father's daughter."

Al-Hashimi nodded. "And what is next for you? Patricide?"

"Not if you are obedient. It will be enough to destroy everything you have built. But if you cause any trouble for us, believe me, they will kill you without a second thought."

"Hamoud is here," al-Hashimi said. "I know that he enjoys killing."

Her brows arched. "You know Hamoud that well?"

"Yes."

"I can control him . . . if you all behave yourselves."

"Once I thought I could control him."

Bahjat smiled bitterly. "You have been wrong about many things, haven't you?"

Ignoring her thrust, he asked, "What about *El Libertador*? Is he a prisoner, too?"

"Yes. He could have been our leader, at one time. But he is as old and corrupt as the rest of you."

"He is a man of high principles," al-Hashimi said. "That makes him very difficult to deal with."

"I will deal with him," Bahjat said.

Al-Hashimi hesitated. "It is true, then. You are actually the leader of this gang."

"Does it seem so strange?"

"I thought Hamoud . . ."

"Hamoud *thinks* he is the leader. He shouts the orders, but he orders what I tell him to."

"I see."

"Go back and tell the others that we have found quarters for them in one of the apartment complexes. But if they cause us the slightest difficulty, the troops will slaughter them all."

"The ways of Allah are difficult to fathom."

"Not really," Bahjat answered, the heat of anger melting her icy indifference toward her father. "When you murder an innocent man whose only crime was to fall in love with your daughter, you should expect that Allah will extract justice for your crime."

The sheikh stared at his daughter. "Ah . . . so *that* is why . . ."

"Yes," she said, her eyes blazing. "That is why. Blood for blood. You murdered my love; you destroyed my life. Now I will destroy everything that you have spent your whole life to build up. Everything!"

And down at the base of the theater, on the huge electronic map, another cheerful green light winked into red, showing that a Solar Power Satellite had been shut down. The Gulf Coast region of the United States, from New Orleans to Tampa Bay, flickered from yellow into deep, sullen red.

Hamoud sat on the edge of the fruit-laden table and noisily bit into a pear. Juice ran down his beard.

"So this is where the billionaires live," he said. Three more guerrillas stood a few feet behind their leader, grinning at Garrison and Arlene.

Garrison glared at Hamoud from his powerchair. "What the hell do you mean, you've taken over Island One? That's impossible!"

Hamoud laughed, leaned forward slightly, and swung a backhand slap at the old man's face.

Arlene, standing beside the chair, stepped inside Hamoud's wide-swinging arm and drove a stiff-fingered blow to his throat. Hamoud went over backward, knocking over the table, fruit smashing and rolling in every direction. Arlene jumped over the fallen table after him, but two of the guerrillas grabbed her arms and twisted them painfully behind her back. She smashed one of them on the instep with her heel. He yowled and let go of her arm.

As she elbowed the other, Hamoud came up from behind the table, gasping, one hand clutched to his throat. Garrison was wheeling off toward the bedroom while the three guerrillas struggled with the one red-haired woman. Hamoud staggered to his feet and reached out. Grabbing Arlene's hair, he yanked her backward hard enough to make her shriek. One of the others slammed a rifle butt into her midsection and she crumpled. Hamoud let go of her hair. She slumped to the floor.

"Come back here or we'll kill her!" he screamed to Garrison.

The old man stopped his powerchair at the doorway to the next room. Slowly, he turned and came back toward them, his wrinkled face white with rage.

Hamoud nudged Arlene onto her back with the toe of his boot. She was conscious. Her hate-filled eyes glared up at him.

"You will stay there without moving," Hamoud said softly to her, "or we will shoot this stupid old man."

Her hands tensed into claws, but otherwise she did not move.

Hamoud turned to Garrison. "A courageous employee," he said, gesturing to the prostrate Arlene. "Her only fear is that you might be hurt."

"You leave us alone," Garrison said, his voice weak and old. "Go away and leave us alone."

"First we must search this house to make certain you have no weapons to use against us." He nodded and the three guerrillas headed off toward the other rooms. "If you stay here quietly, you will live."

Garrison sat helplessly, staring at the gun jutting out from Hamoud's holster. He heard a crash from the bedroom, then ripping, tearing sounds and harsh laughter.

"My men are searching very thoroughly," Hamoud taunted.

They can't get to the art, thank the Lord, Garrison told himself. *They'll never find the underground vault, and*

even if they do, they won't know the computer codes to
open it up. Everything'll be safe.

It seemed as if they tore at the house for hours. Garrison heard smashing, tearing, breaking sounds from every room. Arlene lay still, not moving. But he could see tears of frustrated rage in her eyes.

Finally they were finished. The three youths sauntered back into the living room, rifles slung over their shoulders, shreds of linens and brightly colored tatters of some of Arlene's clothes clinging to their own baggy jumpsuits. One of them had draped a brassiere around his neck. Another was gnawing on a chicken drumstick.

"No weapons," said the bra-toter. "We searched real good."

Hamoud nodded. "Good." Turning to Arlene, "Now you can get up, beautiful lady."

Slowly, barely controlling her anger, she got to her feet. Hamoud nodded again and two of the boys grabbed her arms firmly.

"We take her with us," Hamoud told Garrison, "to teach her a few lessons of respect."

"No!" Garrison clawed his way to his feet. "No! Leave her alone!"

"Can you stop us, old man?"

"I . . . I'll give you something . . . something you'll want . . ."

Hamoud put his hand on Arlene's breast. Beneath the silky fabric of her blouse he could feel her nipple. He squeezed it. Hard. She didn't flinch, but stared straight ahead, avoiding Garrison's eyes.

"I have what I want," Hamoud said. "It's a small price for you to pay for your life, Mr. Billionaire. We'll even ship her back to you when we're finished with her."

Garrison remained standing on trembling legs. Lowering his voice, forcing himself to be steady, he said, "But what I've got is worth millions. . . . You can buy a whole city full of women with just one of the things I can give you."

Hamoud looked at him. "What are you talking about?"

"Treasure, boy," Garrison said, his voice becoming a wheezing purr. "Gold and silver. You won't have to worry about banks and credit checks. This is the kinda loot that Suleiman the Magnificent would've envied."

"Where?"

"Underground. Not far from here. In a vault . . . like Ali Baba's cave, where the forty thieves kept their treasure."

Hamoud's eyes narrowed. "If you are joking with me . . ."

"No joke! More gold and silver than most men see in a lifetime. And diamonds, rubies . . . pearls as big as your fist."

"Near here, you say?"

"Let go of the girl," Garrison bargained. "Tell me you'll leave her alone and I'll tell you where my treasure is buried."

They let go of Arlene without waiting for Hamoud's order. Garrison smiled inwardly, then described where his underground vault with all his art treasures was hidden. He told them how to work the computer-directed locks on the vault door.

Hamoud made Arlene write down the combinations, then grinned as she handed him the paper. "We will be back for you, pretty one . . . after we see the treasure!" He turned to Garrison. "And it had better be as you described it, old man."

They dashed out of the house and headed down the path toward the buried vault.

"Why'd you do it?" Arlene burst out. "They'll rip everything to pieces when they see that it's artwork and not jewels or coins."

"To save your pretty neck," Garrison said. "Never thought I'd see th' day when I'd be so damned noble. Now, get on the phone to the central computer and change those lock combinations, right *now!* We got fifteen, maybe only ten, minutes b'fore they come scootin' back here, madder'n wolverines. We gotta be out in the deep woods by then!"

Arlene threw her arms around his neck. "You old scoundrel!"

He pried her away. "Get to the computer, damn it. *Move!*"

The guerrillas had completed their takeover of the colony. Fifty-two PRU terrorists were now in control of Island One's ten thousand inhabitants.

Cobb sat slumped in his high swivel chair and stared at the screens around him.

"Damned frustrating," he grumbled.

"He's a madman," David said. "If we're not careful, he'll kill us all."

"Even if we are careful, maybe."

David was watching the screens that showed the guards the PRU had set up in the administration building. He counted fourteen of them, all heavily armed, including two just outside Cobb's office.

"What does he want?" Cobb asked.

Pointing to the screens that showed the satellite control theater, David answered, "Power. He's going to bring the whole world to its knees by shutting off the energy from the Solar Power Satellites."

"You're blaming yourself for all this, aren't you? Don't. It's not your fault."

"I told them everything they needed to know," David said.

"They forced you, didn't they?"

Nodding, "Yes, but it's still my brain that they picked. Without me they couldn't have taken over the colony."

"We'll get it back from them." *Somehow,* the old man added mentally.

"They're all going to die," David said. He turned to face Cobb, his head and shoulders taller than the pedestal's keyboard top. Cobb could remember when he sat the lad on his lap and let him play with the buttons.

"What do you mean?" he asked.

David seemed bitter, at war with himself. "I'm going to kill them all. They're all going to die . . . maybe everyone in Island One will die . . . because of me."

"Who's playing God now?" Cobb asked.

David looked back at the old man with rock-steady eyes. "I'm not playing."

Cobb felt his breath catch. "No. I guess you're not. Tell me about it."

The door to the chamber opened and Bahjat stepped in. She looked all around her, open-mouthed, like a pilgrim who had found her shrine at last, a pilgrim in a rumpled, sand-colored jumpsuit, with a pistol holstered at her hip.

"Unbelievable," she murmured.

David went to her, took her by the hand, and led her to Cobb's perch.

"This is the Director of Island One, Dr. Cyrus Cobb," he told her. "And this is the famous Scheherazade, the soul and spirit of the PRU, and its most beautiful leader."

Bahjat looked startled. "You can joke?"

"It's no joke, Bahjat," he answered. To Cobb he added, "Scheherazade is also the daughter of Sheikh al-Hashimi."

"Really?" Cobb said.

"You should not have told him that," Bahjat snapped. "If Hamoud knew he would want to kill you."

"He's going to kill us both, anyway, as soon as he gets what he wants," Cobb said.

"No, he's not," David said.

"I am trying to avoid needless bloodshed," Bahjat said.

"It's too late," David said. "You're all dead. You just don't know it yet. But I've *already* destroyed you . . . all of you."

NEWSFLASH***NEWSFLASH***NEWSFLASH***

MESSINA: World Government sources this morning confirmed that elements of the People's Revolutionary Underground have taken over the Island One space colony.

Among the hostages being held by the PRU terrorists are Kowie Boweto, Acting Director of the World Government, and the Latin American revolutionary leader *El Libertador*. Boweto and *El Libertador* were engaged in a meeting to discuss means of ending the wave of international terrorism that has struck with such devastating force all around the world, including the outbreaks of organized rebellion in the major cities of the United States just two weeks ago.

Official reaction to the PRU takeover of the space colony has been guarded. There has been no response to the terrorists' "non-negotiable" demands so far, despite the fact that energy from several Solar Power Satellites has been interrupted. The PRU claims that it will cut off all energy . . .

• CHAPTER 39 •

Bahjat stood uneasily next to Cobb's high lectern, her eyes locked onto David's.

"Destroyed us already?" she asked. "What do you mean?"

"You'll see soon enough."

Cobb interrupted their staring match. "Looks like your friend Tiger's given up on trying to pry open Garrison's vault."

David turned to the main screens on the wall that Cobb was facing and saw that Hamoud was striding angrily along a forest path back toward the Garrison mansion. His three henchmen followed him at a respectful distance.

"Garrison cleared out. He and his gal are hiding in the woods." Cobb chuckled. "The old coot's got more guts than I thought."

"Hamoud will be coming here," David said.

"Sooner or later," Bahjat agreed.

He searched the screens and located Leo, sitting in one of the tube trains. The man was bathed in sweat; he looked half-unconscious.

"And Leo's coming this way, too."

"What did you mean . . ." Bahjat started to ask again.

"No time for explanations," said David. "I have to go now. I've got work to do."

"I can't let you leave," she said.

"You can't stop me."

"David, don't force me . . ."

He reached out with a blurringly swift move of his hand and grasped the pistol at her hip before she could reach it herself. Gently, he lifted it from the holster.

"I think we've played this game before," David said.

She almost smiled. "It becomes more dangerous each time we do."

Glancing over his shoulder at Cobb, who was still perched up in his chair watching everything, David turned back to Bahjat and said, "Whatever happens . . . I do love you."

"But not enough," she answered with a tiny helpless gesture.

"More than enough—too much to let you go through with this insanity. If there's a way to save you, I'll find it."

"And the others?"

"I don't know. You're the only one I really care about. You're the one I love."

She put a hand on his shoulder and, on tiptoes, kissed him lightly on the lips.

"My poor David," she whispered. "Torn so many ways. Allah protect you."

He didn't trust himself to say another word. And there was no time. David turned and sprinted toward the rear of the room, behind the lectern. Since childhood he had known about the emergency escape corridor back there. Dr. Cobb had threatened to spank him when he had first discovered it and wandered through the corridor to the airlock at its end.

He found the set of four viewscreens that masked the exit door and touched the all-but-invisible button set into the recess between the two upper screens. The door swung outward into the corridor. With a last glimpse back over his shoulder, he saw Cobb watching him, a thoughtful expression on his dour face. Bahjat had already turned away, her head bowed.

She's torn in as many ways as I am, he realized, then suddenly hesitated. *I could bring her with me. . . .* But then he thought that if things didn't work out as he hoped, she would have a better chance for survival apart from him.

"Allah be with you, too, Bahjat," David called as he stepped out into the corridor and carefully shut the door again.

The corridor was narrow and slanted steeply downward. No doors or markings marred its featureless gray walls. Overhead, light panels set every few meters cast enough light to allow a man to run as fast as he could.

David ran.

At the end of the corridor, panting and skidding to a stop, he found the emergency airlock just where it had always been, waiting silently for the moment of need. On the other side of the airlock, David knew, was an escape capsule—a sort of miniature commutersphere, to be used only in case of the most extreme urgency. None had ever been used before in the history of Island One, except for routine tests. There had never been any need. But the escape capsules were attached to the outer skin of the main cylinder, like barnacles studding the hull of an ocean liner, like lifeboats ready for use if the cylinder's inhabitants had to get away from Island One.

The capsules couldn't go far. The spheres could not reach the Moon or Earth. They were not as comfortable as the regular commuterspheres that plied between the cylinder and the work pods. But a dozen people could be squeezed into one of the emergency capsules and live inside it for several weeks, until rescue spacecraft could come in from Selene or from Earth.

The airlock's smooth metal hatch bore a red stenciled EMERGENCY ONLY sign. David yanked the hatch open, knowing that it would set up an electronic yowl in the colony's safety network. Inside the coffin-sized airlock were stenciled directions on how to use the airlock. David studied the small panel of lights set into the metal wall at eye level.

All green. That meant that the emergency capsule on the other side of the airlock's outer hatch was in operating condition and already pressurized with breathable air. David swung the outer hatch open and stepped through into the capsule.

The heat sensor in the capsule's hatch automatically switched on the lights inside when it felt David's body cross its threshold. David found himself on a narrow metal catwalk. Below him were contour couches for twelve people, three rows of four. Supplies were stored beneath the deck plates, he knew. A tiny galley stood at the rear of the deck. Up front was the control cockpit.

Slipping into the pilot's chair, he used the computer link implanted in his skull to refresh his memory of the capsule's controls. They were simple enough, and within a few minutes he had brought the craft up to full internal power. The nudge of a switch released the fail-safe mechanical springs that separated the capsule from the cylinder's hull. Another button ignited the aluminum-oxygen rocket engine briefly and the capsule lurched clear of the colony's main cylinder.

Navigation was the tough part. The capsule's main purpose was to get away from a disaster. It had little more navigational equipment than an ocean liner's lifeboats. But David had no intention of drifting passively in space until someone picked him up. He had a definite destination in mind: the work pod that hovered between the colony's hospital and the farming pods that specialized in pharmaceutical plants. The pod that held Island One's highly advanced biochemistry laboratory. The pod where he himself had been gestated and "born."

He linked the ship's minicomputer with the main computer of the colony, using his own implant as the connecting segment. *Can't go through the spacecraft control center,* he knew. It was in the guerrillas' hands.

He sat at the controls of the empty emergency capsule for a weird few minutes and listened to the tinkling electronic singsong in his head as the computers talked with each other in their own staccato language.

The rocket engine fired two more microsecond bursts, the control jets around the capsule's spherical hull flared, and the craft slued around and headed out toward a cluster of pods hanging high above the colony's main cylinder.

Satisfied that all the lights on his control board showed green and the biochemistry lab was centered in the crosshairs of his forward sensors' viewscreen, David leaned back in the pilot's chair and took a deep, shuddering breath.

There was nothing to do now but wait.

The bright Sicilian sunlight failed to light the spirits of the Executive Council. Two of their members were hostages up in Island One. The empty chair where Boweto sat stared at the other Councilmen like an accusing eye. Somehow, al-Hashimi's empty chair did not seem to bother them so much.

"Well, we've got to do something," said Williams, the American.

Malekoff agreed. "We can't let them hold the Acting Director hostage."

Victor Andersen shook his head slowly. "They are holding more than ten thousand people hostage. In a sense, they are holding the entire world hostage. They are shutting down the Solar Power Satellites."

"We've got to go and rescue them," Williams insisted. "Meet force with force."

"And wreck Island One?" Andersen countered.

"It is winter in the Northern Hemisphere," Malekoff pointed out. "Moscow has a meter of snow on the ground already. At daybreak today, Leningrad's power was cut off. They will kill thousands, perhaps a million or more, in the Soviet Union alone."

"So what're we going to do?" Williams snapped, his voice rising. "Let them take over the World Government?"

Chiu Chan Liu, sitting at the end of the table, separated from the others by the two empty chairs, said quietly, "The first thing we must do is to exhibit some patience. Rash, hasty action would be worse than no action at all."

"And if they kill Boweto?" Williams asked. "Or al-Hashimi?"

Chiu's shoulders inched upward in the subtlest of shrugs. "Regrettable. But that is to be preferred over destroying Island One and the Solar Power Satellites, is it not?"

Williams puffed a disgusted sigh across the table. "Sure," he said. "And then we'd have to pick a new Director, wouldn't we?"

"That is uncalled for," Andersen said sternly.

"Instead of arguing like this," said Malekoff, "we should be sending teams of technicians to each and every one of the Solar Power Satellites to take control of them."

"That would take many days," Chiu said. "Once the PRU realized we were attempting to do so, they could activate the control jets on the satellites and move them completely out of their present orbits. They could even drive them back into the Earth's atmosphere to burn up or crash."

"That would also take days," Malekoff countered. "In the meantime, cosmonaut teams could intercept the satellites and put them back in their correct orbits."

"A few of them," Chiu granted, "but too few. Most of them would be destroyed. Large sections of the world would lose power altogether. It would be a terrible disaster."

"And while that would be going on," Andersen added, "the terrorists would be ritually murdering Boweto, al-Hashimi, and who knows who else?"

Chiu closed his eyes for a moment. When he reopened them, he said, "Gentlemen, our only course of action is to wait. The terrorists are few. The people of Island One are many. Perhaps *they* can solve the problem for themselves."

"And for us," Williams grumbled.

Still perched on his high swivel chair, Cyrus Cobb ignored the insect's eye of compound viewscreens spread all around him and gazed steadily down at Bahjat.

She stood silently by the lectern, barely tall enough for the crown of her lustrous black hair to peep above its edge. Her hands were knotted together, her face a mask of misery, shining with perspiration.

"Do you love him?" Cobb asked.

Startled, she snapped out of her private thoughts and stared up at him.

"He thinks he loves you," the old man said. "I've known him since before he was born. If he thinks he loves you, he's going to risk his life for you."

"What will he do?" Bahjat asked.

Cobb shrugged his bony shoulders. "Whatever it is, he's already planned it out." He didn't trust her enough to show her that he could watch the emergency capsule's flight on the viewscreens. But, looking up, he saw Hamoud striding down the corridor toward his office, dark as a thundercloud.

"Do you love him?" Cobb asked again, urgently.

"No!" Bahjat snapped. "I . . . how can I? We are enemies. Only Christians are fools enough to love their enemies."

Cobb smiled like an inquisitor who had found a raw nerve. "I see," he said. "Well . . . here comes one of your friends."

The door to the outer office banged open and Hamoud stormed into the observation chamber, his face glowering sullenly.

"What are you doing here?" he snarled at Bahjat.

She faced him unflinchingly. "The prisoner—the blond one, David Adams—has escaped."

421

Hamoud stopped a few paces before her. "Escaped? How? To where?"

"I don't know."

"He overpowered your friend here," Cobb said from his perch, "and took off in one of our emergency capsules. I think he's going to hide out in one of the work pods that surround this main cylinder. He can't get very far in an emergency capsule, anyway."

Hamoud's eyes narrowed. "Why are you being so generous with information, old man?"

"Why not?" Cobb grinned lazily. "You'd just try to beat it out of me, wouldn't you?"

Pushing past Bahjat, Hamoud leaned his chunky hands on the lectern. "Then tell me, you who sees all, where have the Billionaire and his red-haired woman gone to?"

"Garrison? Yes . . . I watched that little scene you played at his house. Very nasty."

"He tricked me."

"He told you the truth about the treasure . . . although most of it's in artwork, not cash."

"He gave me the wrong combination for the vault. We'll have to go back and dynamite it open."

Cobb chuckled. "He gave you the right combination. But while you and your pals scampered out there like a pack of little boys looking for buried treasure, he had the computer change the combination."

Hamoud stepped to Cobb's chair and, reaching up, grabbed a fistful of the old man's shirt. "Do not laugh at me!"

Cobb put a hand against the lectern to keep from being dragged off the chair. "I take you very seriously," he said.

"Then where has the Billionaire gone?" Hamoud let go of Cobb's shirt.

"While you and your wide-eyed boys were trying to break into Ali Baba's cave," Cobb replied, "Garrison and his bodyguard took off for the woods."

"I will kill them when I find them. Both of them. Slowly."

"First you've got to find them."

Bahjat interrupted. "We didn't come up here to play games with billionaires. The Power Satellites . . ."

"Silence, woman! We have the colony in our control.

We are shutting down the Solar Power Satellites. In the meantime, I want to find this man and his whore."

"They're in the woods in Cylinder B," Cobb said, "hiding."

"Where?"

With a shake of his head, "Don't know."

"You said you were watching!" Hamoud flung an arm out toward the viewscreens.

"I was." Cobb pointed a gaunt finger to the screen that still showed the empty interior of Garrison's living room. "But they took off a few seconds after you and your boys left the place."

"Where did they go?"

"Search me. We don't have cameras out in the deep woods," Cobb lied.

"The blond one said you have cameras in every part of the colony!"

"Sure we do . . . and a viewscreen in here for every twenty-five cameras. But we still can't cover every inch of the woods out there in Cylinder B. It's too big."

"I want to find Garrison and that woman!"

"Hamoud, please," Bahjat said.

He shook her away from him.

Cobb said genially, "Well, you're welcome to sit up here and punch buttons all you want to, but the chances are nine out of ten that they're not close enough to a camera to be seen. Garrison's no fool. He's gone to ground out in some thick brush where you couldn't spot him even if there was a camera two meters away. And he's going to stay there until either you guys go away or the two of them are driven out by hunger. They packed what was left of their food before they took off; I can tell you that much."

"I'll kill hostages!"

Cobb made a sour face. "Garrison wouldn't care a rat's hind tit how many you killed."

"He cared about his woman."

"And she's with him."

"I'll destroy the colony!"

"No!" Bahjat snapped.

Cobb shook his head. "With what? It'd take a megaton bomb to destroy Cylinder B."

"Let the air out."

"That'd take weeks."

"Turn off the heat."

"Sunlight keeps it warm."

Hamoud stared at Cobb, trying to fathom if the old man were speaking truthfully. Cobb stared back. Bahjat watched the two of them, feeling her own insides burning, her legs weak and shaking.

"Look, fella," Cobb said at last, "this is a *big* place. And it's not very fragile. We built it to withstand accidents and natural disasters. Why, a meteor could blow out half our windows and we'd have them patched up before we'd lost one-tenth of our air. What do you think your little popguns can do to us?"

"I can kill you all," Hamoud said sullenly.

"Wouldn't do you much good. I'm telling you the truth. Just because you don't like it, don't think you can change it by killing people."

Bahjat heard their voices dimly. Her ears were roaring, her head spinning dizzily. And she finally knew what David had meant. *"I've already destroyed you . . . all of you."* It was true. He had.

Turning, she saw the huge form of Leo lumbering through the doorway, a heavy assault rifle in one giant hand like a child's toy.

"You . . . Tiger," Leo called, his voice rasping, his breath ragged. "I gotta get my stuff. *Now.*"

And he pointed the rifle squarely at Hamoud's middle.

Local Couple Are Parents of Island One Hostage

Minneapolis: Mr. and Mrs. Alan T. Palmquist, of the Minnetonka Retirement Village, watch the skies and pray.

Their son, William, is among the more than ten thousand hostages being held by a handful of People's Revolutionary Underground terrorists aboard the Island One space colony.

"We don't care about the politics of it," Mrs. Palmquist told the **Tribune.** "We just pray that our son will come through this terrible ordeal all right . . . and his bride, too."

Young Palmquist was a recent arrival at Island One, having come to the space colony only . . .

—Minneapolis **Tribune,**
8 December 2008

· CHAPTER 40 ·

Pete Markowitz was deeply engrossed in the detective story he was reading. He sat with his feet up on the supervisor's desk, his chair tilted precariously back on its two rear legs, and flicked page after page across the little viewscreen reader built into the desktop. The super would be coming back from his rounds of checking the power transformers in a few minutes, and then going home for the night. The power substation would belong to Pete alone until the dawn shift came in. Plenty of time to finish the detective story and then get into the magazine he had brought with him.

He patted his shirt pocket, where the tiny videotape casette rested. Pornographic picture magazines were expensive, but Pete intended to get his money's worth out of this one as soon as the super left.

The door to the cubbyhole office banged open and the super stomped in.

"Getcher feet off my desk, huh?"

Grinning, Pete complied.

"Christ, is that all ya do, is read? Dontcha ever do anything else?"

"I'm improving my mind," Pete said.

"Yer rottin' yer brain with that crap."

Pete didn't answer. He resisted the urge to tell the super about his magazine casette.

"You oughtta get out on th' floor once in a while an' see what the transformers look like," the super said, reaching for his parka. "Just once in a while . . . do ya good."

"We got all the gauges in here. I can tell what's happening. I don't need to . . ."

He stopped in mid-sentence. The high-pitched shimmer-

ing hum of the power transformers, a sound so constant
that neither of them took notice of it, was suddenly changing. Lowering. Winding down.

"What the hell . . . ?"

Pete felt his mouth drop open as he looked at the banks
of gauges covering the walls. All the needles were swinging
down to zero.

"Jesus Christ," he whispered. "Look."

The super was staring at the transformers through the
office window. All the noise stopped. The entire substation
was absolutely quiet, except for the keening wind outside.

"They . . . they're all out," the super said, his voice
awed. "All of 'em!"

"How could . . ."

"Get on the phone," the super snapped. "Get through to
Central Distribution right away." He himself grabbed for
the emergency radio's headset. "Those bastards who hijacked the space colony musta turned off the fuckin' satellite!"

Pete reached for the phone and punched the red button
that instantly linked their substation with Central Distribution. The line was already busy. Jammed with calls from
other substations that had also shut down.

"Shit!" the supervisor was saying into his headset.
"Holy Mother of Shit!" He ripped the set off his balding
pate. "The rectenna farm's shut down. No power comin' in
from orbit. They either turned off the satellite altogether
or moved its beam all th' hell off the rectennas."

The super still clutched his parka in one hand, Pete
noticed. He remembered the weather forecast he had heard
on the way to work: heavy snow, high winds, near-zero
temperatures. A classic Maine blizzard. And no power for
the whole area. No electricity for heat, for lights, for communications.

The wind outside seemed to be howling louder.

"Wait!" Bahjat cried.

Leo, still holding the rifle in one massive fist, turned his
gaze toward Bahjat. His eyes were red, half-closed with
pain and fatigue. Hamoud stood frozen near the lectern
where Dr. Cobb sat, his right hand resting on the butt of
the pistol at his hip.

"Look at me," Bahjat said to Leo. "I am perspiring also,

just as you are. Flames of pain are shooting through my body. I feel weak . . . *just as you do!*"

"You can't," Leo said. "You're not . . ."

"He infected us! David infected us with something—a disease, a virus, *something*—back in the laboratory by the river."

Hamoud snapped, "Impossible. He couldn't do such a thing. He never had the chance."

"When he ran away from us," Bahjat said, "and we thought he was trying to escape . . . where did you find him?"

Leo thought a moment. "Back in th' lab area."

"Where they kept stocks of bacteria and viruses. Where they had been working on diseases and biological agents."

"But how could he have infected anyone?" Hamoud demanded. "He didn't inject you with anything. He couldn't have put anything into your food or drink."

"He infected himself," Bahjat said. "He is immune to diseases, but he can carry them and transmit them to us—all of us!"

"All?" Hamoud's eyes went wide. "All of us?"

"Yes. All he had to do was to be near us, to breathe the same air we did. He was in the shuttle with us for two whole days—more than enough time to infect every one of us."

Leo's face was pouring sweat. The rifle in his hand wavered; then he let his arm drop. "That white-ass little son-of-a-bitch. . . ."

"He couldn't have," Hamoud insisted. "It's impossible."

Bahjat turned to Cobb. "Tell him," she said.

The old man leaned his elbows on the lectern. "It's not impossible at all," he said with a crooked smile of satisfaction. "The girl's right. David was genetically programmed to be immune to almost every known disease. He can carry the microbes in him and spread them wherever he goes. If he dosed himself with something really deadly, he can certainly give it to anybody he comes near. He's a walking biological bomb—a Typhoid Mary of the megaton caliber."

"He's infected *me?*" Hamoud raged.

"I guess so," Cobb answered sweetly. "It's just a matter of time before whatever it is starts to affect you."

"What's the cure? I must have the cure!"

Cobb shrugged. "You have to find out what the disease

is first. Maybe it's one of those special mutations the lab boys play around with—it could be so new that there isn't any cure yet."

"Find him! Find him and make him tell us!"

"But he could be anywhere," Bahjat said.

Leo slowly let himself down to a sitting position on the floor. "Better find him fast," he rumbled. "If he gave the germs to everybody, then we're gonna have fifty-two dyin' people on our hands."

"More than that," Cobb said. "He can't control the disease transmission factors. He's given it to everybody he's come in contact with—including the people here in Island One. We may all get killed."

Bahjat wanted to sit down, too, but she knew that she must keep some form of control over Hamoud or he would run amok.

"You can see every part of the colony," she said to Cobb. "Find him for us. Where has he gone?"

Cobb waved at the viewscreens. "Find him yourselves. You've as good a chance as I have."

Snarling, Hamoud yanked his pistol from its holster and smashed it into the old man's face. Cobb flew out of the chair and landed with a heavy thud on the carpeted floor.

"You fool!" Bahjat screamed. "When will you learn . . ."

"Silence, woman!" Hamoud roared back, the pistol still in his hand. Blood flecked its barrel. "*I* will find the traitor. Get the Englishwoman in here—quickly!"

Once in the biochemistry laboratory, David had no intention of hiding from the terrorists. But he had a few chores to accomplish first.

The laboratory filled the entire work pod, a vast fairyland of bubbling glass retorts, plastic piping, stainless-steel vats, tubes and ducts and strange crystal shapes with narrow black metal catwalks snaking through them. The kingdom of Oz, David had dubbed it long ago, but the wizardry that went on here was real, and it could spell the difference between life and death.

Hanging above the chrome-and-crystal forest of the laboratory's sprawling apparatus was the monitoring office, a gondola stuffed with desks and computer terminals and viewscreens. Windows all around the office slanted outward so that you could look down on the working hardware below. Doors opened onto the catwalks that wove through the glass-and-metal jungle. Just above the gondola were the heavy steel structural beams that held the pod together.

The desk-like consoles inside the office controlled every facet of the laboratory pod, from the temperature of the air to the speed with which the pod spun—thereby creating its artificial gravity. David spent nearly half an hour going through the control programs of the pod's own internal computer and making certain that he could run the computer with his implanted communicator.

Finally, he sat at the phone screen, pulled Bahjat's pistol from his waistband and placed it on the desktop, and punched Dr. Cobb's number.

Hamoud's tense, frenzied face appeared on the screen.

"You!" the PRU leader snapped. Surprise, anger, relief, fear flashed across his face.

"Where's Dr. Cobb?" David asked.

"Where are you?"

"Where is Dr. Cobb?" he repeated, suddenly afraid. "What have you done with him?"

The view on the phone's screen widened and David saw Leo holding Cobb on his feet. A gash ran from the old man's scalp to his brow; caked blood matted his hair and streaked the side of his face. His lips looked swollen, turning blue.

A flash of white-hot anger burned through David. But to his own surprise it immediately boiled away, replaced by a coldly calculating hatred, calm, clear-sighted, implacable, and as deep and frigid as interstellar space.

"We will kill this old man," Hamoud said, "unless you give us the cure for the disease you have infected us with."

"You know that I infected you?"

"Yes. And you will cure us. Or he dies. Painfully."

"Where is Bahjat?" David asked.

"Unconscious." The phone camera was set at a wide enough angle for David to see Hamoud's hands. They were trembling. Leo looked shaky, too. Cobb was barely conscious, hanging limply in the big man's arms.

Then two more guerrillas pushed Evelyn into the camera's view. She looked sick, as well.

"She will die, also," Hamoud said. "Painfully. And

everyone else in the colony . . . one by one, if you don't give us the cure."

David shook his head. "You won't have the time. You'll all be dead in a few hours, long before you can kill more than a few of the people here. Dr. Cobb is an old man. The Englishwoman . . ." He forced himself to shrug. "What of her? She is closer to you than to me."

Hamoud pounded his fists on the keyboard. "Where are you? What is the cure?"

"There is no cure," David said, "not for you. You're going to die. Maybe I can cure the others . . . but not you, Tiger. You are going to die. Painfully."

Hamoud's eyes burned like coals from hell. "If I die, *she* dies. Bahjat—Scheherazade. I will slice her throat open myself."

David hunched forward in the plastic chair he was sitting on. "You bastard . . ."

"I'll kill her," Hamoud answered in a molten-hot whisper. "You'll never cure her. You'll never see her alive again. I'll destroy her."

David let his shoulders sag. "I'm in the biochemistry lab," he said in a low, defeated voice. "It's the work pod next to the hospital. Get the technicians from the spacecraft control station to put you into a commutersphere and send you out here. The serum you need is here."

Hamoud broke the connection instantly. The screen went blank.

Straightening in his chair, David smiled.

NEW ENGLAND CENTRAL DISTRIBUTION: The main rectenna farm's completely shut down. We're not getting a watt.

NATIONAL POWER ALLOCATION OFFICE: You're not the only one. The whole northern rim is gone. Canada, too.

NECD: You got to do something, and fast. It's below freezing here.

NPAO: We're working on it.

NECD: What the hell are you working on? They've turned off the satellites.

NPAO: Not all of them. Arizona's still getting full wattage on all their rectenna arrays.

NECD: They are? Well, pipe some of it up here—quick. People are freezing here. We've got snow and . . .

NPAO: We've got to go through World Government channels before we can . . .

NECD: What?

NPAO: We need an okay from the World Government office before we can shunt power to you. We'd have to divert what we normally pipe to Mexico and . . .

NECD: Fuck Mexico and fuck the World Government. We need the goddamned power now!

—Read into the *Congressional Record* by
Representative Alvin R. Watts (D., N.Mex.),
15 December 2008

• CHAPTER 41 •

Bahjat awoke and found herself reclining on a contoured couch. She felt weak, her head ached, and a dull, rasping pain was sawing away inside her lungs.

Turning her head to one side, she saw that the Englishwoman was lying on the couch next to her, looking just as miserable as she felt.

"What happened . . . ?"

Evelyn stared blearily at Bahjat. "You fainted. In Dr. Cobb's observation room. David's infected us with some horrible disease."

"I know. Where . . ."

"We're going to him. He's in a biochemistry laboratory or something, out in one of the pods outside the colony's main structure. We're in a commutersphere now, heading out toward him."

Bahjat smiled weakly. "David . . . he has destroyed us all."

"No. He said he has the cure for us."

"Do you believe him?"

"Oh, yes."

"You love him," Bahjat said.

Evelyn ran a weary hand over her eyes, then said, "But he loves you."

"He told you that?"

"Yes."

Bahjat tried to turn a little to make herself more comfortable. But the straps of the safety harness prevented her, and the gnawing pain in her chest groaned on.

"It could have been very beautiful with David," she said, more to herself than to Evelyn. "But it was not meant to be."

434

"He loves you," Evelyn repeated. "He never loved me."

"What difference does it make? In another day, another hour, we will all be dead."

"No, that's not true. David . . ."

"My life ended months ago," Bahjat said. "I died in the explosion of a helicopter. What has happened to me since then has been a dream . . . not real. I have been dead and dreaming for months."

"A helicopter explosion?" Evelyn asked.

"My lover was killed in a helicopter explosion. I died then, too."

"Hamoud said something about a helicopter explosion. . . ."

The pain eased somewhat. Bahjat wondered if she were beginning to die. "We will all die, no matter what. What we have tried to do—the PRU, all this killing—it will catch up with us soon. We will all be killed."

"He told me about a helicopter explosion . . . someone was murdered, an architect or something . . ."

"Yes." Bahjat heard her own voice murmuring drowsily. "The architect. My architect."

"He was killed in the explosion," Evelyn said.

Bahjat could feel her body drifting, drifting weightlessly into darkness. "He died because of me."

"Hamoud committed murder." Evelyn's voice was dwindling, distant, echoing. "He murdered—for you."

With a frail shrug, Bahjat replied, "We have all killed. We are all murderers."

"But Hamoud committed cold-blooded murder. An execution. For you. He told me so."

"No . . ." Bahjat said, scarcely hearing her. "Not murder. We are at war. It isn't really murder. Not really. Sleep now. I must . . . sleep. I am so tired."

Waiting is the worst part. David sat at the viewscreen in the biochemistry lab's monitoring office and watched the commutersphere slowly glide across the emptiness between the colony's main cylinder and the laboratory pod.

Nervously, he swiveled his chair to face the phone and tapped out the number for the satellite control center. The phone's small screen showed him the situation map: The entire northern tier of American states was without power.

All of Canada glowed a sullen, powerless red. Most of Europe was shut down, too. And the red danger area had grown to include a large part of Russia, from the "Workers' Riviera" on the Black Sea to the ice-locked ports of Archangel and Murmansk.

For the twentieth time, he punched Cobb's phone number. At last the old man's battered face appeared on the screen.

"You're alive," David said, the tension in his voice almost visible.

Cobb frowned, then winced. "No thanks to the PRU. Soon as that Hamoud guy heard where you were, he took off like a shot."

"With Bahjat and the others?"

"They're all gone from here. I presume they're heading out to you."

David studied the old man's face. "You ought to get medical attention. You probably have a concussion."

Cobb made a negative wag of a bony finger. "Can't move. They've got guards on the doors. Nobody goes in or out except the PRU crazies."

"But how do you feel?"

"How should I feel? My head hurts. My mouth hurts. I've spent a fortune in preventive dentistry all my adult life to keep my teeth, and now that Arab knucklebrain has busted a couple of them."

"But you're okay. You're alive."

"Unless you've infected me with the same bugs you've given them."

David nodded. "It's a respiratory bacterium that takes a few days to incubate. They used to call it the Legionnaire's Disease, for some reason. The computer didn't say why. It's fatal inside of a hundred hours if it's not treated with the specific antigens."

Cobb's swollen lips hung open. "You don't fool around, do you? They'll be dropping like flies."

"That's right."

"Kind of cold-blooded, isn't it?"

"It's better than shooting up the whole colony, or letting them keep the power off all across Earth."

Cobb looked dubious. "And what happens when they come at you with machine guns? The bug hasn't really hit this Hamoud character, the one who calls himself Tiger. You're not the only immune guy in the world; there are *natural* immunes, too, you know."

David could feel the muscles of his jaw tighten. "I'll deal with Hamoud when he gets here."

Cobb snorted. "Tough guy."

"As tough as I have to be," David answered.

The old man broke into a crooked grin. "By golly, I think maybe you are. I sent a boy out of this tin can and I got a man back."

"Sent?" David snapped. "I had to break out of here, like escaping from jail."

"Do you really think you would've gotten away if I didn't want you to go? It was time for you to bust loose, son, to see the world for yourself."

David stared at him, searching for the truth in his seamed, bruised, sharp-eyed face.

"Then why," he asked, "didn't you just tell me to go out and see the world? Why make a game out of it?"

"Because *you* had to make the decision to clear out of here, not me. If you went out because I ordered you to, you would've taken a quick tour of a few big cities, visited their science centers and universities, and come scuttling back here inside of a couple of weeks."

David started to protest, but Cobb went on: "When a fledgling decides to leave the nest, it's got to be his own decision, not the boss bird's. Kids always have to get sore at their guardians before they work up the guts to fly out on their own. You had to push yourself out."

David grunted. "Myself, huh? Seems to me you called all the shots . . . as usual."

"Not really," Cobb replied. "You did it your own way. All I did was make sure you had the opportunity. And now you've come back—an adult. Strong, confident, tough. You've boiled off your baby fat, son. You're a man now."

"I didn't have much choice about coming back."

"Sure you did. But you came back because you realize just how important Island One is to the future of the human race."

"To its present, you mean."

"The future, son. The future! What difference does all this nonsense make?" Cobb's voice rose, his face set into a grim frown. "So these PRU crackpots turn off the Solar Power Satellites for a few days . . . or a few weeks, even. What difference?"

"Millions of lives."

"Chicken turds. Listen to me. You were wondering what the missing element is—remember? In your Forecasting. You could see that Island One is important to the corporations today, but you hadn't grasped what its importance is for the future."

"You mean to provide more and more energy for all the peoples of the Earth, not just . . ."

"Kid stuff!" Cobb snapped. "That's not it at all. Listen to me. Island One is the beginning, the take-off point. We're Independence, Missouri, where the American pioneers started off on the Oregon Trail in their covered wagons. We're the port of Palos, where Columbus left for the New World. We're Cape Canaveral, where the first astronauts blasted off for the Moon!"

"Easy," David said. "Calm down."

"My backside, calm down! Don't you understand? Island One is the first real step outward from planet Earth. We can see to it that the human race spreads through the whole Solar System. We'll be safe then! No matter what happens to the Earth, no matter how stupid and short-sighted they are down there with the homeworld, we'll still survive. Human beings will live here at L4 and L5, on the Moon, in space colonies out beyond Mars, among the asteroids—we'll populate the whole Solar System! That's the key to human survival—dispersal. Throughout all of space, throughout this whole enormous universe we're in. We've got a whole solar system full of natural resources and energy just waiting for us. Who needs the Earth?"

The old man was panting heavily, excited by his own vision.

"Survival by dispersal," David muttered.

"Yes!" Cobb gasped. Raggedly, he went on: "What do you think I've been doing here—with the early factory modules, all the construction equipment, and the first living barracks we put up for the construction crews? Garrison doesn't realize it; none of them has even guessed. I've held onto them. I'm putting them together . . . for the first expedition out to the asteroid belt. Gold mines out here, boy. And iron, nickel, water, carbon, nitrogen—everything people need to live. We're going to put together a mobile colony and go sailing out there to explore the asteroids—like Marco Polo, like Henry Hudson, or Magellan, or Drake. They'll be gone for years, they'll have to be self-sufficient and big enough to be a *community,* a set of families . . ."

"I understand," David said. And he did, at last. Totally. He understood Cobb's whole scheme, the way it all meshed together. *He's planned the human race's next thousand years!* And David also saw the flaw in that plan, the hollow core of it that would bring the whole edifice down in a crashing heap . . . unless he could cure that flaw.

Then he felt the jarring thump of a commutersphere docking against the pod's main airlock.

"They're here," he said to Cobb's image in the phone-screen. "I've got to handle them first, before we can build any future for the human race at all."

Hunter Garrison awoke when the outside mirrors swung automatically to cast the first rays of a new day's sunshine inside Cylinder B. His aged body ached in every muscle, every joint. The ground beneath him felt hard, damp, cold.

Groaning, he slowly pulled himself to a sitting position.

For a long moment he sat there, blinking watery eyes at the heavy, dark green foliage all around him. It seemed to swallow him up in ominous shadow. He couldn't see more than a few feet in any direction; even overhead his view was blocked by thick clusters of leaves and tendrils of hanging vines.

Slowly he realized that Arlene was nowhere in sight. His hands began to shake.

"Arlene!" he called, but his voice was only a harsh, croaking whisper. "Arlene!"

He was frightened. He couldn't admit it to anyone but himself, but he was frightened of the thugs who had invaded his home. Alone and frightened.

"Arlene! Where are you? What did they do to . . ."

A noise in the brush startled him, but then he saw Arlene push her way through the leafy branches, strong, tall, healthy. She had changed to a skimpy pair of shorts and a clinging white T-shirt. Her hair was rumpled, but she was smiling at him.

"It's okay," she said. "They're gone. We can go back to the house."

She helped him to his feet.

"You're sure they're gone?" Garrison asked.

Nodding, "I checked with Morgenstern and the others. All the terrorists are over in the main cylinder. Everything's quiet here . . . for now. St. George is coming over with a few of his men to help us guard the house."

Garrison stumbled on a twisting root, and Arlene grabbed him by the shoulders before he could fall.

"Guess you think I'm some kind of sombitch, heh? Those were the guerrillas I helped to arm. It's my money that got them here."

"You're not the only one who pumped money into the PRU," Arlene said.

"I thought we'd be safe up here," he mumbled, "away from them. Let 'em tear down the World Government . . . that was all happening down *there*. Couldn't bother us, not up here. . . ."

"It's all right," Arlene said. "They're gone now. Maybe they won't come back."

"They'll be back," Garrison answered. "They'll be back."

"You were pretty damned wonderful back there," Arlene said, holding him tighter. "You were willing to give them your art treasures in exchange for me."

"I . . ." He glanced up sharply at her. Her face was glowing. Looking away, Garrison grumbled, "I lost my head for a minute. That's all. Wouldn't have done it if . . ."

"You did it," she said. "You were willing to let them have your most precious possessions just to save me."

"Don't get maudlin about it," he snapped.

"Of course not." But she was beaming at him.

"Stop that smirking!"

Arlene laughed. "You're not half as bad as you like to think you are, you know that?"

"Not half as smart, either," Garrison said. "I was a stupid fool—a cold-blooded, stupid jackass of a fool. It's one thing to watch them killing each other . . . but when they come up here and break into your own home . . ."

440

"We'll be ready for them now," Arlene said. "We'll be protected."

He shook his head wearily. "But there's no place to hide! Where can we go that they can't find us? There's no place to hide, no place at all. . . ."

A half-million years of experience in outwitting beasts on mountains and plains, in heat and cold, in light and darkness, gave our ancestors the equipment that we still desperately need if we are to slay the dragon that roams the earth today, marry the princess of outer space, and live happily ever after in the deer-filled glades of a world where everyone is young and beautiful forever.

One final doubt mars this vision of paradise. The hunters who killed the mammoths and outwitted the beasts were young men, in their prime. Few lived to be fifty. Those who reached that ancient age spent their days by the campfire while their sons and grandsons carried in the meat. Their business was to teach young men the wisdom of ancient ways. . . . They did not need flexible minds.

Their descendants do. The graybeards who sit around the council fires of nations today need more than ancient wisdom. They must be able to shed the thought patterns of their youth as quickly as an Ona drops his robe when he kneels to shoot. . . .

Cannot these old men bring themselves to realize . . . that the passport to a new life is theirs for the asking, but only if they will discard the traditional caution of statesmen . . . and develop minds as bold and flexible as that of a hunter tracking a bear?

Can they not realize that the alternative to cultural change is not a perpetuation of the status quo, but the failure of a cosmic experiment, the end of man's great adventures?

—Carleton S. Coon,
The Story of Man,
Alfred A. Knopf, 1962

· CHAPTER 42 ·

David stepped out of the monitoring office and walked along the spidery, steel catwalk that snaked between bubbling retorts the size of fuel drums and gleaming metal pipes that glistened with moisture.

Dim all working-area lights to one-third normal, he subvocalized into his implanted communicator. The light panels dimmed, turning the crystal wonderland of the laboratory apparatus into a shadowy, haunted forest.

All radio and phone communications outside this pod are forbidden, he ordered the computer.

Listening to the tinkling singsong of the computer's response, David nodded to himself, satisfied that he could control all the pod's systems with his implants.

The lights in the office gondola still burned at full brightness, and from his place among the shadows of the catwalk, David could easily see through the wide office windows.

There they are.

Leo, Evelyn, Hamoud, and Bahjat entered the office from the airlock hatch set into the ceiling. As they slowly climbed down the ladder to the office floor, David thought, *So anxious to get the cure for themselves they brought no one else with them. They probably haven't even told the other PRU troops that they've been infected. Trying to avoid a panic.*

The four of them looked around the office, Hamoud in obvious fury, Evelyn looking pale and exhausted. Leo slumped in the nearest chair. Only Bahjat was smart enough to peer out the windows, into the maze of tubing and hardware that filled the laboratory's working area. She looked weak, bedraggled. But David saw that she noticed her pistol lying next to the phone console, and she picked it up.

Seal the airlock, David instructed the computer. *Signal the spacecraft control center to retrieve the commuter-sphere.*

Automatically, with only a few clicks and vibrations that none of the others paid any attention to, the pod was sealed and the spacecraft headed back for the main cylinder.

There's no escape now, David thought, *for any of us.*

"Where is he?" he heard Hamoud shout.

Stepping out into a pool of light along the catwalk, David called, "I'm right here."

Hamoud's first reaction was to smash the window glass with his pistol. But the explosion-proof plastiglass merely bounced his hard-swinging arm back at him, nearly wrenching his shoulder.

"Leo!" David called. "You're the man with the biggest problem. Come out here and let me show you where the drugs you need are produced."

The black man was off his chair and at the catwalk door instantly. Hamoud raced over and tried to stop him, but Leo shoved him away and came out on the catwalk. The rifle was still in his hand.

"Better be the real stuff, man," he rumbled.

"It is," said David.

Hamoud stood framed in the doorway. "The cure! We want the cure!"

Half-turning so that the rifle held so casually in his huge fist just happened to point in Hamoud's direction, Leo shouted back, "Me first, brother! I got worse problems than any of you!"

"Stay in the office," David called to Hamoud. "I'll bring you what you need when I come back."

Leo shambled up beside David. "Okay, where's my stuff?"

"Down this way," David said.

He walked alongside the big man, carefully watching his sweating face and the tremor of his hands. *It still won't be easy to overpower him,* David realized.

Deep into the crystal fairyland they walked. The steel

445

catwalk twisted past towering stainless-steel cylinders, metal domes that hummed and radiated heat, strange glass tubes and twisting shapes that murmured and shimmered in the shadowy half-light.

"Here it is," David said at last. "This is the section where the hormones are manufactured."

Leo stood like a dark mountain and gazed all around him. His feet were planted solidly, spaced slightly apart, unconsciously prepared to move instantly in any direction. The rifle was pointing downward, but David knew he could swing it up and empty its magazine with the twitch of a finger.

"This is it?" Leo asked, his voice hushed, awed.

Metal and glass shapes twined around them. Plastic tubes of a dozen colors ran over their heads. Far below the catwalk's narrow steel plates, huge open vats churned and bubbled. The whole area vibrated, gurgled, steamed. The air was thick, hot. Even David was sweating here.

David nodded. *Prepare for emergency spin reduction,* he subvocalized. *Reduce pod spin to one-tenth current value on my mark.*

Leo's gaze settled back on David. "What you mean, this is it? This is what? How'm I gonna get this stuff into me . . . go take a bath in the vats down there?"

"No. The hospital will give you what you need," David said. "That's in the next pod over from here. I wanted you to see that we have the drugs. You can have them . . . after you've handed that gun over to me."

Leo snapped the rifle up to point at David's chest. "You tricked me."

"I'm going to save your life, Leo. But you'll have to surrender first. That's why I wanted you away from Hamoud and the others."

Leo cocked the gun with a heavy thumb. "I'll shoot if I have to."

"You'll be killing yourself," David said. "There's no way out of this pod. It's sealed tight and the sphere you rode over on has been sent back to the docks."

"You white-assed son-of-a-bitch!"

Leo swung the rifle at David's head. He ducked and dived into the black man's legs, sending Leo sprawling. The gun went off. Glass shattered and bullets whined off metal.

Reduce spin to one-tenth. Mark! David commanded as he rolled to his feet and vaulted over the catwalk's railing. Leo was on his knees, turning toward him, the rifle in both hands now.

Outside, the small rockets that corrected the pod's spin flared brightly. The pod's rotation suddenly jerked down to one-tenth of its previous level. The effect inside was to have the gravity suddenly reduced to a tenth of normal. It was like stepping into a high-speed elevator and having it suddenly drop out from under your feet.

David had planned his route well. He vaulted over the catwalk railing and fell in a long, dream-like arc until he reached out and grabbed one of the supporting beams that jutted out far below the catwalk's surface. Hand over hand he made his way, monkey-like, scrambling up to the other side of the catwalk.

The sudden drop in gravity had lurched Leo completely off his feet. He went sailing off the catwalk and into empty air.

David hauled himself across the catwalk and launched his body after Leo's. The black man saw that he was going to crash into a massive glass-walled retort and his old football instincts made him lower his head and hunch his shoulders. He banged into it heavily and bounced off, legs flailing. But the rifle was still solidly in his hands.

David—practiced all his life in low-gravity games— pushed off the glass retort as easily as a swimmer reverses direction at the end of the pool. He sailed out after Leo and banged into the big man's back.

"Let me help you, for God's sake," David said.

Leo was gulping for air, struggling, twisting around, trying to get the gun between himself and David.

"Ain't never been a white-ass son-of-a-bitch a black man could trust!"

But David clung to his back. "I don't want to kill you. You saved my life more than once. I want to save yours. If you don't let me . . ."

Suddenly Leo screamed a blood-chilling animal howl of agony and fear that echoed off the shadowy glass and metal shapes that loomed all around them. He doubled over, blood bursting from his nose. The rifle spun away.

My God, he's having a heart attack!

447

David saw that their long leap through the empty air was taking them down into one of the boiling vats below. Leo was oblivious to everything except the pain torturing him. He thrashed madly as they fell, tearing at his chest and shoulder with his right hand.

Twisting their twined bodies around, David kicked hard enough to alter their trajectory slightly. They hit the side of the vat heavily, with David sandwiched painfully between the hot steel and Leo's pain-wracked body. They slid the rest of the way down to the floor plates.

Leo lay there sobbing with agony, every muscle in his body knotting. David wormed out from under him, his own back bruised and stiff.

He could hear the rifle clattering as it still fell in a long, low-gravity glide. He needed that rifle.

But Leo was dying. He writhed on the metal flooring, nothing but a low, breathless moan escaping from his gaping lips.

I'll have to find the rifle later. With his communicator, David located the nearest first-aid station, raced along the dark, looming vats to yank it off its wall stanchions, and ran back to Leo. The communicator linked him to the pod's emergency medical computer, and David quickly slipped an oxygen mask over Leo's face, hyposprayed the proper drugs into the black man's arm, and then snapped pressure cuffs over his legs to help pump the blood back up from his extremities.

"You'll be all right," David kept muttering. "You'll be all right."

"Damn . . . honkie bastard," Leo gasped.

"Damned foolish black man," David whispered back at him. "All this killing . . . what did it get you?"

"It's . . . our country, man." Leo's voice was muffled by the oxygen mask, but David was bent low enough over the black man's face to hear him clearly as he injected more medicines directly into his chest. *"Our* country . . . not just theirs. But they wouldn't let us have our share. We wanted . . . t'get . . . what's ours."

"By tearing everything apart? That doesn't make sense."

"Whaddaya know . . . about it . . . white-ass? You try . . . bein' black . . . a couple hundred years . . ."

His voice faded away. His eyes closed. David never

noticed as he continued to work feverishly over Leo's prostrate form.

Bill Palmquist stood by the living room window and stared out at the neat rows of furrows that stretched as far as the eye could see. The tilled land was just starting to turn green with new shoots of corn. But the fields were untended. Not a person or a machine moved along the long, cultivated rows.

"Come back to bed, honey," Ruth's voice called from the bedroom. "You haven't slept all night."

"Okay," he said. But he couldn't move from the window.

Then she was beside him, her plain pink housecoat around her shoulders. She rested her head against his shoulder and he could feel the soft warmth of her body.

"Come on, honey. You know they told us to stay inside until the trouble was over."

Bill shook his head. "But we can't just let the crops sit there. We've got work to do. This is an important time in the growing cycle."

"You wouldn't leave me here all alone, would you?" Ruth asked.

He slid an arm around her. "Of course not. But . . ."

"Nobody else is going out to the fields," she said.

"I know. . . . *Look!*"

Her body stiffened as she saw what he was pointing to. A terrorist, dressed in olive-green fatigues, was sauntering along the dirt lane that bordered the cultivated fields. From their fourth-floor window it was hard to tell if the guerrilla was a man or a woman. But they could see very clearly the long-barreled automatic rifle slung over the guerrilla's shoulder.

"He's heading for our building!" Ruth whispered, terror in her voice.

Bill held her closer, his mind cataloguing everything in the apartment that could be used as a weapon. Nothing much against an automatic rifle.

But then he said, "Look, he's staggering."

"Drunk?" Ruth wondered.

"He doesn't . . . he looks like he's in pain. Maybe he's hurt."

The guerrilla suddenly sprawled face-down on the dirt lane. The rifle slid partway off his arm. He didn't move.

449

Bill headed for the door.

"Lock yourself in behind me," he said to Ruth, "and get on the phone to everybody in the building. I'm going to get that gun. Maybe we can at least defend ourselves."

Bahjat awoke to a blazing headache. When she tried to sit up, the office swam wildly around her until she let her head sink back.

She had slept on a desktop with a thick notebook for a pillow. She felt hot, burning, the way she had felt back when she and David had been fugitives in Argentina—could it have been only a few months ago? It seemed like years. He had saved her life then. He had risked his own to save hers.

And now here she was, sick again. Dying. This time because of David. *Lovers and enemies,* Bahjat thought. *Instead of bringing life to each other, we bring death.*

Wearily, she sat up and swung her legs over the desk's edge.

Evelyn was stretched out on the floor, asleep, breathing heavily, her face shining with perspiration. Hamoud sat in a chair, pistol in hand, and stared blankly out through the office windows to the maze of laboratory apparatus below them.

"How long did I sleep?" Bahjat asked. Her throat felt raw and dry. Tendrils of fire laced through her body.

"Several hours," Hamoud said, not taking his eyes away from the windows.

"Still no sign of him?"

"Nothing. Not a sound, even, since the shots and the screams."

Very carefully, Bahjat got down from the desk and stood on her feet. When the gravity had suddenly changed, the three of them had been flung across the room. Walking had become difficult; an ordinary step tended to lift one right off the floor.

"How do you feel?" Bahjat asked him.

Hamoud grunted. "I have a fever. But it is not serious. I am stronger than most . . . even stronger than the giant."

"Perhaps he killed David."

"No. David has killed him. That was the giant screaming, not your precious David."

"What shall we do?" Bahjat asked, leaning back against the desk. She felt too weak to move far.

"You have a gun, don't you?"

Bahjat nodded and put her hand on the holster at her waist.

"Well?" Hamoud insisted.

"Yes, I do," she replied, realizing that he was not watching her.

He got to his feet, slowly, carefully, like a brittle old man. "I am going out to find the blond one. Whatever this disease is that he has infected us with, it has not hurt me as much as you others. I will find him and bring him back here."

"Alive," Bahjat added.

Hamoud's lips twitched in a momentary smile. "If possible."

"Otherwise, we will die."

"You guard the Englishwoman. She might still be useful to us, once I capture him."

Bahjat nodded again, even though it made her head thunder with pain. Hamoud stepped to the door and went through, out onto the catwalk. Holding the railing with one hand and his gun with the other, he started slowly along the metal walkway.

Evelyn opened her eyes. "Is he gone?" she whispered.

Surprised, Bahjat stared down at her. "Yes," she said.

"We've got to get away from him," Evelyn said in a harsh whisper. She propped herself up on one elbow.

"But, how?" Bahjat asked. "The airlock hatch is shut and it will not open. We can't get a radio message back to the rest of the colony."

Evelyn sat up, squinting with the pain of her effort. "David . . . he's sealed us in here, hasn't he?"

"Yes."

"Then we've got to get to him—before Hamoud finds him and kills him. David's our only hope. . . ."

"No," Bahjat said, her voice hardening. "We will stay here."

"So that you can threaten to kill me if David doesn't surrender to you?"

"Exactly."

Evelyn started to laugh, but it ended in a cough. Rasping,

451

she said, "It's not *me* whom Hamoud will threaten to kill. It's you."

Bahjat shook her head slowly.

"Believe me," Evelyn said, "he's already done it. He threatened to slice you into pieces. . . . That's why David told him where he was hiding."

"You're lying," Bahjat said.

"Who would David care about more—me or you?"

"That doesn't matter."

Evelyn struggled to her feet. Watching her, Bahjat slipped her hand down to the butt of her pistol.

"You're such a bloody fool," Evelyn said, swaying slightly as she stood. "David loves you. And Hamoud is better off dead."

"You would like to destroy the PRU, wouldn't you?" Bahjat countered. "That would be the biggest news story you could imagine."

"Don't be silly. You've already destroyed yourselves. When you were a bunch of romantic silly rebels popping up here and there, no one cared enough to swat you down. But now you've terrified the whole world, and the world will crush you. You've become too strong, too successful."

"Have we?"

"Of course. It was you—Scheherazade and Hamoud and Leo—who forced *El Libertador* into the arms of the World Government. Can't you see that? For every action of yours there's been a reaction, equal in force and opposite in direction."

"But we have Island One."

"Not for long, you don't. David's taking it away from you. He'll beat Hamoud out there, you know. Why do you think he's stayed out there and waited for us to come to him? If he can beat Leo, he'll easily beat Hamoud."

Bahjat's eyes flared. Then she dashed for the door in two long, low-gravity, cat-like leaps.

She fired her pistol up into the air. The roar echoed off the pod's curving walls and the tangled jungle of equipment below them.

"Hamoud!" Bahjat yelled in Arabic. "Come back! Come back!"

Evelyn stared out the window. Sure enough, the dark, stocky figure of Hamoud appeared from behind a metal cylinder. *He certainly didn't go far,* she thought.

"Come back!" Bahjat called to him. "Quickly!"

"You fool," Evelyn said to her. "He'll kill the two of us to get what he wants."

Turning back toward her, Bahjat said, "Hamoud is a fanatic, yes. But he would never hurt me. He loves me."

"Yes, of course," Evelyn snapped. "He loves you so much that he murdered your architect for you."

Bahjat's mouth opened, but no words came out.

"He wouldn't hurt you? He murdered your lover. He told me so. He boasted about it one night in Naples when he was so drunk that he vomited in bed. Your father may have ordered the killing, but Hamoud set up the helicopter explosion. It was his doing."

"You're lying." Bahjat's voice was an ice-cold knife blade.

"Ask him. He even arranged it so that you would see it happen. Ask him."

Bahjat turned and saw Hamoud working his way cautiously along the catwalk, heading back toward them. She glanced back at Evelyn and for a split-second her hand tightened on the pistol she was holding.

"I don't believe you," she hissed at Evelyn. But she could see in the expression of the Englishwoman's face that it was the truth. *That is Hamoud's way,* she knew. *He destroys whatever stands in his way and takes pleasure in it.*

Out of the corner of her eye she noticed a blur of movement. Turning, she saw David swooping through mid-air, dropping in slow motion from the top of a maze of pipes to the catwalk, landing on the balls of his feet behind Hamoud.

Leo's assault rifle was in David's hands as he called out, "Tiger! Turn around!"

Hamoud spun to face him, gun in hand, and froze. For a timeless instant they faced each other, perhaps twenty meters apart.

"Bahjat!" Hamoud called, his voice a strained snarl. "Bring the English to the door and hold your gun to her head."

Bahjat stood at the doorway. She could see only Hamoud's back and, beyond him, David's grim, tight-lipped face.

"It won't do any good," David said. "I told you that you were going to die, and I meant it."

"She will die, too," Hamoud countered. "Both of them. You can't shoot me without my killing you, too. And then they will both die of the disease that *you* gave them."

Evelyn had come to the door. Bahjat had her gun up in the air, where David could clearly see it.

"Put your rifle down," Hamoud ordered, "or we will all die—the Englishwoman and Bahjat, as well. And *you* will have killed them."

Bahjat couldn't see the expression on Hamoud's face, but she heard the triumph in his voice. David looked at her, his eyes questioning, pleading with her. Then he lowered his rifle and let it drop to the steel flooring.

Hamoud laughed and straightened his arm, pointing his gun precisely at David's head.

Bahjat fired four times before she realized she had pulled the trigger. Hamoud's body jerked, danced like an insane puppet, hit the railing, and collapsed in a blood-spattered heap.

... and now the news.

World Government authorities have still not released details of the abortive attempt by the Peoples' Revolutionary Underground to seize the Island One space colony.

Other than reporting that casualties were "light," and that none of the World Government or other dignitaries who were visiting the colony have been hurt or killed, no information about the incident has been forthcoming.

The Island One Corporation has maintained a similar silence on the matter, other than to report that a "general uprising" among the colony's residents overcame the handful of terrorists who had tried to seize Island One.

Microwave energy from the Solar Power Satellites was restored to full power earlier today, ending the crisis that virtually paralyzed much of Europe and North America and caused at least seven thousand deaths over a forty-eight-hour span.

World Government Acting Director Kowie Boweto and the revolutionary leader *El Libertador* were unhurt and plan to continue their negotiations aboard the space colony. . . .

—Evening news broadcast,
International News Syndicate,
10 December 2008

• CHAPTER 43 •

So this is how politics works, David thought.

He was sitting at a small round table, representing the host—Island One—while Dr. Cobb recuperated from his dose of the respiratory infection David had carried. On David's right sat Kowie Boweto, on his left, *El Libertador*. Jamil al-Hashimi was the fourth man at the table, sitting opposite David.

Boweto spread his big hands. "My staff has gone over the problem several times in the past week, since we've been here. Our position has not been rigid."

Villanova smiled a calculated, gray-eyed smile. "But not quite as flexible as my people would like."

"We are granting local autonomy."

"In return for allegiance to the World Government."

"That seems only fair," said Boweto.

"Only if local autonomy includes the power to make necessary adjustments in the local economy."

"But you can't tinker with the economy of one nation without disrupting the economy of your neighbors and the rest of the world. The next thing you'll demand is a return to local currencies."

Villanova raised his hands in protest. "No, no . . . the World currency is perfectly suitable. Your monetary policies have been admirable, for the most part."

"For the most part," Boweto echoed in a frowning mumble.

"Gentlemen," David interrupted, "as your host, I must remind you that your conference is due to end today, and the world expects a communiqué of some sort from you. Perhaps you should emphasize the things you've agreed on and continue this dialogue at future meetings."

Boweto grumbled something, but Villanova chuckled. "Out of the mouths of babes," he said.

"What have we agreed upon?" al-Hashimi asked rhetorically.

David answered, ticking off on his fingers, "First, there will be a general amnesty, worldwide, for all members of the Peoples' Revolutionary Underground . . . no further prosecution of them, anywhere."

"But any future guerrilla activities from this date onward will be stamped out without mercy," Boweto added.

"Agreed," said *El Libertador*. "The time for fighting is ended—if we can achieve justice without force."

Before they could start arguing again, David went on: "Two: Argentina, Chile, and South Africa will rejoin the World Government. And three," he added quickly, "the World Government will restructure its Legislature and regional structure in a way to give more local autonomy to the member nations."

"The details must still be ironed out," Villanova said. Boweto nodded.

"Fourth," David continued, "all clandestine support of the PRU by private agencies"—they all stared at al-Hashimi—"will immediately cease. Future support to terrorists will be regarded as an act of terrorism in and of itself, and will be treated as such."

"Agreed." Al-Hashimi sighed.

"I would like to add a final point," David said, "one that hasn't been brought up in your discussions, but one that we here in Island One feel is vitally important."

They turned toward him.

"Dr. Cobb has suggested that we begin to turn as much of Island One's profit as possible into new space communities, which will move outward through the Solar System to develop new raw materials, natural resources, and space industries. Our preliminary calculations have shown that for an investment of seventy-five percent of our incoming profit, we could return to Earth something on the order of a fifty-billion-dollar-per-year increase in Gross Global Product."

"Seventy-five percent of the profits!" al-Hashimi gasped.

Nodding, David said, "We will be able to speed up production of Solar Power Satellites, to beam energy to the Southern Hemisphere nations, as well as construct new space communities. Our aim is to bring the riches of the entire Solar System to all of the Earth's people."

"But the Board will never agree to investing so much of their profits."

"They will have to agree," David said, "or Island One will declare itself an independent nation and apply to the World Government for membership. Just the way the lunar settlers did at Selene."

Al-Hashimi half-rose from his seat, then sat down again, his face a bitter mask of displeasure. "This is blackmail."

David smiled at him. "The Board will still be making a good profit from Island One. But the *people* of Island One want more than profit. Our objective is to make our fellow human beings on Earth as rich—and secure—as we are."

"That is Cobb's objective," al-Hashimi snapped. "The people of the colony don't even know about this yet."

"But they will soon," David countered. "How do you think they'll vote on the question?"

Al-Hashimi didn't answer.

El Libertador broke in. "As you said, my young friend, we must bring this conference to an end. I think we have accomplished much, although much remains to be done."

Boweto got to his feet and extended a hand to Villanova. "I suppose you'll have to become a member of our Executive Council," he said.

Taking the African's hand, *El Libertador* smiled ruefully. "Do you think there is any way I can quietly disappear? I really don't like politics."

Boweto grinned back. "Not likely. You're in politics for life, Colonel, whether you like it or not. You'll probably take my Chairman's seat away from me, sooner or later."

Villanova looked aghast. "I wouldn't dream of it!"

"No," Boweto said, "but your supporters will. And in the end, you will do what must be done."

Sagging back in his chair, *El Libertador* ran a hand through his iron-gray hair. "Then let us hope at least that we can disagree with each other in peace."

Boweto nodded. "In peace," he repeated.

David fled the small, private conference chamber gladly and hurried down to Dr. Cobb's office, which he had made his own headquarters while the old man was hospitalized.

He avoided the inner observation chamber. Cobb could spend all day in his all-seeing insect's eye, but not David. He simply wanted to finish the business at hand and get outdoors, away from offices and reports and politics. He knew how *El Libertador* felt. *Will I be tied to this for the rest of my life, too?* he wondered.

Evelyn was in the outer office waiting for him, sitting on one of the low-slung couches in the quiet, warmly carpeted room.

He had expected her. "It's finished," David said, letting the door click shut behind him. "The conference is over. They haven't really agreed to very much—except to put an end to the violence."

"It's a good beginning," she said.

"Maybe it's enough," he said as he sat on the couch beside her. "Maybe . . ."

Evelyn was wearing a frock of Island One silk, a shimmering sea-green dress that brought out her natural coloring. Already the lines and tensions of the past months were easing out of her face.

She smiled at David, but then her reporter's curiosity took command. "Will they be releasing some kind of statement for the media, do you think?"

"They plan to. But if you want, I'm sure I can get you private interviews with Boweto and *El Libertador* before they leave."

"If I want to!"

"You're in a good position, you know," David told her. "You have the only firsthand experience of the PRU's takeover here."

Her face clouded over momentarily. "There's not going to be any legal trouble about me being with the PRU, is there?"

"None at all," he answered. *"El Libertador* got the World Government to agree to a general amnesty."

"That *is* news! If I weren't blacklisted. . . ."

"You're not blacklisted in Island One. You can file your story from here. Every news desk on Earth will pick it up. You'll be very famous."

Clasping her hands together, "My God, David, that's fantastic!"

"And your reports on the PRU and the conference here

will break the blacklist, anyway. But, why bother? Why don't you stay here in Island One?"

"No," she said quickly. "I can't."

"Cobb only sent you away so that I'd go chasing after you," David explained. "He won't . . ."

"But while you were chasing after me, you found Scheherazade."

He hesitated. Then, "Yes, I did."

"And you're in love with her."

"Maybe I shouldn't be," David admitted, "but I am."

Evelyn was trying to control her face, but not quite succeeding. David felt his own insides wrench as he watched her.

"Island One is a big place," he said. "There's no reason why you can't stay here if . . ."

"Yes, there is," she interrupted quietly. "For me there is a reason. This colony isn't big enough for all of us, I'm afraid."

David didn't know what to say. "I'm sorry," he murmured.

"There's nothing to be sorry for. It's not your fault— not anyone's fault." She forced herself to brighten. "Besides, I don't think I'd ever feel comfortable in a world that's inside-out. I want to see a proper sky over my head, and a real horizon."

He nodded mutely.

"You don't suppose," Evelyn asked, "that you could arrange for me to fly back to Messina on the same shuttle that the politicians are taking? Could that be done?"

He grinned at her. "I'll see."

They chatted for a few moments more, but Evelyn cut the conversation short. David felt grateful. She got to her feet and he stood and walked her to the office door. For an awkward moment he didn't know what to do. Should he shake hands, embrace her, avoid contact altogether? She settled it by reaching up and pecking at his lips.

"Good-bye, David."

"Good-bye," he echoed.

She left, dry-eyed, striding strongly down the corridor, never glancing back at him. David stood at the door and watched her for several moments.

The insistent buzzing of the phone finally pulled him back from the door. He flopped on a couch and touched the phone console's ON button. A life-sized wall screen lit up and Dr. Cobb's face glared out from his hospital bed.

"What's this bull-dingy about handing out seventy-five percent of the corporation's profits to build new space communities?"

David had thought he'd be immune to surprise, but the old man had fooled him again. "How did you . . . that was supposed to be a private conference!"

Cobb chuckled at him. "Nothing's private from *me*, son. Now, where do you get off telling them that it was my idea?"

"But it was," David said. "I just put the numbers to it."

"Seventy-five percent of our profits?"

"That's what it'll take to do the job in a reasonable time."

"Reasonable? That's back-breaking! Wait 'til Garrison and the rest of the Board hear about it."

"When are you going to tell them?"

"Me? *You're* going to tell them. It's your show now. I'm an invalid . . . confined to my sickbed, wracked with disease, suffering from a concussion. You talk to Garrison."

David sat up straighter in the couch. "All right, I will."

"He'll chop you up into little pieces," Cobb warned. "Seventy-five percent of his profits."

Feeling anger warming inside him, David snapped, "I've been chopped at by experts. Let's call him right now. We'll see who does what to whom!"

Cobb was grinning broadly. "I want to see this."

It took almost fifteen minutes to get Garrison to the phone. His mansion was being repaired; work crews were cleaning up the damage done by the terrorists, teams of decorators were repainting the walls, toting in new furniture. *Like the ritual cleansing of a temple that's been defiled*, David thought.

Arlene Lee tried to deflect the call, but both David and Cobb insisted that they had to speak with Garrison himself.

He was up on the roof of the mansion, lounging in a reclining chair, his frail old body draped in an ankle-length, brightly patterned dashiki.

"You'd better have a damned good reason for bothering me, youngster," Garrison growled. "I've been through a meat grinder, partly b'cause of you, and I deserve my rest. I've earned it!"

David squirmed slightly on the couch. Garrison glowered at him from the left-hand half of the big wall screen. Cobb smirked in the other half.

"The political conference is ended," David started to say.

"Good riddance to those clowns. Send 'em back where they came from."

Taking a deep breath, David blurted out, "And I told them about our plan to use seventy-five percent of Island One's profits to build new colonies in space."

David felt as if his heart had stopped beating. He stared at the viewscreen, waiting for Garrison to explode.

Instead, his cold eyes flicked sideways to focus on Cobb. "This your idea of a joke? Using the kid to front for you?"

"For me?" For once, Cobb was surprised.

Garrison's thin lips curled a bare centimeter. "I know you've been stashin' away equipment and supplies. You want to go scootin' out to the asteroids or whatever you call 'em and set up more colonies out there."

"That's true enough," Cobb admitted. "We'll have to do that, sooner or later."

"And it'll take seventy-five percent of my profits?" Garrison's voice rose.

"Only if we do it at a breakneck pace," Cobb said. "Our young friend here seems impatient."

"We *must* do it quickly," David insisted. "There's no other way."

Garrison's gaze was like the hypnotic stare of a cobra. "Convince me," he said. *Or I'll swallow you whole*, David could almost hear him adding.

"I could give you all sorts of computer runs that show the situation very clearly," David said.

"You tell me," Garrison replied.

Taking his hand off the phone keyboard, David said, "Well, we've got to go balls-out. We don't have the time to wait. If there were nothing and no one to consider except those of us living here in Island One, sure, we could afford to take a leisurely pace. But we're not alone. We're not isolated. We never have been. What's happened here in the past week proves that."

Garrison inhaled deeply and then let his breath out in something between a snort and a sigh.

David plowed ahead. "Don't you see? There are nearly eight billion people down there on Earth. And we're not apart from them. We can't live up here in isolated splendor while they slide down into global collapse. *They'll take us with them!* They'll destroy us as they destroy themselves."

"Then maybe we oughtta move ourselves out to Mars," Garrison said, "or wherever . . ."

"No," David snapped. "That's not the answer. Just the reverse. You've got to understand this: space is rich in resources—energy, metals, minerals. Everything they need so desperately on Earth, we can supply from space. They can't make their society work down there unless we start pouring new wealth into them. And the wealth is here! In space! We have the riches of the whole Solar System at our fingertips."

"We give it to them?"

"We've *got* to bring that wealth back to Earth, and do it as fast as we possibly can. Otherwise, no matter what kind of political agreements they come up with, they'll be fighting over food and resources again in a few years."

"They're going to fight, anyway," Cobb said. "We can't stop that. What we should be doing is providing an escape hatch, spreading human colonies throughout the Solar System so that even if they wipe themselves out on Earth, the human race will survive."

"No, we've got to do more," David insisted. "We have the power to help them avoid genocide on Earth. We'd be less than human if we turned our backs on them."

"And it's going to cost seventy-five percent of my profits," Garrison muttered.

"What do you need the profits for?" David challenged him. "You have everything you've ever wanted. Island One is a success; it's self-sustaining. What do you do with your profits? Invest them in Earthbound corporations? They'll be wiped out when the collapse comes. Invest in armaments, revolutionary movements, try to knock down the World Government? You know where that leads—barbarians come and sack your home."

Garrison winced. "You know how to twist the knife in the wound, don't you, boy?"

"Invest in new space colonies," David went on, ignoring

his words. "That's the place to expand. I'm not guaranteeing that we can avert the global collapse by doing this, but I know the collapse will come for sure if we don't."

"Use our profits to expand our space operations," Garrison mused. "Don't sound so bad when you say it that way."

"No matter how you say it, we've *got* to . . ."

"Now don't crowd me," the old man snapped. "I still want to think about this. And there's a healthy chunk I want to invest in the biology research boys—the ones who're workin' on longevity and rejuvenation."

David pressed his lips shut.

Turning to Cobb, Garrison growled, "How long you gonna be loafin' in that hospital bed?"

"A few more days, they tell me."

"All right." Garrison scratched his chin for a moment. "We'll have a Board meeting Wednesday. Be there, both of you. And you"—he looked directly at David—"you better have all those computer runs you mentioned. I want t'see facts and figures, not just fancy talk."

"Yessir," David promised. "I'll have them."

"You better." Garrison snapped off the phone connection.

Cobb's face filled the screen again. He was chuckling.

"What's so funny?" David asked.

"Not funny," Cobb said. "Happy. I'm glad to see you've finally pulled it all together. You're a leader, son. You've got the whole thing figured out and you know what you want to do. I'm not sure I agree with you—you won't be able to avoid the collapse, you know."

"We can try."

Cobb shook his head sadly. "Those idiots on Earth have plundered the planet and overbred to the point where nothing on God's green Earth can save them."

David felt himself smile. "We're not on God's green Earth. That's my whole point. We can stop them from killing themselves."

The old man looked thoughtful. "I don't think you can prevent the collapse, David. Postpone it, maybe. But you can't prevent the inevitable."

Shrugging, David said, "I'll settle for a postponement. If we can postpone it long enough, maybe it'll go away."

"The optimism of youth." Cobb's grin returned. "Well, you've set yourself a big task. I wish you well."

"Now, wait, I'm not in this by myself."

"No, but you're the boss. It's your job. You're the leader now. My task is finished. You can take over from here on."

"But I don't want to take over!"

"Tough. I didn't want to, either. But it's there; the job's got to be done. You'll never be able to let somebody else do it, because you know how it's got to be handled. You can do it right. And you will."

David knew the old man was telling the truth. There was no way he could escape and return to the life he had known before. Yet, instead of feeling a burden trapping him, he felt light, strong, happy.

Cobb was still grinning. "You're already giving orders to Garrison. You've got the World Government and *El Libertador* listening to you. How's it feel to be a mover and a shaker?"

"I . . ." David eased back on the couch. "You know, there are a couple of things I'd really like to do."

"Such as?"

"Well, a first step, at least," David said. "There's a little village of Indians up in the Andes in Peru. I don't want the developers to gobble up their land and turn it into new cities. I want them left alone."

Cobb nodded. "Not too easy to pull off, you know."

"Or, maybe . . . maybe we could build a space colony for them—give them a world of their own, where no one will ever bother them."

"I can see Garrison's face when you tell him *that* one."

"And Leo," David said. "If he pulls through all right and the hospital gives him a clean bill of health, I want to send him down to New York and see if he can start to make some sense out of what's happening to the cities."

"Send him back to New York?"

"Why not? He knows the problems. Maybe he can come up with some solutions."

"That'd be like sending Attila the Hun to a convent!" Cobb argued. "Leo's got too much blood on his hands."

David shrugged. "Name a political leader, a man who achieved power, who didn't get his hands bloodied. George Washington? Yasir Arafat? *El Libertador?*"

"They'll never accept him back in the States, not after what he's done."

"The people will accept him. Even the white leaders will accept him, because he can speak for the whole non-white majority down there."

Cobb shook his head.

"Would you answer a question for me?" David asked on a sudden impulse. "A personal question?"

The old man looked puzzled. "If I can," he said.

David could feel his heart thumping in his chest. "Are you . . . my real father?"

Cobb's puzzled scowl melted away. "Your genetic father? No, son, I'm not." His eyes were the gentlest David had ever seen them. "Don't know who he was, either. Wish I had been, though, 'cause I'm very proud of you. Couldn't be prouder of you if you were my own flesh and blood. Couldn't love you more."

David realized he was on his feet, standing before the life-sized screen.

"Thanks for, that," he said. "I've loved you like a father for a long time."

Cobb coughed and looked embarrassed.

Reaching out, David touched the cold glass of the viewscreen. "Get some rest now," he said.

"I will. Got a Board meeting Wednesday."

The screen faded to a gray blank, leaving David standing there alone. For a long time he remained in the quiet office, cut off from everyone, thinking, wondering.

Then he noticed the electronic calendar/watch on the wall. Abruptly, he acted. With a churning mixture of elation and apprehension stirring inside him, he hurried out of the administration building and found an electrobike in the parking rack outside. He leaned on the accelerator pedal all the way down the trail to the next village.

He stopped only once, at a tiny shop on a quiet lane in the village. Then he pedaled quickly to the apartment building at the village's edge where Bahjat had been quartered.

Bahjat's apartment was hardly palatial, but it was as comfortable as Island One could make it. She had a top-floor suite with a broad, sweeping view of the whole colony's interior from her balcony. The rooms were large and furnished with pieces that Sheikh al-Hashimi had brought from his own sprawling palace in Cylinder B.

She answered the door herself. The only servants in Island One were electronic ones.

"I thought it might have been you," Bahjat said as she stepped back and let David into the living room. The thick carpet was Angora-white. Graceful potted palms touched the ceiling.

"I brought you a present," David said, taking the small package from his slacks pocket.

Bahjat accepted it with a soft smile. It was not wrapped. "A makeup kit." She looked up at him.

'I know you've got your own things now," David said, feeling quavery inside, "but I remembered . . . that night in New York . . . well . . ."

Her smile widened. "A symbolic gift. Thank you, David. I shall treasure it."

With a gesture, Bahjat invited him into the room.

"The conference is over," David said, not knowing how else to begin speaking to her.

"And?" she asked, looking neither fearful nor hopeful, merely totally beautiful and desirable.

"And they've agreed on an amnesty—effective now. There will be no more retributions, no more fighting. The PRU can turn to peaceful means of achieving their goals."

Bahjat walked slowly to the low couch by the windows. She sat down tiredly, dejectedly.

"There will always be madmen like Hamoud who can do nothing but destroy."

Nodding, David said, "Then they'll be crushed like insects. The World Government, *El Libertador*'s revolutionaries, even the multinational corporations—they've all agreed: no more violence."

"For how long?"

He smiled. "Long enough, if we're lucky. If we work hard."

She frowned at him, puzzled. "Work hard at what?"

David sat at her side and began to tell her about his hopes to expand human communities throughout the Solar System, to send whole man-made colonies outward so that they could ship back the resources and raw materials that would make the entire human race wealthier than anyone had ever been before.

Bahjat listened, smiled wanly, nodded. "It is a good plan, a good objective. You can build a worthy future for yourself."

"And for you," David said.

"For me?" She shook her head. "I have no future. I am a murderess."

"You saved my life."

"I helped to kill thousands. And I murdered Hamoud deliberately . . . with joy. I killed him gladly."

He saw the anger flaring in her eyes. And the pain.

"Scheherazade killed a PRU gunman. But Scheherazade no longer exists. Her work is finished. Princess Bahjat al-Hashimi, on the other hand, still lives. She is a permanent resident of Island One . . . with her father."

"I will not live with him!"

"You can live a few miles apart and never see each other. Perhaps in time you'll change your feelings toward him."

"Never!"

"That's a long time."

She stared at him. "Don't you understand, David? I can't love you. Too much has happened between us. I could never love you!"

"Never?" he asked.

She looked away from him. "So I am to be a prisoner, then? Here in Island One?"

"You're my prisoner, Bahjat. I've been yours; now it's your turn to be mine."

"You're serious?"

"Very. I love you and I want you with me. There's nothing for you on Earth except bitter memories. Stay with me, Bahjat." He reached for her hand. "Stay here with me."

"But, David, how can you love me?"

"It's not difficult."

"After all we've been through . . ."

"Especially after that."

Despite herself, she smiled at him. "And you know that I can never forget all that has happened? Never forgive myself . . ."

"There's nothing to forgive. All the past is finished. Look forward, to the future. Help me to build new worlds."

She stared out the windows at the green land curving up insanely, the bright windows where the sunlight streamed through, and the solid green land beyond them, overhead.

"But it's not a real world here," she said. "It's so closed in, so limited. . . ."

David glanced at his wristwatch and then pointed up toward one of the long, cylinder-spanning windows.

"Look out there, Bahjat. Watch."

The light was dimming, slowly at first, so slowly that it was difficult to tell if it were really happening. But then the glaring sunshine dimmed, dimmed, and they could see the bright body of the Sun itself through the polarized glass of the windows, being eaten away by a dark disk.

"It's a solar eclipse," David said. "The Moon is passing in front of the Sun. It happens fairly often here, more often than on Earth."

He heard Bahjat sigh as the Moon's invisible dark shape covered the Sun almost exactly.

"Ohh!" she gasped.

A ring of dazzling jewels circled the eclipsing bodies for a moment, a halo of fiery diamonds glittering in the dark sky, winking and dancing. And the Sun's glorious corona shimmered into sight, an ethereal, pearly pink glow that covered the heavens.

"This may be a little world, Bahjat," David said, holding her, "but it's only *one* little world. We're going to build others. We're going to spread all across space and out to the stars themselves. We can do it. *I* can do it. But I want you here beside me. I need you. I need your strength and your love. We can leave Earth behind us, and yet do more for Earth than anyone has ever done before. Together we can do that. And we will."

She turned in his arms to face him, and he could feel her heart beating as wildly as his own.

Slowly the Sun came back and the light of day returned to Island One.

• EPILOGUE •

—From the journal of William Palmquist

We celebrated Neal's third birthday today, and Ruth's due to deliver our daughter by the end of the month. The reports of the first cycle of crops in *Explorer Able* came in today, too, and everything was right on the button, which means we'll start to set up housekeeping in *Explorer Able* before the year's out.

David Adams himself came over and congratulated us on making all the systems on *Able* work right the first time, including the farms. I got a chance to speak to him personally and asked him if we could bring my parents up to take our places in Island One. He said it was a little unusual to bring retired people into the colony to replace active farmers and technicians, but he'd see what could be done about it. Guess we couldn't ask for more than that.

Neal wants to be an asteroid miner, of course, and not a farmer, like his Dad. That's okay with me. He'll get a chance to see lots of asteroids while we're on *Explorer Able*. He'll be ten years old by the time we swing back to Island One. If we ever do.

It's a big universe out there, and there are plenty of places in it for all of us.